THE GRAIL WAR

RICHARD MONACO

THE GRAIL WAR

Illustrated by
David McCall Johnston

A WALLABY BOOK
PUBLISHED BY POCKET BOOKS NEW YORK
DISTRIBUTED BY SIMON AND SCHUSTER

Another *Original* publication of POCKET BOOKS

POCKET BOOKS, a Simon & Schuster division of
GULF & WESTERN CORPORATION
1230 Avenue of the Americas, New York, N.Y. 10020

*The author acknowledges the help
and support of the following:*

*Adele Leone
Barbara Bravin
Peter Lampack*

PROLOGUE

B ROADITCH of Nigh was watching the bony-backed mules plop-plopping along the muddy trail that frothed under the steady rain. Their sides were slick and the animal reek hung in the sluggish, cool air sharper than the smell of earth. The open cart jerked and creaked along. He wondered if he might not have done better to walk. The cold water splashed over his hood and spattered his reddened face.

The heavy-bearded monk, face obscure in the shadow of his full cowl, held the reins with chapped fingers. His long body swayed with each lurch and tilt as they moved across the open, rolling, flooded fields through the oppressive, unrelieved gray daylight. . . .

"King Arthur's been dead over a year's time," the monk was just saying as the cart labored through a grove of bedraggled, autumnal apple trees.

"As long as that?" Broaditch reflected, without great interest.

"Over a year's time, brother," the other confirmed. "And you say you seek the famous knight Parsival of the Grail? But what can your business be with such a one?"

Broaditch cracked his big knuckles. His massive body swayed only slightly as the team struggled unevenly on.

"I ofttimes wish I were more certain myself," he said meditatively. "The Grail, for all I know."

"You seek *it*? Ah . . . you and the devil, too."

"I left my wife, three children, and a fair farm . . . "

"Well," the monk reflected, just his knotted, wet beard showing, "we say that's a call."

Broaditch folded his powerful arms inside his worn, stained cloak.

"I cannot say," he commented, "but I know the world wearies me. . . . " He shook his head. "I might be like yourself at that, save God has not spoken. Aye, He's been notably silent in my case. . . . Yet the world is weary and stale. . . . So have I thought more and more as my years mount and ride me down. . . . "

"God's voice is not as men's. You hear it and know it not. Yet you are led often to purpose by what seems chance and foolishness." The monk was very matter-of-fact.

"I cannot say. . . . But over the years I find I think of the Grail and Lord Parsival, whom I knew as a boy. . . . Aye, that's sooth. I served in his mother's domain. . . more years ago than bears thinking. . . . Perhaps I but *want* to believe he found it and knew joy and light without end. . . . No doubt I want to believe it. . . . " He sighed and now clasped his hands over his knees, then squeezed the soaked leather. "And yet I love my wife and little ones. . . . " He sighed, shook his head, and smiled wryly. "If this be heavenly advice I've taken, brother, it truly seems ill."

"If it were clearer," the monk said, whipping the reins up to stir the sluggish team, "the end you seek might frighten you away." Broaditch looked at him thoughtfully, but said nothing. "Recall, the devil sought it, too," the monk repeated.

"Did he?" Broaditch wasn't quite amused yet.

"The devil Clinschor—the black wizard cursed of God. He fought to possess the holy cup."

"Is it a cup for certain?"

The monk shrugged. "So some say."

"What would the devil do with such a sacred thing?"

Make it as evil as once it were holy. Use the power of light to shine darkness. . . . So have I heard."

"Well, Clinschor is dead twenty years or more." Broaditch stared into the gray horizon.

"Have you seen his grave?" As there was no reply, the monk went on, head tilting into the rain. "It is said the Grail draws everyone, though the many feel it not, being too mired in the world. The devil, it is said, knows it as a stinging, an irritation. It angers him continually."

Broaditch made fists and drummed them on his knees.

"He must be dead," he declared at length, "or in his dotage." The holy man looked straight ahead.

"To reach the Grail, you'll have to pass the devil," he said.

"Well, that's comfort, indeed," Broaditch responded, cocking his head to the side.

"You can always go back to your farm." The monk shrugged.

"Did you mean Clinschor? What are you hinting at?" Broaditch wasn't sure whether it was funny or frightening.

The monk didn't respond immediately, then said:

"You took this quest up freely."

"Quest?" Broaditch expostulated. "Be that what it is?" No response. "Why mention him to me? I saw him once and saw close at hand the horrors. . . . " He shook his head and refolded his arms. "Let memory sleep in memory," he said grimly.

The cart was just topping a rise where the trees were thick, and Broaditch was startled by a sudden, violent shadow beating past his face with a raw shriek and he ducked away, hands raised up.

"A crow!" he gasped an instant later, heart pounding, glimpsing the creature winging into the gray sodden shadows across the road. "It struck for my eyes!"

The monk turned his loose, soggy cowl to him. Only the bushy, dripping beard was visible.

"Let it be just a bird that meant nothing," he suggested with a faint mocking edge.

Broaditch stayed silent for a while, watching the heavy hanging trees move slowly and unevenly past as the steaming mules labored on.

"Has Clinschor been heard of?" he finally asked.

The monk urged the team along the twisting way.

"When the sun is setting and day dies," he said, "there are long shadows. If you look, you see, brother."

"So you but hint on," Broaditch said, "mystic one." He was irritated. "You and that crow are alike: you stir fear with darkness and noise." He raised his bushy eyebrows. "Quest," he muttered.

For the first time his companion (who'd promised him a ride nearly to Camelot) seemed amused.

"Some things," he said, "are greatly to be feared, brother."

Broaditch turned away and broke off the conversation. He tightened his bulky arms together and tilted his chin down. The cart staggered on through the clinging mire and he gradually fell deeper into a dozing sleep and found himself suddenly flying, higher and higher, feeling his beating wings lifting him soundlessly, circling over the reeling, grayish world, and then, far below, a skeletal shadow seemed to bend its vast angles over the landscape. . . seemed to move like a pair of wings. . . . Then he shuddered, crying out in his throat, starting, jerking on the seat, falling away from the immense, flying, black-winged, red-jawed, clawing, fierce-eyed shape. . . falling, crying out, hitting the rutted mud dully, banging himself awake, seeing instantly (heart racing as he struggled to his feet) that the driver was gone and the mules stood motionless in the traces. . . .

He twisted, looking around. How far had they come since he fell asleep? The day was dying into blurry twilight. Where was the damned monk? In the trees? Shitting? There were dense woods all around here. . . . For some reason he didn't want to call out. . . .

The rain was cold and relentless. He decided to walk. Those animals were too slow, in any case, and no doubt the man would take his time. . . . He knew he was rationalizing. . . . He didn't want to wait, so he started walking, his traveling sack slung over his shoulder, and for a moment or two he fought back an impulse to run, as his broad back felt naked and tingled. . . .

THE GRAILWAR

BOOK

I

P ARSIVAL was drenched. He was sitting on the black, hard
rocks in a saturated gray robe, bare feet callused, cut, and bruised;
face pinched, haggard, eyes deep-set and burningly bright blue.
There were silver streaks in his blond hair and ragged beard. He
was staring out over the rolling moors and fens where dark,
scraggly pines and scrubby brush smoked with heavy fog among
the sharp, bare, tundric stones.

The rain had more or less stopped, and bitter, gusty winds rent
mist and leaden sky. He barely noticed the raw chill on his face
and limbs.

"Nothing again," he murmured. He worked his dry tongue
around his cracked lips, licked a few drops of rain from the corners
of his mouth. "Nothing at all," he said quite clearly.

There was only the raw day and the dark, bitter hills. He sat in
his lean, tireless body, which was like well-worn and tanned
leather; he felt the faint, unspecific gnawing of his long fast. Yes,
much had happened, up to a point: he'd slept on stones, held his
mind fixed on God for hours at a time (as the Irish monks had
instructed him); the months had rolled away as he'd thinned out
and hardened and lost all ordinary sense of time and events that (he
thought) were neither truly real nor truly dream had taken place;
he'd melted from his flesh, heard the voice of rain and earth, the
heartbeat of the sun, whispering of the moon; and since the
endless rains began, he had come upon an inner silence so deep
and intense that he often feared he'd somehow fall into it and be
lost, and lose even the memory of memory. He'd obeyed the
monks, strained, stopped body and breath and fought for peace,
sensed it there just beyond the furthest grope of his efforts. Even

the visions he'd sought had shimmered to nothing and stranded him when he'd risen to embrace them and found only the hard rocks, like the teeth of dreams. Even the demons became rageless shadows after a time and he was stranded without even evil anymore.

He had been watching the two riders across the moor, not particularly curious as to which side of reality they rode from. He partly closed his eyes and saw the shimmering flickers of flame-like gleaming spring out from their forms. Well, his sight had certainly changed, he reflected, though it had not made him loving or good or filled him with the peace and benediction of God. . . . It was a strange shock to realize these were merely men coming, and he felt the density, the earthy solidity, of them and realized how light he'd become. How many months since he'd seen a real person? And then it was as if he could hear them speaking close to his ear, though the distance was still too great, even for shouts.

Am I altogether a wizard, he wondered without fear, *in seeking God to find only strange strength*?

He was still considering this question as the two knights rose, out of a streamer-like exhalation of mist, silvery ghosts, and his normal sight doubted their reality again. They stopped. Visors were up, but their faces were obscure in the steel hollows. They were watching him and he thought they were speaking again before the voices actually sounded so that he seemed to respond to another statement rather than the words.

"Good day, hermit," the first said.

"So," was his reply, "you've come again into my life."

He said this because the last time suddenly flashed in his mind, a whole memory seeming to totally repeat in an instant in his strained and remarkable consciousness: over twenty years ago (though time was no part of the memory) on that sloping field outside the castle walls, nude, the risen sun digging into his aching eyes, a wine headache, the smell of sex on his body (the woman wasn't there; she had been somebody's wife or other . . .), shivering in the bright morning, surrounded by the brigands in castoff armor, castle guards looking helplessly down as Gawain, helmet tightly shut, stood there, the silver faceplate blankly reflecting Parsival's fine, bright hair and scintillant blue eyes. . . .

He remembered saying, "Don't kill me, Gawain." Feeling a need to live, a fantastic, clear, tender beauty, a deep touch that held him and them all: men, sky, hills, sun, caught in a hush of pure stillness, like a voice saying something with a depth no word could skim even an inch from, as if saying everything is beloved and loved, loving itself and touching itself with an endless lover's touch . . . and his heart . . . and sinking and rising, saying, yes, yes, yes, lips still saying, "Gawain, please don't kill me!"

Not from fear (for there was no shadow of death or stain in his mind at that moment), because he was speaking to light and tender peace and he wanted just to share this, to share everything he was and had and felt and would feel and see . . . yes . . . with everything, flower, bird, beast, and man . . . and he smiled and perhaps the other felt it, too, the inexplicable, overpowering, gentle nearness of it. . . .

He was never certain, except that Gawain's voice said, "Then lead us to the Grail, Parsival, my old companion."

And Parsival laughed; he couldn't help it.

"Yes," he said, "but I have. I'll show you."

"Is it here?"

"Yes. Exactly."

"Inside?"

The others had gathered around, scarred, utterly grim and mangy faces.

"Yes. And outside, too, my friends. Anywhere you like."

"Arr," said one, with a slit nose and one eye, "he's mad." He raised his spear to kill him.

"Wait," said Gawain inexplicably. "Let him live."

This notion found no favor with anyone.

"Very well," Gawain stated, "but I'll not touch him. Even naked and unarmed, and slightly fat, as he is, I wonder if all of you might prevail. I say he's no use to us. He will die here and reveal nothing. But a living man can be set watch upon and followed and all his secrets found out. A dead brain is a tomb of truth, you lowborn curs."

Most were convinced. Two were not.

"The Grail is moonshine, anyway," one said. "Let's kill this pretty swine and roast his liver." He had a single eye working, the other a raw socket, gaping, myriad little muscles flickering when the first moved. "I'll skin the bastard!" he offered in conclusion.

He thrust his jagged-tipped spear at the tall, pale, naked man. With breathtaking ease, Parsival stepped inside the deadly jab and effortlessly plucked the shaft from the man's hairy grip and casually cracked him under the ear with it. The outlaw dropped like a stone.

"Now he's armed," Gawain observed dryly. "Even armored as I am, I'd choose some lighter sport to fighting him, if it please God."

Parsival felt wonderful, light, free, and hardly was aware of what he'd effortlessly done. It was true that, though armed, all but Gawain were as good as dead in a fight with him.

He found himself looking warmly at the depraved, glowering lot of them; he didn't actually perceive them as individuals in the usual sense, just saw the sheer life, the undistorted, unconcentrated, innocent pulsing, as if they were little children playing silly games, and he felt this as if the breeze blew it into his naked body, there on that grassy slope in the clear morning sun.

"Violence has no meaning, " he told them. "All that we have and are is borrowed from one another. To strike one another is to rend our own garments and spoil our own substance."

He had no idea why he said that or if he expected any result. It was true, and so he simply said it.

And then, he was remembering, sitting on the rough outcropping as the horsemen came up to him, *and then my troubles really began. . . .* He smiled. *To be touched by that sweetness and peace and then to let and be let go again . . .*

He sighed deeply.

"Holy man," the nearest knight called, leaning down a little, "we seek Sir Parsival, the great warrior."

"So you mock me," Parsival said.

"Pious one," said the other, "what a thought."

"What you mean is clear," Parsival told them, sitting perfectly still as one man dismounted and walked closer, steel suit pinging faintly. Parsival seemed to look deep, deep away, eyes never shifting to them.

"Holy saint," the knight said, "we crave your blessing."

"Don't mock him," said the man on horseback.

"Will you force this senseless thing?" the famous knight inquired calmly.

The horseman moved closer. His shield hung around his neck, wetly gleaming. His war ax lay massively across his lap.

"Give your sermon, holy one," the man on foot said within the shadow of his visor.

"If I could put ears and sense in stones," was the reply. "And I am far from holy." He sighed.

"Best confess yourself, then," the man suggested, "and make what peace you can with God."

"Fools," Parsival said, standing up gracefully. "I want no more to do with all your silly business, your petty plots and hates and wars! Tell your Lord that."

"It can be carved on your tomb, instead, you hypocrite and bastard knight!" hissed the other, who, in one explosive movement, drew his long sword and lashed a savage cut at the unarmed, bearded man . . . which could as well have been aimed at a shadow or the drifting, gleaming fog. Parsival moved as though they'd rehearsed this together for a lifetime; he stepped inside and under the cut, took the helmet in both hands, burst the straps, and tossed away the steel pot, exposing the bright coif of mail, and he flattened the fellow with a terrific blow, gracefully moving behind him as if glued to his back as the sword spasmodically swept around and the ax wielder tried to maneuver into position for a blow. Parsival stooped and picked up the sword now, still not looking directly at anything, moving with uncanny economy and grace. The horseman held back, watching the brooding figure in tattered robes and shoulder-length, wild, golden-streaked hair.

"Why do you seek the Grail?" Parsival had asked Gawain twenty years before, standing naked, holding the spear like a graceful, edenic archangel.

Gawain replied without lifting his gleaming mask. "Why did you, Parsival?"

"I knew not what it was."

"No," Gawain said. "That was the first time. What about the second?"

"I still didn't know—not until today, now. I'm still finding out."

Gawain's flat, seamless visor didn't move, mirroring Parsival's pale body, as if the man within the armor didn't even have to draw breath.

"Whoever has the Grail's power," Gawain said, "can rule all men."

"No," said Parsival.

"Yes," Gawain insisted, relentless, almost fanatic. "Yes,

yes, yes! And he can heal all wounds, and restore what has been lost."

"Poor Gawain," Parsival said, "this is both true and false."

He thought of Gawain's incredibily mutilated face and thought about what was truly mutilated within him. He shut his eyes with the pain of it. . . . So he hoped to cure his torn flesh with the holy, magical cup or jewel or whatever it actually was . . . because no one who said "seek it" ever actually described it . . .

"What will you do now?" the mounted knight asked.

Parsival still wasn't quite looking at him. He weighed the sword in his right hand, musingly.

"I threw one of these away," he said, "years ago. Still they fear I'll swing it again."

"Won't you?"

Parsival hummed to himself.

"Perhaps," he allowed, "for I've failed."

"Then I have to die," said the knight, "to stop you, on my vow."

Parsival flipped the sword up once and caught the hilt again.

"Why?" he wondered.

"I swore to."

"An honest knight. You knew me?"

"No."

"But you swore."

"Yes."

"Who is your lord?" No reply. "I have failed here," Parsival went on. He sighed. He started walking. "The rain will lift soon." He rested the blade across his shoulder, bare, callused feet padding lightly over the harsh rocks.

And all the misery, he was more or less thinking, goes on . . . the brief lives, the dying friends, glory lost and won, O God, O God, if I could but rest still and content in you while outside life passes like a shadow . . . each dying thing leaves me with no pleasure, not in food, drink, woman, or praise; each beginning, each flower of hope, withers as it sprouts . . . a race of fools. . . . God help us all, all us fools and that fool behind me about to slay himself for a fool's dream of honor under a fool's order. . . . Grant us some common permanence to sustain us, give us the grace of your utter love so there's no loss but simply a joy, a joy deep in the heart of all that perishes without end. . . .

The horseman was looming over him, the animal's frothy mouth, shod hooves sparking on the slippery stones, the determined warrior already chopping straight down into Parsival's peripheral notice and his body stepped meditatively aside and the stroke went wide.

"Don't be absurd," he told him, "you can't possibly kill me."

He heard the fellow's strained grunt and the clink of steel as he recovered.

"I must try, curse you!" he thundered and zigged another savage cut. This time his target leaned into the armored horse's flank and tossed him up out of the saddle by one leg. He rolled and banged over the stones. Parsival prodded the animal into a canter and watched it head away across the moors.

"I wit," he called over to the fallen warrior, "I can walk on better terms than you."

The horse jogged into and out of long, undulant strips of fog that streamed across the wild valley.

It was still raining when Broaditch reached Camelot. He stood on the black, muddy track of chewed-up road near the great gate, leather hood over his head. The wind billowed the downpour; the hillside ran with mud. Puddles lay everywhere like ponds and there were rivers where the earth was level, whitish, boiling. Rivulets arced and spattered down the massive castle walls. His legs were muddy to the shins.

How many days of this? he was wondering. It had been well over a week. The earth seemed to be dissolving away. The fields were sunken, sodden, spring plantings rotting pale in the ground . . . rivers flooding all across the country . . . birds barely flew from limb to limb in the forests. . . .

The gate was open. A sentry stood huddled, miserable, leaning on his spear. The vast courtyard was deserted. Broaditch, Oriental pipe clamped, reversed, between his teeth, plodded on inside without even a token challenge from the shivering guard.

Within he learned that the man he sought lived in the town outside the walls on the steep slope of the hill.

The fire in the long, low, stone and log room sputtered and struggled at fresh, wet logs. The steam hissed as they dried. The endless rain boomed at the hide-covered windows.

He stood before the lukewarm hearth, rubbing his damp hair

and face with a rough woolen cloth. His bones ached. Time, he decided, was telling him something about age: there would always be a little pain.

He turned to face the brawny, long, dark, bald armorer who was squatting over a rough three-legged stool, long, powerful fingers working, polishing a sword that lay across his lap. He was surrounded by the iron tools of his trade.

"Well, Broaditch," he said in a raspy voice, "hard to believe you stand before me. I knew not that you were living to this day."

"Like your fire here, Handler," the big, grayed, weathered man replied, "I struggle on with the little heat I have." He yawned and stretched.

Handler cleared his throat with a great rattling hawking. Then he spat onto the lumpy dirt floor.

"The bread's rotting in the bin," he said. "I can't offer you much."

"If this goes on," Broaditch suggested, "we'll all learn to swim and feed like fish or else drown in the open air." He eased himself onto the uneven, backless chair as little winces flickered across his gray-bearded, but still ruddy, face. "Already the first crops are lost. It's the same wherever I've been."

"The priests call it a judgment." Handler looked angry and a little frightened, too.

Broaditch shrugged.

"So it always is," he said ambiguously. "But naming is no cure for troubles." His eyes smiled. "Else I would speak the name of my pain and my bones would be at peace."

Handler's long, slightly out-of-line face tilted impassively at him.

"I wonder," he said, "that you found me. How many years have passed since we fought together?" Broaditch shrugged and said nothing. "My wife's been gone these seven," Handler went on. He cleared his throat again and worked his lips around his few remaining yellow stumps of teeth. "And I have one worthless son living here still . . . another in London town . . . a daughter married in the South, and two dead from fever. . . ." He spat again, then went on buffing the steel across his knees. "I'm a damned grandfather," he muttered. "I wonder that you found me taking breath."

"I had word of you on the road. Anyway, you've prospered since the wars."

The other grunted.

"Or so I believed myself," he said, "until these recent days. Hah. With old Arthur gone and the kingdom fallen to the barons, there's no law left in the land." He spat. "Nor even war, to speak of, just damned raiding and kidnapping. I wonder that you went six miles with purse and life intact."

Broaditch weighed a chunk of soggy, dark bread in his massive hands.

"I've less of both to lose," he said, "than was once the case."

"How many years since the fighting?" Handler frowned, eyes focusing away, as if into time itself. "Some twenty since the invaders came. . . . My mother died nine before this day."

"Is she dead, then?" Broaditch looked up from sipping at a battered pewter cup of home brew. "Old Mol? God rest her."

"Aye," Handler went on, "so if she was living last you knew, why, it's been ten or more years."

"About fourteen, I think. I could still swing an ax easily then. No creakings in the joints."

"Aye," agreed Handler, showing his blackened, spaced tooth stumps, "and you could smell out gold then. And I'd swear you were still too rich to go as a pilgrim in these bitter days. Is your red-haired woman a-living?"

Broaditch faintly smiled.

"She is," he murmured. "And my three doves. But I don't seek gold now, old friend."

Handler shifted on his stool, buffing the long blade again with slow, careful strokes. His manner was watchful. He obviously assumed Broaditch wanted something.

"So you just walk to take the air, then?" he inquired, sarcastic.

"More like to take the water," he was corrected. The ceaseless drumming on the roof paused a moment like a breath, then boomed on again. "I seek someone."

"Ah?" murmured Handler expectantly.

"Sir Parsival, or maybe King Parsival. I know not how he's called these days, or if he lives, for all of that."

His friend knit his eyebrows and shook his head.

"Who can tell?" he said. "Word of even the greatest lords creeps like a worm in these sorry times." He cocked his head to one side. "Why do you seek such a one?"

Broaditch shut his eyes. He held the cup in both his wrinkled farmer's hands. He looked meditative.

"So?" Handler persisted. He cocked his dark face to one side, eyebrows furiously knit. Water was now sluggishly seeping in under the door, filling and soaking into the rills and craters of the uneven earthen floor.

Broaditch opened his eyes and shrugged.

"Let it be, for now," he said.

He raised the battered cup again and drank deeply. The water lapped around his booted feet.

Elsewhere, before the massive, rambling castle that overlooked the walled coastal town called London, the field had been prepared for a tourney, or, as one wag put it: "The mud's been prepared." The rain gusted steadily. A scattered audience huddled in the grandstand-like structure, where banners and garlands drooped and swayed heavily. A hide canopy kept the spectators fairly dry as knights on chargers and squires and suchlike on foot left their wind-rippled tents and plodded through the muck toward the lists. A trumpeter had just sounded a feeble blast into the drenching air.

The first pair of mounted knights moved into position, horses slogging knee-deep. A groom and two soggy pages crouched together under a tent flap, watching.

"By Christ," muttered the groom, wrapped in his coarse furs and hides, "this is fools' play."

"How much longer could they wait?" a page commented.

"Sir Rador," the other pointed out, "in white. He's very strong. I saw him last year break a man's back on the first spear."

"It's a day for frogs to joust ducks," the groom grumbled.

Now the chargers were ready, lances lowered, shields braced, horse breaths steaming, and then the charge began as a bedraggled Lord stood forward on the bleacher benches and dropped a silk scarf into the foaming mud.

The combatants crashed toward each other more like boats than anything else, the groom thought. They came together in skidding slow motion and both lances glanced futilely off the other's shield with a dull scrape.

"Nobly run," the groom remarked.

Now they were plodding back before the apathetic onlookers, prepared to try again.

A tall knight in part armor came out of the tent and stood under the canopy behind the squatting trio. He had bushy, dark hair like wire and a slightly beaked nose. His eyes were sharp and sarcastic with a nervous, concentrated look.

"When do the merchants tilt?" he asked, his voice sudden and harsh.

The pages turned and stood up. The groom glanced back from his crouch.

"After the third matching, Sir Lohengrin," said the first, a puffy-faced boy with a wart under his eye.

Lohengrin looked with disgust at the mud-spattered jousters struggling back to their starting positions.

"Call me then," he ordered, turning to re-enter the tent. "This pains my eyes."

Now the knights were heaving forward again, even more sluggishly churning the muck this time, rocking, bouncing, glopping, mounts grunting, the downpour dinning over them. . . .

Broaditch stood up with Handler, staring at the flooding water that was pouring steadily over the sill.

"Blood and shit!" Handler cried as the door opened and there stood a pale, freckled youth with wideset, dull-blue eyes, snapping, reddish hair plastered flat around his head like a bowl.

"Father!" he cried. "Father, the hill is sinking down! The mud has already carried away the huts on the middle road!"

His father widened his eyes, then grunted.

"Quick!" the young man shouted, darting back out the door.

Broaditch and Handler followed into the endless downpour. The hill did seem to be sliding down toward them from under Camelot castle. A few disjoined homes were broken and tilted out of the muck like ruined teeth. The water and running mud-gravy streamed over their feet in a sluggish torrent.

"God save us," Handler gasped.

Broaditch stood solid as oak.

"I'll help you gather what you can," he said sensibly.

Handler just stared in outraged disbelief.

"Is the whole world turning over?" he wanted to know, gusts of rain spattering into him. "Is this the second flood?"

"It's to be fire, they say," Broaditch corrected. "But any man may be mistaken, much less a holy prophet whose sight is too long for a single lifetime."

The boy was heading across the flooding yard toward the valley.

"Valit!" his father shouted. "Come back here and help us, you oaf!" He shook his head and headed into the house, muttering, "What a son . . ."

Valit was heading back on the double. Broaditch and Handler were already inside, snatching up provisions and whatever else they could grab as the greasy muck, stinking from the barnyards and latrines it had sucked into itself, flowed like porridge through the door.

They were spattered to the chest, looking back across the valley, among a crowd of refugees, at Camelot hill, where the last of the town had been swept away. The castle itself still stood above like (Broaditch reflected) an old man's long canine.

They were standing on the close-set paving stones of the old Roman road where young Parsival and Sir Roht the Red had first come in sight of Arthur's fortress over two decades ago. . . .

A lightly dressed, mud-stained knight was standing a little apart from the motley crowd taking in the relentless, slow-motion catastrophe. He was talking with a pretty commoner girl, barefoot, in a patched dress. Her teeth were bright, and even when she smiled. Broaditch watched her with a certain nostalgia. She could have been the daughter of a girl from old days. . . . He smiled slightly. And then the knight mentioned a name that caught his full, present-tense attention. He moved a little closer to them.

"I could wait no longer," the knight was saying. "Thrice the tourney was delayed by this cursed rain."

"Ah, my lord," she said, "and all these folk here washed out of their homes. What's to become of us, then?"

The knight nodded vaguely.

"You people," he said, "amaze me, the way you can survive ill fortune."

She was partly looking at him, head slightly humble, deferential, with a faint smile on her lips.

"Aye," she said, "but myself, I'm in sore need."

He raised his wet eyebrows with aloof concern.

"Ah?" he murmured.

"My father and mother are dead. And my house is swept away."

He nodded. He was partly looking back at her now.

"And you wouldn't object to a warm roof right now? Hmm?"

"Oh, my lord, and how could I?"

"No," he said decidedly. "Well, follow behind me." He smiled faintly. Broaditch could see he was looking at her feet and legs, brown and shapely under the mud streaking. "Not too far behind me. We'll see what may be done."

"Oh, thank you," she said, curtsying, "good, my lord."

"Sir knight," Broaditch said, and tilted his head forward slightly, not quite irreverently. The thin-lipped man regarded him distantly.

"Hmm?"

"Did you not mention the name of Sir Lohengrin?"

"What of it, sirrah?"

"Was he not at the tournament in London?"

The lord nodded. He frowned, irritated. Then he turned back to the girl.

"I have heard he is a mighty knight, my lord," Broaditch said.

"There are many mighty knights," was the irritable response.

"Have you fought with him, my lord?" she asked. She brushed a wet lock from the corner of her eye. Even here under the trees the rain dribbled steadily onto all of them.

"I would have, had the jousts been run," he said, a little too quickly, Broaditch thought, realizing he was afraid. He wasn't looking at the girl at all now.

Broaditch pondered and made up his mind. It was his first clue in a long time. He'd follow the wet trail to London and speak to Lohengrin if he could. He'd been searching for months now. His family was in the mountains, where they were safe and relatively dry. . . . All right, first find Lohengrin and work from there. . . .

And the next morning it was still pouring. The three of them were huddling in single file, chilled and drenched. Half the time they were wading through the slowly flooding valley. The upper Thames was like a gray, shallow lake under a sky of whitish-streaked beaten lead. Ducks and geese sailed among low huts and houses. Cattle, horses, sheep, and men struggled toward the hills. Some families crouched grimly on thatched rooftops. There was a haggard look of impending doom on every face.

Handler sloshed along in front of his son in Broaditch's wake.

"How far must we go on?" Valit groaned from under the packs and sacks roped to his shoulders and back.

"Peace, boy," Handler said. "Save breath."

"We must reach higher ground," Broaditch called behind, "or float off like kindling."

"Where, then, are you bound?" Handler asked.

"To the coast. London."

"Then our road runs the same way."

"Road?" They were knee-deep at this point. "Road for boats."

After a few days they tried again, except now there was more water than mud. Lohengrin's groom told the story to his wife that night. They were in bed together, the straw mattress rustling in the still, dark room at their slightest motion. The spent coals were a vague purplish glow on the invisible hearth. The rain drummed quietly, endlessly on the roof.

"So," he was saying, his voice amused and harsh and sad, too, "they lined them up again, only this time it were more like to swimmin'. Them fools." There was a slight creaking of straw as he shook his head. "Ten at a time, bangin' at one another out there, fallin' into the water and drownin' if they couldn't get their feet under them fast. Three foot and more ov' muck, an' them in that armor." He sighed. "Great knights die easy as any else." His wife made a small sighing moan. "Yer back again?" he asked her.

"Aye," she whispered.

"Should I rub it with oil, then?"

"No matter. With all this damp, there's no relief in that."

He went back into his memory of the day's combats.

"The water was stained red, as when you slit a hare's throat over the pot. An' then on foot one noble lord took to his heels because he dropped his sword an' couldn't find it. Aye, there were a pretty fix! The other one with the ax chasin' him. It was worth a laugh. Why, you could look away, you see, an' turn back a minute later an' you couldn't tell they moved no more than flies on honey. . . . They looked like they been carved on a church door, one lookin' back, the other with that ax raised up, as if he believed any second he'd strike him low. . . ." He chuckled. "Why, I went to piss behind the tent an' come back an' still there they was, though they'd moved just enough so you couldn't be sure they was actually carved or not. . . . I wit it were dead night, an' still the one must chase the other."

He sighed and chuckled again.

"What of the trial of the common men?" she asked.

"Aye, woman," he muttered without amusement, "they did have their trial."

This event Broaditch and Handler and the son arrived in time to see, soaked and saturated by the mud of days that should have been hours of travel. All the knights had come out to watch. The rain beat on Broaditch's leather hood and beaded down his face. As he came closer he was surprised to see two commoners standing out in the tournament area (in the water, mud, blood, and horse droppings) facing one another with staves, both stripped to tunics.

"What manner of combat is this?" he wanted to know.

The dour groom himself happened to be standing close at hand at the edge of the field.

"Those are merchants," he said, "of great means and have come to trial in the matter of a debt of eleven coppers and a bolt of cloth."

"What?"

"Aye. They would not be reconciled. There's bitterness between them, though I think now that it's too late they would repent themselves."

"I have never seen such a thing in my time," Handler put in.

"But it's the law, in truth," Broaditch said.

"What fools they must be," Handler said, shaking his long head.

Across the field Broaditch could see a screen set up in the grandstand and wondered what it was for. He didn't know that a great lord sat behind it peering through an eyehole so as not to be seen attending such a spectacle.

Broaditch could see the fear, however: the two pale faces, restless eyes, a lost and isolated look, and he knew their mouths were dry and hearts light and rapid; time seemed speeding past them. The shorter one was shivering in the chill downpour. A herald in the grandstand was reading a scroll. The wind cut up the sentences, so Broaditch caught very little of the matter.

". . . justice be proved . . . in God's name . . . His mercy . . . truth be revealed for . . ."

One of them had to die. The terms were absolute. That was really the point, he reflected.

As a horn signaled, the shorter man kicked a glop of mud into his adversary's face and swung a long-reaching blow at his head.

He connected with a hollow thock that (Broaditch noted) did little hurt, as though he'd struck stone. He knew in that instant which one was about to die. He hardly had to watch.

"That rogue wants no helmet," a knight called out with a laugh.

The sticks crashed on one another, crossing, scraping as they thrashed and wallowed, the slight man continually giving ground, slogging back, knee-deep, both already dripping black mud and blood. Then, in a sloshing flurry, the smaller one went down and began half-crawling, half-swimming to escape, but the other, with huge, bouncing strides, managed to get closer and aim full, sweeping blows so that the first was forced to twist and sink down to break the impact, covering his own head with stick and torn forearms. Now his enemy began spearing him, poking him under the surface, straining all his weight into it until the little man howled and sputtered and rolled aside like a wounded whale, blowing bursting breaths. And then, somehow, the sticks were broken and lost, one left poking upright like (Broaditch thought) a pole in a river. . . .

They'd worked their way closer to the onlookers. Covered with muck, eyes wide and white, they clawed and rolled and thrashed. It seemed to Broaditch as if he watched primal men newly raised from the wet clay of creation heaving up, struggling, falling back. He felt pity and sickness. The little man kept trying to scream now as the other rode his back and frantically rammed palmfuls of mud into his face, pressing it into his mouth and nostrils, cursing and puffing, too drained himself to even hold the desperate face under the surface long enough to suffocate him. The little man bit his hand as the other hooked and gouged feebly at his eyes. . . . Then both went under and heaved out of the mire apart, blowing throats and noses clear, like great surfacing swamp creatures.

The little man cried out as he slogged away, crawling and wriggling: "Help me . . . O Holy Mother . . . help me, please, please help me . . . !"

"He prays," someone remarked.

"In season," said another.

They fell and rose again and again, near collapse, until the big man finally caught up with the smaller, who simply lay on his side, chest heaving, spasming. One of his ears was bitten loose and flopped in its blood. His eyes were shut and his mouth gasped breathless words. His enemy hesitated and looked toward the crowd, standing a few yards away. His hollowed, searching look had a terrible, silent plea in it. He had learned something, was seeing something now, and had no way to say it except with his wild eyes—or so Broaditch believed. A massive warrior at the edge of the swampy field shook his somber head.

"You must slay him," he pronounced, "or else die yourself."

"See, see!" cried Valit with fear and excitement. "One rides the other!"

Broaditch turned away as the big man knelt himself upon the other's head and finally forced the bloody face for good under the slimy muck. One great bubble popped up after a long space of silent time. And the crowd shortly began to break up and drift away. The spent, quivering victor remained, kneeling up to his waist over his now-invisible opponent as if, for some ascetic reason, he was praying alone in the reeking field. . . .

Broaditch walked among the rain-beaten tents. He stopped beside a squire who was struggling with the soaked harness of a balky charger.

"Young sir," he said, "have you seen the knight Lohengrin this day?"

The boy glanced up.

"Old sir," he said, "I have not."

"Well, then, would any here know his whereabouts?"

"Yes."

The boy waited, expressionless, sly.

A pause.

"All right," Broaditch said, "do you?"

"Yes."

"Where?"

"In his tent." The boy showed nothing.

He takes me for a bumpkin or a fool, Broaditch concluded.

"Which tent?" he asked patiently. He was looking across the gusty field at the line of them, the fog whipping and twisting. He noticed half a dozen knights in full mail gathered around a tall red tent with black trim. For some reason he understood that was the one. It seemed strange that they'd be guards, he decided. Stranger still was the fact that they stood, axes, spears, and swords poised, facing in on all sides. Broaditch started walking, spungy earth splashing under his feet as he braced into the wind. As the leader (in green-silver armor) signaled, the men sliced and jabbed through the tent fabric, long spears poking from wall to wall, and

then, ropes cut, the whole slashed structure sagged down and
someone was screaming in agony inside, and he thought with
dread and pity how the man must be ignominiously caught under
the material like a netted boar. However, a moment later a
helmetless, though otherwise armored, knight rolled out from
under one edge and stood up, swordless in red and black gear.
Lohengrin, son of Parsival. His wiry, dark hair made him seem
like an avenging devil, Broaditch thought. At the same moment,
from among the tatters, struggling away from the swords and
spears, a half-nude woman emerged, one arm partly severed,
pumping blood. She staggered a little way and dropped, clutching
at herself. The first swordsman to reach Lohengrin swiped at his
head and he pivoted in under the stroke, skidding close with
astonishing speed, catching the levering arm and tossing the fully
armored knight over his back like a wheat sack, his right hand
jerking the sword away as the man came down at the end of the arc
head first, sticking that way, upside down in the muck, kicking his
legs, drowning. And (before the next man arrived) Lohengrin cut
once, savagely, between the legs, splitting him like a hare,
Broaditch thought, heart pounding with excitement and fear. Now
a spearman thrust and the blade deflected the shaft and Lohengrin
hit the helmeted head so hard with the steel hilt that blood sprayed
from the eye slits and the ruined man stumbled in a circle in the
sucking ooze, mailed hands holding his faceplate, rain washing the
gore in thinning rivulets down the armor, until dropping near
the hurt woman.

The others kept a respectful distance now. The massive leader,
in emerald-green and silver plate, moved in with sword upraised,
moved as if strolling forward to a friendly bout. A squire was near
Broaditch and others were gathering around.

"There's Lancelot," one said with awe.

Broaditch's eyes widened. Legends still lived, it seemed.
Lancelot of the Lake, the knight of the cart . . . Incredible! An
aged legend and still one of the most dangerous men on earth. It
was said he was almost defeated once. Once. He was stocky,
bull-like in his armor, short, not even quick. He closed with the
curly haired warrior with a minimum of wasted motion, deflecting
the first cut almost offhandedly, like brushing (Broaditch later
said) a fly away, then chopping a quick, neat blow that traveled a
bare two feet, which Lohengrin barely managed to catch on his

blade and was staggered, slipping backward in the mud. What terrible power! Then Lohengrin came back and flurried so fast that the old champion could only defend with casual shield and edge, planted there, relaxed and almost still. Broaditch felt the thrill of this, the unmoved defense against an attack that would have chopped most men to shreds. One of the other knights had circled behind him now and rushed in as suddenly as the splashing muck would allow: ax zipped down and Lohengrin demonstrated the difference between himself and any ordinary man by simply timing a step back under the arc of the blow and, and the fellow leaned past into space, nearly severing his torso with a backhanded sweep that burst into armor and flesh like a muffled explosion. Blood sprayed into the rainy air as the knight shrieked and blew bubbling wind. . . .

Lancelot attacked again; the rest moved carefully to enclose the helmetless knight in a loose circle as, from behind the tents, a mounted squire led another charger by the bridle in a slow-motion gallop through the onlookers as Lohengrin rushed the warrior farthest from Lancelot, beat him flat into the mud, as though the man had run into a stone wall, leaped up, and held the flank and saddle long enough to be dragged away across the field as Lancelot, visor flung open, shouted orders and curses. As the horses went on out of the encampment, Broaditch could see Lohengrin finally levering himself onto the mount's back. . . .

Broaditch was thoughtful. Well, he reflected, he could catch him on a mule, which these days was as good as a horse, and shank's mare was nearly as swift as that. . . .

The first knight still protruded from the mud, legs bent like a frog's, a rain-stippled stain of blood spreading out from him. The second lay on his face, struggling faintly to crawl as he sank into the ooze. The third was sitting, dazed, bent shield still held protectively up. The sliced woman was being bound by a surgeon, though she clearly was nearly dead. Lancelot stood there, legs planted solidly, staring after his escaped quarry. . . .

Lohengrin and his squire were clacking along a paved road with excellent drainage. The rain was lighter; a dense, smoky fog flowed everywhere, as though the countryside were damply burning.

Lohengrin was smiling sardonically at the pale youth.

"But, sir," the boy, Wista, was saying, "I have heard that even your father had broken his sword and vowed never to raise it again in any cause."

The supple, dark-faced knight, head in a tight leather cap, was amused.

"My sire, Parsival," he said, "speaks honey and gold. But I have seen him at closer range than others. The men he has dispatched to judgment would make a hill to climb with labor." He laughed. "And that without the horses and serfs in the stack!"

"But he has since broken his sword," the squire insisted.

"Yes. And in good time. Who was left living for him to overthrow?" He frowned. "Just Lancelot, and even he feared the old dragon." He poked his finger at the boy. "Do you know how many families have sworn to have my head and my sister's and mother's, too, and any spare cousins thrown in for the sake of my father's gentle deeds?" He was now staring hard ahead into the billowing fog.

"Still, he's come to renounce the life of a warrior and become a holy sage."

"Like a glutted man abjures food, and the pox-struck turns from women." He chuckled. "Why, once I heard a man in the stews swear, with ten whores all about him, never to come in the bawdy house again in God's true name, by Christ's back teeth, by Herod's arse, by Pilate's hands, by the wangers of all the saints who're men, and the boltholes of all the female . . ."

"God's mercy," murmured the boy, crossing himself and looking around nervously.

"Fear not blasphemy." Lohengrin laughed. "Worse things than words go unpunished." He resumed: "So, swearing by these potent potentations, so to say, this poor fellow dared not ever leave the whores if he were to keep both vow and pleasures intact!" He grinned, easy, sardonic, relaxed, his eyes always watching into the folding and unfolding mists. "So even my father's broken blade may be joined again."

"Why does Lancelot seek your life?"

"It seems he loves me not," Lohengrin allowed, grinning. "Thank my great father, I suppose." He was thoughtful. "I should have asked him . . ."

"Your Father?"

"Lancelot, wistful-Wista." Grinning, watching into the fog.

"That grunting dunglump will answer to me in the end. I wait and watch, when need be, and strike at last . . ."

"Have you seen your father since—"

"Peace, break off!" Lohengrin commanded in a whisper. He touched the other's reins as he halted his own steed. The light drizzle trickled over their faces. There was a plip-plip-plop of oncoming hooves. "One rider only," Lohengrin murmured. "And a weighted beast. Here comes my new headgear and chestplate."

A dim, mounted figure seemed to take form before them out of the coiling, insubstantial fog.

"And lance, too," Lohengrin completed the list, observing the long spear held straight up.

The knight came closer, his smooth, gray-green armor blending into the leaden background. Lohengrin was unconsciously smiling.

"Sir knight," he said in classic style, "good day."

The other pulled up and waited in silence.

"Sir," Wista said to his master, "why not pass in peace?"

"Were you weaned in my grandmother's gardens?" Lohengrin demanded. "Are you a girl, in truth, and not just under the blankets?"

The gray-green knight's visor stayed shut. Blank steel.

"Give the ground," he finally said, his voice hollow in the helmet. He sounded somehow weary, too—not weak, but weary.

"Come and take it," Lohengrin invited. He didn't even draw his sword yet.

"So," said the other, "what boots pride?" And he began to turn his bulky stallion aside so as to pass around them.

"No," Lohengrin declared.

The gray-green knight stopped.

"So you force me?" he said as a question answered. He kicked his mount into a tight half-circle, the fog flowing around them like a billowing cape. On one side the land fell away steeply downhill from the road; on the other, dim tree shapes loomed like a wall.

Lohengrin floated his mount sideways, hooves clack-clacking on the stones, then moved up fast to minimize the other's start. The gray-green knight charged, then veered suddenly aside instead of coming straight on and giving his opponent a chance to deflect the lance with a swordstroke. Then he lifted and tossed the massive pole one-handed, like a javelin, the heavy head glancing off

Lohengrin's shoulder, spinning him around in the saddle. As the gray-green warrior closed, Lohengrin just managed to whip out his blade and check the terrific blows that followed, an incredible flurry that bent, then spilled him out of the saddle, cut, bruised, and stunned, onto the hard road, where he clanged and rolled from under the trampling hooves and over the side, bouncing thirty feet or so down the rocky slope before he could stop himself and crouch there glaring up with rage, shock, and respect. His enemy looked through the mists at him, leaving his visor closed.

He called down, "I won't wait and kill you. Your defense was very good. You should be dead, otherwise."

Lohengrin said nothing for a moment. This was no man to vent spleen at lightly, he realized. He was surprised to be alive himself.

"What's your name?" he finally called up.

"What matter?" was the reply. "I have sufficient enemies. Enjoy your life," he said, turning his horse around, "for so long as you keep it."

Lohengrin heard him ride off into the mist. After a while he clambered up to the roadway. His squire waited, holding his mount.

Lohengrin stood there for a moment before getting on the horse.

"I'll find him again," he said seriously, "and stand on better terms without tricks."

Wista seemed puzzled.

"Why fight again, sir?" he wanted to know. "You yourself say that a fight for no profit is for fools."

"So it is." Lohengrin nodded as he mounted. "A sham, the fiction of chivalry and honor. Something for songs and stories, boy." He leaned his sharp face and dark, magnetic eyes close to the other. "But it's my one purity, you understand?"

The squire shook his head.

"No," he admitted. "What purity do you speak of?"

"To test my skill with death."

Wista took this in thoughtfully.

"Why?" he still wanted to know.

"Because," was the answer as they started to ride on, "you live or die, win or lose, and there's no lie in it. There's decay in lies. And all else but this *is* a lie, boy."

Broaditch, Handler, and Valit had found shelter in a narrow

crack of a cave. They'd lost the road at dark, though it could not be far in any direction from where they were. The rain still fell steadily at the entrance and drained noisily away down the slope.

There was no hope of finding wood for a fire, so they crouched miserably around the chill walls in utter darkness.

Broaditch was contemplating the implications of an unusually foul odor in the cave. A wild beast? Long-dead prey? Offal? It was certainly a stench among stenches. . . .

"Well," said Handler, "we'll reach the town tomorrow. You're welcome to stay at my daughter's."

"I thank you," Broaditch replied, "but I may not."

"You mean to go on with the world washing away looking for I know not what?"

"If the world be about to wash away," Broaditch answered, "then I'll sink or float wherever I find myself."

"Why are you whimpering?" Handler asked his son.

"Ah, it's the damp here," was the reply, through chattering teeth.

"Here, boy," Broaditch said, rummaging in his pack, "I've a dry blanket my wife rolled in hide for me."

"Alienor," Handler's voice said in the blackness.

Broaditch found the blanket and passed it across the narrow chamber.

"I miss her," he remarked. "We fit together like mortar and pestle."

Handler chuckled.

"Aye," he agreed, "I understand such things. If I were you, I'd have stayed at home."

"We're good friends. After so many married years, you become friends at last or hate until death."

"Well, with my woman, his mother, it were neither one nor the other." He paused and reflected. "But she were a wonder to lie with, though. An' I lay with more than one!"

"So you did."

"Aye. An' she, as well," Handler said, "she were a woman, though she were never my friend." He chuckled. Then he sighed with memory in his voice.

He sighed as a raspy, penetrating voice cut suddenly through the darkness. Valit cried out involuntarily. Broaditch instantly thought in defense: *he can't see us, either.*

Handler called out, "Who's here?"

"Impure of minds," the voice intoned. "Dark are your worldly souls."

"Who speaks?" Handler demanded.

"The pipe is played, but ye dance not," the voice said grimly.

"A hermit's cell," Broaditch murmured. "Forgive us, holy one," he said, placating with a certain seriousness and calculated reserve. "We sought shelter from the rain."

The shrill voice spoke as if bodiless and unaffected as a ghost's would be to any possible response to it.

"The floods gather and ye heed not! Free thyselves from thy long chains of sin, feel they shame, fall on thy knees and remain so for ten years, cry to the holy spirit ere thy complete destruction is accomplished!"

"Damned fool," Handler complained, "to startle honest men and use them so."

"Abase thyselves, wicked ones! Death gnaws at thy heels, his cold hand is on thy limbs, his chill breath fills thy nostrils."

"Then what use to pray, holy one," Broaditch asked, "if there is no hope of salvation?"

"Ah-ha!" cried the voice with glee and rancor. "Hear, O Lord, how the devil kneads the truth to bake his bread!"

"Since God has left so many hungry mouths," Broaditch snapped, irritated, "peace, hermit. I weary of sermons and misery."

"I'll hear nothing said against God, Broaditch," Handler's voice broke in.

"God?" Broaditch wondered. "God is in your heart, not your words."

"The devil lives in yours," the voice hissed.

"Have you tinder for light?" Valit suddenly asked.

"Aye, boy," the voice declared, "a light brighter than the blaze of summer noon, and ye are the tinder."

"We don't need one like that," Valit said. "Even a candle end would do in here."

Broaditch smiled in the darkness. *Who can burn words at need?* he asked himself. *If we could, we'd all bathe in warmth. . . .*

As Lohengrin and his squire, Wista, were crossing the castle yard, the sun was suddenly out. It was a shock. Men stopped their work; people of every degree could be seen leaning out windows. A stout peasant woman toting a bale of wet sticks stood knee-deep in mud, her lips moving in prayer. Lohengrin looked up into the brilliant warmth and then, just as the standing pools began to steam, it disappeared. . . .

Well, he thought, *it still burns in heaven.*

All around the people suddenly looked depressed and gray again.

"At least the rain has let up," his young light-haired squire remarked, tilting his handsome face around.

Lohengrin grunted.

"At least," he paralleled, "we've come to where the gold is supposed to be. If there's none in the sky, at least some will shine in my dark purse."

He met the Duke in the archway to the throne room. They embraced and formally kissed.

"My lord," Lohengrin said as they crossed the gleaming tiles toward a window seat, "you are well, I trust?"

"My stomach has not eaten me yet," the Duke replied. He smiled faintly. His eyes and hair were matching gray. Even his skin had a grayish tint. He was as thin as a razor and restless under his poise. They sat down together as a man served spiced wine and then quickly withdrew.

"Well," Lohengrin remarked, "I still wait to be resolved, my lord."

The Duke sipped his drink and stared vaguely out at the misty, dripping landscape beyond his swollen, overflowed moat.

"We'll all die of congestion and shivers," he said, "in this cursed damp long before the rains drown us all."

"I have a few things to do still, before I die."

"You're an arrogant and impatient young killer." The Duke sighed and stared at the flooded fields, saw a peasant on a raft out where last year's rye had blown. . . . "In the face of nature, as a wise priest said, these plots seem shadows." In mind was an image of a sunken world with the bloated dead floating everywhere, himself on a high seat watching the water creep up to him. . . . Still, we'll all act our parts even into death as far as God allows. . . .

"I long to be resolved," Lohengrin said.

"Ah, yes?"

"In whose service do I truly stand?"

"You don't think it's me, then, in the lead?"

"No."

"Why not, pray?" The Duke was curious enough to look away from the grim landscape for a moment.

"Your whole soul isn't burning for it."

"Is yours, young man?" When Lohengrin proposed no reply, the Duke went on: "If we are successful, you will soon learn. If not . . ."

"So that's it," Lohengrin said, his dark, fierce eyes leveled, "a falcon in the night. I'm to buy it by the flap of its wings alone."

The Duke was gazing out again at the gray wash of land.

"Do what you must do," he said mildly, "and earn your gold. But use caution."

"Caution? I rarely offer my neck to any blade, my lord Duke."

"Not in your fighting." He turned to squint intently at the dark young man. "Don't press to know what you need not." Lohengrin could see the man was very uneasy, almost, he thought, afraid. "There are worse things than swords, young knight. And many."

Lohengrin raised both eyebrows.

"What things?" he wondered, almost mocking.

"To cross a narrow bridge, look neither left nor right." The Duke turned away again.

He's afraid of something, Lohengrin thought. *He regrets his course. . . . Strange, he was always said to be a hard man. . . . Does he believe the last judgment is upon him? There are fools enough for every foolishness. . . .*

"I'll eat and sleep now, my lord," he said, standing up, "with your grace's leave."

"You have it." The Duke still stared and his sweaty fingertips worked slickly together.

"I'll cross my bridges each in their time." Lohengrin grinned. And he strode away. Still the Duke stared and sighed to himself, watching the water lap at the stones of his castle. . . .

Lohengrin had forgotten her name in the two months since he was first here. She came into his chamber with a cup of hot wine. He was lying wrapped in a dark red robe. The steam from his bath was still in the air. She was very angry with herself, he noted, that she'd come unbidden. But she'd obviously been afraid to wait. She probably thought he was playing a cruel lover's game. He almost smiled. A clever technique, he reflected, resulting from his having forgotten her altogether until this moment. . . .

"My lady," he said, not getting up, gesturing her forward.

She had bright teeth. Her lips were parted in love's sweet pain as
Lohengrin drove the spear of himself harder and deeper into her,
pressing her hips down where she squatted over him. He was
thinking with a certain detachment: How could you blame man for
his fall since he carried the instruments of bliss between his legs?
He smiled faintly as she cried out and rotated her sopping loins.
He held himself back as far as he could and watched her, and then
more urgent thoughts began stirring up from his carnal depths,
images: two sluts in a tub licking one another's breasts . . . two
others together sucking a man's genitals . . . ah, the beautiful
whores. . . . He rocked himself now in her time, faster and
faster . . . beautiful whores. . . . Free and helpless as it rose
within him, lifted him, floated him, and he dug his hands into her
arms and slammed her up and down. She gasped and rolled her
eyes and cried out in pleasure and pain, begging, weeping, and he
cried out as he fell, as it burst beneath and dropped him into
sweetness and a flash of death.

"Bitch . . . ! Ah, bitch . . . !"

Flesh violent and anonymous, uncontrolled now, slamming,
slamming, slamming, and he locked rigid and dropped beyond
light or shape:

"You little whore . . . you have me, you little whore. . . ."

Dim, gray, soggy dawn finally appeared at the cave entrance.
Broaditch's aches had condensed into a general numbness. He had
sort of slept. The hermit's voice had stopped some hours before
daylight. Someone was snoring and moaning. The rain was a faint
misting now. He sighed to his bones and shifted his solid body.

He was remembering the chaotic days, the deadly sickness
stalking everywhere . . . twenty years ago . . . the lawless bands
. . . the endless war devolving into fragments of outlaw horror as
the great armies broke up and the land itself began to reek with the
burning, bleeding, and decay . . . twenty years . . . and after
struggling with pregnant Alienor (the child was lost in that first
year before they found refuge) as far south as possible, reaching
her father's land only to find a drained mill pond, gutted
ruins . . . and then joining the mercenaries . . . pillage, terror,
fleeing, fighting among the scattered, wasted kingdoms . . . his
sack of gold he'd gathered, buried, added to bit by bit . . . buying

the farm in the far south . . . watching the three children grow up . . . the harvests . . . the contentments . . . the longing . . . all this in one moment of memory . . . then the pilgrimage to find the man he'd known as a boy, the "fool" who supposedly found the holy Grail, the perfection of God, something he'd come to insist upon believing and something (like so many others) he hoped to see, had to see, because he understood his life was rolling him to darkness as the snows caught in his hair and beard, as faces changed against the pulsing, ageless seasons. . . .

So, he thought, with his sardonic twinkle (that had never aged a day, either) in those ceramic-chip blue eyes, *here are you, you old heap of bones and meat, as mad as ever Parsival was himself to follow ghosts and dreams after all the blood and mud truth you learned.* . . .

He gathered himself and struggled to his feet. He yawned immensely. The snores went on, then suddenly broke into a fit of coughing and spitting.

"Did you awaken, holy man?" Broaditch called back into the darkness. A snarled curse showed Handler was coming conscious. Broaditch chuckled.

"So," he remarked, "you say your matins with your first breath, like birdsong."

A rank, sickening reek suddenly flowed out of the damp innards of the cave as Broaditch fancied a great gobbet of decay burst loose deep in the intestines of some monstrous beast. Handler, cursing, emerged, closely followed by Valit.

"Did one of you just die and rot a moment ago?" Broaditch demanded, stepping out into the gray drizzle with the misty, wetly gleaming forest at his back.

The hermit came near the opening in a wash of stink and Broaditch considered that this was sanctity you could slice with a sword.

"Stay where you are," he called to him. "We're too sinful out here for your fragrance, holy one."

The skinny, dim form had stopped just where the shadows began to thicken so that his flesh seemed half-consumed by darkness.

"Sinful creatures!" came the cry. "Remove thy impure stains from this sacred spot!"

Handler crossed himself. Valit squinted, still shaking himself awake. He seemed unimpressed, Broaditch noted.

"Bless us, holy one," Handler said to the shadow in the cave.

"He who has touched no water since they baptized him," Broaditch murmured, shaking his weary head.

"Let God give you a test!" the hermit cried. "Suffer, bruise thy flesh, tear the soul free from the body's gripping cage!"

Handler suddenly knelt, facing the cave mouth. Valit inclined his head with a faint, almost (Broaditch thought) sly, smile on his lips. Broaditch turned and was already heading down the slope toward the woods.

Parsival was walking steadily, meditating on the fog and gleaming heath that spread out all around. He heard the panting, the clinking armor for a long time before the pursuing knight actually caught up. He never looked back. He could have felt the man even if he hadn't actually heard anything. He could always do that now.

The knight kept pace just behind him, puffing. Parsival said nothing. They crossed a stream on a tilted, half-submerged log. Parsival's step was sure and effortless, while the knight slipped and teetered.

"Christ!" the man called out. "Wait!" And he fell heavily, feet scrabbling desperately at the slick wood, into the cold, running stream, spluttering as the steamy fog boiled up.

Parsival stopped and looked back as the warrior struggled to his feet and stomped out of the water onto the muddy bank. He waited while the knight stood there dripping and raging, unscrewing his helmet, water pouring out of it and all the joints of his armor. He was young, stubborn-faced, eyes steel-gray chips.

"For God's sake," he said, coughing, "am I some nimble-footed jester to dance over trees like a squirrel?"

"When you track a wolf," the older man advised, "don't expect him to keep to the paved way."

"I don't track you," the young man announced. "You overthrew me." He unbuckled his sword and tossed it in the mud at Parsival's feet. "I am in your service."

Parsival smiled and raised an eyebrow.

"A custom," he said, "met more in tales than in life in these times. Pick it up. I wish no man's service."

"I want to learn from you, sir," was the stubborn reply. "I want to know how to stand naked with better defense than armor."

"Go back."

"I'll follow you until one of us drops dead, sir."

Parsival turned and started walking, saying, "Unless I cross a few streams more."

"Well," was the angry response, "I'll swim if I must." He snatched up his weapon and shook the mud from the scabbard. "Damn you!" he raged at the tall, wide, receding back. "See if I don't!"

With a fixed, grim look of infinite determination, he rebuckled his sword belt and began plodding into the foggy wake of his reluctant master.

Lohengrin stood nude, brawny, brooding by the embrasure staring out into the gray morning. A faint spatter of infinitely strained, pale sunlight flickered, with the tentativeness of a butterfly, on the moist stones.

He was holding his sword, twisting it idly. He turned away from the soggy view. Across the room the woman lay sleeping, snoring lightly in the tangle of covers.

He was wondering if the Duke really stood to gain the crown. He unconsciously ground his teeth, abstractly furious. Why was he always frustrated? What use was limitless skill with limited opportunity? And why did Lancelot, who had the brains of a fly, try to kill him? To run him out of the race? Whom did that ass serve?

He snapped and spun the blade in an explosive, raging cut. He gritted his teeth.

Well, they'd see . . . they'd all see! By God, they'd bleed and see that, too. . . .

He posed, holding the blade two-handed over his head. He forgot everything, even his anger now, easing into it, feeling himself flow out into the steel as if it were all one movement as he noiselessly turned and cut again, feeling a thrill in the release and the grace and force he expressed through himself. . . .

Parsival looked back down the twisting dirt trail to where faint, strained sunlight glowed on the bend of dense trees. Yes, there the fellow was, still coming, struggling on relentlessly in his dulled armor. What did he want? What point in a few cheap tricks? How could a man who knew virtually nothing teach anybody else a thing? Well, let him keep coming and eventually he'd be discouraged. . . . Or would he . . . ?

Parsival turned and went steadily on and on. . . . The narrow way twisted, doubled back through this oppressive, dank forest. . . . It reminded him of those wet lands where he'd ridden for weeks when he first set out for Arthur's court in his rags and impossible innocence . . . so long ago now it seemed but a memory in a dream of a dream . . . so long ago that for a moment tears came to his eyes, remembering. . . . Every play of shadow and light had seemed so vibrant then, had seemed to hint at the momentary unfolding of supernatural adventures. . . .

And now, here he walked, aloof in a world gone gray, having found even magic as dull as mud and wearying to pass through. Yes, he was steeped in magic like a herb in sauce, it had seeped into him with his years of fasting, prayer, and vast, cool distance from the shadow-play of life. . . . Oh, he had learned many secrets, from Merlinus and others, powers . . . he had tried to follow the way to the true Grail, which he now believed was mistaken for a symbol, as well as for a reality. . . . Gawain and the others thought it was a talisman or a weapon or the cup that had brimmed with Christ's blood or secret words to win the world with . . . Ah, but he believed the Grail already pulsed in his heart and that he had to, somehow, unwrap the wrappings and free the golden fire to shine. . . . And all he'd succeeded in was gaining power of flesh and will—the heart stayed dark. . . . And, worse, the process had left him permanently open to the normally impalpable forces that prowled and lurked in sorcerers' shadows. . . .

He was climbing steadily now and the sun was stronger. The rising, rocky ground was almost dry in places. The trees were thinned out and scrubby. He knew he was getting closer to his ancestral home. Several years had passed since he left his wife and children here. He wondered if he'd find them or if they'd returned to her lands in the southeast. He was remembering his childhood suddenly, and the memories were dense and rich, like a jewel wrapped in crushed rose petals. . . . His mother: the slim, tall, youthful woman seemed to float in her shimmering flower beds beside the square-stone castle wall . . . mother . . .

He crossed a pebbly stream bed and then began following it, twisting up the slope. Withered heather lined the sides among sharp outcroppings of dark rock. The place seemed familiar. He walked on, thinking back, and then had it, stood still and gazed around. He'd nearly died here, twenty years ago. Right here, or a few steps on, anyway, he'd lain in his rent and shattered armor, bleeding into the dry, stony earth, watching the day dim and reel around him, seeing the shadowy-seeming knight in jet-black steel (with bright crimson pulsing from the chestplate) lift his bloody mace and stagger another step closer to him, holding it, trembling, over his head, breath puffing and blowing gigantically. . . . Parsival realized his helmet had been battered away and that even a moderate blow would kill him, but he could only watch from a great distance, feeling the outlines of a blissful peace beginning to enfold him. . . . He'd felt like a child after a long, weary day . . . and then the knight, mace high, was pulled over backward by its weight and the last thing Parsival registered or could recall now was the distant clanging crunch of his fall. . . .

. . . He blinked himself back to the present. He walked on a few steps. The band of black horsemen had poured up this way and he'd fought them every inch and slew as in a dream. They had swept over him without seeming end. *I must have died*, he thought, smiling, bending, poking around in the loose stones . . . touched the steel he'd thought he spotted. He pulled a rusted, rotted mail gauntlet loose. Through the rents he could see yellow, bony fingers still clutched within it. He was amazed.

He turned quickly, hearing a distant, approaching crunch and clink. Then he relaxed with a shake of his head. That stubborn knight still followed. For days he'd dogged his trail.

By twilight Parsival had passed the ruined wall, which was as far from home as he'd ever gone as a boy before he ran away to find King Arthur's kingdom on the swayed back of his bent horse, Spavint. He'd traded Spavint for his first charger, Niva, at Camelot. Spavint had walked and wandered him in circles for weeks. . . .

The rounded, spilled stones here had been set in the days of the Pictish kings to hold back someone from something long lost and forgotten. Time went on melting and shifting the landscape. Parsival wondered who and how many had died in defense of whatever at this mysterious border. . . . The twilight flowed in like a tide and the wall curved across the hill into a tantalizing obscurity, as if (he thought) you might encounter the long-lost phantoms by following it into the deepening mists of evening. . . .

A few steps farther on he felt something, a presence. He turned suddenly. A shadowy shape floated or stood back in the violet wash of fugitive light. He felt a strange, steady, pulsing tugging at the pit of his stomach. He used to assume it was fear until he learned it was a wizard's way of touching things, that his inner perception was reaching out to finger or be gripped by forms unknowable to the daily senses.

He paused and waited. He knew he was vulnerable. The price of his powers. The defense of ignorance secured the ordinary man. He began controlling his breathing, clasped his hands over his stomach. He focused his will there to create a kind of shield. *This*, he reflected, *is another kind of jousting.* And his legendary strength was no assurance here of anything.

"You," he called into the evanescent gleamings. No response. The figure seemed armored, the face a seamless reflection of vague shimmers. "You," he repeated, "do you seek to bar my path?"

The figure may have moved, walked smoothly as water flow, or drifted a little closer. There was a liquid shimmer of sword, which the knight apparently held at his side. Parsival still couldn't be certain if it was a substantial form or not. He wondered if the sword could cut living flesh. . . . He wished his master were here: the frail monk Limus whose eyes could stun a strong man with a look. Limus, who'd pushed him half out of the world so that he could never be sure again of the borders of life and death . . . Limus, friend of Merlinus. . . .

The squat, blurry knight was flowing toward him now, rapid, silent, as if wind-borne, as if the fading twilight had condensed and exhaled this phantom. Parsival braced his body, feeling the onrush of terror and doubt, worked his breath as he'd been taught, felt the pressure of the figure's coming, and as it reached him his perception exploded and he flashed a vast, dark, chilling, wing-like flutter so that for a moment he felt shrunk to a speck in a vast and resistless sea of obliteration and his thoughts cried: *Lord God save me! Save me!* And he vibrated like a storm-wrung leaf, and as a scream rolled up from deep within he suddenly, inexplicably, struck back and everything burst in an empty bubble of dream. . . . He was trembling, shaken, and alone in the twilight. . . . He realized this was but the beginning of these attacks or experiences or whatever they were. . . .

"So you finally stopped," a voice suddenly said out of the darkness behind him. He turned, surprised. It was the stolid knight. Too much time had passed, he thought, and, incredibly, he hadn't sensed the young man's approach. A soft glow of moonlight was replacing the sunset wash.

"Where is your armor?" Parsival asked.

The other shrugged.

"I laid it aside," he replied.

Parsival smiled.

"So as to creep up on me?" he wondered.

"No. It avails me naught against you. And it wearied me."

Parsival nodded and started to walk on ahead, thoughtfully.

"I cannot teach you what you wish to learn," he remarked, following the faint trail. "Yet I might show you all the things I don't know."

Why, he asked himself, had he been attacked? What or who would send those powers to harass him? He spoke over his shoulder to the young knight, who was treading at his heels in his faint moonshadow.

"Who was the lord who sent you against me?"

The young man hesitated, then said, "I am bound to keep my honor, sir, as I would now for your sake."

Parsival frowned, then nodded.

"Keep it, then," he said at length. "A thing so rare should be treasured."

In the wan shards of sunlight, Broaditch, Handler, and Valit passed through the grimy, grim gates of London town. The slimy streets were knee-deep in nameless muck. Nearby a mound of rotting fish had been ground under wheel, hoof, and foot. Broaditch was astonished. He'd known a stench or two in his time, and that holy hermit had been a very prince among the lords of stink, but this! God save them! The concentration and monumental excess of this stained collection of huts and houses was beyond natural imagination. Men must swim in the smells like fish in the sea. . . .

He clapped his handkerchief to his nose with a certain futility. Handler's son was eyeing the wonders about him, Broaditch observed, with what might have been a certain surprising slyness. He wouldn't have expected that quality, though he'd barely spoken twenty words directly to the boy. He was pondering a massive cart loaded with bound and sacked goods.

"Consider," he said, thinking aloud, "how many folk must be fed herein . . . all in one place. . . ."

Broaditch gazed around the city walls, where heads and skulls sat tilted on spikes and bodies rotted in chains. They turned a corner. An old woman was squatting, ragged dress lifted, at the opening of an alleyway. . . . A half-naked, blood-spattered, mud-covered boy was racing, splashing through the filth as three larger versions pounded in his wake, two brandishing staffs, one a dagger, coming on in silence and deadly purpose. . . . Behind them a drunken man was dancing on a cart. . . . The boy and his pursuers vanished into a twisting, narrow lane. . . . People continued about their business: a pair of carriers staggered from their wagon into a building under a load of freshly killed pigs, the heads swaying, dangling. . . . A man was broiling something on a stick over an open fire. . . .

Broaditch and the other two worked their way carefully along the slippery, sunken stones that served as a sidewalk. He glanced into a doorway where a man leaned against a wall in the shadows and a woman knelt before him as if in prayer or confession, except, Broaditch thought, she followed a strange catechism. . . . A boggy steam rose steadily from the streets as the sunlight intensified.

They passed a long row of dried salt fish hung under eaves to dry, when Handler said, "He lives near the river."

"Ah," Broaditch responded, "who?"

"My son, Luark, whom I seek."

"My elder brother," Valit put in. "His brain is dented."

"Peace, you vicious rascal," his father muttered. "A full pot don't ring when you beat it."

"Was he born . . ." Broaditch touched his head.

"Naaa," sneered Valit, "he come by it from the king's men. They caught . . ."

"Peace!" And his father's lopping backhand nearly caught the son in the face as he nimbly darted aside. "An empty pot makes noise enough!"

"It's true," Valit insisted, keeping ahead and looking back, "he cut Odd Jack's grain and . . ."

"Heed not a fool's tales," Handler growled.

"It's truth. The king's men cracked his head for his pains and so dented his wits."

"Ah," disparaged Handler, "let me catch you and yours will sag a bit, I promise you. Heed him not. He's a sly, lazy, shiftless . . ."

They ducked against the nearest wall as a glopping of slops

sprayed down close at hand. Broaditch saw the bucket being withdrawn from a second-story window. The lane slanted down toward the river, whose steel-gray sheen was visible through the spaces between buildings and huts.

Broaditch had decided to spend the night with them and set out to discover Lohengrin in the morning. All he knew of Parsival at this point was composite rumor (virtually a tradition already) that he was living in a monastery and that he had the Grail with him, hidden because evil men sought to discover him and its secret.

Well, Broaditch considered, *evil often is just another word for your enemies.*

That afternoon Lohengrin was riding into the city, unarmored, with sword and dagger at his hip. He reined up his charger by a freshly painted red frame building. The windows were hung with black curtains.

He crossed the foul, mucky street with a few long, bouncy strides and mounted the steps to the entrance. A carrot-faced townsman just entering jostled the hook-faced knight, who, with cold fury, shook him by the collar so that his knees rattled together.

"Base scum," he hissed, "heed your course."

He tossed him back with casual distaste and pushed through the rough plank door.

"Ha," the man called after him from the relative security of the street, "but base-born sluts are good enough for your noble pecker! You stinking muck-brain, your face looks like a soggy cod-piece!"

He broke off muttering, taking a few lanky steps out of the path of a dog-cart as Lohengrin's fierce, bushy-haired face was thrust from the doorway, glaring, then withdrawn silently as the door slammed shut.

A second stone jug of wine was going around the rude table under the greasy, smoky tallow lamplight. Broaditch, Handler, Valit, his brother, Luark, his wife, and a burly neighbor with a missing ear were sitting around a tilted table. Luark was slit-eyed and scowling.

"Ah, those were the days," the neighbor, Rova, was saying, "and no mistake about it." He addressed himself mainly to Valit and Luark. Handler nodded agreement sagely.

"What do these youngbloods know?" he asked, swilling down more acidic wine.

Broaditch smiled to himself, leaning back in a shadowy corner of the buckled, narrow room. He was sucking at his long Oriental pipe.

"So let it be my treat, b'God," one-eared Rova said. He winked ponderously. "Pity the married man who has to hold by the hearth tonight." He laughed.

Handler nodded through his semi-stupor. A dribble of wine was drying along the crease of his chin.

"Arr," he said, "pity, pity,"

The wife tossed her square head and looked sour.

"Off to the bawds, are you?"

"What a notion!" Rova cried, laughing. "A great, solid man like Handler, there?"

"Aye," she affirmed. "And will you have him back to his family with pox?"

"Do you hear that?" Rova boomed. "Why, I mean to treat them to nothing of hurt. But it's a dull life without some loving, eh?"

"I hear there's great profit in whores," Valit said thoughtfully.

"Of a sort, boy," Rova said, "though it be a profit that costs a man."

"The boy means whoremasters," Broaditch put in from his corner.

"I know not," Rova exclaimed, "for every man who owns a wine shop falls sick with the drink."

"And all bakers are fat," declared Luark, "and who would not like it so?"

"That's wisdom," Rova said.

"Aye," said the wife, "wisdom. From him, that's eggs from a goat and milk from a chicken."

"It were the blow to his head," Valit assented, as if he'd been asked.

"Shut up," Handler advised.

"Well," Rova bantered, "it's not me inflamed by the devil's lusts."

"You told me," Valit protested, and Broaditch couldn't tell if it was slyly, "you said you even put horns on the head of Christ."

"What words are these?" the woman cried out, crossing herself.

"Well," Rova said and smiled, "not every bride is true to flesh, much less an invisible husband."

"You're the devil's carrier, Rova," she said, crossing herself again.

"Well, stay off my cart, then," was the retort.

"Leading men and boys to the whores," she said, getting angry. "No wonder God drowns the world with such as you in it."

"What does this mean?" Handler demanded, wobbling on his stool. "What is he saying?"

"That vows are not the soul of purity," Broaditch put in quite seriously. These questions mattered to him more and more and were not to be put aside with easy cynicism or dull belief. Were the acts of the clergy of any importance to God at all? Did the reasonings of scholars affect the heart for good?

"Or their seal, either," Rova said.

"You say," Handler demanded, cocking his head to the side, "you say you have lain with nuns?"

"I lay with none who was chaste."

Broaditch smiled.

"That covers all cases," he said.

Rova laughed.

"Speak no more unholy things," the woman said, "or leave this house."

Handler was searching Rova's face with narrowed eyes. He kept licking his lower lip. He was agitated.

"Well," he insisted on knowing, "do you say truth or lie?"

"What?" Rova wondered.

"Nuns. Have you truly lain with nuns?"

She stood up.

"No more of this talk," she said. "Is naught still holy?"

"I heard such tales," Handler went on, "but—"

"Enough!" she cried.

"Silence your wife, brother," Valit said maliciously.

She raised an earthen crock.

"I'll silence somebody," she announced grimly.

Handler swayed on his stool.

"When I was young," he declared, "things were not the same. . . ." He shook his head. "Let me tell you this . . . you worked your lord's land . . . you fought . . . no one but Jews and Italy-men would live in a town . . . things were differ-ent. . . ."

* * *

". . . so the priest creeps close to the crack in the door," Rova was saying as Broaditch, Handler, and Valit reeled up a narrow, mucky alley together behind him, "and sees the lord's prong standing up straight as a club. So he next—"

"Where be the damned place?" Handler demanded. "Must we wander in darkness forever?"

"No surprise in that," Broaditch commented.

"Peace, brothers," Rova declared, "salvation is at hand."

Broaditch felt his drunkenness clamping firm and velvety around him. Well, why not? he kept asking himself. Why not steep himself in nonsense for a night? He'd grown so serious over the years. Why not act the fool on purpose for a change? So the saints didn't do it, it seemed they didn't want to, to begin with. . . . Maybe the only sin is caring too much one way or the other. . . .

"What is this place?" Valit asked.

"Why, you'll soon see," Rova replied, "for if you know not the art of it already, then tonight's your night to be a man."

Handler found this amusing. They'd reached a narrow door in the back alley. A shrewish voice was rending someone around a bend; elsewhere there was singing. . . . They went through a second door into hot, wet air, with a smell of cooking food, cloves, perfume, and a sharp, faintly rank odor. . . .

"Is this an inn?" Valit asked.

"Ah-ha," said Rova, "yet none come to it to rest a night!" He turned to include Broaditch and Handler. "Now, when I stayed in the town of Naples, there was a stew there, the oldest and most magnificent in the country, with girls like angels from heaven . . . girls stolen and lured from the east, from the far north. . . ."He shook his head at the inexpressible wonder of it.

"Was that the high mark of your life?" Broaditch asked him bluntly.

"What's that?"

"The finest house of whores. Was that the high mark of your life's ambitions?"

"Could be worse," Rova said, faintly defensive.

They had entered a high-vaulted chamber lined on either side with canopied beds. Huge wooden tubs of perfumy, steaming water stood every few paces, with men and women soaping and splashing.

"What use will the memory of that be to you," Broaditch said, very sober for a moment.

"What use is any memory?" Rova wanted to know.

Broaditch was now contemplating tender hands soaping him in a hot bath. With age such pleasures became almost profound, he thought.

The richly gowned madam, in furs and silks, flanked by a stout ruffian, thick staff cocked over his shoulder, came grandly down the steamy aisle. Handler was uneasy.

"This place be not for the likes of us," he muttered.

"Peace, friend," Rova assured him. "So long as coin be in fashion here, so am I in fashion."

"How did he come by his money?" Valit whispered to Broaditch, or perhaps only to himself, as Rova walked ahead, all smiles, to greet the puffy-faced woman. "It's known he has more than one of his station rightfully should." As he said this his face (or so it seemed to Broaditch) showed a strange, sarcastic, intense contempt, and that same, subtle slyness, as well.

"This place be not for the likes of us," Handler repeated as his son looked at him with obvious scorn.

"Speak for yourself, old fool," he muttered. "What might suit me, you'd never dream."

Broaditch was just turning around. He'd just heard a deep moan from behind the curtains of a bed across the aisle. The sound smacked more of the rack than delight, he thought. It repeated over the music that was just starting again in some nearby chamber. Violas, reeds, and a tinny drumbeat. A grinding dance tune.

Handler suddenly sat down on a footstool, bent forward, and expelled one brief splash of vomit on the tiled floor. His son shook his head. Broaditch, after hesitating, parted the curtains and the general candlelight softly glowed on the scene within: a young nude woman lay beside a silver-haired, bony man (on the massive bed that could have slept half a dozen), whose eyes were very wide and unblinking, as if he stared at some wonder up in the canopy, a dagger tilted in his chest, rocking slightly, blood jetting weakly like a failing fountain. The blade flashed soft light over the bed, the terrified woman, and the harsh face still in the act of withdrawing behind the rear curtains.

Broaditch took in the bright, dark, snapping eyes, bushy hair, and instantly recognized him and instantly said, "Lohengrin!"

He stopped there, staring with an expression of weary resignation.

"Your mouth has just slain you and this slut, you blocky oaf."

And he leaped forward in one terrible motion (and Broaditch's mind thought: *this is death*.) across the mattress, snatching up the dagger (a sudden bloodjet as it came free), and striking a terrific claw-like slash at Broaditch's throat that barely missed as the big man flung himself back with surprising agility, whipping free his own dirk, crouching, ready, in the aisle.

Lohengrin, leaning out, saw a number of interested spectators and pulled back, cursing and hissing at his escaped victim. "It would be better for you to cut out your tongue! If you speak, I will give you the worst death you could dream!"

The whore was trying to slip unobserved from the bloody bed, breathless with terror. Lohengrin, quite casually, with a vicious final twist, slammed the blade between her breasts, dropping her, with a vague, sighing outcry, to the sheets.

"Please . . . I want to live . . ." she murmured.

Lohengrin's depthless eyes never left Broaditch's face.

"Remember," he said and moved back into the shadows through the rear curtains and was gone.

His escaped victim stood there a moment, then stooped forward to see to the girl, who had managed to crawl partway off the mattress, as if swimming face up, where she now dangled, draining away onto the yellowish tiled floor.

"It came to nothing in the end," Parsival was saying to the young knight called (he'd learned) Sir Prang. "I killed a host of men, won back my lands from my relatives with little difficulty . . . had a son . . . then a daughter . . ." They went on through the dim trees. The leaves rustled softly around them. "I turned to the spirit. I touched the least hem of its garment . . . then lost my grip. . . . I even went to war again, oh, to keep away from home, I admit this . . . and so it came to be that I killed more men. . . ." The woods seemed to be thinning out. Parsival intended to make a point of discouraging Prang, but, at the same time, he was glad of an ear after so many solitary months. "I became a great fellow," he continued, "as, no doubt, you've heard." He smiled sarcastically to himself. "I stood high in the councils of Arthur after he regained his power and was never happy a day with it. . . . And I came to my thirty-sixth year dulled by eating, sleeping, and fucking my fill. Why, I was so dulled that only the memory of the glory I'd touched as a boy had any life. So I joined the Irish monks, shattered my sword, and swore never to cease striving until I walked in that glory again. . . ."

He broke off as they moved across a narrow, moonlit field that sloped up before them. The castle was a dim outline on the crest.

"Well," he murmured, "I've come home again with more gray hairs and a dark heart." He sighed.

"Sir," said Prang, "you have already mastered more than . . ."

"No. I lost it. I lost the glory. Can't you see that? Men who have never known it never miss it and so may endure their lives. But such as I lose both heaven and earth." They climbed up the steepening, gleaming slope. Off to the left was the little village of huts. A single candle seemed to shine down there. "You should understand this," he said. There were no lights showing in the castle itself, he noted. What was it about a place where you spent childhood? A magic? An intensity that never fades. . . .

"I don't know about all you say," Prang demurred, "but I want to fight as you fight. I want to learn that."

"Why?" Parsival asked over his shoulder. *It wasn't that late*, he was thinking, for no light at all to be showing. . . . Perhaps they'd all gone away, for some reason. . . .

The drawbridge was down, the gates open. They passed the first bodies there lying in the gleam and moonshadows around the pitch-dark opening.

"Ah," said Prang quietly, "they went after your family, too."

Parsival knelt by the first man. The blank eyes gleamed in a bearded face.

"I knew this man," he murmured. "He served with me under Arthur."

"How long dead seems he?"

Parsival stood up and headed through the doorway.

"Not long," he replied.

Prang touched the hilt of his sword and followed.

"Why do you say 'they?'" Parsival wanted to know. He'd discovered he could not hear thoughts at will. When it happened, it happened.

"Because more than one seeks your life. So much I feel free of oath to say."

The older man had stopped in the courtyard.

"No," he said, as if to a third party and startled Prang for a moment. "I won't be drawn back into that."

"Eh?" Prang grunted. "What's that, then?"

"I won't," Parsival obscurely concluded and walked on through the inner walled yard, stepping carefully over and around the bodies, armored and unarmored. The raw blood stink was still in the air.

"It seems it were a good fight," Prang observed quietly.

Parsival didn't respond. They'd entered the main hall. He'd been expecting it since crossing the moat and now he finally faced it completely, let the pain and shock in to himself, and realized he would survive it. So it was that he said nothing after lighting a torch and looking at his wife and daughter sprawled together, hacked to bloody tatters. He said not a word. The sooty torch fire billowed around him, flipping his distorted shadow around the bare stone walls. Neither face was intact; his child's was shredded. But the necklace he knew glinted around her neck. He bent and took it, gripped it in his powerful hand as Prang came up beside him.

"Good Jesus," he said.

Parsival just stood there in the flame and dark, the golden chain swaying in his fingers.

"I won't," he whispered and shut his eyes against a terrible outcry he felt gathering within him. He stood there for a long time. . . . And then he felt the movements before he actually heard the faint scrape of steel. He instantly threw the torch across the hall toward the open archway behind them. He moved Prang quietly aside as the arrow thummed past and clinked dully on the far wall. The flames showed an armored, shadowy figure standing there, with others at his back.

"So," said Prang, drawing his blade.

"Wait," Parsival said, trembling with suppressed energy.

The bowman and two or three other knights entered the chamber. Their faces seemed to fill and hollow out as the flames wavered.

"It were well we waited," the leader said, "eh, Parsival?" He seemed philosophic. "You may as well stand still and take it like a man, you and your friend there. No sense in ducking about like a stricken goose."

"Pick up one of these swords here, my lord," Prang muttered aside, "and we'll show them something."

"No," Parsival said. "Follow me. There are at least twenty more without."

"Eh?"

"And armored."

"How can you tell this?"

"I can tell." As the men advanced across the floor in the sputtering light of the thrown torch, the chief knight nocked a shaft and half-drew his bowstring.

"Prepare yourselves," he said.

"Follow me," Parsival hissed. And he ducked back and to the side as the second arrow zipped by, stooped briefly to snatch up a sword and ax from the litter on the bloody stones, and hurled the ax (without breaking stride) at the lead knight, who deflected the terrific blow with his shield (staggered back) into the man on his right, who screamed and went down in a flash of sparks.

"Christ," murmured Prang, "what a recovery."

"Lancelot," Parsival called out, sure of it now.

The stocky knight threw aside his bow, stooped, and tossed the torch into the center of the chamber, where the fitful light outlined all of them.

"There is no escape," he pointed out.

Parsival seemed quite at ease, Prang noted. His own heart was racing as if the whole space echoed with it.

"Why?" Parsival wanted to know calmly.

"Because you're surrounded."

"Why is it necessary?"

"What does it matter?" Lancelot said, advancing. "Why bear yet another burden into hell?"

The stricken knight on the floor was sighing now, very rapidly. Prang could see him kicking sporadically in the wavering shadows. Several more men had entered the place and were keeping close along the far walls, gradually circling to cut them off.

Parsival was silent, unmoving, concentrating, trying now to touch Lancelot in the way he'd learned from the monks: to grip him invisibly with the hands of his soul, to throw off his timing. But he was solidly blocked. A wall of will held him away. He decided the man must have a talisman. His master had explained that a talisman collected power the way a cup held water, that the power could act as if the wizard himself were actually present to baffle spells and deflect attacks. . . .

"Tell me, Lancelot!" he demanded.

"Now!" The legendary warrior signaled and he and several spearmen charged forward.

Parsival plucked at Prang's arm and they retreated quickly toward the stair, though three armored men waited there with leveled spears. Prang was certain they'd be held up long enough for the others to fall upon their rear. He was grimly amused to think he was suddenly on the other side of the fight and about to die for no reward and in obscurity to boot at the hands of the most famous knight in the world.

Except, incredibly, the first attacker seemed to skid, as if on sheer ice, and fall even as he thrust so a way opened between the other two that Parsival smashed through, cutting one sweep over his head that sliced both spears short. Prang jumped over the strangely fallen man and followed this reluctant teacher. The man still struggled to gain his feet, as if he walked in grease. Prang had noticed nothing as he passed, he reflected, cutting one good blow on the upraised sword of the man at his heels. . . .

Once on the landing above, they raced down a twisting series of passageways until Parsival lost the pursuit. Prang followed by sound and an occasional moonlit glimpse as they passed embrasures. . . . They stopped in a high, dim hall. There were columns leading to a pair of raised thrones on a dais.

"I last looked upon my mother on this spot," the older man said. "Sitting here . . . she bid me godspeed in the world. . . . I was impatient to go. I thought I'd be back before too long. . . ." He smiled faintly to himself and shook his head, then sighed.

"Sir," said Prang, "for God's sake, let's be off."

"There's no hurry. I sealed the door behind us."

"What? I didn't see that. Is this magic?"

"There is no magic—only what you cannot understand at the moment."

It was like praying: you couldn't explain why, you couldn't grasp the mechanism of the underlying intelligence and movement of all life, but you could learn to trust it. You could throw it out from yourself and simply trust it. Like walking in the dark with shut eyes, your body would see for you if you totally gave yourself up to it. . . .

"Well?" Prang wanted to know.

Parsival started walking again. They left the chamber. He remembered his mother's face for a moment: pale, glowing, wordless, beseeching . . . wordless. . . .

Well, he knew he'd have to have blood now. The part of his

awareness that was free saw it as absurd, that pain would lead only to pain and resolve nothing. . . . But he had to have it now . . . the chains of custom. . . .

He stopped in a narrow cell. An iron-bound door was bolted shut and locked. A dim ray of moonlight fell there.

"A way out?" Prang wondered.

"Yes."

"Have you the key?"

"There is none. My mother had my father's weapons sealed here forty years ago."

"What? Was she mad?"

"Some said so. But she was not."

Her subtle form floated between his eyes and the glaring world . . . blurred, dimmed its reality.

"Cannot we be off?" Prang said, impatient. "For all we can tell, they may have surrounded the castle."

"I don't think they have," Parsival said, staring at the door. "You will have to stand up to Lancelot while I deal with the others."

"What? What are you saying to me?" Prang was incredulous.

"Don't try to win against him. Just stay alive for a few minutes. Turn and defend, keep turning and defending. If he finds you still he'll beat you flat."

Parsival reached and gripped the lock in his hands. He began to twist it. His body was relaxed, Prang noted, and his face peaceful, as if he prayed—and yet the metal began to bend, and then, after an interminable moment in which Prang's heart pounded, iron and wood parted and the incredible warrior pulled the door open. He lit a torch with flint and they wound their way down a spiral stone staircase in a whisper of fine dust.

Even well below ground level the stones were still smooth and dry. At the bottom they entered a passageway and then a low chamber, where the smoky flames gleamed and glimmered on a wall, hung with old, inwrought armor and massive weapons.

Parsival stood there a long, silent moment. Prang was testing the heft of a mace.

"Your father must have been a strong man," he observed with appreciation.

Parsival was binding on a suit of red and gold chain mail. It mainly protected his torso and thighs. He tied his ragged robes closed over the steel.

"This mace pleases me," Prang said.

"I recommend you throw it at Lancelot ere you come to grips," the older knight advised. "I tell you, dance like a juggler for as long as you can."

Prang looked interested. A flame light hollowed his eye sockets and cheeks.

"There may be fifty men out there," he remarked, raising an eyebrow.

Parsival buckled on the mesh sword belt and took up his father's red-and-black-enameled helmet. The visor was missing, torn away. He remembered the story Broaditch had told him. They had just come back from the village together. The common man had found him hiding in a barn. He must have been twelve years old. . . . He'd been watching a peasant festival day. His mother had forbidden it. . . . He remembered standing on the hillside looking over the bright green valley. He remembered it had been spring but no longer recalled Broaditch's name. He didn't try to bring it back. "Your father fell in a joust," Broaditch had said.

"A joust?" young Parsival had wondered.

"A noble sport, young sir. Not as light as a dance or as easy as sleeping in hay. . . . A lance tip in the face is uncomfortable."

Parsival had made little of those remarks. "My father," he'd said, looking off into the blue-green shimmer of horizon, "loved my mother—as I do."

"A lance tip in the face," Parsival whispered, unconsciously, setting the helmet on his head. The cowl of his robe fit over it fairly well. His father's name, Gahmuret, was worked in gold across the dome.

They went out through the far end of the narrow chamber, Parsival holding the sputtering torch. They stooped through a low tunnel, mossy stones slippery under their steel-shod feet.

"One death may be as good as another," Prang said. "Why don't we fly and take revenge when time and numbers favor us?"

They came out beyond the moat. The moon was low, the night cool and misty. Still . . .

"Why not?" Prang whispered, watching his teacher moving quietly along the grassy slope, parallel to the walls and a long, low growth of pines that stood like a screen beside them.

"I have to bury them," was the quiet answer.

Suddenly there were torches all around. About a dozen

shadowy men came up the slope and through the trees, running, weapons glinting.

Prang saw Parsival move: a blur, a flying shadow, a flashing of steel, spangs, crunchings, screams, sighs, sobs, curses, men scattering and falling like, he thought, rats before a striking cat. Before he could close with anyone, those who weren't down were ducking and running and Parsival stood alone in the guttering light from the dropped torches, sheathing his sword. Prang's heartbeat was rapid. The idea that he had sought to slay this man seemed humorous. . . . The famous knight moved like a phantom and his every blow sheared plate, mail, and flesh. He'd never seen such work. Why would someone with such skill and power throw his sword away? What more could any knight have wished for?

"My lord," he said, a little breathless, "that was magnificent, my lord." He stepped over a faintly moaning man-at-arms who still convulsively clutched his shattered spear in the tangle of his shadows.

Parsival was walking again. His mail clinked softly. Prang followed with the long mace over his shoulder. Lancelot and the others were just coming out of the castle on horseback. Prang estimated fifty or more men, though he knew his fear was prodding his imagination. This was the end. He accepted it. A small army of mounted men with lance and ax. . . . Life seemed very sweet suddenly. He found himself thinking how pleasant it had been a week or so ago eating pork pie, swilling ale, and talking with his comrades, lying and stretching points, describing old jousts and loves. . . .

Broaditch stood listening in the black street. He held his unsheathed dagger. He leaned on a tilted plank fence and strained to see what seemed to move up ahead. . . . After a few moments he went on cautiously. He'd realized he had to get out of there fast and was picking his way back to the house. The streets were quiet: a few voices, distant shouts, and cries here and there. . . .

His legs were smeared to the knee with muck by the time he reached the door. River mist and fog were closing in. He sheathed his blade and tapped on the timber.

The door opened a little on the latch and the wife said, "What now?"

"Eh? I want to enter, woman." He saw the dim firelight and smelled the musky warmth of the room. He wanted nothing more than to lie down, stretch out his bones, and sleep by the hot stones like a dozing cat. . . .

"Who are you?" she wanted to know.

"Broaditch of Nigh. Who do you think? I left here with your kinsmen and husband not two—"

"Ah."

She swung the door inward.

"—hours ago."

"So soon done with your sport, then?" she asked. She stayed in the doorway, the fire glow behind her.

"I'm weary, woman," he told her. "I had little enough sport and the air is chill."

"Men are fools," she informed him.

"That well may be," he replied, tired. "I've seen little to war with that opinion."

"Where are your fine pards?"

"They lingered a little."

"Aye. So they did. Drunk with the whores, I ween."

"Woman, my teeth clatter in my head and spoil my speech. The cold bites me, I—"

"Who was your friend who came before asking for you?"

And Broaditch said, "What?" He said this automatically looking to the left and right down the twisting lane.

"A dull fellow," she reflected, stepping back to admit him and wondering why he still stood there, frowning. "Big and thick of neck . . ."

"He asked for me by name?"

"No. He says: 'Is he back?' 'Who?' I says. 'The big one with the beard on his face.' 'Where would you expect a beard to grow?' I asks him. 'No matter,' says he. 'Is he come back here?' 'No,' I says, 'he isn't.' "

The clammy fog was rising above his knees now. He shivered slightly, thinking of the night before him. Someone, he realized, must have known her husband at the stew and a few coins spread the knowledge wide. . . .

" 'Are you his friend, then?' I asks. And the dull brute says, 'Aye, that. His boon and hearty.' 'What name do I give?' 'What indeed,' he says and goes off. The dull brute, that he was."

"My friend," murmured Broaditch.

"Come in," she said, "before the damp does."

Back behind him he was certain someone had just moved close to the wall. He stepped past her and found his staff and traveling pack. She'd closed the door. He opened it again.

"What's this?" she wanted to know. "Off again?"

"Say my farewells," he said, moving cautiously outside again. "Accept my thanks, good woman."

She watched from the doorway as he moved quietly into the rising, thickening mist. She shivered and went back inside.

One of the survivors apparently had just reached Lancelot. Parsival and Prang paused to listen behind the screen of pines.

"We was set on, my lord!" the breathless man cried. "We was set on . . ."

"What's this?" Lancelot demanded.

"Many men, my lord . . . in the trees . . ."

No doubt he was pointing, Parsival reflected. Now, what would the lumpy brain of Lancelot make of this information?

"Many men?" The legendary knight was still taking it in.

"Aye, my lord."

"I don't like this," Lancelot declared. "Who are these men?"

"I know not, my lord."

"Many, you say?"

"Aye!"

"Shall I ride and see?" a knight offered.

"I wasn't told anything about this," Lancelot decided. "I will see His Grace and then come back. They think I have no wits, eh? They think all I know to do is ride straight and crack heads. Come on!"

And he led his band at a trot away down the hill toward the forest road.

Parsival smiled, wry.

"So he is become a dancing bear," he said. "And who is 'His Grace,' I wonder?"

"A Duke," Prang said almost reluctantly.

" 'What is a swallow?' I ask. 'A bird,' he tells me."

"I am bound to say no more," Prang muttered heavily.

"His Grace," Parsival said. "Very well. You can help me now if you choose."

Duke LaLong and a short, thin, middle-aged Lord Gobble with

a pronounced limp, were walking across the castle yard beside a rutted puddle that resembled a motionless stream in the faint, sharp sliver of moon reflection that flowed through the stretched-out clouds.

The little fellow had an ashen face and overlarge, protuberant eyes that rolled around, as if he were reading the night shadows.

"*He's* impatient," he was saying in an insistent, shrill voice. "He must have results."

The Duke seemed uneasy and, though this fellow was of lesser rank, appeared surprisingly deferential.

"What more can I do?" he wanted to know, stopping suddenly as they were splashing across the water, jerking his foot up with a shudder of disgust.

The little man went obliviously on, eyes still peering around, as if there were much to see. The Duke stooped and stared at something in the dark, greasy muck: some kind of furry animal, he decided, but precisely what was unclear. A little hand-like paw reached through the surface where he'd trodden the shapeless body down. . . .

The other was still limping on, saying, "Lordmaster accepts no excuses. The stakes are too great. The hour is near, very near. Great things are about to happen . . . great things. He—"

"Listen," LaLong called after, piqued, straightening up from the puddle, "I can do no more than what is possible. He must understand—"

Gobble whirled around, eyes suddenly fixed on the Duke, slightly twisted body bent in his direction.

"I can tell you," he interrupted at a fanatical pitch, "he has little interest in what is possible. I can safely tell you, Your Grace, that he means to have all of them dead who might know things that should not be known."

"First he wanted Parsival and his family living. Then the instructions were changed overnight and I have only your word that this was so. I should see the master myself, I—"

"You are free to do so, naturally," the bent man said very quietly, "Your Grace."

His Grace remained uneasy.

"Yes . . . yes," he murmured. "But I, of course, have every confidence in you and there's really no need to disturb him at such a critical time and —"

"Orders were changed," the little fellow said fiercely, shrilly, as if this statement in itself had some profound, universal meaning. "He no longer required their information. He wants them *all* dead! All!" He trembled slightly.

They just stood there on opposite sides of the standing water. The slight moon whipped in and out.

"What of Lohengrin?" The Duke wondered.

The other shrugged, twisted, uneven.

"That is left in your hands, for now." This was said without expression.

"He knows nothing. He and his father shared nothing."

Gobble seemed to smile or at least part his lips, the Duke thought, sweating slightly.

"The responsibility is yours, Your Grace, is it not? After all, the master has full confidence in you."

Was he still smiling? LaLong couldn't tell. He thoroughly disliked this fanatical little spy, as he termed him. He was again regretting his whole involvement in this business, though it was far too late for that now. . . . He stared down again at the dim, crushed blob at his booted feet. . . . They claimed they were about to swallow the world, and he was out of choices. . . . He suddenly spat into the dark pool and watched the faint, foamy white spin and drift. . . .

He would take his chances with Lohengrin for a while. He had to admit he liked him in a way. He saw something of his own overeager self in the skilled, arrogant warrior. You couldn't simply waste your best tools because of these foreign fanatics and their notions. . . . He spat again.

Lohengrin looked absently down at the girl's head, which rocked in his naked lap. The pleasure of her mouth on him, suckling, turning, withdrawing to a painful cool, then relieving him, taking it into her deep, sopping heat . . . the pleasure did not distract the cold line of his thoughts. Even as his body tensed slightly as his orgasm began to generate by degrees, he was asking himself how long they would continue to use him as a paid assassin. Did the Duke actually trust him so far as that? What reward did they plan to offer him, the son, after all, of a minor king?

The woman's head rocked faster and faster now and his muscles started to lock, his breathing tense, and he thought how, for a few moments, he would be helplessly gripped and wilted by the soft and relentless lips of a lady. . . . He looked at her: the curls of unstrung dark hair, the beading sweat on her cheeks, shut eyes, the rhythmic working together of her thighs, her snorted breath, the sloshing of her mouth on his searing hardness. . . . He showed his teeth in an involuntary smile with the distant thought that he was over the brink now, without recourse, he was falling down into the wild abyss of flesh and fire and he had not the slightest power over it, no more than death . . . no more than death. . . .

Prang was sweating in the night chill. His tunic was open. He leaned on his spade as Parsival climbed out of the grave and stood silently looking down into the darkness of it. It gaped like a mute mouth. The setting moon stretched vague shadows on the grass.

"I wish we could have done more with what was given to us," he murmured.

And Prang said, "What?" before he realized the great knight was talking to either his wife or child.

"Regrets are like leaves in the dust."

A long silence ensued and then Prang said, "Is it safe to tarry here?"

Parsival didn't look up.

"What place is safe for any man?" he wondered aloud. He sighed and shook his head. "I have spent so many, many gifts . . . so many . . ." He looked up. "Well, fill this in and we'll be off." He took up his own spade and sunk it in the mounded dirt. "I am always leaving things unsaid. And then it's too late to speak. . . . My mother . . ." He tossed a shovelful of soil into the black slash in the earth. "And other things . . . other things . . ."

Later the moon was on the horizon. They were moving steadily across a rolling plain.

"You know," Prang was saying, "I feared you meant to die in combat . . . out of grief."

They were just coming to the outskirts of a deep forest. A spur of dense trees stood like a wall before them.

"Save your breath," Parsival counseled. "Our troubles are not past."

Prang twisted around to stare back across the dim fields. He thought he could make out the shape of the castle on the line of distant hills.

"I see nothing," he said.

"Be still!" his master hissed, suddenly motionless, facing the trees. Prang tried to control his breathing. He stared and listened and detected nothing . . . a sweet, rich scent rose from the earth. . . . Then he thought a shadow moved, a blot, a darkness at the end of the field . . . or was it his eyesight's strain . . .? His skin prickled and he unconsciously gripped Parsival's arm. He wanted to run. His heart was suddenly racing and he wanted to run. . . .

"What is this?" he hissed.

"Peace," said his teacher, leaning forward, seeming to concentrate intently. Then he stepped forward toward the shadowy edge of woods, slowly raising his long, wide sword above his head, as if an enemy stood before him. Prang saw none but still felt the chilling pressure, as if, as he later told it, an evil wind blew from the trees. He was actually on the verge of bolting and then found himself moving closer to Parsival, as if his body gave tangible shelter from the intangible. . . . He could have taken oath that a blurred, shadowy something reached inexplicably from the night to clutch at him and he heard his voice choke on a scream as Parsival seemed to cut the vacant air with his blade once, a ripping flash, and stood still again, as if leaning on emptiness, and suddenly the moon had set and the dark pressed close against them. . . .

Giddy, blood pounding with terror and shock, he thought he heard the master knight say: "I am not as weak as that."

And then, as though a gate had parted, Prang staggered forward at his teacher's back.

"Was it a demon, my lord?" he asked finally, whispering.

They were moving carefully into the woods. Prang kept stumbling, but Parsival held his arm.

"Have you ever met a demon?"

"No," admitted the young knight, "unless it were tonight."

"Where do you think the devil lives?"

"Why, in hell, sir. Where else but there?"

"Where else?" Parsival agreed, helping the other over a knotted root in the cool, musty, thick late-summer woods. There was a faint scent still of rot from the rains. "But where to find his house, Prang?"

"Is it not under the world where the eternal fires burn . . .? Lord Parsival, how can we fail to lose ourselves in this place? Shouldn't we wait for the morning's light to . . ."

"Prang," declared his master, "heaven, hell, and the world are all one place."

"But I—"

"Peace, yet again, Prang."

They stopped and stood intently listening. After a few moments Parsival relaxed.

"It's all right," he ultimately said.

Prang was cocking his head from side to side.

"I hear no pursuit," he said.

"Pursuit? I feared no pursuit." Parsival was slightly surprised. "Only what's before us, young warrior." He smiled in the unbroken darkness. "I never feared anything," he reflected. "Then I came to dread death . . . then life . . . now something else altogether. . . ."

"I don't understand."

He took the young man's arm and led him on into the dense, invisible tangles of limb and brush and bole.

"What do you want, Prang, before you die?"

After a few moments the knight answered: "Long life. Fame . . . to fight well . . . to have sons . . ."

"I have had all of those but the first."

"Yes?"

His outstretched hand touched a tree and he pressed closer to Parsival as they went around the great roots.

"And I fear," Parsival said, "and I long . . ."

"For love? How do you find your way here? Is it magic art?"

"Perhaps."

"Perhaps which?"

"Perhaps." And Parsival said no more as they worked their way on and on through gullies and over ridges and rocks. . . .

Broaditch was afraid. There was no moon now as he groped through the mucky, stinking lanes downward to the water. Now and then he glimpsed the magical silver moon gleaming between the squalid roofs. It was very late and very quiet. The houses were dark. The clammy fog was rolling in chest-high, like smoke, he thought, from a cold fire. . . .

He held his quarter staff out before him like a blind man. He was listening intently. Danger always cleared the senses, he ruminated, sharpened the world, made each breath a gift. . . . He heard distant dripping sounds, voices . . . a child crying . . . racking wheezes as he passed a shuttered window where someone lay sick or dying. . . . Broaditch stumbled, stepped on something softly elastic, shuddered, then dimly saw a man at his feet, drunk-asleep or dead. . . . He stepped over the form and went on his way. . . .

He came out of the last streets and stood looking at where wharves and ships seemed to drift away as the mists steamed and flowed past them. The marsh reeds lining the shore seemed phantasmal and ominous. The path curving into them could have been the road of shades. . . . Echoes and faint splashes came across the unseen water. . . .

He moved carefully, straining to distinguish outlines along the shore. He was hoping to locate a waterman willing (or with a reason) to sail upstream. But the area seemed deserted. Fear was cold at his back. He was certain someone, at least one, had followed him from the house.

He turned suddenly and crouched behind his heavy staff. He listened, but he heard only the creakings and muffled splashes as the moored vessels rolled and shifted on the tide. . . . Somewhere out on the river a pair of voices were singing a sea chanty. . . . Then he thought he heard a squishing step in the billowing fog just around the bend behind him.

He saw no reason to hold this ground and waded on through the muck along the river's edge. He heard steps coming faster now.

No you don't, by Mary and the saints, he thought, and he ducked down behind a cloudy fence of cattails. He waited, controlling his breath. . . .

The feet were running now and a moment later a tall, lanky figure broke out of the gleaming mists, panting, wobbling a little, then stopping with a stagger. Broaditch stood up, recognizing Valit. His eyes rolled wildly. Broaditch was suddenly reminded of someone from the lost past: the lanky body, the terrorized look. Waleis, who'd died in the snow. The blood brought the image back, spilling from nose and mouth. . . .

"What happened?" Broaditch asked, supporting him by the arms as Valit sagged to his knees in the mud.

"I . . ."—he gasped—". . . followed . . . it . . ."

"What are you saying?"

"I . . ."

How were you hurt?"

"Hit me . . . back there . . . a man . . . he's coming . . ."

"Why did you follow me?" Broaditch was staring around at the ghostly fog gleamings. "Can you walk?"

Valit nodded.

"Mayhap," he whispered.

"Come, then." And Broaditch led him back through the reeds to the edge of the river.

"He was a murderer," Valit said.

"Hush, boy," Broaditch said. He'd seen a long skiff drawn up on the bank through a thinning patch of mist and made for that.

"I want to go with you," the young man whispered. "I . . ."

"Peace!" Broaditch hissed.

They tumbled into the boat and Broaditch poled away from shore with an oar. When a few yards out and melting into the mists, two men emerged and stood on the bank: dark, blurred blots. One seemed to be holding a sword. They said nothing and then vanished behind a billow of chill smoke. . . .

"So close as that," Broaditch murmured to himself.

They drifted for a few minutes on the flooding tide. Broaditch crouched in the bow, listening to every faint, echoing sound. . . . After a time he moved carefully amidships and took up the oars. He plied them with great care and silence. They were drifting steadily, but he assumed the incoming sea would swing them inland against the sluggish current. His idea was to proceed upstream all night, hugging the far shore.

Valit was cross-legged, dabbing at his nose with a bit of rag, leaning against the gunwale. Broaditch spoke in a conversational whisper, bending his wide back steadily, rowing.

"Well, then," he was just saying, "what sent you after me?"

The cottony fog streamed over them as the breeze freshened. Broaditch kept glancing over his shoulder, hoping for a glimpse of the far shore. He wasn't sure how wide the river actually was at this point. "Did your father send you?"

"Him?" Valit was scornful, now wetting the cloth and applying it to his head. "Not likely."

"Then why did you follow me? Or were you just strolling for pleasure, taking in the night fog?"

"Oh, me head," he sighed as the cold water touched it. "A great club he done me with. . . . I'll have an ear like a potato. . . ." He shifted around where he was, tipping the craft a little. "I saw you were clever," he told Broaditch seriously, "and one as knew his way about the world. . . . Sister-in-law said which way you went. . . ."

"Ah. So you mean to adventure with a middle-aged pilgrim?" His elder was amused.

"Adventure, me arse," was the measured reply. "Do I seem a mad knight or a fool in skins? But there's more to you, Mr. Broaditch of Nigh, than just a pilgrim. I'd say you've got your purposes. . . ." There was an air of great slyness about him now. "And can I ask you one thing?" He sat up straight, pressing the cloth to the side of his long head.

"All right, boy."

"Who's after you?"

"By name and face?" Broaditch was sardonic, then suddenly let his oars trail, listening. "Be still. . . ."

There it was—a faint splish-splash not too far away; low voices. . . . Could it be the other side already . . .? A bubbling and creaking and then a huge shadow loomed up out of the mist so that it took him a minute to realize it was twenty feet of sail. He hit his oars and pulled back out of sight. But he'd been heard or seen: a hoarse shout echoed from another off behind them. Broaditch had glimpsed men on the ship, dark and armed.

"So we're bloody well done," Valit muttered, scowling around. "I should o' knowed better than what I knowed."

"Be still," Broaditch repeated.

The voices were directing one another, hollering. Two craft at least were in the hunt. They drifted. . . . Broaditch lightly worked the oars from time to time. . . . Suddenly the fog pulled away and a slim sailboat, tilted under short sail, was bearing straight down on them. Broaditch dug in the oars, pulled, cracked his muscles and back, puffed, feeling as though embedded in a sticky sea, straining as the boat seemed to rush headlong at them. He heard the hue and cry go up, saw men rush to the bows, point and shout . . . on . . . on . . . thunk! Ptuck! Punggg! Three arrows shook in the gunwale. Valit crouched in the bilgewater like,

Broaditch thought, a cringing dog. . . . He felt the next arrow shot clip his hair as the shaft zipped out into the water.

Is this, then, the manner of my death? he wondered. And something seemed to say *no* within him. And then the smoky mist closed between them again. He heard other shots whiz past unaimed . . . heard muffled voices and creaking drift away into the night as he panted and struggled on . . . then stopped and brought in the oars.

"Why don't you row?" hissed the young man from where he lay in the wet hull.

Broaditch gestured around.

"Point the way, then, lad," he suggested. The fog rolled like a wall on all sides.

Valit sat up and looked around wildly.

"Christ's wounds," he muttered, "am I lost, then?"

"No more than I. Still, this fog should lift ere long."

"You have this from God?" Valit asked with exasperated contempt.

"Hmm," Broaditch grunted, sitting there, solid and patient, on the smooth-worn seat. Valit slumped back, brooding. He kept gently feeling his battered head and crushed ear, wincing. "You never told me what you seek, Valit," Broaditch mildly asked.

"The far side of the river Thames, old man," was the surly response.

"Mayhap you'll find the bottom first," Broaditch suggested, "if you mend not your speech."

The fair, sarcastic young man glanced up, as if to weigh this remark, and decided to soften a little.

"I mean to make me fortune," he said, "not plow a long grave in the fields for some lord."

"Then you'd do better to stay in town here, would you not?"

"Poor in the city is poor in the country," was the reply, "without even fresh air, old man."

"And you have a third place to go? Under the earth or out to sea?"

But Valit was done saying much.

"What I know," he said, "I know." And he went back to sighing over his wounds.

"One thing *I* know," Broaditch said, "old man that you say I am. . . ." He eased himself into the boat's bottom and stretched out to rest, fishing out his long-stemmed pipe from his leather pouch. "There's a wind blowing you where it's going to blow you, flap your silly sails as you will." He sighed and sucked the cold stem. "This have I learned, boy. *This* have I learned."

The roads were still soft under a bright, clean sun. The morning's blue and green were soft, the earth steamy.

Modred was feeling ill. The swaying horse did nothing to ease it. Or, perhaps, the wine had been bad that morning.

"That bitch," he muttered to the nearest retainer, Sir Gaf, a cousin of long-dead Sir Kay, adviser to Arthur, the father, by a serving maid, of Modred, who, at forty-one, was the closest approach Britain could make to an heir-apparent: balding, sweaty, pot-bellied and ever depressed.

"My lord?" Sir Gaf answered.

"That bitch aunt of mine. She looks no older than she did twenty years gone. . . . Did you mark that?"

"I had not seen her in those times, my lord," Gaf said, ever so faintly contemptuous.

"She's a witch," Modred declared. "Always was. My father, curse his cold heart, he knew it well. . . . Morgana the bitch witch!" He shook his head. "I sickened on her dinner. I swear it!"

"My lord," Gaf soothed, riding his mount a little closer to the prince-by-default as they worked their way along the overgrown road through berry thickets and dense brush. The hills were gentle and old here, trees scrubby. The earth had been burned out years before and was still, gradually filling back. Twenty years earlier Clinschor's barbarians had razed this countryside. "My lord, she is a wise and gentle lady in her way."

"Bitch!"

"And her advice . . ."—he held the word and pause—". . . is sound."

"Then it has the advantage of her food."

"She means to raise you to your father's throne."

"I'm not my father. And I've troubles enough."

"Britain could fall to the northern devils, my lord," a third rider put in, a bishop by his vestments. "We need . . ."

"Then," said Modred, "put young what's-his-name in power and be damned!" He pressed his thick hands to his belly. "God's mercy, I churn. . . ." Sweat was running into his eyes. He wiped them. It was going to be a hot day, he thought. The weather was so uneven. This would be a miserable ride back to Kent . . . and these fools prodding him. . . . He regretted now even putting on his light mail shirt. The sweat gathered under it. And the links always made him itch. . . . No more of this, he decided, no more—no more plotting and riding all over the damned country. He'd not be used by the damned nobles and church. . . . "I've been poisoned by that bitch," he said, burping violently, tilting forward and burping again, tasting garlic and decay.

The air was still and shadows cool under the bushes. Blackberries glowed in the splintery sunlight.

He sat there enjoying the ripe scents. He toyed with his long mace where it lay across his armored legs. A composite moment from childhood returned to mind: sunny summer midafternoon eating with the family under the trees, shifting on the bench, bored, restless, watching his father slowly, painfully (he thought) eating and sipping wine, seeing his mother's tense looks while her husband stared into space. . . . She would start to speak and sigh and stop. . . . Then she looked for one of the servants and at that moment Lohengrin spun off the bench, still chewing gristly meat, and raced down the sun-brilliant, dusty path into the woods, hearing his father's voice behind him: "Why can't he sit for five minutes? What kind of . . ." And his mother's voice: "Would I could fly thus from you!" And then came his father again, louder, but the words were lost as he leaped a cool, rushing stream into deep pine shadows and hush, forgetting the two of them for the moment, as if they'd vanished from the earth. . . .

He recalled all this, remembered how he drank deeply of the peace. How tense he'd been in those days, for a child, he reflected, how terribly tense. . . .

He reached and plucked a berry, smearing the rich purple on his steel gauntlet, then sucking the sweetness off. He frowned suddenly as a memory ran past where he'd intended: he was spinning his sling in those vivid boyhood woods, the tug of the smooth stone whirling around his head, then released zipping at a bird perched blue, bright, gleam-eyed on a berry bush in the heavy sun just beyond the pine shadows. He'd seen the blurred track, the sudden splash of red as the little head exploded, and then came a feather or two flickering down, and he remembered the smile on his face as he hissed a thought over and over: *that'll teach you something . . . that'll teach you something . . . that'll teach you . . .*

He came alert, heard horses. So his information was correct. Very good. He was ready. This was no bird coming here . . . a what? . . . a capon, maybe. He almost smiled. Lohengrin had refused to turn away from that bird. He'd gone and looked at the headless, awkward ball of fluff caught in the brambles. *This is death,* he'd told himself. *It will happen to me.*

He blinked the memories away and stood carefully upright. He held the mace over his shoulder.

After this, he was thinking, *it might as well be me as any other. . . . I might as well be king myself as some dreaming Duke. . . . We may as well be entertained before we die. . . .*

Modred sighed and wiped his sweaty face.

"Christ," he complained, "is there an inn along this way?"

The ecclesiastic beside him looked remote. The knight shrugged.

"It may be, my liege," he said. "Within a few furlongs there's—"

He broke off as a knight, all in black and red, stepped from the muted sparkling of berry bushes and planted himself before them, long mace across his shoulder.

"You'll lunch in hell, I think, Modred," he said through his visor grate and followed this by springing forward with astounding agility and striking a round blow at the Prince's head.

Modred screamed in fear and threw himself backward, virtually out of his saddle and stirrups, and the deadly blow slammed across his lightly mailed chest and gut and laid him out, winded, lying flat on his mount's spine, head lolling back by the bushy, fly-tormented tail. The horse backed away as the other knight drew and struck at the assassin, who blocked the cut with ease on his shield and smashed another blow, this time catching the helpless Prince across the thigh.

"Ahhh-h-h-h," he sighed as blood drained from the mushed flesh.

The rest of the stunned escort (about eight men) closed up now and the black knight knocked two aside before accepting that he'd have to withdraw with the job half done.

"You were but spared for a time," he said, backing into the brush, "if, indeed you survive these hurts, you fat, oily dog."

And he was gone.

"After him!" shouted the knight, but no one was overanxious. A moment later the escorting knight (the rest were men-at-arms) rode into the bushes, nervous, carefully probing with his sword. . . .

Broaditch was trying to explain things to Alienor. She sat in her wicker chair on the sunny porch and shook her head at him.

"No," she insisted, "it's too late. You can't come home to me now."

"I am so weary, my love," he protested, leaning against a post. "I long for my old joys back. . . . I want to work in the fields and sit at supper with you."

"No," she told him, pointing across the fields, "look."

A cloudy wall of deep darkness flowed slowly in from the horizon, blotting out all the green and blue and gold it touched, seeping the landscape to death, withering the afternoon. . . .

And he shuddered awake as he was telling her: "But, love, my back aches. . . ." And he found himself still drifting in the fog-bound boat, Valit snoring in the stern. Broaditch's bones were cramped and damp. He sighed and looked around: dawn was faintly hinting the mist shapes and nearer waves. Then fear broke through his dense weariness as a low, dark boat came suddenly straight out of the fog at them.

He poked Valit with the end of his thick staff, but the fellow didn't stir. This seemed strange, though he noted it only later.

"Are you dead from the sea air?" he wondered in a mutter.

This boat was odd: no one was visible at oar, tiller, or sail. A single figure in a conical hood and dark, full robe sat amidships.

A craft from the land of the dead, Broaditch thought, *or else I dream*. . . .

Closer now, he noticed the sail was furled and the boat was drifting like their own, but faster, which had given the impression it was under control. Still he wondered why it slowed alongside to match their direction and speed within easy speaking distance. The waves were steepening and Broaditch had an idea they were no longer in the middle of the river. He chose not to contemplate the implications just now. Anyway, he reassured himself that the sea current would drive them onshore once they cleared the river flow.

"Are you lost, too?" Broaditch called over as the other boat rose and tilted over them, then dipped as they went up. . . .

"I have no destination at the moment," a resonant voice replied, "so I cannot be lost."

"You could be lost to the light of God," Broaditch surprised himself by saying.

The bass voice seemed to approve.

"Your own words have chosen you, friend," it said out of the cowl folds.

The thwarts of both boats were inches apart now as they slid up and dropped and rocked in tandem, as though invisibly joined.

"Who are you?" Broaditch wanted to know. He glanced and saw that Valit still slept.

"A man in a boat."

"A sailor?"

"Well, say that I fish."

"Where are your nets and hooks . . . and baits?"

The other laughed, surprisingly mellow and relaxed.

"My fish," he remarked, "know well enough when they're caught." Then the tones became forceful and grim. "If you survive the looming storm, you have a task laid upon you."

"Are you a philosopher, sir?" Broaditch gripped the boat side as the waves steepened and tipped them. "How can you command me?"

"You command yourself. You are a man who only hides from truth because once you understand it you have no choice. You have hidden well, but the sea has brought you where your feet would not."

Broaditch felt intensely alert, though a little dizzy from the gyrations of the waves. This was all so matter-of-fact, and he found himself accepting it in the same relaxed way it was being put across.

"Beware of your companion there," the cowled man advised. "He is blind . . . you follow the brightness and heed nothing else. Find your way and you may pluck what is sacred from the devil's lap."

"Pluck what?"

"It has fallen to you to find what the greatest have lost."

"But what? pluck what? . . . Am I asleep again?"

"When are you ever awake? When can you tell?"

"But *what*?"

"Would you know the Grail if you saw it?"

"So you're a holy man? A master?" He was strangely amused by this, too. "A wizard?" Or a madman.

"What a burden to you these words are."

"Am I far from shore, sir?"

"Farther than you think. If you survive the storm, then you'll learn more. The wind and fury are close upon you."

A black scud of cloud came whipping overhead and the boats heeled in a savage gust. Valit sat up suddenly as the other craft moved off into the wild mist and mounting seas.

"Surrender your life!" the man had shouted back through the veering winds. "And be sustained into the land of death, my broad and foolish fish!" And then the storm broke over them with astounding violence.

Broaditch shut his eyes and then opened them, as if to awaken. He wanted to think he'd been asleep.

"My God!" cried Valit. "We're doomed!"

Perhaps I have done all I can ever hope to do, Parsival thought.

He stared through the narrow slit window at the setting moon. It was early morning. Prang was asleep across the corridor in his own room. They had come to the castle of a man who'd been Parsival's companion at Arthur's court for a time after the Kingdom had been partially re-established. Earl Bonjio. A short, dark, part-Spanish fellow. . . . Arthur's beard had gone silver and his hair was thin. His sister had come to live at Camelot and, it was said by some, supplied the steel for the spine of her brother's prong. . . . *Well*, Parsival remembered, *he never really knew the king that intimately*. . . . Arthur was ever wary of him, for some reason. . . . He remembered riding back from a tourney with Bonjio, the horses seeming to float through a mellow, grayish midsummer dusk, hooves virtually soundless on the yielding turf as sloping fields drifted by. They'd been drinking mead. Bonjio had just tossed away the empty stone flask.

"So," the dark man was saying, "how did you elude Gawain?"

"When?"

"After you'd struck down the varlet, outside your castle. You said you were nude and had just finished with a woman and then were set upon."

"Ah, yes." Parsival remembered. "The details are unclear.

Bonjio smiled. His dark eyes were very shrewd and watchful.

"Wine will blur them every time," he remarked.

"No. It was the next day. I was sober . . ."—he frowned slightly—"and drunk, too. . . ."

"Well?"

"I can't explain this thing . . . but that was the best moment of my life. . . ."

"What?"

Parsival stared across the field at the steep slope topped by Camelot castle. At that time the first peasant houses were going up on the ridge, and new crops sprouted and ripened on what were once jousting meadows.

"Anyway," Parsival said after a moment or two, "Gawain and those men left. I went back to my wife."

"Did you put on a robe, at least?" Bonjio grinned.

"I suppose so. . . . I haven't seen Gawain since."

"They say he's in Ireland or across the channel."

Bonjio carefully wiped off and munched a piece of fruit. He sucked the juices with each bite.

"What happened to the woman?" he asked at length as they were just starting up the long hill on the dusty road. A peasant in a mule-drawn cart was laboring before them as slow as could be. "Wasn't she the wife of a guest?"

Parsival was abstracted. The mellow day drew him deeper into memory.

"What? Who?" he wondered, blinking back.

"The woman you'd lain with." Bonjio licked the wound his mouth had made in the ripe peach. "On the hillside."

Parsival remembered.

"It's been ten years," he murmured, "nearly that. . . ."

Bonjio cocked his head at him.

"Was she slain?" he pursued.

Parsival shook his head.

"I can't recall her name," he said, "but she came back later, wearing a shepherd's cloak. She'd been battered a little but wasn't so bad as I'd expected." He smiled faintly.

"Liked her men, eh? Well, I can understand that, only too well."

"That isn't supposed to be possible."

Bonjio nodded.

"So they say," he admitted, "but I have such a desperate weakness myself that I can understand any other."

Parsival was interested.

"Which weakness?" he wondered. "I lose count of mine."

"Yes, yes . . . but for the flesh . . . the *flesh!*" He shook his head and worked the pit into his jaw and sucked it. "It makes me tremble. My soul is slit when I see a beautiful woman. I must have them, you understand."

Parsival shrugged.

"Most men must," he noted, "it would appear."

Bonjio leaned over and touched his mailed arm. His eyes were intent, a little wild, as if the thought alone released anguish and need.

"Not as I," he half-whispered. "How is it with you, Sir Parsival? No, tell me this . . ."

They were just passing the cart. A bony old woman gripped the reins and didn't look aside from where she stared at the slow hooves.

"With me . . .?" Parsival mused a moment. "I enjoy fucking as much as any other, I suppose. . . ." He looked down over the sweet blue tinted valley as they climbed. The new grain sparkled and rippled. "It's brief enough a satisfaction," he added.

"It doesn't eat you alive? It doesn't make you reel with need?" Bonjio was very serious. "You never want to creep on your knees to suck the bare feet of a young maid?"

"Creep?"

Bonjio partly smiled. His eyes were lidded, sardonic, self-mocking, and serious.

"In a way of speaking," he amended, "though I think I'd crawl on my belly like a serpent if it came to that."

"I don't understand," Parsival said neutrally.

"Then I make you out as both lucky and unfortunate, great knight though you are." He sucked in a deep, slow breath and shook his head, as if to clear it.

"I enjoy it," Parsival reflected and repeated, "as much as the next man, I think." He turned to the other. "Why is it so with you?"

"Ah," said Bonjio, "why, indeed. . . ." He uncorked the wine flask and tipped it up to his lips again. A crease of dribble showed like blood at his lips.

"Is that an answer?"

"No. I haven't one." He tucked away the drink. "I have only the burning."

"That you can't quench," Parsival mused.

"That I can't quench," the other man agreed.

The moon was suddenly down behind the hills. He kept staring out over the lightless castle grounds. He felt his outrage loosening its hold on him like tired fingers. . . . It took so much energy to hate. . . . They were dead and that was that. He discovered he didn't even want to kill Lancelot, not really, not deeply. He frowned. It would be no better, he reflected, than destroying the sword that slashed them. Lancelot was no more than a weapon. And it was done with. . . . All these things seemed like shadows, like the play of vicious children caught and twisted in their ugly imaginings, which, after all, were just imaginings. Waking dreams. . . . He sighed. What would one more dead man prove? . . .

He let his head rest on the cool stone of the window arch. He stood there weary and strong.

Should I weep for all my wasted days, oh, God? I missed my way so many times. Enough for many men. . . . I'm dead to this world and blind to heaven. . . . I but mark days to the grave. . . .

A flash of color moved in his mind, bright, rich green trees flowing past, rocking with the uneven motion of the bony horse under him, climbing toward the massive castle wall that towered to a stunning height above the trees. The holy castle. And, he concluded, it might as well have been imaginary. . . .

"Sir Parsival," a lady's voice said, and he turned.

It was the earl's wife, Unlea, a light-haired, ripe woman, face and body very soft, eyes large and yielding. She had on a rose-pink, low-cut gown. Those eyes were always slightly widened, as if she were about to be amazed. She smiled a great deal and, as he'd noted, wasn't an elaborate or coquettish sort of woman. He'd liked her immediately. He liked frank people.

Whenever he reached an impasse, he thought wryly, smiling, there was always a woman around. Perhaps they were the signposts to detours.

They looked at one another in silence for a while. She didn't seem too uneasy.

"Well," she finally said, biting lightly on her lower lip, "there is always pleasure."

He rubbed his beard with a forefinger.

"Or war," he replied, "or whatever you like."

He just noticed she was holding a long, slender taper. The flame wavered and moved shadows, as of passing time, across her face.

"Or little things that hurt no one," she added.

He sat down facing her on a stool and rocked back and forth. Then he was still.

"I have never, lady," he found himself saying, "felt such an emptiness before or behind me."

She came closer. Her feet were noiseless in furred slippers. A jewelless crimson chain circled her throat. He smelled a light perfume now.

"Why press yourself beyond the natural limits?" she wondered.

"What tells you I do?"

She shrugged.

"It's clear enough, sir," she informed him. "You've been a king, a priest, and God knows what else."

He saw the castle again, vivid, solid in jewel-bright autumn air, the golden, flaming forest, the crisp breeze, the immense bronze gleaming gate across the moat starting to swing open. White, wild swans were on the green-black water, and the startling, towering clouds mounting above, framing the bright towers. . . .

"God knows," he said at length.

"Why not?"

"What?"

"Learn to play?" She was, he saw, quite serious.

"Play?" He frowned. "Like a lad? Ah, I played later than was the rule, they tell me."

"No," she corrected, "not child's play."

He studied her or tried to. He was thinking how he might have her. She was extraordinarily tender and easy-moving, he was thinking. Well, he was always easily attracted, though he didn't creep on his knees, he thought, remembering her husband's old expression. He wondered if he could have her, at that. . . . The mating reflex came back, he noted, as if it had never been suppressed into ice in the monk's mountains. . . . He smiled faintly to (or at) himself again. In his mind he kept seeing the vast gate opening, a glimpse of walls, bright pennants, movement, sun, shadow. . . .

"I've done all those things, as well," he told her.

She shook her head, eyes widening a little.

"No," she said, "I can see you never have."

"Don't speak foolishly, woman." He frowned down at the dull stone floor. *She isn't really interested*, he thought.

"I see more than you know," she told him, reaching out and touching his head, stroking his fine, brownish-blond hair with glints of white here and there. "Poor Parsival."

Her hand was very hot on his cheek. He half-consciously held it and brushed the fingers with his lips.

I feel so burned and stiff and chill . . . and I turn aside again . . . as if I actually knew where I was going in the first place. . . .

The gate stayed partly open in his memory. He wasn't even certain it *was* memory anymore. Time had eaten the drawn edges. . . .

Lohengrin contented himself thinking he must have convinced Prince Modred to take a pilgrimage to Rome, at the very least. Too bad he hadn't been able to kill him, but that was fate and a shying horse. He expected no pursuit and none came. He marched on through the sun-spattered undergrowth among golden wild flowers and buzzing bees.

He reached his mount, loosed it, and swung up. He considered his problem: most men were fools and full of fear. His own advantage largely lay in his lack of concern for what bound, or at least impeded, others. He believed he had no distracting feelings. He was concentrated. Aim truly, fight well, or die. And die, too. The rest was philosophy and poetry. He'd once watched a famous scholar, robes flapping, crawling and moaning over a steaming dung heap behind a barn. The church where he'd just lectured that morning stood across the cow yard, golden cross gleaming in the noon glare. He'd offended the local lord in some fashion, by some phrase or other, and so he crawled in the dung, gasping, choking, terrified as several men-at-arms followed him with their spears. His face and the side of his green robe were bloody.

"Show us your learning, why don't ye?" a round-faced soldier mocked.

"Oh, he's learned, he is," another laughed, a lean redhead with a raw, swollen nose.

Lohengrin had been about fifteen at the time. His father had been away for several months in the Holy Land, it was reported.

Lohengrin remembered his relief that his father was gone. No tension at home. . . . He'd been exploring the countryside on his pony and had stopped in this town to buy bread and cheese.

The spearmen had surrounded the scholar on all sides.

"Go on," one said. "Man must eat to stay alive, eh?"

This remark produced an astounding roar of laughter and approval that baffled Lohengrin until he saw the middle-aged, suddenly broken man, with a spear point pressing into his back, kneeling in the filth, cup a handful of dung and hold it, with shut eyes, before his face.

"That's it, master!" encouraged the round face in greasy leathers and iron cap. "Eat your fill—you need share with no one." Laughter.

"He dallies," raw nose put in, grinning, showing yellowed stumps and gaps in his mouth.

"Kill him," suggested another, jabbing his spear.

"Quiet, brother," raw nose ordered. "He but most properly and piously says his grace."

"Or makes his peace with God," an onlooking farmer said.

"Him?" round face declared, hearing this comment. "Oh, he'll eat his supper, all right, won't he? There's a good un. He wants to live to gather more wisdom." His spear point prodded the man's side. "The grovelin' wretch!"

"I'd die first," said another soldier, a young man with grim, flat features.

"That so, youngblood?" raw nose said. "Why don't you take his place and see how death stirs your appetite?"

Youngblood looked grimmer and uneasy, Lohengrin noticed. Then suddenly he put his spear to the scholar's throat.

"Go on," he said, "and be done with it!"

"Or you'll make him a new mouth, eh?" Round face liked this idea.

"Go on!" youngblood shouted.

The trembling man cried out: "God forgive me, but I must live!" And still with shut eyes, he pressed the rank handful into his mouth and fell forward, gagging.

"Keep chewin', you grovelin' wretch!" round face added.

The laughter died away fairly fast. Lohengrin was impressed. This was something he knew he'd never forget. As the crowd broke up, the young man, as the scholar was spitting and gagging, suddenly ran his spear through his stomach, a blank, contemplative look on his stolid face. The shocked man was pinned to the dunghill, gasping, blood trickling from his stained, choked mouth. He whimpered a little.

"You'd done as well, fellow," youngblood said gravely, "never to have ate no shit at all."

Lohengrin might have dated the formation of certain of his values from that afternoon. He recalled it, for some reason, riding, heading northwest on a dusty track of road.

A plan was forming, step by step. The Duke's actual army was small. He himself had the doubtful loyalty of enough cutthroat knights and others to stand up to His Grace alone. . . . So there was someone behind and above, as there always must be . . . someone with vast power who, for some reason, could not come into the open just now. . . . Why not . . .? Who . . .? As he rode through the lengthening afternoon, he pondered the question: How many had the blood to even aspire to Arthur's seat without having to hold it daily by sheer force . . .? Not many. . . . And he'd already killed several himself, under orders. . . . How many could be left . . .? They'd have to have blood at least as good as his own or his father's. . . . Nonsense, the old bastard had renounced everything. True he'd fought with Arthur and at the gates of Jerusalem for power, but that was long ago and out of despair, or so he said. . . . But, still, suppose the pure great one was depressed enough to want to be in charge of the world again? He wondered if anyone else had thought of that. . . . Well, he'd have to consider it as a possibility only, for now. . . . Lohengrin needed more men. That was a simple fact. Most knights these days, as the saying went, had a bony horse, a one-eyed squire, and an elder brother enjoying the fief. . . . In his own case, his father held what he had through his wife, and the only lands left to Lohengrin contained the old toy castle in the half-deserted north, where his father, Parsival, grew up with a few pock-faced serfs scraping the cold, arid soil. No, thank you! That was no gift, he thought—more of a curse. . . . But there were many such partially disinherited men drifting around these days; that was a thought. . . .

Well, he thought, *be all as may be, let's first see what's to be done about His Grace.*

The rest of the planning he could feel without any details yet. Just a definite gist. It was growing and, he had to admit, the scope of it frightened him just a little. Thinking deeply on these and kindred matters, he hardly noticed the bright, lush countryside flowing by. . . .

Little, limping Lord Gobble was standing beside an overweight knight wearing silks of red and white. Gobble was in dull black velvet that draped over his body, which seemed twisted into a permanent half-turn to the right. Sooty torch light shifted shadow and smoke around the low-roofed dungeon.

Massive Lord Howtlande was gesturing with a jewel-encrusted, ornamental mace. His flabby face was grim and martially furrowed around his surprisingly long, hooked, bony nose.

The naked man hung facing them, as if pinned on the damp stones. The chains that supported him were hard to see in the wavering darkness.

Gobble coughed and brushed his hand at a stinging puff of smoke that billowed from a nearby brazier where long irons were neatly poked into the coals.

The victim's bleeding head lolled. His mutilated body quivered slightly. He made no sound. A hooded executioner was busy nearby working at a jammed hoist mechanism with a tool. He suddenly cursed and kicked it in exasperation.

"This here," he said in outrage and apology to the two noblemen, "this here ain't even of no worth, my lords. . . . I ask and ask for new equipment. . . . This here always jams on you. . . ." He bent over it again. "It ain't rightful. . . ."

"No matter, Jack," Howtlande assured him, "we're done with him now."

"What use to ask, I wonder?" Jack was muttering. "No use. . . . If the master knew how things is done, why, I know some as would smarten up. . . ." He nodded. "Aye, they would. . . ."

Gobble's protuberant eyes rolled restlessly. He never seemed (Howtlande had noted, with contempt) to look at anything longer than a grasshopper sits.

"Dispatch this fellow straight," Gobble ordered in his shrill voice. Jack looked up, alert under his masking hood.

"Aye," Jack agreed, "if he be not gone already, my lords."

"This knight here," Howtlande said, jerking a flabby nod at the dying man, whom the executioner was advancing on with a businesslike step and raising an outsized broadsword, "confirmed what Hinct, the Grail traitor, said?"

"He did," Gobble agreed.

"And what did lord high-holy think?"

"Have a care, lord general, how smoothly you mock."

"Keep yer tools in order," Jack declared to himself, calculating his downstroke with a cocked head. "So I ever says . . . order . . ."

"We're all in this pot stewing together," Howtlande said. "So the traitor claims he will deliver the holy spear or whatever it's supposed to be before we reach the magical castle where the Grail does whatever it does?"

Gobble stared at him for longer than was his wont. He smiled, the other thought, or did *something* with his mouth.

"*I* believe in lord master," he said, his voice shrill as the shadow of Jack's cut crossed them, and neither really noticed the sound of split flesh and bone or the *bunkk* of the severed head on the cobbled floor. Jack grunted with satisfaction. "I believe that this Grail is real. Our investigations reveal that it is a spiritual power center. It has long been in the hands of the weaklings. . . ." His eyes rolled fiercely around the dank chamber. "And they use it to soften the spirit." He took a few limping steps across the uneven floor. "*We* need ruthless strength for our task. . . . I believe that in the master's hands it will magnify *his* will and we then become strong as gods. . . ." He twisted around to face Howtlande, who was simply taking in this strange credo without reaction. Gobble was calm. "Of course, the ignorant doubt this. But I assure you the master knows what he is doing. . . . This, I believe. . . ." The eyes rolled restlessly, Howtlande thought, like those of a troubled fish.

"I never said I disbelieved," he said coldly. "Still, no one ever tells me what this *Grail* is when I ask."

"Our studies haven't hasn't revealed everything. But the master will recognize it. Why, he is more god than man, I sometimes think."

Howtlande narrowed his eyes.

"He's remarkable enough," he affirmed, "though you carry the point far. . . ." He glanced at Jack, who was tidying up now. "And what is the *spear* for, Gobble?"

"The sacred spear," the other murmured, nodding. "Very necessary . . . it is used to defend the Grail. This much is known. The traitor, Hinct, explained these things when he delivered a map of their country to us."

"Why did he betray them?"

The other shrugged.

"He knows their power is fading. We will triumph, rest assured, and you will see a new life begin for the world." He did what might have been a smile again. At least his teeth showed in the grimace.

Howtlande arched one eyebrow almost imperceptibly, but merely said, "Just so we succeed, I leave the magic of the gods to the rest of you."

"Ah," Jack was just saying, lowering the ruined body, "well struck, old lad. Clean and sure as ever. . . ."

Howtlande swung his jeweled mock weapon before his face thoughtfully. It flashed the smoky light.

"You will see a new life begin," Gobble repeated conversationally, eyes rolling left and right, as if following an elusive something in the grim, chilly chamber. . . .

My lady Mary, Mother of heaven, she was thinking, *I was starting to finally believe we were safe. That it would never come again . . . And now it's come . . .*

She was kneeling beside her daughter, Tikla, and youngest son, Torky, at the edge of the wheat. Their heads were just above the grain as they looked across the level field toward where the sunset was gathering and the slow, black smoke billowed up.

They were returning from the lake. Alienor and Tikla had been washing clothes while Torky fished. He was holding a string of hand-sized lake trout.

"Who are they, Mama?" he asked Alienor.

"I cannot tell, son," she whispered, though the distance was great enough to lose a normal tone.

"Are they knights, Mama?" asked Tikla.

"Peace, children," Alienor murmured, straining at the shapes in the smoke-thickened dusk. She was sure she saw a glint of arms and plate. The horsemen were moving across the fields, half a dozen at least, followed by a line of foot soldiers who seemed to her very small, almost child-sized, digging in the potato fields with their spears.

One looked back straight at where they were crouched and she had a fearful impression the man would see her. The dimming, smoke-blotted light cleared for a moment and she thought she saw a silver-pale grimace of a face, terrible, distorted. Her skin prickled. Then the figure on his huge, dark mount moved off in the wake of his fellows.

She felt a lifting of relief. She waited while the stunted-looking marching men moved off into the deepening darkness. A few guttural fragments of speech sounded on the wind. Then silence. . . .

The house was burning down like a torch. There was nothing at all to be done.

"Mama," said Tikla restlessly, "can we go home when the fire stops?"

"Hush, child," Alienor said, embracing her. "Hush."

She already knew what she had to do. The mass of smoke touched by the vague last fingers of twilight high on the local lord's hill told her that. This was no chance raid. This was war. After so many sweet years, that horror was opening before her like a furnace door. . . . She reached and stooped and held her two children close. She stared across the field, as if into the dark, unknown days and nights and miles unnumbered before them. . . .

"Oh, hush, my dears," she whispered, staring.

The Duke watched the underbrush, rocking on his steaming, blowing horse, his light lance held ready. He was unarmored and wore a bright gold cape and hunting furs. Several mounted attendants watched with him. To his right was some Count, to his left, Lord Lohengrin of the shoddy fortunes.

The morning was clear. Dark, swampy trees grew like a wall before them. The dogpack was raving somewhere in the mucky woods.

"My lords," said the master of the hunt, a long, high-shouldered peasant with a pointy red face, "he'll turn soon. But he's lost to us, I fear."

"Nonsense," said the Count. "Why cannot we go straight in now? Hark! Ah, hear? The dogs are upon the bastard!"

The Count bit his lip and smiled with nervous excitement. Yelping screams, squeals, and rasping grunts intensified in the grayish-dark damp woods.

"My lords," the master of the hunt insisted, "in this bottom section the pig will rule the king. A lance cannot be freed to strike straight.

The animal struggles seemed to be moving off and deeper again. There was a sudden, long-drawn-out screech of agony and a momentary pause in all other sound.

"We must call back the dogs," the master said, "or lose the pack."

"And let the porker off?" Lohengrin suddenly shouted and spurred forward into the dank, dark, stinking trees. "I go myself."

The others looked at one another and held back. The master of the hunt leaned close to the Duke to whisper.

"My lord," he said, "don't follow this fool."

"You know I must," was the Duke's reply, raging. "I am bound by custom." He was half-snarling.

"But, my lord . . ."

None of the others looked at one another now as they sat watching the Duke move into Lohengrin's wake, closely followed by the hunt master. The bushes caught and brushed at their legs. The tilted, fallen, dense-set trees forced the big horses into a kind of galloping crawl.

"Rein off," the Duke instructed after fifty yards or so, "and draw the hounds away."

He watched Lohengrin's back dip down the rise before them.

Parsival knelt between her legs on the tight-packed straw. He glanced around at the rich, musty barn. The rank-sweet animal smell flowed up to them from below the loft, which was warm and low-ceilinged. Moonlight poked dimly through spaces in the boards. He kept trying to remember something . . . almost had it . . . something from long ago that this place recalled. . . .

The lady was smiling, head tilted to the side. Her robe was parted and her fluid softness showed dim and pale.

"Are you worried?" she asked.

"You mean afraid," he amended, resitting on his heels, hands resting on her knees.

"Yes," she agreed.

"A bearded, aging dreamer."

"All men are aging," she put in. "Your form is youthful." She considered the streaks and gouts of scar tissue on his lean, wide, powerful body. "Your eyes, Parsival, your eyes caught me. You didn't know that?"

"No."

"Your eyes." She nodded her head. "I look into them and find myself dreaming by the sea . . . waves and shores unseen with magic birds in golden trees. . . ." She smiled and moved her body, as if she were bound in sweet chains. "Yes," she murmured.

"My eyes do this?" He partly smiled.

"So I just told you, sir."

"If those magical places are within me, I know it not."

"But I see them." She delicately fingered his chest.

"I wish no more dreams," he said.

"Ah, but they live in your eyes, sweet knight. Would you blind yourself to darken them?"

He smiled again with a wry half-mouth.

"And lose the sight of you?"

"Yes."

"Never, my lady," he said, and she wasn't sure how deeply he meant it.

"*Never*, sir?"

"It is too late already," he said neutrally.

"So you love me, then."

He tilted his face and shut and reopened his eyes.

"I feel," he said, "I have been cold and stiff and dead for so long. . . ." He sank down upon her, lips almost touching, inhaling her, dizzy with her, feeling as though his flesh were melting wax, except for one insistent part. "For so long," he finished, kissing her cheeks and forehead.

She held him firmly across his wide, scarred back and sucked, and licked, and gently nibbled his lips.

"Oh," he sighed and pressed himself into the burning yielding. "Oh, God. . . . Heal me, my lady . . . heal me . . . heal all my dark years and heart. . . ."

And he believed she could, the sheer touch and intensity of her . . . he believed she could. . . .

Alienor followed the faint sketch of trail at dawn which grayly and sourcelessly began to glow among the dense pines. Their steps were muffled by the soft, fallen needles. The air was almost cold. She thought she could feel the steel teeth of winter nipping just a little.

"Mama," her daughter asked through a yawn, "will we find Papa soon?"

"We'll see, Tikla," was the reply. She held the child's hand. Torky, the boy, went in ahead, kicking up clumps of the brown woven turf, swinging a stick back and forth like a sword. Now and again he cut at some imaginary opponent.

"Got you!" he declared. "How do you like that?"

Alienor was still settling her thoughts. She had only a very general idea of what to do at this point. Her husband's last message had come from Camelot by way of a carter. He had transformed her into a secret literate like himself—in fact, he possessed (or had until the fire) three fragments of books in the English tongue. She still had the scrap of parchment:

MY LOVE. I AIM TO COME UNTO LONDON TOWN BY MID-SUMMER. WEARY. WILL STAY WITH JACK HANDLER'S KIN. B.

Her first problem was food. There were potato fields beyond the hill they were crossing. If the raiders had avoided the back trails, the section would be intact. Well, there was nothing for it but to try for London. She was going to have to face that prospect. She didn't want to think about the war. But for some reason she had a feeling it was widespread. She didn't know why, but she was sure of it. . . .

The Duke's horse was virtually jammed in the rotting beeches. It kept sinking fetlock deep into the black ooze. The eye whites showed as he strained under his master's curses and goads and smelled the rank, raw boar scent.

The Duke, as if the creature were to blame for his plight, kept punching the long head with his knotted fist.

Lohengrin was atop the gully that the other man was struggling to cross. The boar's snorting fury was clearly audible above the dog cries that were circling back toward them.

"You're mad!" the Duke flung at the younger knight. "If the beast turns into us here, why, we're undone!"

"Think a pig may slay two armed fellows like us?" Lohengrin smiled, showing his yellowish teeth.

The Duke's spear was now tangled in the vines that draped the pulpy trees. He tried to keep his grip as the horse pulled forward and he teetered back, tried to hold, then lost it and swore explosively.

The riot of animal sound was close now. The Duke had worked his way up beside Lohengrin on the little spine of ridge. They moved carefully along the top, as if balancing, hooves slipping on wet and mossy stones. Then the underbrush crackled and shook and the baying and squealing seemed all around them: savage, grunting snarls, louder, louder, and then the musty, reeking bloody-tusked, boar broke out of the snapping trees, massive, violent, sudden, seeming to undulate along close to the earth. A hound, tongue flopping, foam spraying, loped out at his heels, and with incredible speed and force the boar doubled back on itself and in one sweep ripped and tossed the screaming dog back into the brush in a rain of blood.

"You bastard!" the Duke was screaming. "You shit-sucking bastard!" He drew his dagger, more out of nervousness than anything else.

The pig had turned again and was virtually below them down the ten-foot slope.

"Where is that fool?" he muttered, craning around for the master of the hunt and seeing nothing but the gray netting of dead trees.

And then he just had time to twist his raging, pale, despairing face around to glare his fury at Lohengrin and swing one futile cut with the blade as the bushy-haired knight braced the handle of his lance under his victim's armpit and tilted him out and down into the steep gully to roll helplessly in the path of the furious beast.

He kicked, pale and desperate, at the tusked snout, flat on his back. Lohengrin looked on with interest and professional detachment. He saw the boar's first hit drive the Duke behind a bush. He couldn't tell if he'd been slashed. He thought the older man was doing very well, considering. But without even a mail shirt, there was no chance, of course.

The dogs were trying, circling, dodging in and out, but the dense, low-slung creature, thumping mud, shaking brush, snorting in a frenzy, came in again as the man got to his feet and took a few wild, windmilling steps through the dense, leafless trees, his outline blurring into a gray shadow. He screamed this time and went down, trees snapping, into a flurry of dogs and squeals and ripping and blood and a voice shouting somewhere out of sight (the master of hunt): "Your Grace! Your Grace!"

Parsival was sitting up, nude, in the damp hay. Pieces of straw were caught in his hair. His body was still smooth, solid, and supple. His scars had faded as much as they ever would. He stroked his beard and, for no particular reason, said, "I'm going to shave this off again."

She was on her back, relaxed, soft and thoughtful looking.

"Come over here, Sir Parsival," she offered.

She touched his wrist with one rounded bare foot. Kneaded his flesh lightly with her toes.

"It's dawn," he said, gesturing with his head at the wall before them where faint, grayish slits of daylight showed.

"The birds are still quiet," she noted.

"But is your husband?"

Her foot went away.

"I've grown fond of him," she said, "in these last years. He's a decent man . . . he understands me."

"It shocks my senses," he said, "when I think how easy it is to put off one life and put on another. . . ." He turned to face her, still squatting. "I was afraid last night, when I came here with you. Did you know that?"

"Yes," she replied. "And I wonder at your frankness. Few men would speak so."

"What profit to lie?" he wondered. "Why, there have been times when I've been incapable with a woman."

"That," she said, smiling with rich content, "is like a rich man talking of his days of poverty, Parse."

"Parse?"

"No one called you that?"

"Perhaps. But it never sounded so fair."

"Does it displease you?"

"No."

A pause.

"What were you afraid of, Parse?"

"Last night?"

"Yes."

He cleared his throat and held back a yawn that sent sleepless shivers down his back.

"A week of days ago," he said, "I sat in the bleak hills alone. This world was distant as a dream in a dream. . . . I sat there immersed in things . . . things beyond the world's borders. . . ."

"Yes?" She was interested.

"Even now I feel only half here, as when I was young. . . ." He yawned again. He wanted to sleep, to float. The word drew at him softly.

"Oh." She was a little saddened.

"And I was afraid I'd surrendered again."

"Ah. Perhaps you have."

He moved to his knees beside her. He watched her smooth face, her eyes, as if some answer to something unasked might float up and reveal itself in those violet-green gleaming depths.

"I'm still afraid," he said.

With a yielding strength, she gripped her surprisingly long arms around his thigh and rested her cheek near his knee.

"That you've lost God?" she softly wondered. "That we're sinning?"

He shook his head.

"No," he replied. "Not so simple, lady, not so simple. . . . The sins I've witnessed and committed in this world would leave this a pale wrong, indeed, in their harsh light. . . ."

"Then *what*?" she wanted to know, pressing softly but insistently at him.

"That I've started another adventure," he finally answered, smiling, serious, but inescapably wry, too. "I want no more of them." He touched her face as if amazed at the sweet, firm warmth and life of the flesh. "They leave me ever with empty hands." He raised her face to his and kissed, his tongue lingering in the hot, silky, fluttering unfolding of her mouth. "And," he now whispered, "more lost than ever . . ."—he kissed—". . . without an ending."

"But," she told him, serious and direct, "there is always an ending."

He frowned. The idea, the fact, pained him. It seemed, unreasonably, a surprise. It was as though underneath all he'd seen, done, felt, and hardened himself to, there was a timeless hopefulness in reserve, a belief in joy unsullied and permanent, as simply, he reflected, as anything his famous childhood had showed. . . .

"No," he murmured, almost too softly for her to hear, "let me only begin and begin forever, my love."

"Ah," she sighed, suddenly clinging closer, drawing herself up to press against his full length. "There's such magic in you . . . you're like a dream yourself. . . . What am I to do? Tell me, love, and do it I shall! Only tell me. . . ."

He kissed and stroked over her, inhaled her spicy sweetness of ripened flesh. Staring into her spring-forest-colored eyes, he could only say, "I want to be with you. That's what I want. I want to learn everything within you."

He released himself now, as if all the years frozen in him were finally melting, and he knew only now how cold he'd been, how utterly cold and lost and remote. . . . As all else thawed and ran, he found one thing suddenly, burningly firm, and letting the day dissolve away, he pressed into the resistless wetness of her, and although there was motion, there was no time: the outer world beyond their bodies shifted in its tides and currents without effect and the sounds came through without meaning and they rocked together as if to fuse seamless and forever, fragments of words and images flashing by. . . . His body snapped into her faster and faster, deeper, fiercer, as if something were within reach, as if in this tender violence there was bliss and space, both struggled in a frenzy to free within themselves. . . . He heard the loft rock and creak with the strain, the rhythmic rustle of the hay, the sop-sop-sop of their loins, his breath, heartbeat, smelled the sweat, juice, and uncanny fragrance on her breath . . . raised himself higher and hurled himself into her with images of golden fields and white, rich blossoms raining through his mind unbidden . . . the waves of a shimmering sea swelling and peaking . . . delicate, translucent, shining beings in a prismatic world embraced and praised and sang wordless and wept gold with joy . . . a flower like the sun unfolding . . . a tender animal, all warm fur and flowing, forest eyes, quivering in his grip. . . .

"Ah," he gasped, "I'm you . . . I'm you . . . I give all . . . I give all . . . I give . . . give . . . ah! . . . ah! . . . ah! . . ."

"No!" she cried, fluttering fingers clawing into his pulsing buttocks. "No . . . no . . . no . . ." Rolling her head distracted, throwing up her legs to lock behind his neck so that each stroke of him pounded against her innermost recesses, so she cried in pain now, too: "Harder . . . no, no! Oh, harder . . .! Heaven and earth . . . harder . . . kill me with it . . . kill me . . . kill me . . . kill meeeee . . .!"

Because it was there and for a moment neither knew where the other began and ended and there was no telling mind from flesh from soul. All one fabric stitched through them. And he thought (though never remembered) or said: *I am we are this joy only this only this only this only this* . . .

Lohengrin rode out of the swampy woods into the cool sunset. The master of the hunt followed a few minutes behind with his lord's body. The retainers were waiting. Lohengrin noticed his squire had finally arrived. He wondered if he'd accomplished his purpose. He couldn't ask him just yet.

"A terrible mischance," he said to them all, his face set, eyes cold and steady, not quite looking at any one of the half a dozen present. No one said anything. A chill, damp wind blew across the over-lush rot of the field. Autumn was coming in on the season's tide. "My lord Duke, His Grace, is perished." The men just looked at him. "He fell bravely, gentlemen, saving me from the pig. I owe him a debt of life." Silence. The cool gray shadowless twilight filled the woods around them like rising water. "I slew the brute killer, of course." He let his horse drift a little closer to the vassals. Two lower barons sat at seeming ease, eyes slightly restless in bearded faces. "The Duke's last words—unfortunately heard only by myself and the good God . . ."—he crossed himself—". . . were that I take hold of his affairs and act as uncle and regent to his unformed son."

He idly wondered if they could hear his heart. Would they let this pass for now? He was basically demanding neutrality. He smiled slightly, unconsciously, thinking how one might as well risk a kingdom as a castle. . . . Why a king but treats the world as any man might treat his family . . . The same stick can strike a thousand backs.

He didn't realize (as he noticed, relaxing slightly, that they weren't going to resist him just now) his smile had decided them. His mouth had curved and parted unselfconscious, as a shark with no thought to terrify: it was his utter cold amusement at the fact that life and death hung on this moment, and that flash of slightly too long teeth had been enough for men who still believed their lives and families and politics led somewhere to something beyond the void and trackless blackness those eyes stared into and the bleak, bitter depths that mouth smiled from. . . . They weren't prepared to defy him face to face.

"Fortune's wheel," he was saying, not smiling now, spurring his horse lightly past, the bloody spear resting across his lap, gesturing for his squire to follow, "astounds us all."

He felt warm, comfortable, a little light-headed. A bold stroke. So far successful. It was a good game and would stave off those melancholy hours when he was done with combat, sex, chess, eating, and sleeping, those hours of staring into the blackness that was always there gnawing at the heart of the brightest day like flecks of sore and poison. . . .

As they moved along the dimming path toward the castle, he tilted back to speak with the younger man.

"Well, Wista?" he demanded.

"I learned nothing, sir," Wista replied, seeming vaguely curt.

"No trace of that great fellow, your sovereign hero and saint?"

"I know nothing of that. But there was no word of your father, sir."

"So he no longer fasts and prays his days away in the sweet eye of God?"

"I know not. He may, for all I know, seek God in some other place."

Lohengrin turned to face ahead into the dusk. A few stars already showed above the very tall, very massive battlements.

"My father," he muttered, smiling, "and God."

Later in the morning Parsival lay there watching thin fingers of sunlight grope slanting through the boards and probe the musty shadows of the barn. Unlea was dozing, tucked close beside him on the matted hay.

Now what was he going to do? The same question again. Always the same. . . . The world outside without this woman in his life seemed bleak and relentless. And dead gray. . . . He was suddenly afraid she might not care as deeply as he did. His stomach tensed with the thought, which was instantly almost unbearable. Why, was this the same Parsival, he wondered hopelessly, who'd put aside the frail vanity of ambition and strife and tried to feel the pulse of the steady, infinite heart, who'd seen human goals and achievements become a child's snow-carved figure at the start of thaw . . .? Was this himself (who'd heard the eternal whisper once) in a near panic because a woman might have whims . . .? Why, his inner eye had learned to poke through the shadows that seemed mortal substance and . . . his powers. . . . He frowned, said *no* to himself, then tried, concentrated on her, tried to hear and see her mind as he'd been taught. . . . Nothing. . . . He strained . . . nothing at all. . . . He realized he probably had lost everything already. And he was ashamed of himself for the impulse. *Of course I'm losing them*, he thought. *I've dropped to earth again . . . no wonder monks flee from women.* . . . He smiled. And here she was, alive and close. He felt a peace and hope suddenly like an image from the sweet stream of endless dreams, of the infant sleeping at the full and tender breast. . . .

He had to be with her now. Impossible as that was, he had to be with her. He blinked and sat up straight and eased his cricked back. He glanced into his lap at his limp organ, shiny with dried juices in its nest of dark, gold-tinted hair.

Look at you, he thought. *Dead flesh. . . . What passes through you, what fire to raise you up again?* He shook his head. *Your time comes and passes quickly. . . . Well, I'm bound to her and you are the key to the fetters and to her gate, through which I must pass. . . .*

And he thought that, perhaps for the first time, it was not merely the animal who wielded it. . . .

"Awaken, my love," he said, and then, relishing the sound with tender embarrassment: "Unlea." He touched her lightly. "It's full day without."

She stirred.

"Ah," she murmured, "you let me sleep long . . . in the eye of death."

"Bonjio," he said quietly.

She looked up at him.

"I'm not really afraid," she said, "as you see."

He nodded.

"What will you do?" he wondered. *What will I do?* he thought.

She shrugged.

"You must say," she told him.

He hesitated, tried to meditate. He kept asking his soul to ask *What's right . . .? What's best . . .?* Nothing. His years, his talks, his readings, his lives before (because his life had been so cut into sections) had provided nothing for this day and need. *What's right? What's right? What's right!?*

He kept staring at her now, as if the answer lay in the sweet curves of her face and those subtly changing eyes, whose briefest attention seemed precious in the fugitive gleam of a sunbeam. . . . What did he want from her? he kept asking himself. After all, she was just another woman: flesh, blood, thoughts, and the food passing through came out as shit, not nectar. . . . She hoped and feared and had ugly places in her secret thoughts like everyone else . . . would shrivel and die with the years and mark her passing with a set of crumbly bones. . . . But these thoughts were reason without substance. And they were blown away by each hushed moment in the fullness of unstirred time, the glory and wonder of finding out what she saw, knew, and had known before, the world marvelously reflected through her, the new life of her flesh to his stunned, strong hands. . . . He felt the calm of her nearness with the hinting fear that she could go at any time . . . saw with his naked heart that no one could love without willingly, rapturously embracing death. . . .

"So I must say," he repeated.

He remembered in a flash with sight, sound, smell, and something deeper, remembered the actual, tangible presence of the movement from childhood: a spring morning, fresh, drying, cool dew, sun and shadow startling, yellow flowers blinding on the hill, where the clouds and air and green lushness seemed a single flow and extension of his own rippling pulse, and only the stiff, darkened part of him walked on the tilted ground at all, and he could have cried out with each breath and heartbeat as he heard his mother singing, turned (as if the day simply flowed and engendered a new image in the gleaming air) and was blinded by her gown and the burning dandelions and buttercups at her feet, for a moment within the unimaginable soul of the day and so within her, too, felt her being like a floating cloud and needed no names . . . needed nothing. . . . Suddenly, without seeming break, the song became her, saying, "Good morrow, son."

"Yes, mother."

"What will you do today?"

He was mildly surprised. He felt drawn by the stream where it curved, shocking crystal blue, into the deep green, overhanging old woods. Every day he had been following it a certain distance, looking, learning, as the sunlight or gray tints shifted imperceptibly, and finally his mother's voice would reach him and call him back out of that calm suspension and he'd discover he was hungry again. . . . There was so much to see and smell and touch . . . never the same, each day wrote its own story of shape and shadow, insect flickerings, animal tracks, and glimpses. . . . But today a thought kept troubling him.

"Mother?" he asked.

"Yes, Parse?"

She lightly stroked his fine, ash-blond hair.

"Mother, is there something . . ."

"Yes?"

". . . something I *ought* to do today?"

She shook her head, keeping her fingers tenderly on him.

"No," she told him. "*You* have to say, my boy. When you say for yourself without fear, then you'll speak from love and will do

no hurt to anything. I cannot teach you goodness, Parsival." She
shook her head again and briefly shut her eyes. "Oh, and what the
world waits to teach . . . oh, my son, what the world waits to teach
you. . . ."

He listened to those sweet sounds that didn't really satisfy his
questions. Then he went lightly down the resilient hill slope with
the sweet-scented, sun-vibrant breeze in his face. . . .

He remembered all this now in that single flash.

"So I must say again," he said again, lifting her to a sitting
position. "Am I still too poisoned by time to find a true tongue in
my mouth?"

She was smiling, relaxed, dreamy.

"You are magical," she said. "You're my gift from the lands
beyond sleep." She kissed him with her over-soft, bruised, wet
lips. "You . . .! How can I tell you what you are?"

"What will you tell your husband?"

She blinked. He was fascinated by the color and changing tints
in her eyes.

"Ah, love," she said, "I had better be practical."

He smiled, helping her up and into her chemise and robe. He
dusted off the hay as best he could. He picked it from her hair.

"Try only the possible, my love," he remarked, "as a wise man
once said."

"Who was, no doubt, a priest of ice who never loved a whit."

She kissed him again, lingeringly, as they stood there. He was a
little wobbly.

"This is new to me," he said.

"Love? At your age, sir?" She looked up into his face and
stroked her long hands over his shoulders.

"I have learned a few things," he told her, helping her down the
tilted, splintery stairs to the musty floor of the barn. The cows
lowed; chickens bawked and shifted. Outside the bell for morning
mass was sounding. "In barns, particularly," he concluded.

"The priest stirs," she remarked as they came to the door, which
stood ajar. Parsival squinted into the brightness: an old man was
toiling across the muddy yard, a load of firewood tied to his
shoulders. Farther off a bony man was kicking a stiff-legged,
motionless mule. Two tiny red and blue birds suddenly landed in a
bright swirl and nervously pecked the earth . . . then whirred
away in a blink. . . . "The serfs will be coming here shortly, I

should think. I confess I am not expert in rustic ways." She smiled
to reassure him. "But I take walks some mornings dressed as I am.
There's less danger than you think—unless we make love again."
She smiled and watched him.

"Again?" He enjoyed the notion. "So I might meet my death
either from love or your husband?"

"You? With your magic and strength?" She looked up into his
face and nestled close into him. He held her cheeks in his hands
and kissed and kissed and kissed . . . and she rubbed herself
against him, as if drugged. . . . He felt need like a hunger and
thirst now just for her spicy taste and firm touch and the pulsing
stir of his body, a hunger and thirst, he knew, that could never be
assuaged . . . though it might cease someday. . . .

Broaditch had decided to trust fate since, he reasoned sourly,
there was no choice, in any case.

Valit was clinging to the side as the wind slashed and cracked
and hammered the spray into them. Broaditch wondered if he'd
stopped vomiting. The howling air isolated them. Even a shout
was lost a foot away.

He kept an oar in, trying to hold the bow into the storm. He'd
learned this fishing in his youth. He remembered the last storm
he'd ridden out in a round-bottomed carrack, toppling and slipping
over heaped herrings, tangling in loose nets, raging, struggling,
bailing. . . .

The waves seemed to be rearing up and up, lifting them with
sickening speed, flipping the boat like, he thought, a loose plank.
The oar bent as he braced against it . . . hummed . . . snapped,
and they began spinning into sheets of breaking foam, calf-deep in
chill water. . . . He'd never known a storm like this for sheer rage
and intensity. . . . He saw Valit's mouth moving, gaping, soundless, terrified. . . . for a moment the boat was lifted free of the
waves that were too huge to actually smash it, so they sailed out
over an immense trough before falling to the bottom, which
bounded up into a madly tilting crest again. . . .

Broaditch wasn't even afraid now. And except for stray words
and images that moved volitionlessly through his mind, he wasn't
actually thinking. *Impossible to survive . . . so it's over . . . so it's
over.* . . . He was merely waiting now, watching, holding on only
because there was no good reason not to.

And the rain finally struck, sheeted, hissed, boiled over them, and the boundaries of sea and air dissolved. It was all one thing now and there was only tumult and heaving, slopping, sloshing, spinning . . . and then a deeper roar. He knew in a moment the rocky coast was close, and the frail, leaking, half-swamped craft was already leaping among the reefs and he fleetingly considered that simply to drown would have been so gentle. . . . The roaring water exploded all around, the fog was blown to shreds, and gleaming black rocks, like (he thought) terrible teeth in the slash of mouth formed by the bay curve of cliffs, were about to grind and rip them to bloody tatters. . . .

The hull struck with a terrific shock, shook, spun, fell in half, and instantly disappeared, as in spasmodic terror. Valit flung himself into Broaditch's body and locked there, gripped tighter than death, and, like one doubled person, they tumbled into the icy, deadly surf, tumbling into choking darkness, and Broaditch clutched Valit in return, as if the helpless, fragile flesh of another could preserve him, in a blind reflex that may have had wisdom in it, too. . . .

He waited, totally relaxed now except for his arms, for the first rip and battering. For a moment he went free of himself, for a moment (as the body churned and drowned) he was somehow apart, watching, and it was as if time and space had shrunk to something he could encompass and he felt/saw the future before him like a dark land where here and there misty scenes were dimly lit, and he couldn't be sure if this were life or the country after death, then grasped it was both: saw himself and others he seemed to know climbing a steep cliff beset by formless shadows; saw deep, interminable woods where he wandered and struggled; his wife and two children crouched over a guttering fire under cold and windy skies; a strange knight watching him from the edge of a clearing; blinding light streaming from something he couldn't look at and a shimmering figure in shining armor floating above the trees and then an incredible, bottomless longing that seemed to stir from the roots of all time, and he perceived inextinguishable life unfolding joyous and forever, life after life upon life, the music of grass growing, the conversations of the sea, the maternal flexing of these waves. . . . He felt free, fearless, immortal because this seeing reached far, far beyond his death as he (and the other body he didn't realize wasn't his own) smashed heavily into mucky sand

and rolled up a short beach into scraggly pines that tangled them so that the backwash of the immense surf couldn't drag them back to the fangs of rock. . . .

How beautiful, he found himself thinking, panting, *how perfect . . . how effortless . . . like plucking two frogs from a pool. . . .* He was sure for the rest of his life that he'd felt the hands—the literal hands—guide him on the shocking, terrifying, and magnificent tides of arrangement. There was no chance. Chance was lost to him. He'd felt the mother's touch in all the terror. His bones and blood knew those fingers, knew the fierce compassion of the sea. . . . *I died*, he thought, *that's all it took, that's all there was to it. . . .* There was no point in thinking about it. Thinking couldn't do a thing. It was too immense for reason.

Lohengrin's squire, Wista, was standing at the well in the luminescent dusk. A young serving girl was just drawing a bucket. Another girl in her late teens, wearing the silks of nobility, had walked him across the yard and was sitting on the low stone circle of well wall. Her face was roundish, dim, gleaming in the lingering violet-tinged light.

The serving girl filled the pails on both sides of a yoke and started trudging back across the hard-packed earth without having seemed to noticed their presence. She moved toward the vaulted doorway. Fireflies drew brief bright stains on the dusk.

"Take it to the second level, Lina," the girl commanded, "the bath chamber."

Lina barely nodded and went on steadily, balancing the two pails.

"She's surly," the girl announced.

Wista was staring, trying to see Lina's bare feet in the dusk. He'd noticed how shapely they were when she was drawing the water. He found himself fascinated by women's calves and feet recently, as if the part somehow stood for more than the whole. There was a familiar pressure within his codpiece: his flesh had started to harden. *This*, he thought, *is what frightens priests*. It was so intense for a moment that he wished he could fall to his knees and kiss the girl's sweet, sleek, bare arch and calloused instep. He felt an unformed desire to totally prostrate himself, to surrender in worship, shame, and ecstasy. . . . He shook his head, as if to snap a spell. . . . The girl beside him—what was her name? Frell—that was it. . . . What was she saying? He tried to catch up with her words, hoping the pulse of pleasure would subside, except that every step rubbed it against the stiff material and thus served to make matters worse, or, if you chose, better, according to his now widely fluctuating point of view. . . .

". . . so I told him, I said: 'Rein up your steed, sir, for you ride alone this even!' " She laughed lightly. "I stood ready to brain him with a platter of brass. A man of *his* years. And he called me a tease." She flounced her head. Wista studied her profile, upturned nose, fullish face. Pretty. . . . well, prettier than he first thought. Well. . . .

They were climbing the stairs inside the main building. Torches were lit along the halls. He studied her covertly. Her face was smooth, but a little too red, he thought.

Lina was just ahead of them. Under her shapeless dress he could see flashes of bare, brown leg. The effect, as they went up the half-spiral, brought him to a sweat and flash of adolescent dizziness. . . .

". . . so," Frell went on, "I told him: 'Sir, you are gray at the temples, and yet you long to revel with a poor maid such as I. Where is your religion, sir?' "

"Ah, religion, yes . . ." murmured Wista, watching the legs winking out of the shadows as the yoke swayed and the water sloshed. "Well," he said, not completely making a joke of it, "perhaps he thought himself Noah and you his daughter."

". . . so, he soon reconsidered. Indeed, he did."

Her hand fleetingly brushed against him. He wondered if there were any significance to it. He glanced at her again. Her body seemed good enough, he decided. He wished her feet were visible, but her velvet buskins were closed. *Why are feet so important?* he asked himself.

"I am writing poems and learning the lute," she told him.

"Ah," he said, glancing at her and then back up at Lina. But now they were in a level hall and the view was nothing much. He had to be content with just the ankle and below in the uncertain light. The sooty torch smoke made him want to sneeze. "Is that so?" he lamely finished.

"I am really quite taken with it. I think it really can reveal the divine side of people, as the Italian poet said."

"Did he?" Wista wondered which one. "I write somewhat

myself," he remarked as they entered a long, low-roofed chamber filled with steam. In a huge tub his master's dark, bushy-haired, hook-nosed face glared from a mound of suds. He faintly smiled. A young, fair-haired page held a mug of mulled wine to the lord's lips. Lohengrin suddenly darted his hand from the water and gripped the slight, graceful boy by the cheek and pulled him until he leaned over the tub side.

"You're a pretty wench of a lad," Wista heard him say.

Lina, the serving girl, was emptying the two buckets into a copper caldron that was steaming in the fireplace.

Wista watched her, abstractedly, thinking: *religion . . . she said something to that knight about religion. . . .* Then he knew what he wanted to do. Then he considered it pointless and hopeless. But the idea caught his consciousness: see Parsival, his master's father. Ask him about his doubts, about knighthood. . . . But did he want to be a priest? Was that an answer . . .?

"I want to give myself to something," Frell was saying, "completely. I don't want to waste away." She looked with nervous intensity at Wista.

"Yes," he said vaguely, "I see." He was wondering if it really were possible to see Parsival. He couldn't dare mention the idea to Lohengrin, who was somehow suddenly a great lord with a hundred men posted in and around the castle, as if he expected imminent attack. He supposed it was possible that vassals of the late Duke might mount a raid for revenge.

"I think perhaps poetry is the best thing for me," she continued.

Lohengrin was looking at them now from the steamy depths of the tub.

"What are you two about there?" he called over. "Exchanging chivalrous pleasantries?" He grinned sardonically.

Frell had just lightly touched his arm and looked up into his face with an almost pleading expression. He was surprised and uneasy. She was somebody's sister and they'd met last night at the feast. She seemed oblivious to Lohengrin's remark. There was naked need in her face.

"We were having a conversation, my lord," Wista said, with the sullen self-control his master always goaded him into.

"I must seem foolish to you?" she said, concerned.

He shook his head, though a little uncertainty showed.

"Not at all," he murmured.

He hoped she wasn't in love with him. The idea was awkward. On the other hand, if it were just hot blood, that would be interesting . . . a relief, anyway. . . . He wondered if he could get around the serving girl, though, who was leaving the chamber without looking past or at him with her expressionless brown eyes. It wasn't easy, he realized, to get something started unless you were a great knight or lord. What could he offer a peasant beyond a fair appearance of vitality? He sighed. He realized this wasn't really like him. Was he changing, suddenly? He had never been so woman-haunted.

"I want my life to truly count for something," she was telling him. "I don't wish to walk in my mother's footsteps. . . . But is this not foolish?"

"Why, no," he demurred, half paying attention, noticing the bent servant who had just added a copper pail of hot water to Lohengrin's bath. The pretty page had left. The servant suddenly straightened up as the bather was delightedly easing himself back and gesturing for Wista and Frell to approach him. The servant threw off his sack-like cloak and in one swift and supple motion laid the edge of a curved dagger across Lohengrin's throat and held it perfectly still, saying nothing. *A rising of commoners?* thought Wista.

Lohengrin's eyes were cold and furious. For an instant Wista believed he would somehow brush aside the incidental mortality of his naked flesh and tear the man apart in the hot gouts of his own blood. Wista saw the vivid image of it: the bath spilling over with reddened water as the slashed throat gaped and sprayed and the inconceivable fury itself like a force apart from the dying body it merely animated, locking the limbs upright and clamping the hands in a death-lock on the slayer's throat. . . .

Lohengrin didn't stir. Only his eyes showed anything. The man didn't speak. Wista noticed his face was grayish, doughy, squinty, utterly without expression.

Frell was startled. Wista heard the faint scrape and jingle of armor behind him and knew not to speak or turn. He involuntarily gripped the girl's arm and held her still.

Two feline-stepping, slim men in elaborately worked light chain mail and silky, flowing robes, wearing what he didn't know were called turbans (he first thought them bandages), padded past on slippered feet, followed by a pair of taller, wider knights in black plate armor with slitted face masks shut. They all stopped around the tub.

Where did they come from? Wista wondered. *How did they pass all those men at arms?*

One of the servants, a round-faced, curious fellow, tending the fire took a few steps nearer.

No! Wista thought. *No!*

The nearest dark, bony-faced warrior dipped, half-turned, drew (what Wista didn't know was a scimitar, either), whipped out and back, and re-sheathed his curved blade in an unbroken casual motion. For an instant nothing seemed to have happened. Then the servant, whose hands had flown vaguely up to his throat, took a weaving step backward; another, a thin smile of blood creasing his neck, then toppled into the flames, where he thrashed very little, smoked, and roasted as Frell gave a choking cry. He pressed her close and held her upright and motionless. He felt death very close, silly, incidental. . . .

"Shh!" he whispered. "Shh!"

"So," the taller knight, the captain, said through his face slits, "accept my homage, new Duke."

Lohengrin just stared, then said, "How did you pass? Did all my men turn traitor at once, or were they never loyal?"

"Many are loyal, new Duke," affirmed the captain. His voice had a tinny echo from the steel. "Take your ease and answer a question, for if you answer well, you'll come with us a little way. If you answer poorly, you may remain in your bath."

Wista realized his master wasn't going to immediately be assassinated. So these men weren't necessarily agents or relatives of slain enemies. Lohengrin obviously had worked this much out himself. He almost smiled.

"Need I have steel at my throat?" he wondered. "It corrupts my speaking."

"It had best sharpen it," was the helpful rejoinder from the slightly less massive man beside the leader.

"Ask your questions, then," Lohengrin returned, "make a London scholar of me . . . or tell me who you are."

The dead man in the fire was hissing and bubbling now like a roast on a spit. Dark, stinking smoke was seeping into the room's steamy air. Wista gagged, but he stayed perfectly still. He felt her erratic breathing against his chest.

"You may think of me as the devil's dearest friend, for all it matters," was the captain's reply. "Who bade you to slay the Duke?"

"Myself prompted me," Lohengrin instantly replied.

"And what reward did you hope for besides death?"

"Death?" He paused. "Reward?"

"Answer," the knight said without emphasis.

Lohengrin knew that doom was grinning at his shoulder. He could almost hear the cold teeth clacking together.

"What about those two?" He indicated Frell and Wista. "Need they hear?"

"Want them to live?" the lieutenant asked.

"Why waste them?"

The leader leaned over the sudsy water close enough for a whisper to reach him.

Wista felt her trembling steadily. He held her. He noticed, peripherally, that she seemed strong-boned and firm-fleshed. He was starting to believe they had some chance to live.

"Easy," he whispered near her ear, "easy, I pray you."

BOOK

II

ACROSS the level dirt field, the woods and hills were going red and gold in streaks and blotches. The bright air was comfortable but cool. Parsival, in fur and velvet, sat on a bench chewing an apple and watching several pairs of young squires engage one another with wooden swords on foot under the eye of stolid Prang. The battlers wore full armor and shuffled, panted, and attacked with awkward ferocity. Unarmored Prang suddenly booted one in his steel backside and sent him flat on his face with a great clang.

"Never lean forward when you stroke!" he shouted at his victim.

Parsival looked up as Earl Bonjio laughed behind him, then sat down on the bench at his elbow. Parsival uneasily ate the fruit. He wasn't certain of his feelings when he thought of her as this man's wife. Custom, he reflected, fenced off the fields of life. And men were continually climbing over. . . . Custom fences you into security and dullness, but, drag your feet or clutch the rails as you will, life sweeps you toward the unknown because, in spite of everything, the heart burns to live, to send you racing free over the mysterious earth in the very eye of death. . . . He smiled, remembering many things. *Yes, until you crash into the next fence after that,* he thought.

"He's very good," Bonjio remarked. "I'm pleased you recommended him. But he says he's unwilling to stay and serve me when you leave." He glanced shrewdly at Parsival. "Either he loves you in some unnatural fashion—" he grinned with his sarcastic eyes—"or believes you have much to teach him."

"Why not say, 'Or both'?"

Bonjio chuckled. Out in the field Prang was demonstrating a step and cut. His grunts and the tearing air as the blade sliced and spun were plainly audible. He glanced over at Parsival when he finished.

"I appreciate your hospitality," Parsival said and the words embarrassed him. He tossed away the apple core and one of the Earl's hounds (which had been resting on crossed forepaws), levered himself to his feet, and crunched the tidbit in lean jaws. "Well . . . well, I'll speak to Prang, if you wish."

Bonjio was studying the form of the sparring squires.

"No," he said. "I prefer to let a man follow his heart and inclinations." For an instant Parsival thought the phrase had a special meaning for him. "But what are your plans?"

Parsival cleared his throat. Nearly every remark seemed a reproach or hinting. What a horrible way to have to live, he thought.

"Plans?" Parsival stayed neutral in response. He watched and waited.

"Where are you bound? What will you do . . . ? Ah! Good, good, there!" He called out where one squire had struck another with the hardwood blade, dented the helmet, and dropped the fellow to his knees, as if to pray, stunned. "Well struck," he added as an aside. "So, then?"

"Agreed . . . though he hesitated a little."

"I didn't notice. But I meant: What are your plans?"

"Yes . . ." Parsival stared at the grassy turf, as if to read an answer there. A flash of color caught his attention: a butterfly, trembling, lying flat in a hollow of hard, dark earth. It was nearly dead. Looking closer, he made out, with a slight shock, a swarm of black, glossy-gleaming ants intricately enmeshing and picking the fan-like spray of yellow and orange to pieces so that it seemed to dissolve, as though fallen from some pure, sparkling height into a glittering, dark, acid stream. . . . "I really don't know," he said, knowing that he lied. He tried to remember if he'd told a lie before. He was certain he must have, but this one burned his tongue.

"You went into a monastery?" Bonjio asked.

"For a time . . . yes. . . ."

"Unlea mentioned it," Bonjio said, watching the combat. "I wasn't really surprised, from what I knew of you. How long since I'd seen you? Eight years?"

"Perhaps."

"When did you take your vows?"

Does he seek to know if I'm still bound to chastity?

"Five years ago . . . I think . . . I lost track of time," Parsival concluded.

"Well," Bonjio considered, "I last saw you near Jerusalem. You told me you were looking for your brother. I didn't know there was such a one."

"Yes. A half brother. Part Moor. So my mother told me."

He remembered: a collection of huts and tents in the blinding-white desert heat, sitting atop his horse, roasting in his armor among the sleepy mules and swaying camels and close-wrapped easterners, squinting at a garishly embroidered portrait on a silken sheet that the burnoused infidel was holding up. It was supposed to be his brother Afis, the prince who would never be sultan. He waved his sunburned hands at the flies that arced and darted into his open visor and buzzed maddeningly inside the metal pot and zipped viciously around his head. The other Christian knights with him were resting in palm shade across the road. The face meant nothing: lean and long with black hair, tilted eyes, and a thin moustache. It could have been anyone from that burning country. . . . He'd promised his mother to embrace his brother once before he died and tell him certain things about his father. . . . He'd glanced away from the embroidery and stared at the white road. The surface danced and swam in the midday brilliance, but he thought he saw a small animal there . . . looked closer . . . started: it was a hand that seemed to be reaching up from under the earth, clawed, distorted. "What's that?" he asked the man in broken Arabic, and the fellow shrugged, said something incomprehensible, and redisplayed the fluttering square of cloth. Parsival ignored him and rode closer. The hand was stiff and still, though for a moment it had seemed to move in the heat mirages. It was a wrist and fingers. "Do they bury men here in the roadway" he mused aloud and poked it with his sword tip. It fell over. A severed hand, but for a moment it had seemed a terror and a portent. . . .

"What a vile place that was," Bonjio was saying. "We were fools and dupes to ever be led there like sheep by mad priests. We roasted and bled in the desert while our women played us false at home. You were lucky, indeed, if kin or stranger stole not your lands, as well as your wife's cunt." He smiled with half his mouth. Parsival recrossed his legs and shifted in his seat, not looking at anything. "Most returned home crippled and in begging rags. . . .

Well, why did you go east, Parsival?" He grinned. "To hunt the *Grail* apace?"

Parsival frowned.

"Trouble me not with the Grail, Earl Bonjio," he said. "I've had sufficient questions and jokes for a thousand years were I to live them."

"But why did you go?"

"Well," he said, "to say truth: because it was far off."

Bonjio nodded.

"An honest reply," he declared.

"I was weary of . . . of things."

"I came back with ten of my hundred that left with me and found a cousin in my house and bed." His eyes went distant and cold. "He escaped me, but she did not."

A pause. The squires were taking a break in the field.

"Your wife?" Parsival finally had to ask. And when Bonjio nodded, he said, "Unlea?" His heart was frozen and pounding at the same time.

"Who?" Bonjio smiled. "No, no, my friend. My *first* wife." He suddenly seemed engrossed in Prang's demonstrating shield-without-a-sword, taking the clanging blows of three opponents at once without seeming effort.

"I see," Parsival murmured. He was thinking that he really wasn't guilty at all and that was why he felt uneasy. What was between himself and Unlea was between them. It existed like heat in a flame and had nothing to do with anything else, person or custom. . . . It was good and sweet and . . .

"I was sick with pain for a year afterward," Bonjio said. "My heart was never in the blows I dealt her, God knows that. . . ." He shut his dark eyes to remember. "I wept . . . I lay down on the cold stones beside her with my cheek in her blood and I wept. . . ." His eyes opened. Parsival couldn't tell if they were moist. "She was a woman . . . a *woman* . . . more than any since. . . . But I had to do what I did. How could I not?"

Parsival shrugged. *Custom struck the blows*, he thought, *not this man.* . . .

"Yet all the while I killed her, Parsival, all the while, I tell you, I felt apart and watching myself . . ."—his eyes were closed again—". . . and, this is passing strange, and, all the while I felt so distant and yet so close to her and I kept thinking: 'I don't mean this, my sweet wife, I don't mean this!'" He opened his eyes and just sat there for a time, lost within himself. "As if another struck," he finally murmured.

Yes, thought Parsival, *distance. And another did strike*. . . .

"At any moment I could have simply stopped," Bonjio said. He sat and stared. Then he pulled himself out of it.

Parsival was looking for the butterfly. His eyes scanned and found just ants trickling away. Not even a speck of yellow remained to stain the earth with memory. . . .

"Who's this?" he heard Bonjio say in a different tone of voice.

Everyone was watching a mounted knight in dark green armor enter the field from the distant woods. He came on at a walk, a very even pace.

"Were you chaste, then?" Parsival wanted to know.

"Eh?" Bonjio was shading his eyes, trying to make out the rider's shield device. "You jest?"

"No," Parsival replied, frowning slightly, "I do not. Why should not your wife have slain *you*?"

Bonjio was suddenly irritable.

"She was a woman," he snapped with a different meaning from a few moments ago. "Or are you still the original fool?" He smiled in mitigation of his comment.

"That's possible," was the murmured reply. "But I've slept under all manner of skies since then." He looked up at the rider, who was crossing the jousting field now. "Except, I heard a knight say once but that we wield a sword and they bear a sheath, men and women have more alike than otherwise."

"Except that we're different, we're really the same, eh?" mocked the Earl.

"Who made man's pride worth a murder?" Parsival was serious: he imagined Unlea being slain. For what? For need? For a dream? Custom . . . created by men ages ago stepping out into the world fresh and saying: I like this, so this is good. I hate that, so that is wicked. "In the name of *Christ*?"

The Earl crossed himself.

"I'm a good Christian," he said, irritated. "Enough of this!"

The mounted knight had stopped now among the training squires. Parsival was frowning, thinking: *It's not just up to men because there is a voice in all things . . . I've heard it. . . . And that voice tells you if you listen how each shadow sorts itself, how each blade of grass finds its proper space*. . . .

Bonjio stood up and stepped forward to confront the newcomer.

Like something in the corner of the eye, he found himself always conscious of Unlea. Parsival knew that, like a miser with his coins, he could think of her with secret joy and vague insecurity. Even the edge of anxiety was welcome because it brought the image to life. . . .

The green knight didn't raise his visor. The grille was wide so his voice was fairly clear, and familiar to Parsival, who tried to place it.

"Greetings, gentlemen," the knight was saying. His armor was glossy plate.

"I suppose you're hungry and in need of sleep," Bonjio said with formal disinterest.

"This covers all cases of mortals," was the wry and brisk reply, and Parsival stood up. Could it be? Still living?

"But your particular case stands before me," Bonjio returned. He obviously didn't like the custom of having to feed any stray warrior who happened by. *Custom is what you happen to prefer*, Parsival reflected.

"Is this an inn, then?" the newcomer wanted to know.

Prang had come up to him.

"What manner of insult is that?" he asked.

"One well chosen," the knight declared, "unless my wit has soured." He seemed perfectly at ease. Parsival was almost certain now he knew him.

"I turn no man from my gate whether he be," said Bonjio coldly, "gentle or a thankless and insolent son-of-a-bitch."

"I've too many years nailed to my back," was the reply as the fellow shifted slightly within his armor, as if, Parsival thought, to scratch some patch of skin. *He always itched*, Parsival thought. "Too many years to be that."

"Are you under a vow," Prang asked, "or will you show your face? Your device I know not." He referred to the single eye on a green triangular field painted on the round shield. It was odd, to say the least.

"It should tell you that I seek to see," the knight told him. "My helmet stays closed for now." He turned directly to Parsival. "How are you?" he asked.

"Well enough, Gawain," Parsival answered.

The knight nodded.

"Gawain?" Bonjio seemed reasonably impressed. "I suppose this is an honor, though it is said you died in Brittany."

"Sir, I am always dying somewhere."

Was Gawain still a little mad? Parsival wondered. He seemed his old self. But it had been so many years. . . .

"Parse," Gawain said, "I see much gray in the gold." He walked his massive steed closer. The horse seemed as relaxed as the man. Smooth. Steady. Gawain rubbed himself inside the plate again. "Yet are you still God's child?"

"As much as any else, I think," Parsival replied.

"I look forward," Gawain said, chuckling, "to renewing our friendship."

"Is that what it was?" Parsival asked neutrally.

"Come, come, I ever was fond of you." Gawain seemed a little hurt. "We had slight differences." He gestured vaguely, depreciatory. "Are you training these lads here?"

"Did you follow me again?" Parsival asked.

Gawain cocked his steel head.

"After all this time?" he said. "For what?" He nudged his stolid horse on past. "We'll talk anon, Parse. I'll hear the news . . . no . . . the *history*. It's gone past news by now."

Broaditch and Valit, as night fell, were struggling across deserted, boggy stretches of flatland. The wind was chilly. The strange, erratic weather was in full sway, Broaditch thought. Late summer intercut with fall and winter . . . endless rains . . . then spring. . . . He'd learned, with his years, that these portents had real significance. The stars and weather and men's fates mixed all together. Something was coming, something vast and perhaps terrible. . . . He believed the old man in the boat had meaning, too, but the reality was fading: the problem was to march to shelter, not meditate metaphysically, and to start for home once he discovered the direction.

God, but how he ached . . . sheer misery. Shock had silenced his young and bitter companion for the time being . . . on and on and on . . . sucking bog everywhere, mists, stink . . . Valit's gasping breaths, his own rasping. . . .

Suddenly Valit gave a cry that ended in a burble: he'd sunk to his face in the clinging mud. His hands sloshed feebly at the surface.

"Help," he bubbled, spitting and shaking his head.

Broaditch stood perfectly still. The fast, cold clouds were streaked with whitish-gray. Last light gleamed vaguely on the bog and spiny, dark clumps of marsh weed. He squatted and reached his hand out carefully, bracing his feet as best he could. The young man strained for it. Fingertips brushed. Broaditch tried to shift closer. He couldn't tell where the firmer footing ended. He knew it would be abrupt.

"In the name of the saints," Valit sputtered and begged, "I'm lost . . . I'm lost . . ."

"Are you still sinking?"

"I cannot tell . . . I'm lost . . . oh, mother . . . mother . . ."

Broaditch felt his nearer foot slide and splash over the slick, sudden edge. He jerked it back.

"Be quiet," he snarled. "Is that the only tune you know?"

"Lord God," the young man spluttered on, "I'm lost . . . mother, help me . . . help . . ."

"Hold yourself without stirring and you may yet live!" Broaditch commanded. "Stop whining at every turn. I scarce believe you the son of a brave man. Don't stir or speak."

While delivering himself of these sentiments, Broaditch was moving carefully, groping in the mud until he found a thick, twisted stick which he dragged from the sucking earth and duck-walked back to Valit's head and wildly reaching, long, pale hands and arms. Each breath he drew sputtered and bubbled. He seemed, Broaditch later thought, a creature born of mire and seeking escape, except, he thought, *men make their own mire and sink themselves . . . and beg to be pulled free. . . .*

The stick was clutched with white-knuckled desperation. The rescuer leaned all his weight into the effort and pulled steadily. He set his mind to pull and never relent. He realized what he was doing was virtually impossible. It would take a sound mule. So he set his teeth and gradually squatted himself upright as Valit gripped with both mucky hands and sobbed and wheezed.

"I'm doomed!" he cried. "I'm not budging. . . ."

Broaditch pulled and concentrated. Eyes bulged, muscles cracked . . . bright spots burst in his eyes. A nightmare: endless straining, slipping, pain, and then, infinitely slow, the soggy, slim young man began to inch free. . . .

The last stain of twilight had long since drained away to pitch, moonless darkness before Broaditch could get a grip on those pale, long, groping hands and twist and haul him free. . . .

They both lay gasping on the chill bog for a long time. Broaditch could hear the young man's teeth chatter. . . .

Need I be reminded so often, Broaditch thought at one point, *of how death is at the end of every movement? Breathing in is living*, he thought, as his lungs labored, *breathing out is dying*. . . .

Finally they staggered on. Valit was trying to stay directly behind Broaditch.

"And if I go under," Broaditch asked him, "will you raise me free?"

He was using the stick to poke before him. They seemed to be on a ridge of relatively firm footing. A step or two off the line and the stick dipped deep. He kept probing to find the solid lane which suddenly twisted left and after that turned every so often, as if they walked, Broaditch didn't say, on the spine of a gigantic snake. . . .

The nightmare continued. The sea wind freshened and chilled. The bog seemed endless. In the hills before them a faint spot of firelight winked redly like a furious, demonic eye. Broaditch assumed a fisherman must live there.

On and on along the serpentine track, glopping ankle-deep in cold mud, wobbling on, Valit even past complaining, holding on around the big man's back like a babe . . . and on . . . the hills crept closer and then the crescent moon rose behind them. Broaditch could see solid, rocky ground less than fifty yards ahead. . . . A few straining steps more and he slipped: the footing gave as if the spine moved, and he left the stick poking irretrievably in the mire. So he had to probe with feet only now, and, for the first time, he considered surrender, to lie down and wait for the inevitable turn of the tide that would lift the muck and drown them. . . . But he went on, thinking just a little more and he'd quit . . . just a little more. . . . Valit held his leather belt and slipped and stumbled in his footsteps. . . .

When they were about twenty yards from the solid shoreline, his leg went to the knee on all sides without bottoming. The submerged ridge was finished. There was no way to be certain how deep this final channel was. So they stood there as the moon swung higher. . . . He knew he was being tested again. So soon . . .

At the moment of certain doom, he'd let go and surrendered to the sea. There had been despair in it. Now he wondered if he had to have faith without even surrender. He lacked the energy to even cynically smile at himself.

He shut his eyes. He'd never really prayed except in battle. But prayer wasn't really needed here—not faith, because faith meant you hoped, believed, but didn't really know. . . . Magical help was worthless. He had to do this himself. . . . He somehow knew something was aware, watching him, and would refuse magic. . . . This was the moment he had to *know*, had to plunge into the slimy, dark, sucking ooze of the earth and *know* his path, vivid and real as blunted bone and battered flesh. . . . Now he smiled. It didn't simply *seem* mad: it was mad. He stood listening to Valit's chattering teeth and sobs and then shook his head and stepped forward off the edge, sunk waist-deep, and sloshed foward with the young man hanging on, still too miserable to even complain as the stinking slime oozed up steadily. . . .

Lohengrin went with them. He dried and dressed in a loose silken robe and they walked him out. First came the helmeted leader and massive lieutenant whose black beard hid most of his face. The turbaned, cold-featured guards followed. As they went out, Lohengrin turned to Wista, in the doorway.

"Say nothing to anyone," he ordered. "Wait for me."

"Ah," remarked the lieutenant, "here's an optimist."

"Wait," Lohengrin repeated, his voice firm as stone.

And then they were gone into the hidden door, the guards' torches moving away down the corridor, an unsteady splash of light, and then the door swung shut and there was only blank wall and no visible seam.

"What does this mean?" Frell asked, still clutching Wista.

"Nothing splendid, I assure you," Wista returned.

"My sister says your master is bound to be a great man."

"Well, in any case," Wista said, "he's not very pleasant."

"He's handsome," she said, "in his way. Do you know his father?"

"No." Wista wrinkled his nose at the stench, then turned toward the fireplace, where the dead man lay charring and smouldering.

"Ugh," she said. "He smells like meat."

"Anyway," he said absently, "you had better stay with me for now, I think."

The captain led the way down a spiral passageway that ended among the dank foundations where the wet, massive stones seemed, in the wavering torch gleam, like the beams and buttresses of the earth. Lohengrin reflected how this would be a fitting support for what the world was: the slimy stones, the vague, scuttling things that rattled and scraped across uneven floors, the dungeon hollows where skeletons could be glimpsed dangling in rusted, brittle chains. The cold air was stale.

"So," he said as they crossed the vast cellar toward a barred cell where a faint taper gleamed, "You mean to butcher me here? Why waste so many steps?"

He didn't really think this, though his heartbeat proved he feared it.

The bushy-bearded lieutenant glanced at him, grinning with deepset eyes.

"Why, your new Grace," he said, "we may only leave but part of you here and take the rest back with us."

None of the turbaned men laughed or reacted. Lohengrin had an idea they knew no English at all. He suddenly realized how much he wanted to live. And, yet, how long? A few more years flickering past in the remorseless face of eternity? Why live at all, except like the flame that can't help but burn until wick and wax fail and the night closes over without effort . . . ? Life is all effort, he believed, and his hapless urges forced him on and on. . . . He thought of all the dead behind him and living to come after, thought of the life and pleasures they'd taste, the days they'd see . . . and the pain. . . .

They passed through the grate into not a cell, but a narrow tunnel steeply slanting down. The walls were rough blocks with pressure mud slowly seeping through.

A startling flash, a red eye near the passage roof. He thought, for an instant, a giant demon loomed over them. Then it flicked and fluttered away. *A one-eyed bat*, he thought. *Or something like it*.

Down and down and down they went in single file. This, he thought, was more a mineshaft than anything connected with the castle above. He had a feeling this way had existed for ages. But could even the Druids have done this work? A deep puzzle. . . . Was there truly magic, as his father insisted . . . ? Who could have carved this passage that corkscrewed down like, he thought, a length of bowels? *God*, he thought, *but this air is dead and stifles the breath*. . . .

They suddenly came to a wider space. Most of the guards had dropped behind; he hadn't noticed where or just when. Lohengrin, the captain, and bushy-beard went on, lower and lower. There was decay on the draft rising into their faces. He just had noticed it. *Now we're through the belly*, he thought, *and soon we reach where the shit of the earth gathers*. . . . He smiled grimly to himself. Then the idea set him chuckling for an instant. Well, he *was* nervous. Bushy-beard looked at him.

"God help us, Morgon," he said, "he finds this light and full of fancy! Why, he comes to the devil's hole like a lover to his lass!"

"Even so," the leader said, "it may be sooth."

They passed through a mounting stench now that slammed into Lohengrin like a damp, filthy hand. He gagged and almost staggered. They were in a wide chamber, like a carved cave. The bedrock was dark and damp.

"What is this place?!" he exclaimed. "A tomb loaded with corruption?"

"It may be a tomb," the leader said.

"Move along," ordered bushy-beard.

The corridor was suddenly a narrow crevice. The chill walls seemed barely shoulder-wide.

It may have been from the hot bath, but Lohengrin found himself shivering. Up above, the captain had whispered, "Come and meet the king. If he approves you, there is no limit to what may become yours." There was no need to say what happened if he did not approve.

He was startled. He blinked. The wall before him glowed a dim, evanescent green. An unsettling phosphorescence. The corridor had ended and only the captain stood beside him now in a room that seemed to be the bottom of a shaft not much larger than a good-sized well. It rose straight up into greenish haze and then darkness. Could it actually go all the way to the surface? How could it have been made?

For the first time he was aware of his fear. There was no dreaming of escape here.

A single guard with a long spear in the passage behind could hold any number at bay until he fell asleep. If this were a prison, it would be the worst imaginable. The idea of being left alone in here set off a chill sweat. He tugged his light robe closer around him. He had certainly blundered. He'd never expected to fall so easily. He'd planned to hold the castle and negotiate with whomever the real master was . . . and then these demonic fellows walk out of the walls . . . ! And he falls like a sheep. . . . He shivered under his crossed arms.

He noticed a thin slit, an embrasure in the round wall. No light showed beyond. At his side the captain suddenly bowed and sank to one knee.

"Lord of the earth," he said, staring fervently through now raised visor at the slit.

Is this the devil's home—are we as deep as that?

For an instant his mind wanted to believe the fairy tales he'd always scoffed at. Then a resonant, rumbling voice, slightly muffled by the stone, sounded from behind the dark slit they faced.

"So this is the dangerous man?" it said.

"Yes, Lord master."

The captain was very strong. He reached up and gripped Lohengrin's wrist and yanked him to one knee.

"Neglect not your homage," he said.

"Lohengrin," the voice rumbled, meditative.

"Yes?" he responded and waited in the silence without a reply.

"Son of Parsival the fool," the voice reflected. Lohengrin nodded irrelevantly. "You have done well," the voice allowed. "You are powerful, yet now your life hangs by the merest thread." The voice digressed. "This is ever the way with men who have not mastered destiny. . . . Have you ever considered the workings of fate?" Lohengrin had, but he realized this was a rhetorical experience; thought he heard the captain sigh faintly beside him and shift his bent knee, as if anticipating a long session. "Fate is history. History is the past. There are little waves in the sea, currents, and finally tides. Individuals are little waves. States are currents, but, ah, what are the tides?" In spite of his uncomfortable and slightly absurd situation, Lohengrin found himself getting interested in this strange lecture. The voice had a compelling quality, a feeling of endless power flowing into it, an impression of utter conviction that seemed greater than human. "All the individuals flowing together!" The voice seemed pleased with its effortless syllogism. "So, human life is mainly chaotic, fragmented, given only momentary shape by each petty purpose and belief and by the force of the strong. But is there an ultimate purpose? Is there a universal goal? Only the tidal man can know this!"

"The which?" Lohengrin murmured unconsciously. He was

drawn in, surprisingly. He was still shivering and afraid, yet the circumstances made him strangely receptive.

"Power comes to the man who disciplines and develops himself . . . power beyond the blood and mud of mere body and brain. So if all men are joined, made one . . ."—the voice became louder and louder until the walls in the chamber rang with it and a shivering, not of cold only, swept over Lohengrin, and for an instant he had an urge to stand up and shout with the voice to reinforce it, merge with it—". . . if the tide moves irresistibly forward, then what ultimate power of the totality of all men will manifest?" The voice soared now. "All united, all one movement! All one mind and heart! Any dedicated man can do miracles, consider hundreds of thousands! Consider!" It was a cry that stunned. "Then, and then only, can the gods return to earth. Then, and then only, can the world be made perfect, as it was in the beginning. But it is not possible for you to understand this yet. No . . ."

The voice paused and Lohengrin started to speak, but was nudged to silence by the kneeling captain beside him. Apparently the voice was not pitched for ordinary conversations.

"But hear me, fellow," the voice went on, "I was master of the Duke you slew. He was a fool, or you had not slain him. So you may replace him. You shall be given certain tasks. If you leave this place, you are the Duke and my trusted servant, sworn to me and to me alone! And I task you then to find your father. Your predecessor failed in that." A pause. "What do you believe in, Lohengrin, son of Parsival?"

"Believe?"

"In God? In the devil? Answer!"

Lohengrin allowed himself a grim smile. It seemed right for the moment. And he was still trying to digest the strange message that the thrilling voice had driven into his consciousness. . . .

"In my skill," he said, "and in death."

The voice was not so pleased as the bushy-haired knight expected.

"Don't parade ignorance!" it cried. "You know nothing of death! And consider where your great skill has brought you. . . . But, before you leave here, if you do, you'll learn more of living and dying, my young sage." The voice was amused.

Lohengrin started, suddenly aware that the man beside him was gone. He turned: the entrance was now sealed by a stone door.

"What means this?" he asked. His heart raced.

"My purpose," the voice boomed electrifyingly, "is not as yours! Your thoughts and powers are petty and pale. You strive for shadows. . . ." Lohengrin hoped there wasn't going to be another lengthy digression: awed, frightened, and fascinated as he was, he still realized the "master" talked too much. . . . And he was a little strange. But still, the sound alone, never mind the words, the sound alone was stirring and seemed to pour energy into the hearer. You felt swept into fervent wrath, somehow. . . . "*I* strive for the ages to come! Beyond death!" The voice paused, as if shaken to stillness for a moment by its own eloquence. Then: "Now comes your first lesson in what a shadow you are, Parsival's son. Yes. From this time forward the daylight world will seem dim to you, if you survive. From this time forward the world will begin to fade . . . like a dreaming . . . like a misting. . . ."

"Who are you?" Lohengrin asked, tones shaking a little from the violence of his heartbeat.

"In these days," was the conversational reply, "I am called Clinschor of the South."

But this was a name, a legend, a tale to frighten children with, his mind was telling him. Clinschor was dead and gone in his father's time. For some reason his knees sagged.

"What," he started to say as the fugitive, greenish gleaming faded out. "Wait!" he cried in open fear. "Wait! I . . ."

And then it was dark.

"Compose yourself," Clinschor said. "At this moment you sway at the abyss."

Lohengrin felt a tingling prickling all over his body. Something seemed to invisibly pull at the area near his heart and stomach, and he had an impression that if he failed to lock his arms and set his teeth against it, he'd be twisted inside out.

Now he was falling, very slowly, as if the air had thickened to support him. Everything crackled like static electricity and he tried to scream now, but no sound came out. He was sure this was the end. . . . He never seemed to actually reach the floor and had an impression that it had opened up, that the earth itself was engulfing him. . . . He could not tell how long the falling went on. . . . Then he could suddenly see: a vast, dark, level plain lay all around him, littered with sooty cinders of rock. The ground was black and glassy. The sky burned red as furnace flame (though he felt only chill) and somber clouds massed and towered.

The chill was like watching eyes, somehow. He felt something icy and pitiless piercing him. He realized he was drifting forward like a feather drawn by a draft . . . floated on and on across the cindered flatness. An immense distance away, vast mountains rose into the boiling sky, and then he reached the lip of what seemed a gigantic mouth for an instant: it was a rock-rimmed, bubbling crater, flaming from the depths. . . . At the rim stood a black, armored figure with its back to the fires, squat and wide, resembling, he thought, a warrior frog on its hind legs. . . . There was a steady roaring sound everywhere. . . . Now he was close, facing the creature who turned a blank, dead-black faceplate to him. . . . There were no eyeholes. . . . Was it blind . . . ? It held a wide-bladed sword naked at its side. The blade appeared molten. Lohengrin realized he couldn't feel his body and couldn't move his head to study it. He had terrible fear about his form. Was he human, or had he changed? He felt cold and transparent and feeble. . . . He kept telling himself this was not the world, that he was asleep, and then the black, blank thing sprang at him on its bowed legs and raised the flashing, burning sword and he thought: *Killer! Killer!* And he found himself in a dream-like panic, striking what seemed his fists against the goblin horror, striking what seemed to have the mass of a mountain, felt forces moving all around him that shrunk him to an ant against an avalanche, a minnow in the wild surf, dust mote in a whirlwind . . . felt a moment of unbearable terror and pressure, saw the dazzling blade slice into himself, felt himself pop like a bubble, and then he was falling again and scene after scene, landscape after landscape flashed past: lightless crags where pale beings wailed; jungles where scaled shapes wallowed in rot; limitless fields of ice; rivers of blood flowing through a land of shattered bones. . . .

"What do you believe, Lohengrin the Duke?" the voice demanded. "Speak!"

"In   nothingness . . ."—he   mumbled—". . . in   nothingness . . ."

He was sitting crosslegged in the well-like chamber. The long slit eyed him from the greenish wall. The voices seemed part of the roaring in his head and he couldn't tell who asked and who answered. . . .

". . . so you begin to learn," the roaring said.

A moment later he recalled this was the voice of the legendary, demonic Clinschor, who'd nearly conquered Britain before he was

born. Clinschor, the terror of children. "Clinschor will get you if
you don't watch out," the saying went, "and you'll burn in the
bottom of the world! He'll take you from your bed; you'll wish that
you were dead . . . !" It went on. . . .

"Nothingness," the voice was saying with almost purring
pleasure. "And pray, tell me, nothingness, what would you have
from this world? The gold of nothingness? Power over other
nothings? Are you so sure now that you even know how to die?
Are you so sure you can ever die? How do you destroy
nothingness?" Clinschor was delighted. "For how long will you go
on and on in shadowy and helpless forms? For eternity?" A pause.
"What power must we have, sleeping fool?" the voice suddenly
thundered at him. It was like a blow. He felt himself tremble. His
thought raced and circled weakly. "Consider, consider, Duke,
what coin would you be paid in if there be no end to the filmy
nothingness of endless lives and deaths? Consider!"

Lohengrin's mind kept spinning, overloaded. He knew he was a
captive of unending and unrelenting time . . . saw death was no
escape, no end . . . felt the insubstantial dreaming he'd called life
thin and fade . . . tried to think and speak. . . .

"Give me . . ."—he started to say—". . . I need strength,
master . . . I need . . ."

"Peace and mark me, Duke, mark me well. Abandon
everything—everything! I give you my hand to grip." The voice,
Clinschor's voice, was now so firm and concentrated that it seemed
the sound alone lifted Lohengrin to his feet, where he stood, wide
eyed, thoughts scattered like dry leaves in a windstorm. He found
his arm reaching up toward the blank, glowing wall, unconscious
of the chamber's moist stench, reaching up to shoulder level,
fingers extended, trembling, as if he actually expected Clinschor's
hand to spring in return from massive stones. He felt a new,
sparkling energy vibrate through him. "You will be the greatest of
my captains," the voice announced raptly. "Grip my hand and
never turn it loose!"

And Lohengrin stood there, arm out straight, reaching. . . .

Gawain was out of helmet and armor, sitting at ease facing
Parsival in the close chamber. A comfortable fire on the hearth
soothed away the chill castle damp. Gawain wore, Saracen-
fashion, a light turban with the last wrapping looped to cover the
half of his face that was sliced away. The effect wasn't bad: under

the silk his head seemed just slightly too narrow on the left side and only one eye showed.

He was sipping a hot cup of spiced wine and munching a piece of meat pasty.

"Well," he was just saying, "Parsival, there's no place to hide when the truth goes a-hunting."

"Which truth?" Parsival wanted to know. "Yours?"

"Listen." Gawain leaned forward confidentially, though the room was empty. "Do you know what's going on?"

Parsival frowned and shifted in his chair.

"Where?" he asked.

"I've been riding in and out and up and down the country," was the oblique reply. "I've learned much." Gawain seemed well satisfied that this was indeed the case.

"No doubt . . . I haven't seen you in . . . in, isn't it *decades*? Two almost, anyway, and you renew our friendship, if that was what it was, with riddles."

"Decades," Gawain mused. He sat back solidly. He seemed infinitely more patient than Parsival recalled. The eye that showed was still a sharp, biting steel-gray. "Well," Gawain continued, "I met your son, for one thing. He must be older than you were when our paths crossed. Remember, in the woods, you knocked some bastard on his arse that day. . . . I liked you, Parse, I always did. . . ." He seemed earnest enough, the other decided.

Parsival stared into the fire. You knew people and then they were gone. Still, he reflected, if you lived each time fully, then it was all right. Then you didn't regret or miss anyone or anything . . . as after a day's good sport no one regretted the setting sun because the day had been enough. . . .

"So you met Lohengrin?" Parsival said, looking up. Half his face was molded redly by the firelight. It smoothed the wrinkles, blended the frowns of care, and, as he was again smooth-shaven, startled Gawain with the ghost of that lost, infinitely expectant innocence.

"On the road." Gawain's mouth was covered, so only the eye showed that he smiled. "He's strong."

Parsival stared back into the flames that wandered and sputtered over the crumbling logs. The embers glowed, he considered in passing, like the floor of hell. For a moment his fancy saw tiny, dark figures moving where the shadows fluttered and flowed. . . .

"I have not seen my son in a long time," he said at length, "though I've heard he fights well."

"He gave me a few bad moments . . . I recognized his crest." And to answer Parsival's anxious look, he said, "I left him alive. He favors tricks, as I did myself when young. Not like you . . . you were simple and terrible."

"Terrible?" Parsival was surprised. He'd never imagined himself in such a light.

"My God, I was afraid of you. Didn't you see that? And I really feared no man to any great extent." The eye smiled again. "I was younger then. Now I fear them all." He laughed and shook his head. "But you, Parse, you were so *simple*—no, not in the mind, in combat. You wasted no movement, like a killing beast. One mistake was all with you and the other was dead."

"I never saw myself," Parsival said, "as others saw me."

"Few do."

"You saw my son. . . . But I never knew you felt fear, Gawain."

"What an ass I would have been to let it show. Besides, I think I might have gone to the curtsy in a dance of blows with you."

Parsival nodded.

"I have many regrets about my son," he told Gawain, who waited, sipping his drink. The fire popped and hissed steadily. "The time went by so quickly . . . I really was never close to my wife. I was just married . . . and then there was the boy and later the girl. . . ." He stood up suddenly. "I regret so much now, Gawain, so much . . . though I've not often spoken of it."

"Times change," Gawain said. "My God, *I've* changed. For years I was maddened by my hurts and I tried to use you then, as you know." He shook his head. The eye was distant now. Parsival shrugged. "I thought only of the Grail," Gawain went on. "You put it into my mind. . . . Why, I would have flayed you alive and roasted off your limbs to get it in my hands, or whatever you hold it with. . . ." He chuckled. "Mayhap you stand on it," he snorted, "or sit. I know not." He sighed and shook his head. "I was mad and there was only myself in my thoughts. Myself . . . *myself* . . . !" He slammed his scarred, knotted fist on the stained, warped planks. "I tell you I am weary of myself." He snorted. "After so many years the company's worn thin. . . . Why, I wandered through Europe and the East and saw things and

learned . . . bah . . . ! It came to nothing. . . . I thought I sought
the cure for my face, but I know better now." He laughed straight
out. "I sought the cure for *myself*."

Parsival looked at him with wonder and a faint remnant of
suspicion.

"I understand you," he said, pacing closer. "I understand. I too
was cursed by the Grail. I gave my family almost nothing while I
dreamed and stalked it . . . while I tried to forget it, too . . . but it
was always there. . . ." He leaned over the table, face to face with
the other knight. "I looked in the sky while my garden withered
under my feet!" He took a deep, uneven breath and straightened
up.

Gawain was intent.

"And now?" he asked.

Parsival shook his head like a man distracted.

"I don't know," he murmured. "I'd like to see my son at this
moment. . . ." He shut his eyes. "Love . . . I want to love and
wipe away all dreams and sorrows and free my feet from the mud
of life. . . ."

They both remained in silence for a while. Gawain finished the
wine. Left the pie. Parsival stood brooding by the waning fire. He
was thinking about Unlea now. Though he knew he didn't mean it,
he almost wished he could run and ride away from here alone. Was
she really what he hoped? Did she truely care? What had those
words of her's really meant when she last said . . .

"Parsival," Gawain broke in, "let me try to be a friend. I've
learned much, as I told you. Let me learn this, too, for the curse is
spreading again."

"Which one?"

"Yours. The Grail curse. Well, all right, then, ours. . . ." He
was serious. "Who will be king now? Who will squat in Arthur's
seat?"

Parsival shrugged.

"What care I," he said, "where a dog shits?"

"Where?" Gawain's eye was ferocious. "It's not just for the
kingdom. I crave no power at court, either. It's the Grail. The
devil is back."

"This is the first I learned he'd ever left Britain."

"I mean," his voice dropped, "Clinschor—the balless wizard."

Parsival grimaced.

"After all these years? You jest, Gawain. What, did he crawl up out of some hole?"

"Be like he did."

"With all those black knights?" He smiled. "Why, they must be older than *you*."

"I see no humor in it."

"At your years, neither will I," Parsival said, enjoying this moment, of having the wit's edge on Gawain himself.

"Parsival, damn it, I fought them. I remember what they were like! We all had our . . . well, our excesses, I mean, in the army, the blood runs hot. . . . But what those devils did I won't even speak of!" He threw himself back in his seat. No face showed in the hood.

"How do you know it's Clinschor?"

Gawain closed his hand and thumped it on the table. He was staring toward the fading embers now.

"I smelled it out," he said ambiguously.

"Did you see him?"

A pause.

"No," Gawain said.

"Well?"

"I smelled it out . . . I can't prove it yet. . . . In the south I met British and heathen knights moving inland together—together . . . !" He drummed his fingers on the planks.

"Still, does that prove . . ."

"No—not prove. But I tell you I'm right! I lay behind a screen of bush at night to hear what I might hear. And I heard two of this host speak as they marched by."

"What did they say?"

"They said someone they both knew had seen *him*."

"They said his name?"

"Ha! They dared not."

"That doesn't prove it."

"Ha! You don't want it proved." He glared at Parsival. "You're too busy with the lady, I think, to want it proved."

Parsival was certain he blushed but clamped his teeth together and ignored the comment.

"I want no more wars," he said, not quite looking at the other knight, who leaned back and seemed thoughtful.

"I'm tired of combat," Gawain said, turning his empty wine cup on the table. "I tried to be killed. Did you know that?" He glanced up. "No, how could you. . . . It's true, I tried and tried. . . ." He shook his head. "But I lived, Parsival, I lived to this day. So I believe in something at last. I believe there is a reason." He rocked in his seat, groping for expression. "I believe I was . . . was chosen. . . . Oh, I know not by whom or what. . . . I know little of God, for I've known too many priests to trust religion . . . but I believe I was spared for a purpose by something greater than my skill. . . ."

Parsival was interested. He sat down on the stool again, facing Gawain in his strange, white, bandage-like headdress.

"I had fallen in battle on the great desert." Gawain went into his story. "I stood to my knees in the hot sand, helmetless, gripping a shattered sword. . . . Parsival, I was a dead man! And well I knew it. . . . Those swarthy devils jostled one another to see who made the kill. . . . I was dead, and I swear, I smiled with the half of this face that can show a human look . . ."—he gestured with a brief, choppy flick toward his head—". . . and said to myself: 'So at last the dreary business is over.' And, mark this, they thrust their spears and chopped their blades at my bare head. . . ." He rubbed the right side of his face with his hand. "I shut my eyes and waited. That's right! Gawain, the fearless terror. . . . In the past I'd have charged and died with my teeth fixed in some bastard's neck—why not? I was all pride"—he snorted a brief laugh—"save when I was cunning. If I could flee, I'd flee, but there I was done, as I said, and weary of everything, of blows and tricks and lies, and saw no other prospects. . . . I was not even angry anymore, as when I knew you. . . ."

"I saw you were changed, Gawain," Parsival put in.

"So I stood there like a pig waiting for the serf's notched knife. . . ."

"And? Did you die and become resurrected?"

"Ah," came the reply, the fierce eye seeming to flame deeper than the reflected light of the fire at Parsival's back, "did I not?"

Parsival frowned.

"Well?" he pressed.

Gawain shrugged.

"I know not." Gawain expelled a deep, almost racking burst of held air. "I know not . . . save that I felt the blows. . . . I swear to you, I felt the steel smashing through my skull. Have I not felt lesser blows before . . . ? I felt the blood burst from my brain and

I sank from myself into the waiting, bleak land of death. I tell you . . ."—he virtually shouted, leaning over the table, the terrifically intense eye startling even Parsival, who imagined he'd seen all intensities in his time—". . . I tell you I was slain! And I awoke unhurt . . . ! In the night . . . the sand had all but covered me . . . you know how it blows there and fills the armor joints and grits and grits to send you mad . . . but I was unhurt . . . ! Unhurt . . . !" He threw himself back in his chair. He waited, as if to see if his listener dared even comment. He didn't. He waited, too. He thought he'd understood, because though swords could not slice spirit, spirit could bend the keenest blade . . . *unless he were fevered from the heat and dreamed it all.* . . .

"Have you been to the land of the dead?" Gawain asked without humor.

"No."

"Mmm," whispered Gawain, letting his face tilt forward so that his eye was lost in a ridge of shadow, as if its luster had withdrawn into the obscure depths of his head. "So I believe there's a reason, you see . . . ? I have heard no voices, seen no light . . . but I'm watching for . . . for . . ."

"A sign?"

Gawain nodded.

"Ah," he affirmed, "I have no religion left, so I don't know what to seek or look for. But now I've seen the devils are back and I think they concern me . . . I think the Grail concerns me, too, though I feel I'll never see it." The head tilted up and the eye flashed again, concentrated on Parsival's face. "As you will."

"You still trouble me with that?" He was shaking his head. "I want nothing to do with it. You may say or do what you please about it, Gawain. I want no more." He folded his arms across his wide chest. "It's said the angels left it and flew back beyond the stars. Let them return and take it away, for all I care."

Unlea, he thought, *I long for you, to touch you . . . Unlea . . . Unlea . . . I love even your name, the trembling of it on my tongue!*

"We'll see what we will see," Gawain muttered. "But nothing will put me off! To the moment of my true death, I swear to you and to whatever God is: nothing will put me off!"

His breathing was violent now, as if he'd run a great distance or fought a fierce combat.

"Nothing!" he cried, standing up. He caught his breath, stood there. Parsival wondered if he might not be mad. "So," Gawain said with a partial return of his old sarcasm, "you see what even an iron-head like me can come to, eh, Parse?"

Parsival suddenly found himself stepping forward and reaching across the table to take his friend's hand, as if he meant to bodily wrench him from some danger. They stayed like that, silent in the dancing shadow light. Parsival didn't completely understand why, but he felt tears burn in his eyes. The two powerful hands stayed locked in their now-speaking silence. . . .

Broaditch plodded on until his vision shook with purplish flashes and his lungs burned and seemed flattened to his ribs. He was conscious of Valit clinging to his massive back, mumbling continually, though Broaditch assumed the ramblings were from the random workings of his own fading consciousness. . . .

The firm shore was only a few steps away when he felt something fat and cold slip along his waist, and at first he thought he'd walked into a thick rope just under the surface, except it moved and he knew it coiled with sentience.

Christ! he thought and suddenly sank in watery mud nearly to his chin as Valit screamed. It wasn't much thicker than water here. They could have swum. He would have rejoiced, save for the reddish eyes that flashed in the moonlight set in a fat wedge of head arched on a long neck that was body, too. *Christ! Has there ever been such a snake save in tales?* There were fangs that flashed like curved daggers. It hissed and yawned its jaws. Valit didn't even scream this time. He was already climbing up over Broaditch's back, as if he meant to submerge him or perform an acrobatic trick. *I want to go home,* Broaditch's mind was saying volitionlessly, *God and the sweet saints, I want to go home!*

The dark creature wriggled massively through the muck. Broaditch realized he'd but felt the last coil of the seemingly endless tail. Straining, sloshing, gasping within three feet of the slimy bank, calling on unplumbed resources of energy and resistance, Valit clinging to his head and shoulders, he stretched out his arms as the jaws snapped down and the astoundingly long body churned the muck to foam. A reflex: the empty, burning eyes zooming close (resembling, his mind distantly registered, a ship's lanterns looming over a drowning sailor), firmer bottom underfoot, Valit, superhuman in his panic, actually standing on his shoulders and head now, leaping onto the shore as Broaditch, without hesitation, as if his will was vast enough to disregard his panting, fainting flesh, heaved up from the slimy water and seized the huge, slippery neck, shouting something like a wordless and primal war cry, as if the sound itself could stun the terrible beast from the dark, submerged, mucky terrors of existence, smelling its stink and (in a strange insight) feeling its life as he might have with a harmless domestic creature, thinking in a corner of conscious-ness: *it's not evil, it's just blind*. . . . Among a welter of dissolving impressions, feeling the immense strength, as if the black tides of the earth flowed up into it, his arms jerked, half-dislocated, pain, back muscles cracking, feeling himself lifted almost clear of the water surface, slammed against the bank, stinking swamp breath in his face, mind crying out: *No! Not like this! Not in these idiot jaws!* And somehow he got his feet braced again and threw himself into a berserk, scrabbling run like a mad bull, raging against it all, all muck and terror, and for a moment the neck gave and slipped aside and, feet digging in, sliding, plopping, straining to the verge of blackout, he reached the top of the mossy embankment and smashed his fist into one redly luminous eye just above the snapping, hissing jaws, the impact deflecting the downstroke, which caught his shoulder glancingly and spun him over the top. He rolled into the clutching of a spidery hand and arm in the deep marsh grass. It locked across his chest. He screamed, threw himself upright, flailing to free himself as Valit was crawling on hands and knees deeper into the dense, mist-smoky reeds. He paused and twisted around to look through a thinning of the fog at the ghostly figure of Broaditch, black with muck and paled with mist, leaping and twisting in what seemed a violent dance with a flapping, clacking, living skeleton, the gleaming jaws snapping at his neck. Valit opened his mouth, then shut it, and kept on crawling without another glance behind into the stinking fern and reed. . . .

Broaditch, shuddering in his panic, conceived that the water serpent had transformed into this horror, reached blindly behind his back, staring into the fleshless face that gaped and grinned over his shoulder with empty eyes and flashing teeth, and, starved for breath, he staggered, vision ripping open, and his last thought was: *so now he takes me, after all*. . . . And fell into unending darkness, fell through the misty, dim stuff of the world. . . .

He awakened and groaned: demons of the netherworld were

jabbing their spears and daggers into his body. He knew this and so was surprised to see the moon still in the sky above the swaying reeds.

He groaned and rolled over, plucking a sharp point from his side and another from his ample buttocks. *Sticks*, he thought, *no, bones*. Why, he'd fallen and crushed the skeleton that his fear had obviously animated.

He groaned and sat up, sore and soggy with weariness and reeking of swamp. And at his age the muscles took longer to recover. He knew he'd be stiff for days.

He looked around and listened, then probed the cracked skull at his feet with the toe of his shapeless, mucky boot.

A fine omen, he said to himself. *Anyway, where's that foolish fellow?* He'd wanted to learn about life, he'd said. Well, he was certainly finding out a few things.

"Valit," he called. He'd a hundred times rather have had Handler along than this peculiar, insinuating, sharp-tongued son.

So far I've met all too many signs to guide me. If I meet yet another, it will be my end.

He pictured home as it was the day he'd left, almost a year ago: just after rain, the air clean and scented, sun-sketched clouds towering over the hills; the harvest laid by in the fields beside the curving road; rich, full trees; a country dance tune being played on distant pipes. . . .

He slogged through the reeds and soupy muck through a mounting din of frogs and screaming insects that fell silent in a little circle around him and filled in again as he passed.

"Valit," he called louder. Nothing. Just the momentarily hushed throbbings. He wobbled on, wondering if he'd actually fall asleep moving upright. And he was hungry, desperately. "Valit!"

Devil take you, he thought. *Well, mayhap he has*. . . . A little tune kept bouncing through his brain: dum-dum, dum-dum, dum-da-da-dum. . . .

Suddenly the earth was stony and firm and he was mounting the hill he'd seen from out in the swamp. A few scrubby trees were scattered around the coarse, grassy soil.

Topping the rise there was a gleam of winking, reddish light. For an instant his mind imaged a single, evil snake eye blinking. . . . He narrowed his focus and saw it was a lantern inside a hut. The open door swung back and forth on a loose latch, blocking, then showing, the smoky light.

He went closer. Silence. Just the steady dinning down in the marsh and the creaking of leather hinges. . . .

He went inside, wrinkled his nostrils at a special stink, even smeared with reeking mud as he was (he'd wiped only his face and hands somewhat with reeds), so that he imagined he looked like one of God's false starts where He cast the clay aside. . . . The air was rank, as if foul old meats had been charred and left to rot. . . . There were embers on the hearth and the place was fairly snug, the wattles tight. In the dim glow he made out a gourd of water and a crusted cheese set on a sway-backed table. He crumbled a handful and ate with wincing, ravenous bites, drank deeply, and had barely wiped his mouth with the back of his hand when he (or his legs) decided to sit on the lumpy, unclean pallet (where his own mud would add little or nothing) and rest a moment. He vaguely wondered about who lived here. His eyes were numb. He had a faint urge to get back outside into purer air. . . . His sight now doubled all he saw: along the dim back wall hung what seemed skinned bodies . . . must be meats . . . not even a crack of window in here. . . . Were his eyes still open . . . ? He waited a little too long to be sure and his last impression was that two red-gleaming eyes were looking in the door, and he thought: *but there's only one flame* . . . and then darkness swallowed Broaditch in one soft, sinking, gentle blot. . . .

Night. Alienor and the children were huddling around a fire with a dozen or so other refugees, as it turned out. The night was drizzly, chilly. They were partly sheltered by pines overhanging the road. In the distance orange flame light made an ominous mock sunrise.

It was really happening. She had accepted it by now. From what she'd heard on the road, bands of armed men and knights had sprung up all over the country and no one was safe. Nobody knew "which was supposed to be fighting why," as one wag put it.

The people huddled miserably. No one said much. A friar sat opposite Alienor. He was middle-aged, with a soft look on his face. He kept licking his lips nervously and shaking his head at the flames.

"What these eyes have seen this day," he said without really looking at anything, "ah, what these eyes have had to see. . . ." He shook his head. "I confess . . . I confess that Christ became but a word to me today . . . but a word. . . . I could not even

pray . . . my tongue cleaved to my mouth's roof. . . ." He shook his baffled head. "I could not pray. . . ."

"Well a-day, priest," said a dour, spare, long-faced fellow with sour, washed-out eyes and a long, beaked-nose profile to Alienor, who was holding her dozing son and daughter.

The befuddled friar sighed. His beard was but a white-sewn fringe on his chin. He didn't look at the quietly furious peasant beside him with streaks of blood and mud on his crease-graven cheeks.

"Aye," the fellow suddenly went on, "all you priests living so soft in your dreams. What do you know, old kneeler? What learned you today? Eh?!"

Alienor realized his rage was not actually directed at the older man. It was much worse than that: it was passion without hope, a fury that expected nothing back but its own eternal echo. "Old kneeler, why don't you just dream you're back in the damned church, all warm and safe, with Jesus blessing your fine wine? Eh!?" His long, uneven teeth flashed.

"Oh, let him be, why don't you?" Alienor put in.

"Let *him* be?" the man returned. "Let him first but call down Jesus Christ to make the damned stones bread! Or restore me son and wife and me brother . . . aye, like He did his pard Lazer. Let *him* be! Why, he let *me* be all these days to this one!" He showed his teeth again, but *only fancy*, she thought, *would take that grimace for a smile.* She turned to the burning horizon that gleamed on the low-lying clouds.

"Oh," she said, "let him have what dreams he's got, fellow. They don't bring you harm." *God knows we all need them . . . or at least can't help them. . . .*

"Let him wake up," the man said. "Let him greet all a man knew burned to black and forever gone! Aye, let him wake up, the full-fed old bastard!"

"Curse not a holy man," a wince-faced farmer interjected.

"I could not pray," the friar said wonderingly, eyes stunned. *As if*, she thought, *Ave Maria or Pater Noster would restore the world again* . . . no . . . because, she understood, if he could have prayed, he would have been safe from it. And there was surely God enough to prevent that. *Bah, I roll my mind like my poor husband, as though my thoughts mattered beyond finding more potatoes and shelter tomorrow. . . . I'll not lose my precious ones—I'll not see that, not while I draw breath in this miserable world.* . . .

The long-toothed man spat into the flames.

"Respect what's holy," wince face repeated, wrapping his rags closer around himself, "can't you?"

"I were dumbstruck," the friar said, clenching his hands convulsively before him, as if about to cry, shout a prayer, mouth trembling wordlessly, a dark gape in his smooth, weary face: nothing came out.

Alienor was planning her route. There was no safety in a group. There were troops everywhere, and who knew (or cared) which side was which? And the heathen, merciless, quick, she'd been told. . . . She'd have to risk finding a bag of food and then keep to the forest until she came near London. . . . If he wasn't to be found . . . no . . . she wasn't going to think about that just now. . . . A bag of food—that was first. And they'd survive. Her mind was fierce: they'd survive, by Christ, with or without prayers!

Wista had gone to his own chamber with Frell. She was watching him from the bed, where he'd told her to rest and recover. He sat on a stool at the foot of the low four-poster.

The windows faced the inner courtyard. The guardsmen's fires lit the massive walls. Clouds blotted at the stars.

"Are you somewhat improved?" he asked her.

"Marry, I think so," she said. "I am a very nervous person, as is my mother. Why, my father often sports with us on this score, which likes me ill. I . . ."

"Do you want a cup of wine or brewed herbs?"

"No. But I thank you, sir. I find myself content for now. Ah, but what do you think will be our lot, seeing what fearful things . . ."

"Think not of that," he insisted. He was watching the courtyard. A normal enough evening. If they were to be attacked, there was no sign.

"When will you keep vigil and be tested?" she wondered.

He rubbed his nose. It was stuffy and his eyes felt funny. He wondered if he were getting a cold. It would always go to his chest. . . . His sister used to rub it with aloe and oil and . . . Roxine . . . he suddenly realized she resembled this girl slightly. . . .

"Hmm?" he absently responded.

"I asked when you might be made a knight. A fellow I knew, Sir

Johnn of Laberdee, received his armor when he had but sixteen years, and handsome, as well. He were a true Sir Trist, and . . ."

"Why have never I heard of his fame?" Wista was faintly bothered.

"Mayhap and because he died, I ween," was the answer.

"With great glory?"

"Alas, and he were slain by a goat."

"What? A goat? By the horns of a goat?"

"Nay. By the flesh, which he ate of at the lists, heedless that the August sun had been full upon it for the day. He . . ."

"Peace," Wista said, straining to see something below: it appeared to be Lohengrin. He'd been gone seven hours and was just emerging from an archway across the yard. Wista briefly wondered why he half-expected to see him there. . . .

"He's alone," he murmured.

"Who?"

"They let him live." He was surprised at his mixed feelings: he was relieved and accepted that he respected the sarcastic, brazen, cold-blooded devil; but he also felt a peripheral gloom because he knew he was going to let himself be towed into the darkening he sensed ahead. . . .

Wista's older brother was a well-versed priest. They had discussed religion and chivalry many times. He owed most of his education to the man. And so Wista understood that Lohengrin had taken him on not so much to train him for knighthood, as his family assumed, but to influence him for his own reasons, to pull down his beliefs and aspirations. So, as he was a tougher and more stubborn young man than he seemed (and perhaps for deeper reasons than he knew, which he would not have denied, either), he stayed and resisted and frustrated his putative master.

"Where are you going, Wista?" she asked, sitting up as he headed for the doorway.

"Shouldn't you be with your sisters?" he asked in return.

"I suppose. . . ." She seemed depressed. "I wanted to speak with you, I . . ."

He hesitated by the door. Why was he resisting her? He wasn't sure. It seemed a small enough business and she was pretty and friendly . . . a small enough thing and perhaps a great relief and pleasure, as well. . . . Was it manly to pass it by . . . ?

"I'll see you later," he said, splitting the difference, and went out, hurrying, feeling strangely bold all of a sudden, anxious to confront Sir Lohengrin the Harsh.

The Harsh was in his private chamber by the time Wista arrived there. The old Duke's clerk (a black-robed, bald-headed layman semi-priest) stood by the bare high desk holding a length of parchment, and, with a slight, automatic sense of superiority, observed for the thousandth time how their desks were always clean because their minds were empty of learning. Lohengrin slouched in the high-backed chair, but, Wista noted, for once his feet weren't propped up on the desktop. The squire thought he looked very pale and his stare seemed strangely hollow. When he turned to him the eyes were slower, not so piercing.

"Bring me all the lists and records," Lohengrin was ordering, "and scrolls marked with falcon and fetter crests."

"But, my lord, the last Duke . . ."

"Bring them," Lohengrin said, almost dreamily, and murmured something to the man too faint for Wista's ears. There was something new about his master: the sense (he thought) of waiting was gone. He seemed purposeful, confident, knowing. The clerk left quickly.

"Well, Wista the Wistful," Lohengrin said, smiling shark-like, "perhaps your prayers were heard."

"Which ones, sir?" He wasn't quite impertinent. He never was.

"Those for my safety." He smiled. "Otherwise, either there's no God at all, or he loves me, though I do seem to be the devil's pet." He showed his teeth. "*Did* you pray for your poor lord, sirrah?"

"I hoped they wouldn't slay you . . ."

"Just rack me for a bit, eh?"

"I hoped they wouldn't harm you. And I still hope that you might convert your heart . . ."

"Wista, Wista." Lohengrin shook his bushy-haired head. "You hold a lance well and swing a sword fair, and yesterday I meant to send you to the knights of the holy cross, for you are a priest at heart. 'He may as well douse himself with cold vows,' I said to myself, 'and be done with it.' You've a fanatic's eye, Wista. That's right."

Wista was surprised to discover his master had spent that much considerate thought on him. Was it a play or tease to confuse?

"My lord," he said carefully, "that were yesterday. What of today?"

"Today?" The flat, black eyes seemed to mist distantly. Dreamy. He was the same, Wista felt, but concentrated in some fashion. . . . "Today my mind is changed, lad, my mind is changed."

"Why?" Wista came closer to the desk. "Was it because of those men?"

"Today," Lohengrin said, eyes far away, where dark fires darkly burned, "today I stood where the world ends. . . ."

"My lord?" Wista cocked his head, troubled. What *had* actually happened?

"I'm new today," Lohengrin said, principly to himself, the shock still lingering in his inmost nerves. "It's true . . . I feel like . . . like a dull sword that's been ground keen. . . ." He pointed his finger at Wista, in profile, left eye locked fiercely to his squire's. "That's why I won't let you go now. Too late, too late, my scripture boy." He stood up, like uncoiling steel. He clasped the boy's arm, his fingers digging deep. "I want you as he wants me."

"*He*? What means this?"

Lohengrin seemed to be looking through him. The hearth flames were reflected on the surface of his black eyes.

"There *is* a purpose." He seemed still almost disbelieving; immensely excited and relieved. "There *is* a world fit for gods and giants possible. . . . I was born for this! To be shown this!" He sucked down a deep breath and smiled distantly. "It will be terrible . . . more terrible than you can grasp or dream, Wista," he said, almost tenderly, holding the uneasy boy in that unyielding hand. "And out of that forge and flame and pounding will come a beauty . . ."—he shook his head; words failed—". . . a beauty. . . . He showed me that . . ."

"Who showed you, my lord?" He could see his words were barely noted. The grip was starting to numb his arm. And then several armored men entered the chamber and Lohengrin put him aside.

The men seemed huge and ominous to Wista. They seemed to press on him with their very presences. He felt stifled in the shadowy room. They were grim: some bearded, with the reddish fireglow wavering on their steel and hinting at their faces.

Lohengrin appeared delighted.

"Welcome, my lords," he said, "welcome all." He was now smiling that disturbing, unconscious smile. He was happy, Wista realized, beginning to understand what might be his own role in all this: not just to drag his feet and twist in the traces, but to come directly to grips with it, with him, because he sensed something you couldn't passively oppose: *if ye are not against me, ye are with me.* . . . For an instant he almost saw an image, the fleeting shadow of a shadow rising with red fangs, with screams and madness and smoking blood . . . a landscape with red lakes and charred hills and stunted figures fleeing or warring . . . bitter ashes where winds swirled . . . a world choked and smoldering. . . . He shook his head to shake the flashes away and watched his master bending over the desk as the vassal lords gathered close around him: one short man in dull mail, limping heavily (Lord Gobble); another tall and fat (Lord Howtlande) in swollen plate armor flashing golden stars and burning rubies in the general, flickering shadows, a thin beak of a nose belying the soft-fleshed face; others, massed around the Duke like an iron wall.

"I don't want to be a knight," he whispered to himself, backing, then walking out of the chamber, recalling Frell's question. "But stay here I shall, even if I know not why yet. I will not flee from this," he vowed, "I won't flee. . . ."

"He knows," Unlea said. "His manservant told my maid. He spoke of it to his chamberlain. He heard it." She passed Parsival a hunk of roasted boar on a wooden plate. He was munching a handful of salad greens at the moment. The long table was covered by green linen with silver and gold service. The day was clear and not too chilly for sitting under a tree at lunch. The Earl was present. Apart from servants and a tired-looking matron, there was only a red-faced, ill-favored page with squinty eyes halfway up the long board who (Parsival thought, but couldn't be sure) seemed to peer at them covertly. His actual eyeballs were, however, invisible in the folds of his skin. "He knows," she repeated at length.

"So, indeed," Parsival muttered, nodding. He found he simply accepted it. It had to happen, and part of him wanted everyone to know, in any case, mad as he knew the impulse was.

"Is that all you wish to say?" she wondered, widening her eyes.

He pushed his plate aside and blinked at the mild, pale day.

"I have no taste for meat," he said. "Too many years among monks." Or was it his mother's blood in him?

"Well," she said, voice pitched low but displeased, "it might have been better for me had you lost other tastes, as well." She didn't smile and that wasn't like her, he felt.

"Do you wish me to leave here?" he asked. For a moment he actually considered it. He wondered if he possessed the resolve.

She shook her head, idly fingering the extended, plucked wing of a broiled squab.

"Parse," she asked him, "what's to become of us?"

He laid his palms flat on the tablecloth and studied the leathery, wrinkled knuckle skin, where his age and life clearly showed.

"I know not," he said.

"You cannot stay." She looked at him, up and down, over and over, with an ache and sigh in her eyes.

"Nor can you," he told her.

"Peace," she whispered, looking up.

Prang was coming. He crossed the grayish-green field, the castle behind him. When he reached the table, he greeted the matron and then Unlea. Parsival was aware of his vague coolness to him.

"Well, Prang?" he wanted to know, watchfully.

"He said to ask you," Prang explained ambiguously.

"Whom? Ask me what?" Bonjio? What? His heart accelerated.

"I challenged him."

Prang seemed remote, defensive, and dense. What was bothering him? He was very proud. And like most proud people Parsival had known, he was sensitive mainly to himself. He vaguely recalled a story Prang told him on the road here: something about his father . . . yes, his father played and sang music, mastered as a minstrel but was weak with the sword and was killed in an ordinary joust. . . . Prang had declared a man must do only one thing, and that as perfectly as possible. . . . He was proud and determined . . . forever sensing injury where none was generally intended.

"No doubt you had good cause," Parsival allowed. "Who is the unfortunate?"

"Your pard, Gawain. But he said I had to ask you or he wouldn't stand up to me. . . . I don't understand."

"Why did you challenge him?" Parsival stood up. "What offense did he give?" For an instant he feared this was indirectly aimed at him, but no, he trusted Gawain now. Without effort. . . .

Prang's face showed nothing. He met the older man's eyes directly. Parsival was certain he was angry now.

"I mean to test his skill," the young knight stated.

"And you think his age will spare you?"

"He said to ask you. Are you answering?"

"What is it, Prang? What's the matter?" He realized how much he'd come to like him. He was honest, strong, well intentioned. . . . Hard to believe he'd once come to kill him, hired by some Duke he'd never named for reasons he didn't know; and Parsival no longer troubled himself about the plot and plotters. He knew Prang expected him to gather men for revenge against Lancelot and to find the Duke himself with the aid of his broad hints. . . . He wanted a new life, a life apart, yes, and with Unlea, and let the whole past lie as a filled-in grave! Yes . . . one blow and then counter-blow and then on and on into dull, warped, embittered old age—if he survived . . . no, never again . . . ! A new life and Prang would come to see, if not share, it himself. . . .

"I meant to learn from you," Prang was saying. "Perhaps I'll learn from Gawain."

"Or have your head broken." So that was it: Prang felt ignored. He knew that Parsival had recommended his services to the Earl. He felt unwanted. . . . Was this what he'd done with his blood son? The insight jabbed into his mind. Had Lohengrin ridden off to spite him, too? He recalled a fragment, a conversation, an outcry: Lohengrin (about thirteen or fourteen) slim, dark, standing, brooding in the rain, wild black hair plastered down, face crisscrossed with trickles in which if there were tears, they were lost. Parsival, wrapped in hides against the storm, was turned on the stopped horse just outside the castle gate. The animal seemed mired in the muddy roadway.

The boy had run from the main keep and Layla, his mother, was coming across the yard in pursuit of her raging son, who was now shouting, 'Why don't you answer? You never answer anybody!'

And Parsival: 'I have to go. It's my duty.'

'Duty, shit!'

'Lohengrin!' his mother cried through the muffling rain.

'You care for nothing! You care nothing for mother!'

'No.' Parsival remembered his blank anxiety upon hearing this. Why couldn't this wild boy understand? He was of age. Layla would explain. She had almost arrived. 'Go back with your mother!' he shouted. 'I've no time for this.'

'You never have time!' the boy raged. 'Why don't you go and chase the Grail again, you stupid fool! You fool . . . ! You fool . . . ! Fool . . . !' And then Layla caught him and swung her palm flat into his face with a resounding, liquid crack. 'He *is* a fool!' Lohengrin kept shouting out. 'Everyone knows it . . . ! Everyone knows it . . . !'

"Prang," he said, "don't make this error."

"Is it?" Prang asked. "But for which of us? They say he has an empty sleeve."

"A hand off only, but his sole arm is more than two for you, lad."

Unlea was studying them both.

"What's the harm," she asked, "of a friendly bout?"

"How friendly would it be?" Parsival wondered. "Or am I wrong?"

"A fight is a fight," said Prang.

"Well," Parsival said, "avoid this one, Prang. You're not ready for such an opponent. I agreed to teach you, and you agreed to heed, so . . ."

"Then we'll go on from here together?" Prang said, relenting slightly.

"I . . ." Parsival glanced at Unlea. Away. At Prang again. Away. "We'll speak of this later," he said lamely. There was no choice. He and Unlea had to be alone, if only for a time. The young man would understand this was a special case: his future, his heart, his soul depended on it.

"I see," Prang said distantly.

My soul depends on it, Parsival thought. *I have no choice. . . .*

He touched Prang's arm.

"I am passing fond of you," he said. "Never doubt it." The young man was just watching him now. "We'll speak of these things later," Parsival finished.

Because my soul depends on it. . . .

Prang said nothing. He allowed the hand to grip his arm. Watched his teacher's face intently. Parsival released him, a trace awkwardly, and turned away.

It does, he thought, *it does in truth . . . it does. . . .*

Except he didn't talk with him again. There wasn't time. Early that morning Unlea stole from her chambers and met Parsival in her sewing room. Barefoot, in sweeping gown and robe, she fled breathless through the dark, chilly halls. Need excused everything: no, not even excused, because that suggested consideration of a wrong, and, in fact, there was only need. She did not belong to

herself. Her limbs and heart moved at his whim (which was stirred
only by love), so there was no one to excuse. She accepted this fate
with a strange fervor, so that even the shadow of doom that
haunted these halls and her daily consciousness was no more to her
than death to a marytr, who's immersed in holy image and
brightness like a moth with the brilliant, killing flame light. . . . So
it wasn't lust, which would have been cautious, but rather a call, a
necessity of blood and soul, a struggle for life itself, like the
drowning reach for the infinite relief and bliss of breath. . . . So
she was given and was not her self's self . . . she joined his will to
move, to fill flesh and mind so that, coming in the doorway,
shutting and half-closing the bolt, she was already tugging down
her gown so as to be full naked for him instantly, flinging herself,
wordless, burning hot and fierce, and limp, too, into his close,
crushing, tender, frightened, frantic grasp. . . .

Neither of them heard the door swing open or a footfall in the
narrow room. They lay naked and silent, tangled in rolls and
bundles of silk and samite cloth, a fluffy down and unseamed
quilting so smooth that there had just been moments when
Parsival not only couldn't tell where he and she left off, but where
the soft, sleek world around them began, either.

So they lay, breathing themselves back to earth and ordinary
time.

And her voice was whispering, "I care not . . . I care not . . .
all other moments are dried and dead for me . . . I am only this,
my lover, and care for nothing else. . . ."

Her lover was half in a dream: the grasses grew waist-tall and
were a soft gold that shimmered faintly; the sky was rose-pink and
the air itself seemed to condense into rainbowed, vaguely winged
brightnesses that flowered overhead; violet blossoms rang like
music in the sweetly dipping, endless fields; he felt the soft
sleekness of the fronds and rich air, and the hush of all things was
like a tender voice; his body was smooth and easy and seemed
without weight . . . then something behind him: he could somehow see it and spun around to confront a form black and red, like
burning iron, a suggestion of armor, massiveness, of bowed and
twisted limbs, of blackened weapons poisoning the scene, flowers
and grasses withering and staining dark from its glowing drippings,
and then the squat, toad-like shape lunged for him, seemed to cry
out: "Die now! Die at last! Die with your secret!"

And he awoke, gasping out distinctly, not comprehending his own words: "Are you the mirror of me? Are you . . ."

And he found himself staring up at a tall man in the dim light of the single lantern he held; heard Unlea moan with dread (though he didn't know it was simply dread of having no more time with him, not of destruction itself).

And then a male voice, both sympathetic and cynical, was saying, "I pray not . . . nor would *I* be so foolish as to stay in the bear's cave to eat his honey."

"Gawain," Parsival said.

"How little you've changed," Gawain reflected. "Nor do you yet appreciate my puns and wit and turned meanings."

"What do you intend?" Unlea asked practically. But, then, she had only the one fear, so all else was easy for her now.

"What is hardest to stand," he replied. "Advice."

"Advise, then," Parsival said, sitting up.

Gawain was shaking his head.

"When ere we meet," he remarked, "you are riding the same steed." He dropped to one knee. "Even with your gifts, O Samson, you cannot win here. There are enough men to cut you down. And if you escape, what of her?"

"My head has been far from clear," Parsival admitted. He turned to her. "You said he knew."

"Yes," she responded.

"Why did you tarry here?" Gawain was puzzled.

"I cannot say." She clung close to her lover, unashamed of her nakedness.

"Well," Gawain urged in an intense whisper, "I say *fly!*" He nodded self-agreement. "Fly, in Jesus's name."

He rode with them until the dawn, which broke as they were topping a high hill. The castle had receded to the middle distance in the long valley below.

The lovers had come away with horses, a pack mule, and precious little to pack. The mounts were halted and everyone was still and silent here at the first moment of sunrise: the delicate rose tints and pale blues, wisps of streaked clouds, red, gold, and green leaves, the breathless hush of first light. . . .

"Well," Gawain said, finally, "fare you well, though you're mad as geese, withal."

Parsival reached over and grasped the knight's bare hand.

"And what of you, my friend?" he inquired.

Gawain's sole eye looked quietly from his improvised burnous.

"I mean not to wander and fight till the end of my days," he said thoughtfully.

"Nor I," his friend said.

"But I think there'll be no escaping what's to come. It may find you, Parsival-the-lover, go where you list. It may find you still."

"I want no more warring. No more."

Gawain nodded. Parsival released his hand now.

"You want love," he said. "Well, I want something myself. And I am hard to discourage."

"Want?"

Unlea was looking back at the silver-green flow of the morning valley. The sun was just poking streams of rich light into the folds of unstirring mist. *Fare thee well*, she thought. For I cannot explain what I do . . . I care deeply for you, O my husband. . . . She felt a sting of tears. *O, fare thee well, and hate me not . . . hate me not, sir . . .*

"If I gain it," Gawain concluded, turning his horse aside to return, "I promise to let you know." His eye smiled from the veiled shadows of his face. "In one world or the other."

"Aid the young knight," Parsival said, in parting, "as you promised."

"I swear my word again." And then he was heading down the long, steep slope into the shadow of the hill.

Parsival looked ahead as they started forward. The trees were thinned out here and the view stretched wide before them, bright, fall-stained woods, a long, swinging, curve of river, soft, gleaming fields, a last misty hint of water among the horizon hills. . . .

I have but one lifetime, he was thinking, *and no more to waste . . . no more. . . .*

So this time it had to be everything, nothing merely pleasant, half-felt, part-intended; this time he had to burn, to taste and totally savor everything . . . everything. . . .

He looked at her as the brightening sun enhanced the honey of her face, her loose hair glinting under the wide-brimmed traveling hat, the slight parting of her rounded lips that he so cherished . . . savored her with his eyes. *Yes*, he thought, *everything*. . . . He stretched out his arm and took her hand as they rode and said nothing. . . .

BOOK

III

W HEN Broaditch awoke, the door was closed. He lay on the hard, bare clay floor in his mud-stiffened clothes. He decided he must have rolled off the pallet. He blinked, snorted, stretched his limbs . . . listened to the wind puffing and moaning through the eaves . . . thought briefly of waking up beside Alienor . . . thought of things they'd shared, of her barbed humor . . . smiled and was sad, too. . . . He stared for a time, shook his head over and over before his consciousness really caught up with waking. He smelled broiling meat and realized he was famished.

He grunted and eased himself upright. Every bone and muscle throbbed. His neck was out again, too. He sighed and started to massage it, roll it loosely, grinding the spinal buttons together. He stopped, staring at what he instantly knew was his host, as daylight and raw wind burst through the doorway, rattled pots, cupboard doors, and an astonishingly round man whirled in with fierce speed, dwarfing the room with his mass, holding two dead, skinned, bloody bodies (that Broaditch only later realized were full-sized goats) casually over his shoulder. The ball-like man, he saw, was nowhere soft. Broaditch had the feeling that any blow or full-tilt charge would rebound without marking a dent.

He was suddenly motionless, studying Broaditch, who felt as if he looked up at the weight of the world looming above: the face was round, nose a bulb, mouth a puckered "O." One eye was red-rimmed, perpetually widened, surprised, and furious. The other was a smear of inflamed, crusted scar tissue. The hairless head gleamed. The door rattled behind him as the draft clattered around the room and raised a smoky fog of dust, sucked and worried the fire. Then the door blew shut with a bang.

"Good day," Broaditch said hopefully, not rising. "God keep you, good man. I am called Broad——"

"What cares Balli for a thief's name?" The creature's voice was high-pitched, irritating, nagging.

"Pardon," Broaditch went on, getting painfully to his feet, "but I am a stranger cast up by the sea, and this were the sole shelter at hand, thus——"

Balli could stand no more. He knotted a fist nearly the girth of the other's head and struck him. Only years of training and natural quickness saved Broaditch's nose bone. He jerked back and, as it was, felt the blood spatter over his face, choked, stumbled, and sat down violently against the back wall.

"You bastard!" he cried, spitting blood and holding his nose, feeling it swell into his fingers.

"What cares Balli for lies?" the round being asked, tossing the two goats into a corner of the hut and advancing with that blurring, fluid speed to the fireplace, where a whole goat body was roasting in its bubbling fat. Balli squatted there, tearing chunks loose (Broaditch wondered how his mouth could stand the heat), chewing, bolting, licking his fingers, seeming to suck the food into himself, burying his face in the steaming intestines now, sucking the long lengths continuously so that, the witness thought, for a moment it might have been his own innards coming out.

Broaditch was so astonished by this performance that he didn't think to flee at first, as the cooked flesh vanished with crunchings and oozing noises. This was more disturbing, almost, than the pain in his nose. . . . The blood had stopped trickling down his throat when he gathered his legs under him, picking a moment when the gross being was bending low, dipping his whole head into the belly of the ripped meal, and charged for the doorway. Balli, the last foot of colon flopping from his mouth, effortlessly sped to the door, which stuck as the fugitive tried to fling it wide. He simply tossed two-hundred-pound-plus Broaditch the length of the hut into the far wall with another crash, and sucked in the tube like a giant noodle.

Then he spoke: "Balli knows how to deal with thieves."

Broaditch had no doubt of this. He sighed. He'd cracked his head on the boards this time, adding a headache to his list of woes.

"Listen, Balli," he said after a bit, trying to communicate reasonableness, "cannot we talk this through as just men?"

The single, round, glassy, outraged eye peered at him from over the fingers the pursed mouth was sucking clean.

"Never fear," Balli declared. "Soon we hold trial."

"Trial?" Broaditch said.

But Balli, still working a few last tasty fragments around his teeth with his tongue, was presently squatting his immense hams over a bucket and unwinding a coil of droppings that, for size, length, and stink, gave Broaditch a passing notion that only the great Homer of the Greeks (whose translated work he'd struggled through when he was taught to read) could deal with the scale of it. . . .

"Mary, save me," he murmured, "a trial?"

Valit was squatting on his haunches, peering through a screen of dwarfed, withered pines down the barren slope, over the herd of sluggish goats, at the windowless, sagging hut. He'd just watched the vast Balli enter, swinging the two carcasses like hares from his fist.

Now, he was telling himself, was the time to run. Valit wasn't superstitious, all things considered, but the sight of Balli raised basic doubts: if there were trolls, then that was one. So the thing to do was run, head inland and go back to London. He'd been an ass to begin with, following Broaditch. There was safety back there with those dull wits. Since the first, he'd been batted on the skull, half-drowned, attacked by serpents. . . . He cursed and sighed, toying with a handful of pine needles, crumbling them to dust in his nervous fingers. Anyway, where *could* this farmer past his prime lead him? What profit would there be, in the end? A fool's choice, no doubt of it. . . . Still, the grayhead was intelligent. Valit was tuned for traces of that. He felt, in that respect, he was often groping for precious stones in a chamber pot . . . *Think how easy it would have been were I born of quality*, he mused. *But my fortune can be made, like Cay-am said, at any time if you watch and wait. . . . But one certain thing—it won't be made back with me Dad and that ignorant lot. . . .* He nodded self-agreement. Best to go on with grayhead, after all. Logic said it. . . . However, from where he lay exhausted last night on the slope, he'd seen Broaditch enter that hut. . . .

He stood up, turning these matters over in his mind. His limbs were sore, but bearable. And he was hungry. He smelled the

broiling meat from the smoking chimney. He idly considered
whether the troll man was cooking up his companion. . . .

Some of the goats had strayed close to the trees. There was a
female standing in the dappled light, full-bellied, jaws working
sideways, eyes calm and round.

Milk, he thought. Yes. Then wait and see. Perhaps there was no
danger. Give it some time. He didn't want to think about being
afraid just now. . . . The whole business could wait a few hours.
No sense in trotting down there by daylight. A few hours just to
get the feel of the situation . . . that made sense. . . . So he
moved stealthily toward the goat, carefully not looking at the
center of the problem. . . .

Balli, it would seem, was largely nocturnal. He settled down to
sleep with his monstrous back to the door. And was soon snoring.
That and the stink from the befouled bucket were enough to push
Broaditch toward desperation. He pondered the round, disturb-
ingly smooth head for a while. The "O" of pursed mouth sucked
air with a strange, irregular rhythm so that, from time to time, his
captive was almost certain he'd died . . . until a subsequent gasp
exhaled away all hope. . . .

And were he to die there, Broaditch reflected, *I'd needs must cut
a hole through that gross flesh, for never could I budge it.*

He'd noticed Balli wore a knife, but wondered (even if he might
snatch it) if any thrust would reach a vital place. *Through all that
blubber and rind. What does this retarded lump want of me? Is this
my great purpose, to be thus butchered at the hands of an obscenity?*

Was this another test? What an idea! After the drama of the sea
and toiling through the endless bog and the incredible escape from
the serpent to be victim of a defecating, gluttonous mound of
witless anger! He stared at the shut eye, at the scar tissue that
seemed to have been molded like clay over the neighboring
socket.

He must weigh five hundred pounds, or I'm a nobleman. . . .
Well, what now, Broaditch, messenger of the gods? he thought
with all the irony and self-mockery in his power.

Might as well sleep and be less sore later for the "trial."

"And what is the penalty, then?" he'd asked, with fear and
sarcasm. "At your little assizes?"

"What does he say?" Balli seemed to ask his unseen companion
of the same name.

"At the trial—what will it cost me to be guilty?"

"Hmm?" Balli had frowned. "Balli knows. He does. . . ." The eye scowled. "Thief finds out pretty soon . . . pretty soon."

"What do you do here?" Broaditch asked for reasons he considered hopeless. But he'd try.

"Do?"

"You keep goats?"

"Balli keeps many goats."

"Have you seen my comrade?"

"Keeps many goats?"

Balli had sat down at this point with his back to the door.

"Is there a village close at hand?" Broaditch persisted.

His host-jailer shrugged.

"Balli stays here. Eats, shits, sleeps. What else?"

There was a time, Broaditch considered, *when I had more likeness to this dull lump than is comforting to recall. . . . Mary in purity, lend me heaven in need!* He sighed and shifted his sore bones. He inched over to where he could reach the skin where the cheese was wrapped. *And what happened to Handler's strange boy . . . ? And what am I supposed to do . . . ? Wander for all my days waiting for a sign . . . ? Dung and blood, I must go home! Am I a mooncalf . . . ?* He sighed, exasperated. *I heed old men in boats who speak darkly in hints. . . .* He sighed. *Why am I ever caught like a cat with a piece of string? Why must I ever chase something just because it moves . . . ?* He shook his head. *I must expect something . . . something, but what . . . ?* He stared at the torpid, erratically snoring sack of flesh blocking the exit. *He's like a cork in a bottle. . . . God send me a corkscrew!* He sighed yet again and closed his eyes in frustration.

At dusk Valit forced himself to walk down the slope. He did not hurry. There didn't seem any clear reason. He had no idea what he meant to do, either. Notions of knocking, calling out . . . or sneaking a peek, yes, that made some sense. No point in blindly pushing into this business. . . . He felt something was almost driving him when his brain said: leave it. Somehow it was important. He kept sensing so many things he hadn't done, hadn't seen, lying green and bright before him, and this rashness might end all that. . . . Why, he'd had only one woman three times so far in his life; there had to be more of that, and once he had gold and property . . . life would be so sweet. . . . He didn't want to

die, he realized, simply because there was so much to miss. . . .
He resented Broaditch now . . . resented whatever was forcing
him into this confrontation.

He stopped, cocked his head, listened a few feet from the door.
He thought he heard voices. He carefully inched closer to listen.
When his ear was virtually pressed to the clay-sealed wall wood, he
heard a moist, high-pitched, strident voice saying: "Balli accuses
the thief!"

Inside Broaditch was still squatting on the floor. His host and
accuser sat at the table, eating another whole goat, pulling it to
pieces and stuffing it into his mouth, speaking through his
voracious chewings. He held up a forelimb like a lord's wand of
high justice and brandished it, making his points.

Clearly, the defendant realized Balli had seen trials and been
impressed. There were odd smatterings of legal procedures even
more twisted and, he thought, senseless than the plain originals.
Broaditch had himself seen a few courts of justice.

This belly and gorge, he thought, *might do well in many a town
proceeding. However, he sticks far too close to the meat of the
matter at hand to have studied professionally. . . .*

"Balli accuses," came the mouthed statement, "and my lord
condemns you—"

"Wait! You deem this a trial? Where is the lord who—"

"Balli is lord and judge. He condemns—"

"Evidence? What of evidence?"

Broaditch half-stood up, but his lord judge raised high the leg of
goat and he squatted back where he was.

"You were in this house," Balli said.

"True. But—"

"Ate Balli's cheese."

"But I was lost and starving and—"

"So lord Balli sentences thief to hands cut off and ears
cropped." Balli wiped his mouth and drew his rusty, wicked,
fat-bladed skinning knife. Broaditch felt fear, sweat, and rage at
the same time.

"You mad, bloated, foul-breathed simpleton! You curds of
scum in a sack! Brainless . . . ! How came you mad and ugly as
this? How—"

"Balli came mad," was the conversational reply, "from his
mother. Balli was hurt by men. Burned his face." He touched the

lumpy scar tissue where the right eye had been. "Balli likes to watch the justice from the wall."

Balli remembered how he'd sat day after day for months in the open courtyard, rain or sunshine, mud or dust, forgetting for long hours even the chains that bound him to the castle wall, squatting, sitting, and lying; wearing the befouled, ragged hides of a fool, feeling the tearing pain gradually stiffen and fade into cold scar, the memory of the boy in the cart dimming so he clearly recalled only the shock of the stick on his skull, then reaching up, gripping, and then the boy seeming to float away into the ditch, then the sound his head made on the rocks like a splitting gourd, then the faces of the men, the hot, flashing pain. . . . He'd lie there watching when they brought out the lord's bench and the cases passed before him and he heard the words over and over and the deeds likewise of the law, all of which engrossed him as did, at other times, the various slantings of light through the stringy trees along the wall, the birds wafting about the castle towers. . . . Eventually he would wait impatiently for the law to commence and then tilt his head and cock his ears to study every movement and word of it, an expression (often remarked by onlookers) lucid and intent on his face whenever judgment was pronounced. . . . After a time he seemed to have been forgotten there, faces changed around him, and he was a part of the place like a leashed, familiar hound. . . .

One day, in sheets of rain, serf boys with jackets pulled up over their heads were standing there in the misty downpour and one voice he paid no special attention to was saying, "How d'ye like it, witless? Like them chains, do yer?"

"His mama was had by a right troll, she was. Lookit him," another added.

"They're goin' to burn out your other eye, y'lumpy bastard!"

And stones hit him that at first he didn't realize were being thrown: a sharp blow just under his nose, a white flash of pain, and he was up, charging into their laughter, yelling, bellowing, tasting his blood, not even noticing when he reached the end of his chains and kept going after a single, blurred, terrific jerk that barely broke his stride, feeling their panic as they slipped, and skidded and splashed away, himself panting after, mouthing the words over and over, following one straight out the open gate, the guard's spear sailing past his ear as he brushed the fellow aside and didn't pause to watch him tumble across the mucky yard, hard on the heels of the terrified boy he'd singled out, roaring into the mist and twilight, his bellow overriding the boy's shouts of mortal terror. . . .

"The justice . . . Balli wants the justice . . . the justice on you . . . on you . . . on you . . . ."

He was now on his feet standing over Broaditch, the ragged knife ready. Broaditch felt like he was gazing up at a mountain. He glanced hopelessly around for a weapon. He couldn't accept this as happening. He felt strangely inert in the face of this absurd fate. . . .

Balli, stooped and snatched him by the neck, Broaditch twisting, punching, kicking viciously as he was effortlessly turned on his belly, and a crushing knee flattened his back and ground his face into the packed clay floor. He felt like a squashed bug, like a child, once again totally powerless. . . .

"Mother of God," he gasped, "pity . . . pity me . . . ."

He felt a stinging grip tug an ear flap out and ready for the blade. The sweat and fecal stench of Balli was upon him. He wanted to vomit and scream. . . .

"You promised, father," Modred was fuming and moaning in pain. His injuries, over a month old, still had him bedridden: ribs split, thigh bone cracked.

His aunt, Morgan LaFay, red-haired and taut looking, leaned over the bed, pale skin vivid against a black samite gown. Only faint lines at the corners of her mouth and eyes betrayed her age in the soft candlelight.

"Don't remain a fool a day longer than need be," she recommended, "though coward you must ever be."

"You promised never to slay me," he sputtered, eyes raging and afraid.

"What is a promise to a dead man worth?" she wondered. "And yet, I swear, lamb, I want you to be lord of Britain. So, lamb, content yourself. I mean to discover who did this thing to you, if I can."

Modred's eye remained uneasy, but he let himself feel somewhat soothed. He tugged the wrinkled covers up under his chin and stared into the dark, vacant recesses of the chamber. His advisor, Sir Gaf, and the glint-eyed bishop were standing close at hand.

"In the event you overlooked it, my lady," the knight said, "there are worse troubles upon us than this."

Morgan was smoothing her nephew's forehead, murmuring.

"Are you making magic?" he fearfully wondered.

"I need not have come here for that," she replied, smiling mildly, "had that been my desire. But, you know, magic is but another way of paving the road, and you must still pass over it yourself. . . . Gather your strength, lamb. I will make it all as easy as I can."

"Yes," the prelate put in, "Sir Gaf here says well. There are powerful forces against us—an army." He squinted one eye almost shut and stared with burning fury. "With Godless heathens in their midst."

"Our vassals are gathering," she said, still keeping her gaze steadily on the Prince's upturned face. In the shadowy, uneven flame light, it seemed to be melting into the pooled darkness of pillow and quilts.

"One of my priests came upon a dying knight on the old high road to Camelot," the bishop half-whispered, moving closer.

"And?" Morgan queried, unstirring, bright red hair loose along one pale cheek.

"And the knight told him—"

"How did he come to be dying?" Sir Gaf asked uneasily.

"The priest was no doctor . . . though he declared blood flowed from mouth, nose . . . eye, and ears, as well, I think he said."

"A blow to the head, then," Sir Gaf said, "no doubt a blow to the head."

"Never mind the delightful details," Morgan put in, straightening up. Modred followed her with his eyes.

"He told the priest," the bishop continued, narrowing both eyes now, "that he were struck down by three knights all in jet-black armor wrought with bright silver—silver shields with a device of sharp fangs in a gaping mouth."

"In Freya's name," Morgan snapped, "get to where you mean to go!"

"I shall," said the undisturbed lord prelate. "I remember such knights as these."

"The mouth design?" she asked.

"Nay. That were new. But the armor."

"And man can put on what gear he pleases," she contended.

"Yes, lady," the bishop said, "but hear this much more: when the knight demanded their names and conditions, when laid low, they spoke not a word, even when he cursed them. . . . Not a single word spoke they!"

"Well . . . well . . ." she demurred. "So they were under some vow, mayhap."

"Ah, but spoke not among themselves, either! And battled in silence, as well."

"Why did he engage three thus?" the knight wanted to know.

"It seems he tried to pass them by, so he said, but they followed. He felt they may have been an advance guard because, he said, he glimpsed many others in armor yet hidden in the trees, seeming to wait. Then he fell. And passed on to heaven in the arms of that pious—"

"He spoke with long breath for a dying wight," Morgan felt.

"In silence all the while?" the knight mused, frowning.

Modred raised himself on his elbows.

"I know what you're saying here!" he cried. "The devils are back! The black devils! That's the meat of it!"

"Peace, lamb," she soothed. "This is far from proved."

"But there's yet one thing more," the bishop said.

"Yes?" she asked.

"He was a stout fighter, this fellow, and well known—Sir Alfred of Dornn."

"Yes?"

"I know the name," the knight affirmed.

"He swore to the priest, dying as he was, that before any were close enough to deal a thrust with lance or sword he felt a terrible blow in his heart that stunned him so his limbs went weak as water. So he swore, ere he rose to glory, being shriven and—"

"A stone struck him?" she wondered.

"He said it were the devil's fist," the bishop stated. Modred's eye rolled. Sir Gaf fidgeted.

"But," she suggested, "he sought to excuse himself for falling so and leaving no other in the dust with him. A fancy, no more." She shook her imperious head. "Wool and moonstrands."

"Yet he so swore with his failing breath," solemnly pronounced the prelate, "on our lady and the cross."

She hesitated. The chamber was silent for a few moments. Outside a watchman cried the hour in the distance. Midnight.

"This fellow seemed to say more in dying," she finally pointed out again, "than many in much life."

The lord bishop shrugged.

"It were God's will, then," he said, "that this tale be told."

"Magic that smites an armed man in his seat," Modred said, excited, "is more than paving a road, dear aunt."

She frowned.

"Fear not, lamb," she murmured, touching his hot forehead again. "I'll raise you to greatness." She looked coolly at the others. "Fear nothing." It was a command.

Tikla was fascinated by the dust rising in a great, sun-shimmered mass across the cultivated valley. The oncoming riders seemed, to her fancy, the feet of the cloud, as if the cloud detached itself from the dark smoke (that she couldn't tell was a burning village) and rolled at a gallop toward them.

She was clinging to her brother, who was clinging to her mother, who was clutching the seat of the mule-drawn cart. The long, lumpy-faced driver was lashing the twin animals into the best run they could make on the winding slope that ran into the dark pine forest above.

Tikla stared back at the glitter of dark armor and bright weapons storming across the potato fields where the four of them had just filled a sack.

"I said they was all over here like fleas on a hound," the driver, Lampic, was expostulating.

"Would you rather o' starved on the road, then?" her mother responded sharply.

Her brother was watching, too. She was trying to see which of the men would reach the trail here first.

"Look, Torky," she said, "I couldn't count how many!"

"I wish I was a knight," he said.

They heard the pounding now; the hillside shook under the mass of warriors.

"You can't be a knight," she informed him, big eyes watching, making out the helmets now. "You're lowborn."

She felt her mother turn and start slightly.

"Mary help us," she breathed, digging her sharp elbow into the driver's ribs. "We're undone in a moment."

Most of the men, to Tikla's vexation, veered away down the

valley road on other business while a few continued up the slope in pursuit.

"We're nearly safe," Lampic said.

"Safe?" her mother wondered. "On the lap of heaven, mayhap, or the devil's knees!"

"Never you mind," the man growled, heading the madly rocking, bouncing cart between two twisted trees. Now they were on terrain that favored mules over any horses: round, slippery stones and loose shale. The riders crashed on behind, but Tikla was disappointed to see them dropping gradually back.

They rocked and tilted on, Alienor thought, *like a ship in a storm.* . . . After a time they were able to jog along a fairly level stretch of rich river bottom that was lush with hedgerows and willow trees. Tikla had given up on the men and was dozing against her brother. The day was bright overcast. Swallows rose and swirled; a flight of geese thundered over. . . . Torky dusted off a raw potato and crunched into it. . . .

"Well," his mother was saying to the driver, one hand smoothing at her iron-gray-and-red hair, "how far, brave chappie, to London town?"

"Ah," that worthy replied, "and if they ain't moved it since, my dear, and we don't cross a deadly fate of knights and cutthroats, I say two Sundays hence you'll see the city wall—though it's no place I'd be going alone with young chaps and me a woman."

"With things as they stand in the open," she jabbed back, "I'll go indoors for now, thank you, very much, goodman Lampic."

The man smiled, digesting her thought.

"Aye," he said at length, "but these wars come and go . . . go and come. . . . If a lad keep out of the way, why, it comes to but tavern talk in the end."

"Not this time," she said.

"Ah," he said, rubbing his pointy chin, "so you're a seer of future things, are you?"

"I'm a woman with memory and common sense. When Arthur and them fought the devils' why, where were you then?"

He looked a little uneasy.

"Well, well," he said, "but them was long-gone times, my dear."

"Then the sun runs backward now," she said grimly, glancing back once, then staring straight ahead, watching the pleasant, still-lush countryside unwind before them, watching the birds drift, wishing she and the children could rise and soar over the country. *Oh,* she thought, *but to rise over all what's to come . . . to rest like a gull on the easy shoulder of the wind. . . .*

"Who told you these things?" Lampic probed, shrewd-eyed, alert.

She shook her sardonic head.

"Birds," she responded. "Birds."

Parsival sat up in the furs and silks, watching the single candle burn slowly down in the center of the round tent. His fancy made of it a watching eye. He imagined it lidded and moved when vagrant drafts wobbled the dull orange spot of flame. The air was cool on his bare torso. He felt her warmth under the covers close to his legs. He wondered if she were asleep yet . . . remembered, as a child, sitting up watching his mother work on a piece of embroidery by candlelight. He remembered her long fingers, sure, delicate, working with unending precision. Fascinated, he'd see the patterns emerge: a picture, a landscape with a man and woman (or boy and girl or two angels; he couldn't recall); the bright colors and spacious beauty of the scene had affected him . . . night after night he'd watched it grow, waiting, as if he were going to come to truly know the people (that he didn't yet realize were lovers) as the dots and lines and specks and shapes of textured color spread steadily, clarified the forms, as if some secret of that imaged world would open to him, as if (he almost had thought) some night they'd move and complete their graceful, though ambiguous, gestures. . . .

"Are you troubled in mind?" Unlea asked, startling him somewhat.

"No," he returned, still staring.

"No?" She stirred slightly beside him.

"I am thinking about nothing . . . I don't dare think. If I thought . . ."

"Yes?"

He shook his head. The eye of flame held him rapt. She tugged him free from his reverie and down to her and kissed and spoke with her lips close.

"I dare not think, either," she whispered and smiled. "Were you thinking . . . I mean, *not* thinking about what I told you?"

He knew what she meant.

"About your lovers?"

She nodded. Her little "mmm" of agreement made him fancy that a fuzzy rabbit spoke and he smiled. *"Why, the very sounds that pass through my lady are enriched."* He remembered a minstrel's quote.

"No," he said. He kissed her lingeringly, held her close.

"Never have I known a man with such a need," she murmured, adjusted herself beneath him, opened her sweet limbs. He ran his mouth down her body, feasting, lapping, kissing right to her feet, which he lightly bit and fiercely kissed. . . . She sighed and writhed on the silks.

"Oh," she asked, "what do you do to me? Oh . . . oh . . . never have I known your like, sir . . . oh . . . oh . . . ah, sir . . ."

He turned her over and ran his cheeks and face up and down her sleek length while his hands led and followed after. . . . It was no longer an exploration: it was an attempt (and he almost knew this) to mark her forever with himself, his being, as if he could penetrate the water of her flesh and feel the inner magic of her with his own inner senses, to mark himself with her, too . . . to keep it, inscribe the flowing water . . . and as he mounted her in their mutual breathlessness, at the far edge of his awareness and sight was the quivering speck of fire that fluttered, winked like eye or wing, again . . . again . . . went utterly out just as he felt himself hard and sure and lodged home again, rocking in their darkness, seeming now to be searching for the rhythm, pulse, pace that fled, unreeling, before him, as if he could lock himself deep enough to join now to forever. . . . He hurled himself into her gossamer finger touches, heat, resilience, into her cries and wordless words, gripping her shoulders and back, until he no longer knew whom was penetrating whom. . . .

"Why are you here?" he asked later, holding her, because, as he knew, time always came back.

"Because I cannot help it, which you know right well."

He stared into the darkness. His eyes kept drooping shut with sweet weariness.

"What can we do . . . ?" he muttered. "What . . . ?"

"Nothing," she said. Her arms were wrapped firmly around his body.

He was partly in and out of dreaming now: sudden bright

sequences flashed and startled him awake. . . . He was riding to
joust against a knight in mirror-gleaming armor. He couldn't
properly take aim, had to keep twisting away and shielding his
sight from the brilliance . . . then the dark tent, her warmth . . .

"We'll find a place to live in peace," he whispered, trying to
garner a plan from his fading, separating thoughts. She didn't
respond. "Unlea . . . ?"

"Yes?"

"Did you hear?"

"Yes."

"Then?"

"If you say so, my love, I will believe it."

"But you *don't* believe it," he said or possibly thought; he
wasn't sure because now there was a castle, a blinding shimmer
like diamonds, towering up so that hazy clouds hung well below
the topmost, dazzling spire. He was rushing forward up the long,
sloping hill, as though a wind blew him across the crystal silence of
the landscape. . . .

He awoke with a shudder. He couldn't hold his thoughts in a
line. . . .

He was certain she'd just said, "There's no place for us to go."

He answered (or thought he answered), "Our love makes us
pure."

He knew the connection was tenuous and now he saw her just
entering the thousand-foot-high castle gate, in the smoky, golden
sparkle of her trailing garments. . . .

"Why are you with me?"

"Stop," she seemed to reply. "Stop this."

"Why?"

"Stop."

"I want you," he was sure he was saying, except it was dark and
the stars were rushing toward him, silver-hard eyes of light glinting
from the vast, cold, empty night. "I want you." The cold and
something else convinced him he was suddenly full awake and the
stars glared in through the tent flap (which had blown half
undone), and a large, shadow-dark figure (in armor that melted
into the night and glinted here and there with points of silver like
stars in chill water) stood in the entrance and seemed to watch
him. . . . Parsival readied himself for combat; he felt a pressure,
as if something heavy, velvety as drugged sleep, were pinning him

motionless to the bedclothes, found himself straining to lift the weight, feeling he could die, smother under it, which was like lifting the world itself. . . . He concentrated, and suddenly burst to his feet, naked, crouched in the chilly air facing an empty opening, the wind flapped, felt a little stronger, though tired, and heard her saying: "What is it, Parsival?"

And he thought, as he reassured her, *I'm more asleep now than I was a moment ago.* . . .

Next morning in the silvery-gray of first light, he studied the ground around the tent for tracks. The first birds were tentatively twittering here and there back in the mist and shadowed woods.

He discovered nothing, no certain traces separate from their own footsteps. But he remained positive someone had actually been physically present. He'd gone to the opening and redrawn the flap. No one had seemed to be nearby. He'd sat awake for an hour and waited, listening to the wind and her steady breathing. . . .

He went over the problem as they were breaking camp. She wasn't much help, he noted. Well, she'd never lived in the field before except with livery. He felt she was putting up with the discomforts of their flight (if it was that) pretty well.

Nearly a week later they were camped by a river just downstream from a low series of falls. The water roared steadily and there was always cool spray and mist in the air.

He was broiling supper. The overcast sky was dimming its pale grays and hinting tints. She was still in the tent. He was going over the total situation again: he was cut off from home because whoever aimed to assassinate him was bound to have set a watch there. Also, could he really live with Unlea over his wife and daughter's graves . . . ? He sighed, then turned the split fish on the forked stick. He didn't want to recall his family. The only hope was in the here and now, he told himself. The thing was not to make those mistakes, not to get distracted again and imagine it was somewhere else like a man trying to grasp the moon's reflection in water. . . . This time, he said to himself, was going to be different, this time. . . .

He stood up and stared at the rushing river: a bright leaf flashed past, spun, submerged, surfaced, whizzed out of sight around the bend. It felt so good just to stand in the evening's peace, to feel her safely nearby. He felt pleasantly hungry and hopeful. . . . For some reason he suddenly thought of Lohengrin and a frown rippled around his eyes. He'd missed so much there . . . so much . . . the boy had been an incident . . . so much of life had seemed incidental to his dreams. . . .

He shut off his thoughts and turned to the tall, rose-pink, silken tent. There was a rent near the flap now (from the wind) and the sides were already weather stained.

"Unlea," he called, "have you no appetite?"

No reply. He pitched his voice well above the water roar.

"Unlea! Come out! Else the fish go back as they are to where they came from."

Mayhap she's shitting in the brush, he considered. But then she came to the opening and said something he couldn't make out. He went closer when she didn't move. He noticed her hair was only partly combed and arranged. Her gown sat unevenly on her. She was shaking the hem at him.

"Look at this!" she said hotly. "But *look* at this!"

"At what, my love?"

"This. . . ." She fluttered the cloth. There was a reddish wine stain on the light peach fabric.

"Oh," he said.

"I have nothing left—no clothes." Her eyes blinked nervously. She'd been scratching an insect bite on her neck. Left a streak of blood there.

He sensed there was more to this. Well, he had been a husband, however poorly, for years enough.

"So soon?" he mitigated.

"After weeks of wandering in wilderness," she exaggerated, "is it a wonder? Look at this!" She yanked at the cloth until he caught his cue and embraced her comfortingly.

"My light dove," he told her, "it has been less than two." He felt her silently crying. Perhaps it was her time of the month. He only vaguely understood the mechanism of it, but he was all too familiar with the effects.

"But what may we *do?*" she said. He felt the heat of her breath, her wet cheek. He tenderly stroked her neck, looking over her head at the twilight glimmer of water. *So soon,* he thought. "Oh," she said, "my lover, what's to become of us?"

"Fear not," he assured her. "We have a goal now. No more of this aimless drifting. Listen, we make our way to the coast and thence take ship to France. We'll be safe enough there." As he improvised he realized he might have suggested this course before. Why hadn't he? They'd simply ridden and camped almost every day in the same moment-to-moment spirit they'd sneaked to the hayloft or sewing room to make love in. . . . it hadn't bothered him; he'd felt complete and content. . . . But it was an obvious mistake! Why hadn't he seen that . . . ? Still, no matter what reason said, the complex idea of actually trying to leave the country seemed unreal. He knew he'd have to force himself to follow through. . . .

"I'm sorry," she was saying, "I'm weaker than I knew." She pulled a little away and looked up into his face. She smiled wanly. "But I am content," she said, "when you hold me."

He nodded, studying her expression as always, looking for flickers of he knew not what.

"I'll try to be braver," she said.

She's just giving herself to me again, he realized. *She doesn't want to say yes or no to anything.*

"Otherwise," she continued, "there will be no pleasure for you."

"Pleasure? Is that all?"

"Well," she explained, brightening, "we aren't together to call up glooms like doddering scholars." Her smile smoothed over and polished bright the rough places of his dissatisfactions.

He sniffed the air and spun away from her.

"The fish is burning!" he cried, running the few steps to the dark, smoking fire. "God's wounds!"

She was laughing behind him and then shouted something and the fear brought him around, thinking: *I should have sensed it what's wrong with me,* seeing the armed, mounted knight come around the bend, sounds wiped away by the seething river roar. Well, still, if he were alone or with a party, unless it were an army, what should Parsival fear? Yes, but still he should have felt the presence as before. . . . What was dulling those mysterious perceptions . . . ?

He stood waiting. The rider stopped near the fire, where the fish was now hopelessly aflame.

"You spoiled our meal, sir," Parsival said in greeting, a trace irritated. Unlea stayed motionless near the tent. When the stranger didn't answer through his blank, closed helm, Parsival prodded him, wishing his power to divine thoughts had not faded. "Do you mean us ill, sir?"

"Hah," the knight said, "I won't begin to march in that circle again, master."

The visor was flung open with a hostile bang and Prang stared coldly at his teacher.

"Well, then." Parsival frowned. "You always find me. Is it a scent I give off?"

"It was the perfume, too," Prang returned, "but you're not hard to find. You don't appear to have fled in haste." He was expressionless.

"What perfume?" Parsival wanted to know.

"Of your lady, for whom I have a message."

Parsival overlooked the sarcasm.

"So," he said, "you stand in the Earl's service."

"More like in yours as is the steeple bell that warns the late sleeper."

Parsival folded his arms. Unlea came a little closer.

"So," Parsival said, "his worship comes on apace?"

"He comes," Prang confirmed.

"Prang," Parsival said, moving close to him until he stood by his stirrup, "I am sorry. I intended to—"

"I came not," his pupil interrupted sarcastically, "to learn your intentions. I am no spy." He turned to Unlea.

"You misread—" the teacher began.

"My gracious lady," Prang was already saying, "your husband sends his greetings and says you have ridden overfar for your exercise and he grows concerned. He will escort you back home if you come but a little way with me."

"Back home to God's bosom?" Parsival suggested. "Beware of fair words that mean doom."

I can't let this end badly, he thought. The idea made him weak and sick for a moment. *I can't let it come to that*. He shook his head slightly to himself.

"No," Prang insisted, calmly, "he declares he knows no fault in her. . . . But his thoughts are less kind for you, Sir Parsival."

He was watching her face. He could see it: there was a wildness and relief there, a hopefulness unexpected. His heart and belly were chilled and sank. He anxiously looked out over the river. The last mists and twilight were dimming together. The white spume gleamed. The firelight became fuller and rich. The cindered fish smoked and stank. *No*, he thought. *No*.

Prang waited, expressionless.

"Well, my lord?" he finally said, glancing at Unlea, who twice had seemed about to say something, then checked herself.

"You feel betrayed," Parsival finally got out. He had never felt so sick with depression and anxiety. . . . It was true, he hadn't really tried to get far away, they'd drifted . . . drifted. . . . He felt shame because it was up to him. . . .

"I?" Prang was remote. "My lord Earl has a better claim to that."

"Parsival . . ." Unlea began to say. "I—"

"I accepted you," he was saying to the young knight, "so I ask you to wait." He stared and blinked.

"Wait?"

Parsival sighed and shrugged and shook his head.

"In any event," he said, "Unlea and I will go on." He didn't quite look at her but saw her expression where the firelight traced her face on the deepening shadows. She nodded agreement, but, it seemed, after a fractional hesitation. Well, never mind that. "We have to go on," he told Prang earnestly, advancing half a step more so he was looking straight up into his face. Beyond the fellow's hurt and assumed dignity there was still a feeling, a sadness, even, Parsival detected.

Prang took a long, deep breath and glanced from the now silent lady back to the man. She had nodded again.

"We must go on," Parsival repeated, eyes intense and wide. "For love . . . for love. . . . There's no turning back."

"God shield you, then," the young man feelingly declared. "I will be silent and say I've seen you not. And for her sake."

Because Bonjio doesn't care to slay a second wife, Parsival thought.

"No," he said, taking a few steps in pursuit as Prang, with a bowing farewell to Unlea, turned his horse and headed back into the thickening night along the river bend. "No," he repeated, not even caring if Prang heard him. . . .

He kept his back to her. She didn't speak. He watched the faint fire gleams on Prang's armor fade to a hinted afterglow beside the dimly silver rushing water.

My God Lord Christ, he thought over and over, *am I losing this, too . . . ? Am I going to lose this, too . . . ?*

Broaditch felt the rasping first sawstroke of the ragged knife split his ear; felt the blood spurt and run down his cheek into his beard as he struggled in Balli's soft, irresistible grip, feeling smothered in the overwhelming, rotting, fecal stink of the mad halfwit. He didn't register the other voice at first as Balli drew back somewhat, blade still poised to saw again.

"Hold!" was the shout. "Hold! You wit not the true law!"

This, Broaditch noticed, seemed the right tack, for he was tossed aside, bleeding, stunned, as Balli turned to face the newcomer. He was surprised to see Valit in the doorway, albeit ready to fly, yet theatrically and still arrogantly there.

"Balli knows law!" the mountainous being cried in anger. "Balli has seen. Balli has heard."

My God in the highest heaven, Broaditch thought, *but this creature is the whole world in more than his vast and unyielding size.* He gasped and pressed his sleeve to his wound, which, while shallow, stung terribly. *He's as senseless!*

"No," Valit insisted, sneering, petulant, "he has a right you cannot fail to grant."

What? To cut his own ears off? Broaditch wondered. *Better if he'd argued with the tort of a twenty-pound stone, he felt . . . though that might have won no judgment considering the knotted head in question, he dimly concluded.*

"Balli grants no rights!" was the reasoned reply. "You're a thief yourself! Balli—"

"Balli me great arse," Valit sneered. "You fat and witless shithole." This seemed, for some cause lost on Broaditch, to check the giant again. "Be still and hear me! You say you must follow law?"

"Balli follows law. Yes. So I take this thief's ears and hands and—"

Ah, yes, I'd forgotten the hands, thought Broaditch.

"But he may call on God to judge the case, fat sack," Valit pronounced, leaning almost jauntily against the door frame, the starry night at his back.

"God?" Balli was uncertain.

"The combat," Valit said triumphantly. "He has the right."

"How?" Broaditch groped. "What? Whom?"

"The combat?" Balli frowned, squinting up his single perpetually surprised-looking eye.

"It's truth," insisted Valit.

"Trial by combat," Broaditch said, trying to regain his feet, "against this monstrosity?"

Valit shrugged.

"Well," he said, "could you be worse off than at this moment, brave Broaditch?"

"If so," came the muttered reply as the brave finally got to his feet, "you've found the way." He stood stolidly there, dabbing at his ear.

Balli, for his own convoluted, fixed reasons, had to accept, and the prospect gradually was coming to please him. He nodded after a little time.

"Balli is just," he declared. "It shall be as you say. Balli has seen the knights do this combat. . . ." He beamed, for the first time so far as Broaditch had witnessed, and the effect was not encouraging. "It shall be as you say. And you are his fighter!" he told Valit, who went white.

"What?" he said. "I—"

Balli, with his terrible, fluid speed, had leaned over and yanked the young man inside.

"Now choose weapon," his roundness said. "Cudgel? Fine blade?" He held up the notched knife. "You choose. Balli has justice." He was drooling a little, batting his reddened eye, pursed lips working like, Broaditch imagined, an anus, sucking in and out. . . .

He's the very world, Broaditch said to himself again.

"There's only one way to defeat the world," he called to the terrified Valit, who looked wild-eyed at him. "And I thank you for coming in good time, young sir."

"What?" Valit wanted to know. "What way?"

"Trick it and run. Else we fall overmatched by a mountain of vicious dullness."

"Choose!" Balli insisted, shaking the reluctant defender of the innocent by the shoulders. "Choose!"

"Choose," Broaditch confirmed gravely. "It matters little enough what. But choose as the world tells you."

Morgan LaFay was fully armored and rode better than a man, Sir Gaf remarked to himself. The bishop was convinced she wanted Arthur's crown herself, but Gaf knew better: she had a purpose, a belief, a plan for the country, something Arthur had failed or refused. She never spoke of it openly, but he knew the idea was ever with her.

The clouds were low, stretched out, gray. The leaves were going gray and brown now. A chill drizzle was falling, rattled faintly on the fallen leaves.

Gaf glanced behind at the line of mounted and marching men. They'd gathered troops from half a dozen minor lords in the past weeks and more were promised. They were building a fair-sized army. The problem was there seemed to be no clear concentration of the enemy. In a way, no one was sure just who the enemy was: British warriors were apparently fighting isolated, savage raids with other scattered lords . . . and then there were the supposed masses of foreigners in the south. . . .

Morgana seemed confident: she'd said they'd engage a main body well before the first snows. . . . Well, he reflected, that had to come from magic arts, because, speaking as a seasoned fighter, there simply was no solid intelligence of the enemy. . . .

"There's nothing to go on," he said to the armed bishop, who turned his fanatical glance and hooked, bristling eyebrows on him. "We hardly know where we're riding or into what fate."

"God will make it plain, soon enough," was the somewhat impractical (he thought) reply.

"Well, well," Gaf said, "she leads us, as if He whispered in her ear."

"The lady is a good Christian. She long since gave over her heathenish arts and necromantic studies." The bishop nodded in full agreement with himself. "Unlike," he added, "that false and conjurous Merlinus Magnus."

"Ah, Merlin," Sir Gaf said, curious. "And what was his fate, pray? Has any of your listening priests heard? They say only Arthur knew how to summon him."

The prelate crossed himself, shifting in his saddle. The light rain beaded on his armor and frock.

"That wizard," he said uneasily, "lives with his father, the devil."

"But," objected the other, "Arthur was a great and Christian ruler and would have had no traffic with—"

"The likes of Merlinus Magnus," the other explained, "can deceive any mortal not armed and sheltered by His angels."

Sir Gaf considered a moment, watching the misty, drab forest flow past. Hooves and feet were muffled on the damp turf.

"So," he murmured, just loud enough for his religious companion to hear, "any of us might well be deceived by a witch or a warlock." He smiled, not having to actually mention Morgan by name. He enjoyed the Bishop clearing his throat, looking uncomfortable and displeased.

Frell had just said something resoundingly inconsequential, Wista realized. Recently this sort of thing mattered less and less to him. Without really thinking about it, he came to spend more and more time with her and found himself relaxed and often talking freely. Well, she was pretty, he thought, looking at her profile again: delicate, haunted by nervousness, graceful. . . .

She sat beside him on a ram skin. They'd just finished an outdoor breakfast. The light rain had stopped; the earth and air were still dampish. A few strokes of sun broke through here and there and brought steam from the ground.

He felt warm and blurry from the wine. He looked at her again: he liked her gentle hesitance, her flashes of warmth. . . . Sometimes she seemed so foolish, and yet who was not in their turn?

"So," she was now saying, "have you had word of your lord, Lohengrin?"

"Hmm?" Wista frowned. "Lohengrin . . . ? No . . . nothing in a fortnight." Impatient with talk, he impulsively took her hand and tugged her closer and she looked nervously at him across sudden inches.

"Oh," she was saying, "I wonder that he left you behind . . ."

"I'm not sorry." Which was true: he didn't want to have to deal with what was inevitable. The future loomed dark and amorphous over him. . . . He had awakened one night from racking, chaotic dreams, panting with fear, feeling certain he was caught, bound to some fate beyond all will and choice, that he was an instrument . . . no, worse: no choice because he would himself refuse it. . . . *To do what?* he'd wondered, but he was afraid he knew that, too. He wished he'd gone away before. Run . . . home . . . anywhere. . . . He'd sat alone in bed with a pounding heart and realized he didn't want to be alone. . . . And beside her now he realized it again. Frell seemed a hope, a possibility. . . . He thought of summers by the lake on his uncle's manor. His father sent him there many times during his childhood. His father was always in service with no land of his own and his mother had died at his birth. The image of those summers suddenly came to him condensed into a single brightness and warmth of long days, sweet smells, floating on the lake, fishing in the reflection of green hills, swimming underwater among the wavering sprays of greenish light that seemed as though the sun were shining up from the bottom . . . fish flashing past and darting off into their secret recesses. . . .

He leaned over and kissed her again and (feeling almost a fear) held her long, firm arms and opened her lips with his, insisted with himself, insisted, stopped her in mid-sentence and felt, after a moment (with vague shame because of fear he couldn't show for a motive), her come back soft, fluid, with a trembling yielding that told him how important this was, was going to be, that she already had known she was lost in it . . . concentrated himself into her summery taste and feel, lapsed his thoughts, felt only her presence, eased back on the warm fur, as if this could save him from all his tomorrows. . . .

He heard her saying, "Oh . . . my dearest . . . my dearest . . ."

He reached her to him, as if he actually could save himself. . . .

Balli tossed them both into a penful of goats, holding each by an arm. Broaditch told himself he was inured to stenches at this point. The goats bleated and stirred around. Valit was now backing through them, swaying under an outsized cudgel Balli had handed him. His chivalrous opponent was advancing, with his rolling gait, brandishing his own weapon, as if it were a twig.

"Well, Broaditch," Valit was saying as the goats swarmed around him so that he seemed waist-deep in a living stream, "what do you suggest?"

Watching Balli's puckered face, Broaditch tried: "We might both fly in different directions," he called over from where he stood on a mound of filth with his back to the askew railings.

"So he will surely have one of us," Valit cried, gasping, ducking away from Balli's first great, sweeping blow. The next swipe barely missed and Valit toppled over the back of a scrambling Billy goat.

Balli waded in, hurling animals aside, long club upraised.

"Justice!" he bellowed in imitation of the knight's war cry. "Justice!"

Valit hurled his club with both hands: it glanced off the giant's head without breaking it or his stride. The young man simply sprinted around the pen, falling over the terrified beasts, rolling, ducking, getting up, the swarming animals the only defense he had. . . .

Broaditch strained his mind. There had to be a way . . . had to be. . . . What . . .? What . . .? Force was useless. . . . Balli even had the speed on them for all his mass. . . . *Christ Jesus, it's a miracle I have lived these past few days.* . . . He fingered his ear. The blood was finally clotted and stiffening. It hurt.

"Justice!"

Valit was now crawling under the huddled beasts, cursing without actual words, frantic, hopeless, maddened as the fleshy mountain plowed toward him, vast hams and hips spilling the mangy, bony creatures.

Do I simply pray now? Broaditch wondered. *Make a vow? Shrive myself and him with short shrift?*

He suddenly heard the young priest's voice in his mind, the one who'd taught him to read. He remembered sitting on the cold stone sacristy floor, late-afternoon light slashing in the single slit window beyond which part of the outer wall of Queen Hertzelroyd's castle showed; the year Parsival was born. He remembered listening, running an unconscious finger under his stained leather serf's collar, absorbed, picturing the rocky valley, the two armies looking down, picturing himself as the young lord in the tale, the sheep-pard with his sling and stone facing the Philistine giant whose voice shook the pitiless, stony desert earth. . . .

And he thought he had it: thought perhaps God or a messenger had stirred this memory at this moment. There were no stones in this foul pen that could do the job, even if he had the skill and force to crack that smooth knob of solid head . . . no . . . but . . . but . . . but . . .

He tore off his cracked leather vest and rapidly knotted it to form a crude, wide sling.

"Hold on!" Valit, he cried. "Roll, curse it, roll, lad! Roll!"

For the which the young man needed no encouragement: he was holding a bleating, terrified goatling up as a shield, ducking, scrambling, panting, tripping. . . . Broaditch noted he wasn't quitting so easily anymore. The lad was improving.

He loaded the makeshift sling with hardened lumps of goat dung and frightened, slightly amused, infinitely determined, he shouted, "Balli! You! Balli!"

He held the loaded sling behind his turned side. Valit had leaped for the fence in final desperation, where he was surely doomed. The trial's scales were tipping against him, except that Balli twisted his head around in time to catch Broaditch coming through a cluster of noisy, terrified animals, winding the sling around and around his head, feeling an almost dreamlike feebleness. He was certain he'd gone daft, and so this was as good a way as any, and Balli's incredible charge no doubt would have proved this true. . . . *A load of dung against this monster! The eye or nothing.* But as Balli sprang, one oversized old billy with a solid set of horns had just had enough and elected to ram the vast hams (which wasn't particularly effective) and then sink his long, gritty teeth into the swelling, bare flesh of buttocks under the loosely flopping hides and wrench and twist and tug and the giant howled ("Mayhap he had a boil there," Broaditch commented later) and the immense roundness began to spin (*like a top, in truth,* Broaditch thought) and spin and spin in an effort to strike the animal, seething howls all the while, the goat gripping like a bulldog, centrifugal force whirling it almost straight out from Balli's behind. . . . Valit was already over the fence and going. When Balli flailed himself, slobbering and shouting, to his knees, reaching back in vain for the billygoat's neck, Broaditch point-blank fired the load of dung (he knew he had gone beyond necessity's dictates, but he gave no damn) into the fat, agonized face and blotted out the single eye and gaped mouth with a wad of shit. Then, deeming this sufficient, he climbed with dignity over the sagging fence and jogged steadily on behind Valit, who was fast disappearing into the moonshadowed forest on the crest of the hill.

Once puffing among the dim trees, Broaditch started guffawing and shaking his head. He heard Valit crashing on ahead and Balli's outraged cries drifting on the sea breeze up the slope. He knelt down, holding his sides, shaking, almost toppling over in a gush of relief and absurdity, staying on his knees past the point of absolute safety, repeating the image: the round face, round eye, round, bellowing mouth, thrashing futilely at the maddened goat, the sudden, clotted spat! that blotted out the face. . . . He shook his head and held his sides. . . .

"Well," Parsival was telling her, "I am no woodsman proper, though I can hold my own."

They were following the river, which was meandering roughly east toward the coast. He was fairly certain of that, though he had no clear idea of how far it was ahead. Unlea was just pressing him about it.

"My flesh is full sore," she told him, perched, bouncing sidesaddle in his wake. "My mare wearies."

"Yet I have no wish to be beset by your husband."

"Nor I," she agreed. "Is it not past noon?" She shielded her eyes to consider the sun. The river was gradually slowing as they moved through more rounded, still densely forested country.

"We'll rest in good time," he said back over his shoulder.

The water was a rich, jeweled, cool blue under clear sky. The golden-grayed trees and bluish-green pines were a reflected hush all around. The ground was still damp.

"Parsival," she said decisively.

"Yes, love?" he said, backlooking.

"I . . ."

"Yes?" He knew, had known, was waiting for this.

"I cannot . . ." she said after a pause.

He reined up and waited. Her palfry halted beside him.

Helmetless, he looked at her, concentrated on her eyes. She was haggard, sad, windblown, but beautiful: soft, full lips, a speck of peeling, a faint streak of mud dried on her cheek, eyes like (he thought) a sunny summer glade. . . . He reached out as from far away to relish the softness of her cheek with bare fingers. . . .

"I love you, Unlea," he said quietly.

"Yes," she said. She shut her eyes. "When you touch me . . ." She gave a little flutter of a gesture. "When you touch me, I . . . I can do nothing. . . ."

"Then I won't release you."

She seemed to silently plead while nuzzling his palm with her lips, and her arms came up to take his shoulders.

"Oh," she said, tearful, "you bastard . . ."

"No," he said.

"Please."

"No. No, I cannot. Don't you see that?"

Because everything was in this. He didn't care how he bound her because he knew the end would prove itself with lucid, simple beauty and peace. The idea of being alone now terrified him. He didn't know what he'd do . . . didn't know. . . .

"I cannot let you go," he said. "I cannot . . ."

She wept, silently, nuzzled his hand, tender and miserable.

That night when he slipped under the quilts (that were beginning to need washing) in the uncertain light of a single candle, she kept her back to him. He moved into her warmth and lightly bussed her shoulder.

"Mmm," he murmured, stroking her long, bare arms and back. She didn't respond.

"Where are we going tomorrow?" she asked palely.

"Are you ill, love?" He was concerned.

"I think not."

"Your voice . . ." He broke off. He had never known a woman so rich with luster and life, and day by day she seemed to be fading. Rain was suddenly drumming on the tent roof and he sighed a curse. "Again," he muttered. "I'm grown weary of the sound." He frowned, thought fleetingly of Prang, Lohengrin . . . his dead wife and daughter . . . Gawain . . . Bonjio. . . . He moved restlessly. He recalled he'd meant to ask Prang if he'd been at the tent flap several nights ago . . . realized it was impossible, at the same time . . . no doubt a vision from sleep. . . .

"Parsival," she said quietly, "where will we go to tomorrow?"

"Onward," he replied, pulling her closer to him, putting his hand over her breasts, almost roughly.

"Have a care," she said, "you're pinching."

He relented, then turned her around in his arms, untwisted her nightdress, and reached between her legs. He poked, not ungently. He found her wet enough and was puzzled and relieved. Her arms, almost unwillingly, came up around him.

"I cannot help but be your whore," she said flatly.

He stopped.

"That's no pleasure to hear," he told her.

"I'm sorry," she said and kissed him. "I know you love me."

"Unlea," he said, narrowing his eyes, as if his expression would reinforce his moderate conviction, "hear me well. We make our way to London town and from there take ship to Brittany. I've been working out the plan of it. From there—"

"We have no silver and gold," she broke in.

"What? I thought . . . ?

"I gave the few coins I had to the guards to seal their lips. I'm no thief to steal more from him I wronged."

"Wronged . . . ?" He sighed. "Say no more to me. I'll find what we need." He sat up, the covers falling away from his bare torso. He stared at the steady candle flame. The rain rattled steadily. Small leaks broke out here and there. He could hear the pit-pit-pit on the damp rug. He sighed. "I'll—"

"How?" she wanted to hear, rolling over again so her back was to him and the slight illumination.

"I don't know yet," he said impatiently. "Trouble me no more, woman."

Silence, except for the rain and dripping. . . . She turned onto her back again, restlessly . . . sighed. . . .

"I'm miserable," she said, rolling her head on the stained satin pillow. "I'm so miserable. . . ."

"Things will be good," he insisted, looking down into her face now. "You love me. You said you love me."

"Yes," she returned, "yes. . . ."

"Then what? *What!*" He felt haggard in the faint, wavering stain of flame color. She kept her profile to him. "Tell me!"

"I know not," was the best she could do. She was weeping again.

He was baffled, maddened almost. He took her by the shoulders, saw her wince with pain. He held hard, anyway.

"Are you content?" she asked him, face turned away.

"What . . . ? I . . . ?" His eyes tracked back and forth. "How could I be? With you as you are. . . . But it will be good, we have to *try*. . . . I . . . I *know* it will be good. . . ."

Her eyes came to his at last. They seemed a little frightened. She said nothing through her parted lips, then went between his legs, gripped his sagged flesh, kneaded it, shut her eyes, as if on all facts and fears and waking things, because her face seemed asleep to him, lost in the faint flame, warm-edged shadows. Both her hands now worked together and he grew and firmed under her touch and she soothed: "Peace, my love . . . peace . . . peace, my sweet love. . . ."

And he let himself fall back with his face by her heels and he held both her feet, biting his lip, rolling his eyes, body arching rigid as her burning hands gathered irresistible momentum, and he heard himself gasp, and in flashes, as his head swayed, he glimpsed her serene face rocking slightly on the pillow, and for an instant it reminded him (though the thought was swallowed and lost whole) of his mother praying in a rapt, sweet, totally vulnerable, utterly remote calm. . . .

"Oh, good Christ!" he cried, bit his lip, opened his mouth, as if to bite and swallow something in the rosy, shadowed air, and her accelerating hands lifted him out of himself. . . . "Aaaaah!" he cried. "Aaaaah . . .! Aaaaah . . .!"

It was still raining steadily the following day. The river was a wide, gray-white, seething sheet. The earth was sodden and flooding in places. They were down to nearly level ground now, so Parsival assumed they were nearing the coastline. They went on side by side with the pack mule between them. The rain tinkled on his light mail links and boomed on the open helmet. The smell of damp, oiled steel always took the edge off his appetite. It was midafternoon and Unlea wanted to eat. As soon as they came to some shelter of pines or whatever, he'd oblige her, he'd just said.

They'd spoken very little, otherwise. The weather was depressing. And he didn't want to risk reopening last night's wound. . . .

"I think we're lost," she suddenly announced from under her traveling hood.

"Lost?"

"Yes."

"But we've been following the river," he protested.

"It keeps turning."

"But it has to come to the coast in the end. It's the way of rivers."

"You haven't been able to see the sky for nearly two days together. I think we're lost."

"Nonsense, Unlea," he soothed. He wished she wouldn't frown like that. It made her seem like a stranger, somehow. . . .

"I have a feeling," she said.

"Never fear," he began, "I . . ." And broke off, reined up, halting the mule in the same movement. She stopped a pace or two on, the river behind her. He was staring through the rain at a line of trees that lay like a wall almost to the water's edge. He felt the pressure in his stomach and knew someone or something very powerful was there. He immediately assumed this connected with the dark figure in the tent opening the other night. He bit his lip as he felt a prickling chill.

Is it mortal or some other form? he asked himself.

He didn't want to stir up that other world anymore. Let it sink into the past.

Broaditch and Valit had gone on into the dark woods for several hours, picking their way over ditches, around fallen trees and boggy streams. The swampy area was gradually yielding to dry country. As the moon was about down, Broaditch decided there was no point in pressing forward. Valit was wobbling, in any case.

They sheltered themselves on a nearly bare hilltop among outcroppings of glacial rock. With their backs against cool stone, they could look back over the flatlands. The sea was dimly visible in the starlight. Broaditch imagined he could distinguish the light in Balli's hut; anyway, it was a single, wavering, faint reddish glint. . . .

Neither said much for a while. Then Broaditch broke the silence.

"Well, lad," he said, "you're getting to see the world, in a certain way."

"Is that what it is, then?" Valit came back with, seeming in better spirits than was his wont.

"I know the road home looks fair to you now," Broaditch added, wishing he still had his eastern pipe for smoking herbs. He was unique in these lands, where only a few stray crusaders had imported hookahs from the infidels. Suddenly he shook his head and chuckled.

"Was that so mirthful a remark?" Valit wanted to know. Broaditch noted he didn't seem normally surly.

"I was going over my last moments with our former host and lord judge." He laughed.

"That ain't funny itself. I had no regrets leaving the mad bastard, I can tell you. As for the road home, I want none of it. I didn't come this far to go back to nothing."

"Well," Broaditch said with some surprise, "I've got no better advice than that. . . . And I thank you for coming back for me, lad." He didn't add his surprise at that, either. He slouched down and stuffed his hide cap under his head. "No better, that is," he concluded, "than to join me in the place where we're most alone—I mean in slumber, Val." Whereupon the massive man folded his arms and set himself for sleep. "I tell you this, young Valit-Varlet," he added, eyes comfortably closed, "I need no more old wizards with whiskers full of hints and mad mischief. It's home for me, and the devil with the devil's own!" He sighed and shifted, trying to wedge himself down in a better way. "I say this much: I were wiser when much less I knew." He yawned with a slight shudder.

"What wizards was that?"

"Hmm? None, my lad . . . none. . . ." He yawned. "Just my own fevers, I expect. . . ." Sleep waited warm, empty, and safe. He let himself slide down into it a little at a time . . . gradually faster. . . . *Thank Christ for sleep,* he thought, *for there the world ends for a sweet time. . . .*

"I ain't tired," his companion complained.

"You're over-young," Broaditch muttered, fading fast. "But the cure for that is inevitable. . . ."

God grant me, he prayed, mused, *relief from the snakes and great, fat fellows with one eye. . . .*

And this was the last thought for now, and restless Valit heard the first, buzzing snore commence. . . .

Except he was wrong this time: he felt uneasy, cold, and exposed . . . tried to turn and struggled down into himself for warmth and safety and realized he was standing up, somehow. He wanted to lie down and blot out the bright, silverish dawn light. He saw Valit sitting up, tapping the earth with a stick, brooding, and, without even being surprised, because he wasn't precisely thinking, his mind in the strange silence of a dream, he saw a big man wrapped in coarse, muddy hides lying beside him, a lumpy, dead-looking hunk that he knew was himself an invisible wall away. . . . Now he wanted to sleep desperately, and before he could act or move in any way he noticed a third figure (that resembled the old man in the boat) standing nearby with arms crossed over a grayly shimmering cloak. And Broaditch felt the wordless dream-voice say: "Do you recall us?"

He instantly had an image of the bottom of a long tunnel lying on his face among naked, toiling workers in chains when he'd been a slave for Clinschor's conquering hordes many years before. . . . He'd escaped by feigning death, but for a time believed he had truly died and had spoken with mysterious beings. . . . He gathered this bearded figure had been one of them. They had exorted him to do something he never quite understood. . . .

"You were chosen then and now."

"But . . ."

"There's no time for indulging yourself. You are in the sea and had better swim."

"But . . ."

And a moment later, without perceptible interval, he was looking down on a rugged terrain lit by the same sunless, silver-blue, even glow. He seemed high enough to see all the country and the gleam of distant ocean while at the same time scenes appeared close at hand and startlingly vivid. The bluish color sparkled everywhere like some underwater sunlight. He floated, feeling sweet and peaceful and tender and free . . . saw battalions of mounted knights moving along intricate paths to take up positions in the almost circular mound of hills and piny forests. Each figure seemed to radiate a warm, goldenish glow into the general washes of color. . . . He perceived men working, felling trees and moving stones to block the winding roads, and then it seemed as though the sun were coming up through the misty, glowing earth itself, because in the heart of the land below there was a towering, hazy outline of what might have been a castle dissolving into a golden-white shining, a blinding radiance whose streaming beams seemed pressing to burst free from their compressed space and ignite the universal twilight. . . . He found himself caught up in the play of light and drifted, watching the pulsing . . . drifted. . . .

"Stop dreaming. Pay attention to what is important!"

But it was so beautiful, and all that he was, was past, and what he had done was done, and he strove somehow to soar higher and float (for the rays went freely straight up) into the rising flame of the melting castle. . . . In a flicker it was stark night. . . . No, the light was simply darkness, a darkness that sucked all illumination into itself, and he shivered and trembled and tried to escape, go back, wake up, anything . . . sleep . . . yes, that was it . . . ! Go to sleep . . . sleep and escape. . . .

"Fool, pay attention!"

Yes, the darkness was not total; he saw that now. There were outlines, crawling flickers of flame, like embers of a burned-out country, and the flashing far-near vision showed intermittent shadow-flashing glimpses: dark-armored men marching . . . burning towns and castles . . . smoke rising and spreading everywhere . . . the darkness was smoke blotting, drifting. . . . He saw a beautiful knight lying on his back, as if asleep or preserved in death within a clear crystal dimly lit by flame glow. . . . He wished he could help the knight break free as the smoke and fire closed in all around him. . . . For an instant he thought he recognized the face, though greatly changed with age, and tried for a name in a state where names and words were not. . . . The knight in full armor lay as if enchanted (he heard thunder that seemed to swell into a pulsing incantation), and he tried to call out his name to him to rouse him from what seemed a solid, blinding river of crystal. . . . His sword lay beside him. . . . The vision was rippling now, shaking like a sheet in wind, and he felt pulled and shocked and torn as the energy failed or was somehow attacked, and he glimpsed a man dipping his bare arm into a bowl of fire and removing a handful of flame that lit his long, wide, soft, bony, pale face and bright, cat-like eyes and upcurled moustache, standing in a strange, round room . . . no . . . prisoned in a blackened iron ball, and then the universe popped like a bubble and he woke up, sat bolt upright on the damp turf, thinking he was screaming and finding himself silent. . . . The stars were silent overhead . . . the sea wind cool . . . Valit was snoring quietly. . . .

He just sat there for a time. His fingers were trembling slightly. . . . He was heavy, dense, dull at first, then, gradually, lighter and lighter, until he suddenly feared he might lift into the air and repeat what he didn't yet call a dream. He breathed deeply and slowly until he felt more controlled.

He still wasn't thinking thoughts: there were no words in his mind, no images, just the same flowing awareness that seemed to take in near and far as one. . . . He felt the world moving, not physically, but in a flowing order where every movement melted into every other so there were no seams anywhere . . . sitting there, air bursting crisp and rich into his lungs, feeling his blood so fierce that, despite his aches and battered places, he stood lightly up with an urge to dance down the hillside and race back again, bounce and half-fly. . . . Nothing was impossible . . . it was all true. . . . He would do it, whatever it was, because he could ride the flow and reach the end, that the goal was intended for him before he was born, that time and nature had been moving toward this moment forever. . . . He grinned, then laughed aloud, feeling as tall as the hill and as wide and inexorable as the world. . . .

He sat down again, feeling peaceful and ready to really sleep. He was starting to think again, but that was all right now. . . .

The goal, he thought. Well, he'd fill in the details tomorrow. Great Christ, but he felt well! *I accept,* he told something, the earth, air, night, *I accept.* . . . He'd fill in the details. . . .

He shut his eyes and was instantly, sweetly asleep. He floated away. . . .

Morning was bright gray. Broaditch woke up feeling refreshed and not too chilled. His new energy seemed to have survived the night. He stretched deliciously and nudged Valit with his toe. He got a grumble and stir for his trouble, then a muffled curse.

I'll make an effort with him, he thought cheerfully. *Every person's worth every effort.* . . . He smiled at himself for thinking that.

"I accept," he whispered. He stood up, shaking with a yawn, opened his codpiece and urinated against the rock, looking out over the blustery autumn day.

"Wake up, lad," he said. "Welcome to the first day of my life . . . and yours!"

Valit had rolled over, blinking and bleary-eyed.

"Dung and blood," he muttered, rubbing his eyes. "Fields of scum . . ."

"Ah, the cheery bird greets the morn!"

By midafternoon Valit was trudging and Broaditch was musing. He'd cut a fairly straight sapling and made himself a staff that he swung, marching along over fields thick with berrybush and long grass. So far they'd passed no habitations. They were climbing gradually toward a low wall (they didn't know it was Roman) which followed the curves of the landscape.

"But where *are* we going?" Valit was saying, repeating.

"Over there," Broaditch said, pointing with the stick.

"And then? I don't understand what you said back there. Where—"

"Valit," Broaditch said, "what do you want? What do you hope for?"

"What?"

"Come, come, you have ears."

After a few thoughtful paces, Valit said, "I trust no one."

"A happy condition," Broaditch reproved.

"With reason," he nodded in dour self-confirmation, eyes fixed on the green-gray earth. "Yet I trust you, Broaditch, this far, since you helped me twice and I still owe you—not that I would stand to the depth with any to witness."

"There's no depth that matters," Broaditch assured him.

"Be it so or nay, I trust you so far to say that many think me a fool because I would not work at bending iron like my father."

"Well," Broaditch pointed out, as they reached the square-stone wall, "there's no better trade and few as solid. For . . ."

"I know all the words to that song I oft have heard," Valit cut in impatiently as they climbed to the wide top, which commanded an impressive view of the deserted barren highlands. Broaditch suddenly realized the storm had blown them a remarkable distance north. "But," Valit continued, sitting himself on the edge, "I care not for it. I trust you this far: I have watched the Jews."

"The Jews?"

"Aye. I made a sort of friend, Cay-*am* of Camelot. I have seen swords beaten from gold, aye, and found them much keener than steel."

"But," Broaditch said, frowning, not catching the meaning immediately, surprised by the fact and manner of these revelations, "Gold is soft and will be a poor . . . aye, I see. I see." He was more impressed with Valit now. "So you mean to become a Jew?"

"In a way. If I can. I trust you this far, but I'll say no more."

Broaditch was certain he wouldn't. He cocked his head at the serious concentrated young fellow and half-smiled and half-frowned at him.

"Well, well a-day," he said to himself. He thought it funny, but for some reason he wasn't really amused. He made the remark, anyway: "And how many will your sword of gold slay, I wonder, lad?"

The watchful eyes took him in as they began walking the paved road that ran along the wall across the wild, mist-strung hills.

"I trust you this far," Valit reaffirmed, "but no man more."

"Not even your friend, Cay-*am?*"

"Him less."

It was pleasant to be sheltered from the edged north sea wind. Broaditch tapped his staff on the smooth paving. He whistled a little tune and watched some crows circling high.

"Whatever you wanted," Broaditch suddenly told him, "lay it aside for the time. Trust me and there'll be more than riches."

Valit just looked at him without a word. Broaditch was surprised by what had just come out of his own mouth. He felt wry and very serious. How was he going to explain this?

"Suppose I told you," Broaditch offered, that wizards and angels direct me?"

"Ah," the young man responded.

Broaditch tapped his stick a few times on the paving blocks and went on whistling tunelessly. He revolved a number of approaches in his mind.

"They seem to be leading you on an uncommon, hard route, master Broaditch," Valit suggested deadpan.

"Never mind wizards and angels," Broaditch said, suppressing a chuckle.

"I rarely do," his companion remarked. Broaditch shut his eyes and shook his head.

"Strike not the fallen." he said, sighing, "though they make the most tempting targets . . . apart from wizards and angels," Broaditch cocked his eyes sidewise to hold the other's tongue in check, "Which were but, in a sense, a way of speaking—"

"Why trouble yourself?" Valit cut in. "I might as well trail behind you than wander by myself. I care little for the nonce, whether it be demons or mooncalfs you follow. But I pray you," and for the first time since they'd met Broaditch saw the crinkle of a friendly smile, "find guides who favor these stone roads, and friendly folk."

Broaditch laughed.

"So," he said, "but I swore to Balli we'd return to swim in his swamps and meet all his kin."

Valit's expression went dour except for his eyes.

"Even if every sprite in heaven and earth," he assured him,

"pointed to that bloated dung bag's dwelling with fingers of fire I'd let the invitation age a lifetime before I took it up."

Broaditch appreciated this rush of eloquence; then he became serious. Smokey streamers of fog flowed over the wall as they marched steadily on.

"Still, lad," he finally came out with, "this is grave business, I think. And, uncertain as I am of how I was led on, for I may even be bent and battered in my senses and straying with the moonbeams, nevertheless, I am fixed in my purpose, though unsure of it . . ." He looked at his companion. "Well, I'm not mad, lad. But I cannot make this plainer until it's made plainer to me." He gestured with his staff along the sweeping walled road. "For now, we walk south."

"To end where?" Valit asked, neutrally, "or know you not."

"I *almost* know," Broaditch said, shook his head and smiled, "I'll discover when I get there."

"And then? The angels and them will lay it plain out?"

Still grinning, Broaditch clapped him on the shoulder.

"Valit, lad," he declared, "you'll have to bide impatience."

"Oh," was the reply. "To see this I am more patient than the sea has waves." He considered. "Or Balli rings of fat."

"Or sins in London town," Broaditch added, "regrets in hell, fools in the church, devils in the government . . . pray, don't make the list as long as the wait."

Valit's face had closed down again, his eyes and expression withdrawn into his inner haunts. They went on without speaking for a time, up and down and around the steeply writhing roadway.

"There's often truth in strange prophecy," Valit suddenly came out with.

"And," Broaditch said, "no doubt there are lies in common hindsight for all of that."

"But what think you?" Valit persisted.

"Aye, there's often truth."

"Even in things unmeant?"

Broaditch shrugged with the stick.

"Commonly," he replied, impatiently, "so it is said." He was staring across the moors: he thought something had moved. *Perhaps a buck deer,* he thought, *who knows? . . .*

"So," Valit said, with the triumph of a true abstract reasoner, "I may yet come to solid profit by way of your insubstantial vaporings!"

Broaditch was delighted again.

"Valit," he cried, "I'm grateful for you! I swear it! I think the world's about to be chawed, swallowed, and shat out and there you are prepared to grope and finger for pearls in the steaming dung!"

Broaditch saw Valit was just watching him so he waited. And the young man said at length:

"So you don't deny it?"

"Deny what?"

"That I may find solid profit?"

"What?" Broaditch was laughing hard. "No, no, lad, I swear, I think you'll find all you seek . . . and more . . . much more . . ." laughing at the same time feeling a warmth and sense of responsibility. He thought of his children . . . repeated their names to himself. Would he see them? He had already accepted the alternative possibility if it had to be. Well, time would explain itself if he kept breathing and walking. "Solid profit," he said, grinning.

Parsival waited; the pack mule rocked uneasily; Unlea's palfry mare was agitated as two mounted, heavily armed knights in dark armor inwrought with silver loops and blazes wearing flat, blank, silver masks, cantered out of the line of trees and halted. He could see the steam rising from the dark chargers.

Just two of those again? he wondered, recognizing the armor from twenty years ago. *So Gawain was right . . . flesh and blood at last.*

"Who are they?" Unlea asked nervously. Her lover shrugged.

"If they be who they seem, they stand undernumbered to trouble us." He took a deep breath. Felt ready. For the first time in years he looked forward to the release of combat. Sensed it had to do with the pressures of recent days . . .

"Are you of the unholy mutes?" he called over, easing his horse toward them. "But then, if yes, you cannot say so."

They were silent and still almost as carvings; only the horse-heads slightly moved.

Now a third warrior emerged from the foggy, dripping trees. A stocky man in polished silver steel and a white and black horse. He looked familiar. He came steadily, one hand on the over-sized hilt of his broadsword, the other holding a lance upright.

"And you?" Parsival demanded. "Name yourself!"

The man made violent snortings inside his helmet. He clearly had a headcold. Voice doubly muffled and obscure when he spoke.

"I know you," he said, sniffing and swallowing. "Well," he went on thickly, "you're not my proper business anymore. You don't recall me, then, Parsi-bird-head?" he laughed and sniffled. "But let's just have one passing play?" he let fall his lance, drew his blade, then came in quickly, the sword casually poised, and Parsival felt the fellow's skill like a pressing, tangible force, and he unfocused his eyes to widen his awareness and let his body relax to the steady rhythm of his breath, sword still undrawn. Parsival didn't even bother to slam his visor shut. He knew if a man like this struck home, he might as well be bare-headed. This was a fellow master and death was one or two cuts away. He heard the knight's raspy mouth-breathing, he seemed too close but forced his mind to wait and watch and let the body fight: which it did, exploding, leaning into the short, irresistible cut, drawing, twisting in one shimmer of motion, tested to the limit, beyond, and not in the perfect shape for it he'd have been in even a month ago. Both cuts became parrys and as the horses passed close he felt a flick across his throat and turned at the same time to see part of the other's gauntlet sheared away and felt a trinkle of warm blood under his neckpiece. To Unlea it had seemed a flash, a whirr, a heartbeat's terror . . .

The stocky knight unhinged his visor, sneezed violently. It was Lancelot, with a beet-red nose. They just sat and looked at one another.

"Magnificent," Lancelot said, "I'd kill you in time, but—" he rasped up some more phlegm. "This a witch's curse laid upon me! Dame Morg or some shit-sucking sister . . ."

"Have you forgotten you've murdered my wife and child?" Parsival asked, waiting, watchful, thinking that fate was going to force him into further pointless combat. *Custom again,* he thought, *the custom of pride and pain* . . . Unlea by the gray river's edge, blurred by the drizzling rain, seemed a wisp of lost hope receding like a smoky shape of fog . . .

"What?" Lancelot wanted to know.

"At Castle Tratinee. Where you found me first."

Lancelot sneezed again. Wiped at his moustache with his steel glove improving matters very little. The hairs remained caked and shiny.

"Why, I had naught to do with any of that," he declared.

Parsival knew Lancelot was not terribly clever, and was aware he never had been known to lie. "What he has for brains makes the flowers grow," Gawain had said, years ago.

"Ah," Parsival said, "you and your men were but there to watch."

"No," Lancelot pronounced gravely, smearing a finger under his nose again. "Not to watch. To slay you. As I then openly declared."

The other thought it through.

"Very well," he said. "Who slew my family then?"

"I know not," Lancelot shrugged.

"And you are no longer bound to kill me?"

"This is true. But I would joust with you betimes for the sport."

"Who sent you to slay me? I knew not your sword was lightly for hire."

"For hire? Who dares say for hire!" The famous knight's face instantly swelled, blue eyes snapping.

"For honor?" Parsival was almost incredulous.

"Aye!" stormed the legendary warrior. "A debt I owed. To Duke LaLong who did great service for me and the dead King Arthur." Lancelot spat phelgm, turned his horse and prepared to depart, still frowning and obviously debating whether to reattack here and now. "The only King who was a *man*," he added. "Say no more to me Parsival, you bird."

"But how came the Duke to lift the obligation of my death?"

"By means of his own," Lancelot said impatiently.

"And whom does *honor* bid you serve now?" Parsival wanted to know, indicating the silent pair of black knights.

Lancelot's frown was grim and cold. His red nose sniffed.

"What's this you're saying?" he demanded, hand on his hilt. "Ask them, then!" he raged and spurred his mount away back into the trees.

"Because they're mute?" Parsival called after. "Are they?" he shouted as the blocky knight was gone, muffled hoofbeats fading. The other two followed after.

Well, what is it to me? he thought, looking back at Unlea, who was staring at the water, sad and lost-looking among the faint wisps of fog and the general grayness. . . . *What matters black or orange knights to me? All that's behind. . . . I'll find a place for us. . . . I will. . . .*

He stared at her, imagining her happy, walking in a garden of lustrous flowers, a golden-haired boy-child playing nearby, a flash of brilliant blue eyes looking tenderly up at her, in radiant streams of sunlight, as if wading in the shimmering colors . . . and as if to seal his vision with an omen, the sun broke through the grim cloud cover and flashed, sparkling on the water, and touched her face, and his mind knew something was wrong, although he was too caught up looking at her to bother with it. . . . She was staring at the sun then away across the flattening fields ahead, frowning.

He rode close to her, smiling with new confidence. He nodded to himself.

"You are so lovely, Unlea," he told her and was surprised she was shaking her head and not looking at him. "Unlea?"

"No," she said. "Please . . . let me go." He opened his mouth and then sighed through it. "Please, Parsival, before I come to loathe our sweet hours and hate the sight of you. . . ." She was terribly urgent. "It cannot be, Parsival. Cannot you see that?"

"But . . ."

"Oh, you . . ." She shut her eyes. "You child, who are yet a man, too. . . ." She opened them with tears this time that caught the already fading sunlight as the rainwater drizzled over the wide-brimmed hat. "This is the *world*, Sir Parsival," she continued, weeping and trembling and yet strong; he saw, for the first time, how strong she could be, a woman could be.

"But I love you," was all he could find to say. The tears burned in his own eyes now. "I love you, Unlea." He suddenly felt that this had been his last chance and now it was lost. He'd failed again, he kept thinking, and *no . . . no, there has to be something I can do,* which he knew was his mind moving in the reflex of the already dead, like a just slain body that seemed to breathe and stretch its limbs. . . . "But I—"

"Look," she said, pointing at the fading sun, "are you so entoiled by this that your senses are darkened?" She faintly smiled. "My child and tender man . . ." He saw her bite her lip. He found himself hanging on each slight sign, each hope of hope that somehow love would be magically enough. . . .

"Unlea?"

"Look at the sun," she insisted; just as it was lost again, it hit him. It was not east, but west. West. . . . *The river must have circled,* he told himself.

"This is the green plain," she said. "My home is just beyond. The fog hid it from me until now. The land looked different from this direction."

"Then we must turn around." He knew she was going to shake her head. Of course. "Please," he heard his voice saying, "please."

"Free me, Parsival," she virtually begged, "for love, if for nothing else. . . ."

"No," he said, knowing it was yes. *Yes! Yes! Yes!* He shut his burning eyes.

"There's no hope," she was telling him and herself. "This is the world of waking, my sweet, lost one. . . ."

He said nothing . . . waited.

"Let me free," she pleaded again, though (he noted) her voice was quite sure now . . . and he finally nodded. He wouldn't look at her looking at him now. "Turn away," she said, desperate, too, "turn away or I cannot go. . . ."

"And," he said at length, "will you be safe?"

"He'll not injure me. . . . He never has."

He knew it was true, knew . . . it was a coldness in his stomach. . . .

"And this is all?" he murmured.

She didn't answer, didn't need to. So he turned his horse and started away.

"But don't you want the mule, too?" was the last thing he heard her say, and silently seared with tears, he shook his head, as if that mattered, still clinging to every last contact and already, as the rain closed around him, feeling the memory begin. . . . When he finally looked back there was nothing but rain and mist and the seamless gray earth and sky. . . .

He went on, drifting now, looking down at the wet ground as the well-paced horse slogged on. He'd left the river and was crossing a wide, rolling, muddy plain.

He didn't look up as the animal minced on the bank of another stream running flat, greenish-dark, straight. He didn't look as the riders caught up with him. Every so often tears would overspill his eyes. He paid no attention to that, either. He barely noticed the voice shouting and the tinkle and clink and bang of steel and horse sounds. . . . When he finally glanced bleakly through hopelessly reddened and blurred eyes, he blinked at dím, gleaming figures. He didn't trouble to count them. He blinked on, but his eyes had been wept out of focus and, for all he knew or cared, forever.

He really didn't listen, either, just politely awaited until the voice stopped raging, blinking his fogged eyes. He had never been depressed to such depths. And distraction. Oh, he knew remotely that the voice ringing in the open helm was Bonjio's, but that fact connected nowhere because he was replaying images of her softness in the first hay, the bed, the tent silks, under moon, stars, and sunlight . . . kept wanting *her* voice, kept wanting to turn and go after her, try again, not knowing what he'd say or do. . . . The future was so vacant and terrifying now. . . . Sometimes he worked together perfect speeches that would win her back with eloquence alone. . . . How could any other have equaled their passion . . . ? It was hard for him to care just now about the Earl and his men and all that, so, as he made up his mind to say something (because there was a silence), he peripherally perceived the shadow of the ax stroke arced for his open face mask, and he drew and slashed at the arm in one motion with that unearthly reflex speed, and ax, hand, and wrist sailed past his face, the streaming blood spattering his cheeks like red pox, the chopped arm still held out straight, as if in stunned salute, blood jetting, splashing over him, as if (his mind said in a blurry corner) that was the real attack: running, pooling; dripping too thick for the faint drizzle to rinse, and then, with a bellowing scream, the stump was snatched back, and desperately, futilely, a metal-bound hand tried to stanch the incredibly rapid flow as Parsival, in terror, understood what had happened, wanting to scream himself and pray to have the blow taken back, to have those few moments returned, that fragment of unyielding time (there flashed a memory from what seemed a thousand years ago: a buck deer jerking its polished antlers, speared through the chest, collapsing in a shimmering splendor of sunshine and himself wanting the cast back, feeling the pain, begging life for life there, the first time. . . . *Oh, my God in heaven,* he thought heavily, *it's always a moment too late . . . always. . . .*

He looked wildly around, blinking, blurred.

"Bonjio," he said desperately, "Bonjio."

Bonjio had fallen from the saddle and lay in a seeping red stain

on the greenish earth as men fumbled around him, working to stop
the bleeding with strips of rag.

Parsival knew he could have avoided the blow if only his eyes
had been clear, if only he'd been paying real attention. . . .

He stared, blinking, at the foggy figure before him.

"Forgive . . ." And he couldn't even say "me." He was thinking
it was custom again, and pain, too, and . . . and the man had been
his friend . . . and . . . there were no more *ands* because this was
the low point, the end of roads. . . . He tore off his helmet,
pressed at his eyes, and pounded his forehead: it wasn't just
Bonjio, either, or her . . . or any certain thing; it was the hole in
life, the absence . . . weight of world and whirring of time, like a
chariot's wheels, each day sinking down to the next and the brief
exalted moments of rest. . . . For the first time he couldn't trick
himself with a hope, a prospect, a goal ahead, and so it all
slammed in on him and he felt swept forward on and on like a
swimmer caught in a dark river at the brink of the shadowed falls
gazing hopelessly back to the far shore, where the sun still flamed a
sweet rose and gold over the enduring earth . . . no woman . . .
no work . . . no vision . . . and nothing, no mother's sweet word
or the unimaginable voice of life spoke to him as he turned in
stunned bleakness, bare head inviting blows that never came,
though he would not have moved a fraction to escape now . . . no
voice, no words, no touch—just the faint, drizzling chill keeping
the blood undried on his steel shell. . . . He rode on into the
blurring, his horse wandering along the darkening, sharply curving
stream, and when the animal reached the bottom of a steep
U-bend and halted to nibble at the pale, bleached grass, he
dismounted, his sight now different in each eye so that what was
clear in one for an instant was bent by the other, and he was more
deceived in his steps as he walked along the bank than if he were
totally blind, everything deceptively refracted so that when, in his
restless, frightened grief, he strode out onto the clustered lily pads
and ripples, he saw only firm earth and thought fleetingly that a
spell had struck him as the ground opened, air a wet shock, and
then he was under the surface, dragged steadily to the mucky,
weedy bottom by his armor's weight until he was looking straight
up through several feet of sluggish stream at the grayish twilight
paling around the shadowy masses of water plants whose
strange roots clustered and swayed all around him. His eyes were
cleared by the shock, and he felt oddly comfortable as driblets of

air slowly oozed from him . . . the mud was as soft as cushions
. . . the water moved over him like a cleansing wind. . . . He
wondered what it would be to breath it. . . . not the gasps and
swallows every swimmer knows, but to suck it deep and cold into
his fluttering lungs. . . . He wondered, vaguely, as the air within
him became a burning pain, if at the end his body would struggle
to rise and save itself, because he knew his mind wasn't interested
anymore, the body could do what it had to, the mind cared nothing
and was waiting now because, perhaps, there would be an image
still to come or the voice . . . the word . . .

Gawain and Prang had stopped to water their mounts. The older
knight had leaned over the stream's edge to cup a palmful of water
as the horses dipped their muzzles a few feet downstream.

The setting sun was just breaking out of a level layer of clouds,
and a reddish gleaming appeared all around, as if the world lit
itself from within.

So he thought it was simply a reflection at first, except, even
diluted, the metallic taste was obvious. He spit out a mouthful and
frowned at the pinkish stain streaming in thinnning clouds around
the bend.

For some reason he stood up, decided it wasn't an animal, and
pushed quickly upstream through the whip-like, wiry brush and
bare prickers. . . .

"The last beams of the sun touched the water," Gawain was
saying to Prang where they both sat in the warm shifting ring of
firelight, sipping mugs of hot meat broth, "through a space in the
trees . . . which was the only reason I saw him." They both
glanced at Parsival, who was lying perfectly still on the mounded
earth, the flames gleaming on his silvery mail. His eyes were shut.
"It shocked me, boy," he continued, "to see him lying just as he is
now on the stream bottom . . . the blood I took for his, still
washing away. . . . His eyes were open, turning to me, I say, as
the last bubbles issued from his drowning mouth. . . ." He shook
his head.

"But what do you make of it, Gawain?" Prang asked. "Was he
injured? Bound by a spell?" Prang looked nervous and crossed
himself abruptly a second later.

Gawain shook his head.

"I must tell you," he went on, "his eyes looked at me, yet he troubled not a single limb to raise himself from watery doom. . . ."

"So you pulled him out."

"Just so," Gawain said, nodding, "but not before he breathed in and shut his eyes."

Lay in the last, lingering blood-red sunbeams that illuminated him on the dark bottom among the shadowy water plants, arms crossed over his chest as if keeping vigil, long golden-silver streaked hair unwinding into the easy currents that seemed to flow the darkness over him and blot out the last thinning thread of life as his shuddering chest inhaled the chill and then it was night. . . .

"Have you ever dragged a caparisoned man from four feet of water?" Gawain wanted to know.

"Nay," said Prang, shaking his head and staring at Parsival.

"Well," Gawain concluded, "I got him to the bank, as you saw . . . with my one arm."

They both had finished the job. Then Gawain had stood on Parsival's back and pressed a sloshing amount of stream out. And though he seemed to breathe, from fitful time to time, he had not reopened his eyes. At least two hours had passed and Prang, for one, was convinced he never would. Gawain seemed sanguine, however.

The waning moon was up, the fire now crushing itself to violet embers, Prang half-dozing, before Parsival actually looked at them from the dim shadows.

Gawain was turned away, working on a frayed saddle girth, wrapping it with wax twine to make a new join.

Prang thought himself asleep: across the faint blowing sputter, the large gray-blue eyes were suddenly fixed on him, seeming to magnify the vague illumination with some cold, inner brightness. He pinched his cheek, frightened by the distance in that look, frozen by it, as if something not altogether mortal gazed dispassionately at him. The feeling passed somewhat a moment or two later.

"Sir," he said, meaning Parsival, though Gawain looked up.

"Eh?" he wondered, then saw where Prang stared. "So you've come back," he stated, as if with secret knowledge, Prang thought.

Parsival didn't speak immediately. He breathed deeply. He finally said, "Yes. Back."

Gawain nodded (Prang felt) knowingly. But why?

"Are you recovered?" Prang asked, feeling irrelevant.

"That's another question altogether," Gawain said. "It's enough he's come back." He tilted his head toward his friend. "So now you know this, too?" he asked, rather gently, Prang thought, all in all.

Parsival gingerly touched, then rubbed, his face, as if surprised to find flesh on the bones.

As well he ought, Prang commented silently, *considering what has been.*

"Yes," Parsival said to Gawain. "Yes . . ."

"You speak as though he's been off on a visit," Prang put in.

"Do we?" Gawain said wryly. "He wanted to let it go," he directed at Parsival.

"Yes," that calm man affirmed. His hands fell back onto his chest again. He breathed deeply. "I'll sleep now," he said and shut his eyes.

Gawain seemed pleased. He settled himself down close to the last embers, wrapping his woolen cape around him.

"Tomorrow, young *Prong*," he said lightly, "you'll find out where we're going . . . and it won't leave you any choice . . . to speak of."

"What?" Prang said. "What?"

But Gawain muffled himself up and said no more.

Lohengrin was only a day's ride behind the main force by nightfall. The road he was following with his bodyguard troops (about fifty horsemen) led over a rise northerly across the sunset. He was puzzled by how long it was taking the deep red glow to finally fade from the dark, massed clouds. They clattered over a narrow bridge and he saw dark shapes in the sluggish, gleaming water. A moment later he realized they were scattered bodies. He glimpsed a woman and child among the rest as they thundered past, up the steepening slope. Earlier in the day they passed under rows of gibbeted men and women where trees overhung the road. He'd wondered in passing what their crimes had been. In the late, angled sun, their bodies had cast long shadows that swayed gigantically over the bleak, autumnal fields.

Atop the ridge of a long line of hills that curved on either side (as far as he could see) to enclose the valley country below, he reined up, shocked, staring because the sun had nothing to do with this light: what must have once been a good-sized town and sprawling castle beyond were sunk in a sea of flames. There, even at two miles' distance, he felt the heat. The air, sucked toward the center of the towering firejet, whipped the trees and long, dry grasses. The forest beyond (straight along the valley with open fields) was cut with long, blazing rivers as dry wood and leaves literally exploded and clumps of pine roared like torches. . . . The dense smoke gathered, filled, and spread out over the sky. The crackling roar broke like thunder.

As they followed the road, wincing and turning away from the furnace across the field, Lohengrin spotted a peasant woman with a young boy and girl crouching in the flame shadows behind the low, broken wall. It was poor cover, he thought, but the best in the vicinity. He pulled out of line, motioning the others on, and crossed over to them.

He sat his horse, looking down at the frightened little girl, the pale, defiant boy, and the red-and-silver-haired woman. She had a sharp nose and almost ferocious hunger in her expression, a dauntless desperation too concentrated to show fear. He could see she wouldn't die easily, and he respected that.

"What happened here?" he demanded, flipping up his visor.

"Where?" she said, watching him from hungry, shadowed eyes. She was lean and ready, he noted, hands hidden within the folds of her cloak.

She has a weapon under there, he thought.

"Was there fighting here?" he pressed her.

"I saw only one army today," she replied, "with none to oppose them."

That's true. This whole section is undefended. But why would we destroy anything here? Killing a few rabble to keep order is one thing. . . .

The children were watching the line of horsemen, dark shadows against the wall of fire in the distance, passing in single file at a steady trot.

"How did the fire start?" he wanted to know. Her eyes, he realized, never left him. He frowned, feeling vaguely uneasy, almost unsafe.

"Try your wits to guess," she couldn't help saying.

Who was the stupid general to allow this? You kept good order at least until after the battles were won. *What fool let them have their head now?*

"So," he said, mainly to himself, "the troops got out of hand."

"No," she said.

"Eh?"

"They threw everybody into the fire," the little girl suddenly said in a too-high-pitched voice. There was a scream haunting the timbre. He realized she wasn't afraid of *him*. She kept staring past even the flames and horsemen. "They threw . . ."

The woman *(mother,* he thought, *had to be)* pressed her hand to the child's lips.

"Hush," she said. "Hush," she said, watching him, just watching him.

These are our villages, he thought. *Why?*

"Did any attack the troops?" he asked, floundering for logic.

"Attack?" she returned, watching him, "As cattle attack the butcher."

The line of men was past now and receding.

"What stupidity!" he said. Well, the master would hear about this. He was supposed to join the main armies here, northwest of London, which Lohengrin had assumed was the main objective. From here and Camelot, if need be, they could establish rule over the south—that was, unless more idiots persisted in burning out the rich countryside to make the conquest worthless. . . . As he reined his charger to follow the men, he glanced, scowling, quick-eyed, back at her. "How did you survive?" he wanted to know.

Just as he was sure she wasn't going to answer, she spoke.

"Always some survive," she said. "Anything."

He started to speak, then shut his mouth. He scowled, nodded, and headed back to the road, thinking about what he'd say to Lord Clinschor later, thinking about the great plan and purpose that had changed his life, had turned a faithless adventurer into a dedicated emissary. Yes . . . but he really needed to see the master again, to clarify some things, as well as to complain. . . .

Broaditch knelt over the dark water. The moon's image shook slightly in the deep pool near the riverbank. The silver-black lacework of clouds glowed around the blotting outline of his head. He heard Valit sigh in his sleep under the overhanging willow tree.

He waited, watching under the surface. He wasn't sure anything would happen. It was an instinct, he thought, or a voice without words urging him. . . . He waited as the moon sailed in and out of the clouds and mounted higher.

He thought wonderingly for a while . . . half-dozed . . . then sat very alert, without a stir in his mind for an instant as moon and shadow formed shapes like rough-wooded and bone-bare hills; a lake; the narrow river (he was sure) right there, where it wound away from their direction. . . . He seemed to see the best approach across the plains to the almost-round mass of high country they had to penetrate. . . . He was almost certain he glimpsed that circle of brightness again that was (or shone through) a fortress, too. . . . And then he blinked himself, he thought, awake as his face touched the cold water and he grunted.

This was no dream, he told himself. He was sure of the direction now. The place was surprisingly close. And then he was frightened a little. What happened when he got there? Because whatever it was, it would be the worst and hardest thing yet. . . .

"What are you doing?" a voice asked and Broaditch started, twisted around, and recognized Valit a moment later.

"Ask your eyes," Broaditch remarked.

"Praying to the water?" Valit wondered.

"Praying for more wisdom and fewer young asses." Broaditch stood up, went and sat under the willow.

"You think me simple?" Valit wondered.

"I was studying our future. Do you believe that?"

Valit shrugged and settled himself down again.

"You are not light in wit, Broaditch," he replied. "So I'll watch and wait."

"For your profit, Valit?" Broaditch grunted.

"What better thing for man to watch and wait for?"

After a time, Broaditch cryptically remarked, "If you truly mean to be like Jews, you do better to take on their trust in heaven and dauntless spirit. For even though they be in error, yet they defy all the armies of man and time. For if they truly cared for profit alone, all would've turned Christian ere this."

There was no reply. Broaditch smiled, turning on his shoulder and wishing he could turn aside the constant fear that haunted all his waking time. *And,* he wondered, *God knows what each night's sleep may bring in these times.* . . .

Wista was riding north along the same track Lohengrin had followed several days before. Wista had been summoned and two warriors accompanied him. They were poor companions: one of the turbaned Orientals who spoke spare fragments of English, and a stocky, tough, old veteran commoner, a mounted sergeant, foul-mouthed, taciturn, and world-weary to an astonishing degree.

Wista was thinking about Frell. He'd been sorry to leave her, it turned out. She was a sweet taste, a tense, awkward, wonderful experience. . . . She gave herself so intensely in the end, and, surprisingly, with few words and long, tender, stroking hands . . . he remembered. . . .

The air was brisk. Time was crossing into winter, though it was still too warm for snow. The pale sun barely pressed through a misty sky. He noticed a castle on a nearby hilltop. He'd seen it a number of times before. It looked like an empty shell, was his first thought: gutted, blackened, walls thrown down, shattered, gaping.

"Was there a siege here?" he asked Grontler, the sergeant. "So near and yet we heard not of it?"

"Hah!" the soldier replied. "That was orders. You'll see yer fill of such sights on this road, laddie."

"Was it a battle, then?" Wista pursued.

"Hah! Not fucked much a one."

Despite Wista's efforts, the man had no more to say on the subject.

Toward noon they stopped to rest by cultivated fields marked off by low stone walls. Wista sat on the soft earth chewing a small loaf of hard bread that slipped from his bite and rolled into a furrow. He dusted it off on his sleeve, took another mouthful, then spat it out. It burned. He swigged water from his leathern gourd.

"Salt," he said, half to himself.

Grontler looked amused.

"Don't you care," he said, "for the seasoning?"

Wista was poking and digging in the crumbly soil. It glittered in his hands. The fields had been salted. Ruined. He looked up in outrage at the crafty veteran.

"More orders?" he coldly asked.

The man winked and spat out a crumb of food. The Saracen sat a little apart, eyes gleaming, inward, dour, remote.

"Well, laddie," Grontler said, "the great lords are doing the world like eating pig: after the slaughter, they salt and roast it."

Wista just looked at him with disbelief and outrage. He started to speak, then checked himself.

"You're on a fucked road, laddie," Grontler advised, "you best get used to fast and fine. You ain't in your fucked mom's bath getting in a toe at a fucked time!"

"But what sense does . . ."

"Hah!" he came in, tilting his head toward the hard-faced, fanatical-looking son of the desert. "Do yer hear him? This youngblood wants to know answers." He clucked, cocked his head to Wista. "He don't speak our talk unless anybody curses him." He nodded sagely. "Y'see?"

Wista shrugged.

"But," he whispered to himself, "why spoil all this good land? For what cause?"

"Why, the poor black bastard." Grontler indicated the Moorish-tinted fellow with an expressive drinker's eye. "He's in a worse plight than you, yourself, eh? Or me, eh? Why, he don't know the north winds in this land blow from the devil's ice asshole." He nodded, uncorking a stone jug. Wista felt the stinging aroma. Grontler sucked from the mouth and shuddered a little. "Ah," he said, wheezing, "I freed this from a fucked priest. . . ." He offered a taste to Wista, who declined. "Don't let none of this trouble you, laddie." He shook his head grimly enough. "What's the fucked point of that, I ask? Hah?" He sucked at the brew again. "None," he concluded. "We'll all be mush and muck soon enough. . . . Did y'ever see the dead in the field? Hah? With flies crawlin' and buzzin' in an' out of the fucked head? Where the eyes used to be? Hah?!" He chuckled. Wista felt uneasy. He shook his head. "Well, you will. And show me one fucked feller who don't come to that end. . . . Hah!" He corked the jug with a self-satisfied twist. "Fact is fact, like the wise wanger saith." He gestured at the Saracen again, who was on his feet, impatient to be off, it seemed. He looked, to Wista's imagination, like a brooding spirit of desolation. "What's he doing here? What's the good of it? Hah! Any fucked bastard can ask ass's questions, laddie. . . . And who cares? What fucked difference makes it if you die here or there?" He grinned and stood up, heading for the horses. "Ask the devil that while you're fucked mouth is full of air." He mounted and rubbed the animal's neck. He looked confidentially at the boy. "Did you ever prod a sheep, laddie?"

"Hmm?" Wista frowned, puzzled.

Grontler guffawed.

"Sweeter than a lass's hole." He grinned, pointed. "Bet he's done them camels in the sand, eh? Ain't you, you black sod?" The Saracen frowned, watchful of Grontler's almost-mocking manner. "Well, I knew a feller who prodded a mare. That's the devil's truth, or God's a pond frog." They were moving back on the road. The haze was bright, the day chilly. "Well, he had a dangler the size o' my arm. He stood on a stump with her all tethered fine. . . ." He shook his head. "It were just like any other thing: he rams it home, gives a joyful cry, and she shat a load down the front of the poor bastard!" His mirth shook him in the saddle. "But that's ever the way with love, ain't it, boy?" The Saracen eyed him, watchful. "What a sight!"

Wista said nothing. He stared across the faded fields that he knew now were dry and dead beyond winter's worst. Nothing green would start from that earth, no sparkle of flowers. . . . He tuned out Grontler's sounds and thought about nothing for a time as they passed through the hazy afternoon into a lingering, distant, charred smell that varied on the shifts of dampish breeze. . . .

The hazy sky seemed to have joined a strange ground fog, so that a pale, grayish whiteness gradually closed in Broaditch and Valit at the center of a blank circle. And, Broaditch noticed, it seemed to be darkening, too, as they headed more directly south, although the sun was still high and the disk visible.

Open country now: long, almost flat, stony stretches of faded grass and scrubby trees.

Good country for goats, Broaditch mused.

Valit was staring around uneasily, frowning, skeptical.

"We'll be needing them wizards and angels of yours," he remarked, unsmiling.

"Never mind that," Broaditch returned shortly. He was getting a little worried himself. This was promising to become the blindest march yet. *Sweet Christ,* his mind sighed.

"What tells you where we're going?" Valit asked. "Not that I doubt at all, holy prophet."

The holy prophet noticed a faint, disturbing smell on the southern breezes that stirred the fogs.

"You are free to go your own way at any time, lad," he pointed out.

Valit was faintly amused, it appeared. Broaditch believed he'd felt, from time to time, what in another he would have been sure was warmth.

"But I am not guided by heaven," that fellow asserted, "and this may be my sole chance while living . . . but so far," he went on to reflect, "heaven seems to have led us to the center of a fog."

"This is more common than you know," Broaditch rejoined.

But afternoon? he asked himself. *It's passing strange that these mists should swell and cling like this. . . . I swear there's smoke on the wind. . . .*

"It has stink," Valit said, "like a burned supper."

That would I deem tolerable, Broaditch mentally commented, *if so.*

"We will no doubt wander in a circle," Valit decided, straining to penetrate the curved, grayish, billowing wall that surrounded no more than fifty feet of clear field in any direction.

"Then we'll sup with Balli, mayhap," Broaditch teased. He enjoyed Valit's responses to this subject.

"You *will,* I ween," his companion hastened to say. "For I'll dine with that dungbag at his funeral feast and toast the working worms that draw him to smears and tatters."

Broaditch grinned. . . . He was just wishing his stick were an Aaron's rod to part these curtains. It definitely was darkening, he noticed: streakings of sooty browns were thickening the mix to a gritty porridge.

So, then, he said in his mind, *now you've led me here. Can I stare a view out of these cloudy shapes?*

He half-began to try, watching the folding and unfolding, the shifting outlines that imagination effortlessly filled. Too effortlessly. He glimpsed his wife's face . . . a vast, warring host . . . a beatific profile . . . a long-jawed demon . . . crumbling castles and towns turning to smoke . . . dissolving landscapes. . . . He shook his eyes free of the images, but one stuck. He blinked, but it stayed, seeming to congeal into ghostly substantiality thicker than cloud and fainter than flesh: a fairy coach drawn by godlike steeds; rounded sides like a keg; a sprightly, lean figure *(mayhap Mercury himself,* he thought, with *peaked, winged helmet . . .)* seemed to lightly cavort in the air just above the carriage, and what seemed lovely, glowing, ethereal goddesses leaned from the sides, long tresses hanging free and appearing half-mist. . . .

"Look there!" he said, pointing with the staff.

"Where?"

The wall was blank again, closed over the images which he had an idea were meant to guide him.

"Nothing," he muttered.

"What did you see?"

"Nothing. A trick of the fog . . . or eyes."

"One of your angels?" When Broaditch didn't respond, Valit said, "What point is there in going on? We might as well camp here. . . . We should never have left the road. . . . And what to eat? A rind of Balli's cheese left and half a crust. . . ."

Broaditch had veered to the left and went straight on this new course. Valit shook his head.

"This is stark mad," he declared. He stood there, but as his large companion started to dissolve into the heavy, blurring wall of smoke as (if he strode out of the world), he hastened after. . . .

Broaditch had decided to aim for where he saw the "vision." *Follow them,* he'd said to himself a moment ago, *it's as good as any other misdirection.* . . .

After an hour or so they were close to actual groping. Visibility was down to a few steps in any direction. And there was definitely a brackish smoke in the mists. It smelled, Broaditch agreed, like smoldering meat.

Suddenly he staggered, slipped, and only prevented himself from falling into a sluggishly flowing stream by sinking his stick into the goppy muck of the embankment.

"This were a good way to come," Valit allowed.

They couldn't see the other side, *if one there is, and this be not an arm of the sea.* They squatted there for a few minutes.

"I'll not be turned aside," Broaditch said and spat into the stream, which had a foul, cloying smell. "No more of that."

And, poking with his stick, he worked his way into the moderate current. Valit followed, resigned to everything.

It was fairly shallow, just over the knee as mean. The fog shut down to arm's length, but the flow itself guided them.

Valit's scream was a shock that spun Broaditch around to see the other thrashing and kicking, white-faced, terrified.

"It's got me!" he cried. "Mother save me . . . ! Mother . . . !"

And then Broaditch felt a heavy something strike him behind

the knee. He whirled and his frantic staff poked, cut, lifted free a bloated, eyeless face and crooked, frozen arm. Bodies. A riverful of bodies. Dead and immersed long enough to partly decompose. How far had they flowed with this befouled stream?

Valit was charging, thrashing past him . . . suddenly going down, tripped by another, whose arms seemed to flail and grapple. . . .

"It's safe!" Broaditch called out. "They're all dead!"

But Valit, half-swimming, half-running, had reached the far bank and was gone in the mist folds. Broaditch paused to stare as several corpses, whose age and sex was long lost to relentless process, rode steadily by. . . .

So many, he thought, *Sweet Mary, what portends this? Why so many? So many.* . . .

A dense mass like (he was thinking) jammed logs went past, slowly tumbling and spinning, forms bunched, stiffly reaching out through the vapors, as if struggling for place and advantage. . . . A limb crossed his thigh and broke away from the force of his storming past and up the far bank, where he stood looking back, wild-eyed, feeling utterly trapped in the obscurity . . .

Am I hard upon the gates of hell?

His nose itched from the smoke in the cold mist. He watched the bodies still passing, dimly, as if their numbers were inexhaustible, until he had to turn away and called after Valit, who was beyond the tight circle of his vision. . . .

The three of them had been riding all day in the bright, hazy air through the still forest. The drying leaves rattled under the horse hooves. Gawain kept sniffing the wind and frowning. Prang rode beside him and Parsival followed a little to the rear. He had barely spoken since his recovery, and Gawain was leaving him in peace.

"What troubles you?" Prang wanted to know.

"A stench of death."

"I smell nothing," Prang said, sniffing.

Gawain glanced back at Parsival, whose face was fixed on the ground.

"Parse," he called back, letting his mount slow slightly as the other looked at him, "do you smell it?"

His eye weren't quite looking at Gawain when he replied: "No—I *see* it."

And Gawain nodded, shutting his single eye, briefly in something between a wink and a prayer.

"So," he said.

"See what?" Prang demanded. He knew there was something private between the two older knights that he should understand. He felt excluded. He still wasn't totally reconciled to Parsival. . . . He also sensed something frightening and wanted reassurance that his stirring anxieties were needless. . . . "What mean you?"

"Be patient, ladling," Gawain told him. "Soon enough, I fancy, you'll discover all you need to know."

"Where do you lead us?" Parsival asked. Prang found his voice remote, austere, and, in a strange way, disinterested.

"Nowhere," was Gawain's answer. "That's up to you now."

Parsival seemed to shiver slightly. He folded his arms across his powerful chest and looked back (Prang thought) at nothing.

"To chase one shadow after another?" he asked without really asking.

Now Prang picked up the smell. *Charred meat,* he thought it to be. He squinted: vague threadings of smoke, almost too faint for sight, coiled sluggishly here and there along the leaves, fallen branches, and dead grass. . . .

"To waste the rest of my days?" Parsival was saying, sighing, almost a moan. "I cannot even have . . . even have love . . . not even that. . . ."

"Yes," Gawain said, "we are both cut off from the sweet days . . . the springtime . . . forever. . . . It's lost, my friend, lost . . . forever. . . ."

"Yes," Parsival almost moaned, "yes. . . ."

"There's smoke," Prang put in from up ahead.

"The boy," Gawain said, still staring at Parsival. "So there's no choice, anyway. There never was, for you."

"I loved her," the sad knight said hoarsely. "And it's ashes forever. I don't even weep now . . . I don't even do that. . . ."

"You don't want to hope."

"It's getting stronger," Prang called back, riding on further to investigate. Even the leafless trees were too dense here to see far.

"That is true, too," Parsival said. "I don't care to hope."

"Why live?"

"Because you pulled me from the water."

"Well, then," Gawain said, biting off the words, "go back and drown, then."

"It's not important enough." And he meant it.

A long pause.

"Then it holds," Gawain insisted. "You lead the way, because for sooth and all else we might as well *try.*" He touched Parsival's cheek at arm's length with almost a lover's gesture. "We both know what lies ahead . . . but we might as well try."

Parsival shut his eyes and sighed again.

"There must be a great fire before us!" Prang called back. He had mounted a small rise where the trees were thinned out.

"I lost it, Gawain," Parsival murmured. He looked vaguely stunned.

"We'll try, then," Gawain repeated, without even pressing now. He waited. His voice broke slightly when he spoke next, and for an instant his friend thought he might cry, though he didn't, half-whispering, "It's all we have . . . to seek it is all we have. . . ." The single eye was wild, misty, desperate. "There's too much blood flowed . . . I could sink under in the blood. . . . For what am I?" he suddenly cried. He snatched away his hood and showed in full daylight what Parsival had but dimly glimpsed two decades ago in the shadowed moonlight: the naked, raw half-face sheared from left eyebrow to point of jaw, teeth forever exposed in death's mirror grimace, the rills of scarring. . . . Parsival closed his eyes. "And you, Parsival, my friend, are cut as deep and badly. . . . So I still say: to seek the Grail is all we have!"

His friend was already nodding, not looking, although that was no entire relief because in the flesh's darkness he could see the flames like the afterglow of a light. Ever since the river he could see the flames . . . and more. . . . Gawain seemed to understand this. He grasped that his companion had changed, had been opened in some mysterious way.

Parsival felt the power flowing within him, the unfathomable strengths and tides. . . . He sensed there may never have been a choice for him, that, like Gawain, he couldn't even die because the power, like a great river, needed a channel to pour through. . . . *But,* his mind insisted, *without joy . . . I could have power over the whole world now and without joy. . . .*

"Yes," he agreed, nodding, looking at the hazy day again, letting it in. "Yes." He was feeling the strength swell and mount until he feared the flesh would burst asunder from the electric pressure, spurring his horse violently forward toward Prang on the hill. He'd seen him again, and the black nightmare shape that haunted him was seeking the same brightness, too; he realized that. He'd meet it where the brightness was. It was a race. He understood the urgency. The power had to meet the dark there. Nothing could prevent it; the power showed him that. He'd have to fight, the last fight, perhaps. . . . He'd have to fight the black, shapeless shape and fight alone. . . .

He passed Prang, thinking: *poor young lad drawn along by the flood like the rest of us.* . . . And Gawain wouldn't be there. He knew that, too . . . saw an image of everything, earth, sky, seas, all men sucked, swirled in a vast whirlpool into smoking, fuming, unguessed bottomlessness. . . . "Yes," he repeated back over his shoulder.

Wista was coughing, holding a damp rag over his nose and mouth as the smoke billowed. The horses were skittish. The wind shifted and, past Grontler's shoulder, he glimpsed a sight that left him trembling: the stream that ran alongside the road was literally choked with the dead. The water oozed and flowed and spread to work its slow way around. A few drifted slowly, rolling a few feet at a time.

"Lord Jesus!" He breathed, muffled into the cloth.

Hundreds and hundreds . . . the water running red . . . and then the smoke closed over again.

"Lord Christ Jesus . . ."

Grontler looked grim and restless. He wore his cloth knotted behind his neck.

Alienor and the children were keeping to the hills, staying above the smoke and clinging fog that poured steadily across the lowlands and collected in the valleys. She thought the whole world must be burning.

They'd met a few panicked, soot-stained folk after leaving the man with the cart when his mules collapsed in the traces. Not long after, the strange knight (she never knew he was Parsival's son) had spoken with them on the road.

She wished it might rain now that it was needed. . . . At dusk the distant flames showed at the bases of towering black clouds, the smoke settling miles away and joining the vapors of the earth.

The sun set a hideous, distorted blood-red behind the smoldering world. . . .

They'd stopped to rest on a high hill in a deserted stone-and-log church. Even this high, the air was biting and reeking.

She was startled by an apparition at the glassless window. She was seated on a bench, where the children had curled up to sleep. It was an old woman's face that was drawn and sucked inward around a toothless mouth. She had one blind, blasted, bluish-white eye and the other keen and penetrating as a cat's.

Alienor crossed herself and stood up facing the tall, arched opening. The last lurid wash of twilight seemed to float the puckered features there.

"Praying to God, dearie?" the face asked neutrally.

Alienor was relieved and chided herself for unreasoning fear.

"Resting, grandmother," she replied. "You're welcome to share it."

The toothless collapse of a mouth worked its gums.

"Time enough to rest in," it said. "Where be ye bound, dearie?"

"South."

"Ah. To London?"

"Aye."

The red-and-black duskglow deepened behind the face. A trick of shadow wiped away the good eye and left the glazed, blank one staring. Alienor wanted to terminate the conversation and lie down on the bench. Weariness was seeping into her, she vaguely thought, like water into soaking earth.

"Well," the womanface said, "the stars have promised this."

"All?" But Alienor was really too tired to care.

"And more still. . . . But there's some what know the secrets and will be safe enough, dearie."

"No doubt . . ." Her eyes felt weighted. Too many days of struggle and strain and the horrors of the way. What was this old silliness talking about? *Let her be done, in St. Hyla's name. . . .*

"Never pass up such a fine chance, dearie. For it means yer life be marked by the high stars." The head nodded and the unseeing eye seemed to wink.

"Aye," Alienor murmured. "But I must rest a little. . . ."

As she moved back to the bench, she heard the old voice telling her: "London's burned down, dearie."

She was already on her back and falling rapidly toward sleep.

The stinging smoke-reek was mixed in there with the general mustiness.

"Ye knew me not when ye saw me," the raspy voice said. And Alienor registered only the first words, and then blank blackness blotted her out entirely. . . .

A few scattered hail stones were cracking on trees, bouncing on turf, smashing on stones, and pinging off the armored riders. Out of the smoke and fireglow of that fearful evening, soot was falling in a steady rain.

Lohengrin was amazed: every wood and castle town they'd passed was ablaze or smoldering. The smoke and fog were closing in as though the whole earth were a cindering coal. . . .

He knew they were very close to the main army now. They'd passed straggling detachments on the road and at the outposts.

He kept his visor closed against the ashes. . . . As they rode, the obscure billowing gave way to brilliant, roaring flame and his eye slits framed several hundred footsoldiers and clumps of black-armored horsemen in a cordon around a collection of burning huts. He glimpsed people in there, heard rending, shuddering screams, and when soot-black, seared villagers tried to escape, they were speared or driven back into the hellish streets to roast.

Lohengrin stormed over to the officer knights who were grouped a little behind the main action, overseeing the work. He snapped his helmet open and raged at them.

"What means this?!" he cried over the flame roar and howls of agony. "Who's in command here?!"

A big, serious, long-faced fellow with a bent nose and steady eyes gazed from his own helm at Lohengrin.

"This is my command," he said laconically. "Who in hell asks?"

"Lord General Lohengrin! And I demand to know—"

The man was patient, calm, sure of himself.

"My lord," the captain said, "I have my orders."

Lohengrin noted a number of his own men had stopped on the road and were looking on.

"Have you?"

"You might do well to attend to your own business, my lord," the captain said, without pressure either way. But Lohengrin noticed he was glancing sidelong at one of the ever-silent black-and-silver knights, whom nobody (it was said) had ever seen without their grotesque visors tightly shut. There was a story they were sealed because the heads within were vacant skulls. . . .

"If we slay everyone," Lohengrin reasoned, "then whom have we conquered? If we lay waste the whole land, then what have we gained?"

The captain shrugged.

"I know not, my lord general," he said, glancing over at the elite warrior again. "But the lord master must." Was the man slightly, ever so slightly, mocking? His expression was perfectly bland.

"I doubt," Lohengrin cried, raising his voice over a sudden swelling of screams, "he countenances this . . . this utter waste! I spoke with him. . . . He'll hear what's being done in his name! I promise you that!"

As he turned to spur away, he heard the fellow's last comment: "We all do what we must, lord general."

Lohengrin gagged as a gust of hot wind brought a reek of seared flesh. . . . He galloped down the road, gesturing his lagging, uncertain men to follow on into the churning, fiery darkness ahead. . . .

The sun was just setting as Parsival and Gawain sat their mounts beside Prang on the hill's steep edge and looked out over the country ahead: a sea of flames was working its raging way from the southeast over the densely wooded landscape. The horizon was a sheer wall of blotting blackness. Heading roughly north, on both sides of the spine of range they were atop, was a hoard that seemed, to Parsival, dark, gleaming streams of ant-like demons, as if the smoke which billowed and flowed over them was part of the invasion, was given off by their burning contact with the earth. . . .

"Look," Prang said. "But look . . ."

"This pales imagination," Gawain muttered.

Parsival shut his eyes. Paused. Reopened. Before long, he was thinking, it would be the same with them either closed or staring wide. Flames. . . .

"Well," he said finally, the strength pulsing through him (and relieved, too, because now he could plunge ahead into the fire and steel). "Well, good sirs, I'll hardly need to guide your steps." He pointed northeast to an area the holocaust seemed to already half-surround. "We all seem bound the same way. . . . Ride and follow!" he yelled, suddenly aiming his charger down the long hill

spine that made a rugged high road in roughly the direction they
wanted and would give them an edge in travel time.

"Whither does he lead us?" Prang wanted to know, calling over
to Gawain as they followed.

Gawain spurred his thick-bodied horse and called back, amused
and still stunned, too, by the panorama below.

"To the end of the earth," he said. "Cannot you see that? My
lad, this is the battle to possess the fairy dream!" He barked a
laugh with almost a hint of hysteria in it. "The dream war! God
shield us!" And farther on, he said to himself, "And one I believe
in at last . . . with all my heart. . . ."

All around now, lit only by its own fitful, tortured glow, the
great cloud mounted upward . . . upward, massing like an un-
thinkable mountain range, dwarfing the world. . . .

Broaditch saw a dim, hinted outline ahead in the sluggish,
twilight smoke mist. He gripped his staff and plodded grimly on.
His heart sped when he recognized the high, strangely rounded
coach and steeds he'd seen before. Real, they were real! A mule
snorted. He rapped the wooden sides with his knuckles when he
got there. . . . Not fairy wood, this. . . .

He grinned at himself. A rough-planked traveling wagon. *For
jugglers and players.* . . .

Helmetless, Morgana was staring into the almost-impen-
etratable haze, holding her mount steady, frowning. Across the
smoke-flooded fields, her army was charging parallel to the forest
edge, ripping through the clouds into the lines of dim enemies that
had just emerged from the valley into this prepared ambush.
Modred, Gaf, and the bishop were close to her.

"We have them, lady," Sir Gaf said, following the blurry action
through his open helmet.

Modred was disturbed by her strained expression as the ghostly
seeming troops collided in a churning obscurity of shouts, screams,
and clashing steel. Horsemen were trailing billows behind, as if it
were their own cloudy substance against which the overwhelming
grinding sounds were the more terrible. . . .

"What's wrong, Aunt?" he demanded.

Her face was tensed, jaw trembling with effort as her mailed
hands clawed at the air.

"Damn him!" she gasped, leaning forward, as if straining into an invisible wall as the troops lined up in reserve to their right along the forest wall suddenly seemed to sway, then sag inward as thousands and thousands broke from the trees directly into their flank, and the men and knights began to melt away like sand figures in a foaming surf. . . .

"Aunt?" Modred yelled.

"Curse him! Curse him!" she screamed. Her red hair shook.

"Aunt, what . . ."

She stared wildly around at Gaf and the other lords.

"Bring me a head!" she shouted. "Anyone's will do . . . anyone's!"

"Aunt!"

Gaf and the bishop looked at one another.

"We're taken in flank!" the former cried. "We must—"

He reeled back (her wide eyes were seeing no one) as she drew and with terrific speed and perfect aim thrust her blade into his open visor and tilted him, howling, out of the saddle in a burst of blood and followed him to the ground, sliced his helmet loose (even as he struggled into his dying moments), and with several desperate chops hacked his head free. Gripping his dark, curly hair, she remounted and lifted it high.

"Magic for magic!" she shouted, snarling. "Magic for magic, you bastard! I'll not be beaten!"

Modred stared for a moment at the bleeding face, the shocked features, the eye that seemed still seeing (the other had been stabbed through), dimming as he watched. . . . Then, gagging, he turned his horse and fled blindly into the burning forest. . . .

His horse plunged into a sudden eddy in the charging waves of stabbing, spearing, hacking soldiers. As the smoke opened and closed, Modred saw men fleeing from one death to another: reeling from mace blows into spear thrusts; kneeling with upraised arms, begging for mercy as swords chopped them to shreds; tight clusters of desperate foot troops fighting hopelessly as wave after wave broke over them in flame and smoke and steel. . . .

His panic had him mumbling and jerking the reins like a puppet, gurgling in fear as he crashed out of a roll of smoke, choking, wheezing, blinded, into a wedge of spearmen who closed in as he flung his blade and flailed and he screamed inaudibly in the blasting of battle and fire. They hamstrung his horse in a moment, and, leaping free, he was racing, tossing his sword away, tripping, rolling, crawling, and saved for now by another black, dense cloud . . . but he heard them following and he ran and fell and ran. . . .

And he was still running, panting, scrambling along a stony gully now, his bejeweled armor baking him alive as a furnace of exploding fir trees hemmed him in to his right. Tripping on roots, slipping on stones, babbling breathlessly, he fled. . . .

Above, to his left, swarms of black-armored knights and Saracens in their flowing robes and headdresses were hunting him. . . .

The last image kept repeating in his brain: Morgan LaFay, in the flashing, darkening day, fading into blurring haze, holding the severed head aloft, steaming gore spilling down over her face, bare, uptilted to the rain of blood, rocking in steady rhythm, voice penetrating, incanting into one chilling, hypnotic, seamless flood of sound that he could hear and feel over the bray and shriek of combat and the fire's thunder. . . .

There were mounted men a turn or two behind him, crashing along the dry wash. He felt his bladder go slack and warm . . . whimpered, tried desperately to scramble up the gulley sides, failed, fell back, panting, trying to loosen his armor, searing his fingers on the steel, weeping and cursing. . . . A great torching tree dropped and sealed the way behind, cutting off pursuit and dooming him as the flames ahead leaped across this narrowing crease in the unyielding earth, and he ran berserkly in mad spirals up and down the sides, up and down, like a frantic bug trapped in a hot kettle. . . .

Broaditch sensed something moving behind him. He whirled, staff held at the ready. A lanky figure and what seemed a pair of down-turned horns emerged from the choking fogs holding what seemed a massive cudgel at his side. A few more steps and he saw him clearly: a middling young man in a fool's cap and bells, dangling a lute.

So, thought Broaditch, *so.* . . .

"You're a troop of entertainers," he said by way of greeting.

The jester's long face looked sour.

"Some of us, big man," was his answer, "but not all equally."

"Well, sir, I could stand some gambols in these times, I swear."

The jester set down his lute, leaning against the back steps of the wagon.

"I fear," he said, "you've met me at the end of my wit and gamboling." He sat down on the wagon steps. "Though I have one bit of humor left in me: the world's burning down. So it's like a suckling babe at the mother's milk-heavy breast."

"Forgive me," Broaditch said, sitting down beside the fellow on the other edge of the step, "if I contain my side-shaking merriment."

"It's a riddle."

The expressionless jester spat neatly out into the swirling clouds.

"So, then?" Broaditch rested his head on the plank door at their backs.

"Why, good sir, the world truly has what it most needs."

Broaditch smiled faintly.

"You're as hard a judge as the archangels," he told him. "But where are you bound?"

"To entertain the dead."

Broaditch guffawed and nodded.

"Why, sage?" He couldn't resist.

"Two reasons: there are more of them . . . "

"Yes?"

"And more likely to be light of heart than the living." He spat again. He never turned to look at Broaditch, who nodded grudging approval of the gloomy answer.

"Where's the rest of your troop?" he wondered.

"Within," was the reply, accented by a jerked thumb.

Broaditch heard steady, rhythmical creaking sounds, then noticed the wagon was rocking slightly. He heard a low, muffled moan. For a moment he took it for pain, then smiled and said, "Well, that's a music not made on a lute."

"That is entertainment." Deadpan.

"But not for the dead, I think."

"Aye, for the dying."

Broaditch stood up.

"Well," he announced, "I'll be off before I lose all hope. You're a jester fit for the audience you seek."

He was still not looking at Broaditch.

"How will you find your way? Now it's nightfall and all the more obscure."

The door of the wagon opened and a barefoot, rather pretty, long-haired, youngish girl wearing a parted chemise-like gown leaned there. Behind her in the darkness, the love making sounds intensified.

She hung a lit lantern on a peg beside the door and stood there. He bit his lip lightly, feeling a rush of tingling blood to his groin, looking at her smooth, bare legs, the dark blot under the long sweep of her belly, one smallish but purely rounded breast showing, inviting a bite, a lick, a caress, a pinch . . . He felt a little weak. . . . *So young and fair,* he thought several times.

Her large, dark eyes just looked at him, watchful, features expressionless so he couldn't tell anything about her feelings. She was so casually lewd *and in her middle teens at best.* . . . The jester stayed as he was, his back to her.

"That's Minra," he said. He lifted his lute and strummed the open strings, which were badly mistuned. He seemed to enjoy the twanging, because a trace of a smile creased his lips. "She entertains."

She was working her jaws slightly in a chewing motion. Then she opened her mouth and picked something from her teeth, which were unusually bad, even for those times: gapped, chipped, discolored.

The jester began to bang the strings in earnest, thumping the wood, rocking slightly. "The horrid sound smote my ears full sore," Broaditch quoted to himself.

And then, as it became virtually unbearable, the worst happened and the fellow broke into unrestrained song. "She entertains, I ween; her ways are all obscene; her twiddie's quite unclean. . . ."

And on in this charming wise, Broaditch later was to say, but he was held by the girl, whose mouth was shut again in the smoldering expressionlessness of her face and knowing eyes that went far beyond ideas of vice and hopelessness. He felt she had never imagined hope or good to begin with, so there was no pain or despair at their loss. . . . He was a little afraid, because in a terrible way she was innocent. . . . He'd never conceived of such a thing or the frightening beauty of it. He had a recurring impulse to prostrate himself before her, to embrace, devour, and worship that untouchable dark intensity . . . and another impulse in no way contradictory was to try and reach the innerness, the tender place somewhere within. . . . He never had felt such a thing, never desired before to instantly immolate himself in such gulfs of ferality. . . . He felt weak.

She rested one hand on her hip, fully opening the thin garment. There was a mild draft of warm air stirring the cloth, spilling from within. He assumed they must have hot stones in a crock inside. It was strangely painful to look up from her graceful feet along the young, round legs, dark wildness of groin, sheer sweep of open torso, graceful neck and oval, impassive, maddening face.

Not Eve, Lilith, he thought, *the dark one . . . daughter of the dark moon. . . .*

He almost wanted to say "I love you," but meaning he knew not what, dared not know what . . . and the dreadful song went on as she didn't smile even a fraction, turned gracefully, and went back in, leaving the door open as a male voice cried out in the throes of sweetest dying.

"They'll do what they must, for no man will they trust. . . ." The song broke off and the jester sat there holding the lute loosely, still staring into the fog. "There's little enough trade out in these lost parts," he said conversationally, "so you can have her for a pair of coppers."

Broaditch took a deep breath. "Ah," he said, his voice breaking. Then he grinned at himself, staring through the partly opened door. He made out a dim gleam that must have been another lantern or a candle.

"There's others, as well, traveler," the jester said, spitting again, watching the gob fly out into the shifting outskirts of the fog. "But Minra's a pearl. You can have her suck it. You can ram it in her bung or her twiddie. Why, you can do anything you please with the little whore. What's a pair of coppers to that, eh? That tasty child? Man o' your years best take his pleasures while he may." He strummed one final, cacophonous chord for emphasis. "You only taste your food in your mouth, which comes at the beginning. From then on it starts to be shit."

"Well, jester of whores," the other replied, breathing deep, resisting, even as his hand strayed to his leather pouch, where his farthings were stored, "all the more reason to eat sparingly."

The fellow laid the tortured instrument aside and stood up, stretching.

"Your young one's within," he said. And to Broaditch's interrogative frown, he explained, "He come by an hour before. Said to look out for a big, old wight."

"Old?" Broaditch couldn't help but snort.

"He said that would be if the river devils spared you, as he doubted they would. He were sore afraid when he come. But Lottali, a slave princess of the distant East, a dusky heathen bitch woman who'd suck the juice from all your fruit, old wight . . ." He grinned now, tugging and cracking the joints of his fingers. "Lottali, as you just heard, brought him to peace and calm."

Broaditch went up the steps. Well, he could have called out, but he was curious, anyway. No harm there. So he pushed inside, into a perfumed dimness. The sweetness drowned out, rather than replaced, a raw understink.

He blinked to focus. He saw heaps of silks, three dim bodies tangled in one mound, and Minra, totally nude now, was sitting across the way, chewing on what looked like a chicken wing. The round walls made him a little uneasy.

He watched Minra suck the grease from her surprisingly short fingers.

There were paintings on the walls he'd never seen the likes of: clearly foreign . . . exotically done in gold and silver, like a church mural . . . women and men wearing strange headdresses, bound up in acrobatic acts he first mistook for combats. . . . He bent closer to follow the images: women with men (*miraculously endowed,* he thought) in a wonder of possibilities . . . he had to admit in the warm globe, smelling the reek and perfume, that incredible girl a reach away, these images left him a trace giddy . . . women woven with women, which didn't so much shock as puzzle him . . . at first. . . . Well, he'd heard of such things and no doubt they went on across the water. . . . It certainly was interesting in here. . . . He moved along the walls, leaning over the three he had taken to be asleep (two women and a man), seeing what seemed gods and devils now joining in an astounding mass copulation with children and beasts thrown in; he drew away, stunned, overloaded. . . . He felt fear and excitement. The images stayed with him as he stepped back. He felt a touch on his left leg. Minra. She offered him a sweetly spiced mug of liquid. He took it, then realized he was trembling and sweating. It seemed to be brandy wine. He drank a searing gulp.

"I thank you," he said, still reviewing that final picture, still seeing it. . . .

But it's just the flesh, just the food served strange and spiced, but still only food. . . .

"Why not sit?" she offered. Her voice was neutral as her expression. He wondered if anything or any man could really

touch her heart, and then understood: *she gives herself like all do,
but gives herself somewhere else . . . to something other. . . .
Think what you like, every wight has an open place . . . even the
devil, I don't doubt. . . .*

It was very warm and he was used to the stuffy smells now. He
sat down but not too close to her.

"I might as well rest my bones," he said, not directly to her. He
felt those inscrutable eyes on him. "It's too dark to go on now."
Even if I knew the way . . . Well, he'd solve that tomorrow. . . .

"Ah," she said.

"Where did those works of art come from?" he wanted to know.

"I know not. . . . This be Flall's wagon."

"The jester?"

"Is he?"

"Well . . . what is your town, then?"

"Ah. What, indeed."

"Where be you bound?"

"Should I trouble for that?"

He looked at her, bit his lip. He'd been in the stews more than
once: to be stewed with drink, water, and women . . . but this was
different.

"Want me to undress you?" she asked. She must have sensed his
tension and conflict. "You may as well travel on with us, in any
case. Flall . . ."

"Good old Flall."

". . . says there's war and destruction everywhere."

"Then you are traveling wrong, as the smoke blows *from* the
south."

She shrugged.

"Will you undress now?" she persisted. She slipped one cool
hand under his belt and reached down across his belly.

He half-turned and set one large, hard hand on her silky
shoulder. There were faint pox scars on her cheeks, but he'd seen
far worse a thousand times. . . . She was beautiful. He ran his
unchecked hand over her body almost as if he were molding her
form, somehow in a potter's or sculptor's gesture rather than a
lecher's . . . or lover's. . . .

"Do you have money?" she asked.

He smiled. She was trying to undo the front of his baggy
trousers. He leaned back and held her hand away, looking up at
the shadowed bulge of ceiling. There was a picture there, too.

Very like a church, in its way, he thought. The images were again hard to make out, but seemed to show men and women bound in chains to various instruments of torment while other men or demons (he couldn't be entirely certain and realized a lot of this might be drawn by his imagination) seemed to burn and whip and flay them . . . seemed. . . . He squinted, but years of candle smoke had darkened it beyond certainty. Perhaps it was simply more sex, he reflected, bemused. But it surely *looked* painful. . . .

"If you cannot fuck me," she said conversationally, "I can do what might please."

"You're a child, after all," he told her, feeling deliciously sleepy and suddenly at ease.

"Ah. You want one of the older chips."

"No. They'd be just women. You see that?"

Her face remained unaffected.

"You can look at the pictures," she offered, "and do what all . . . or watch us others together. . . . It won't cost you more."

Valit had just sat up on the mounds of covers across the way. A big-breasted black woman, sporting golden rings and circlets, was draped across his lap. A red-haired or blondish, over-round young matron was soothingly rubbing the Nubian's feet.

"Broaditch?"

"The devil's spared me," he said, "but will they spare you yet?" He rubbed his eyes. "How came they to part you from a single farthing here?"

"Ah. Well, I struck a bargain—a bit of trade."

"St. Michael defend their end of it!" Broaditch laughed. "That's all I can say."

"This be rare good fortune to come upon these folk," Valit declared. "Did you fuck yet? What a rare time I had. . . . A bit of good fortune after what's been, eh?"

"Mayhap so," Broaditch murmured.

Except it may prove harder to escape from these than Balli. . . . He felt sleep starting to close over him in the stuffy warmth. . . . *Am I truly chosen for something . . . ? Is there any true proof . . . ? Or are we all sad, poor bitch and bastards . . . ? Without hope . . . aye . . . save for the pity . . . no, save for the mother that never quite dies in a woman and the father in every man and the child in all . . . there's that, there's always that, damn you . . . there's always that. . . .*

He sighed and let the darkness come sweetly washing over him.

. . . and fine pictures of saints or whores, either, won't help me . . . not a poor bastard without hope except for that glimmer of father and child. . . .

He tugged Minra's hand over to his lips and gently kissed it.

"God defend you, my child," he barely said, and was asleep.

She just looked at him, his wide, browned, and ruddy face, quick, light eyes where the smile (when open) never completely died. She watched him wordless as he began to lightly snore. And she stroked his graying hair and touched his cheek once, quite tenderly. And she sat there as Valit sank back down between the other two.

She looked now at the dusky, barbaric woman across the musky dimness. Pale Valit was pressing his face to the purple-dark breasts, but she was looking back at Minra and smiling with lidded, knowing, sleepy-seeming eyes, a smile ambiguous and profound. . . .

Wista couldn't sleep. The other two were curled up like true professionals in the shelter of a crumbling wall of what was once a rambling stone building.

The constant stinks and puffs of stinging smoke were almost too much for him, though it was less intense here than some other places they'd passed.

He was pacing along the rutted road in a light, misting drizzle that would have no effect at all on the omnipresent fires. . . . He saw how the passing army had churned the earth to half-damp porridge. . . .

Yesterday's shocks haunted him. For a time he'd feared he might go mad, but finally steadied his whirling mind. He was beginning to feel anger, not hot, but chill and deeper than his thoughts could reach. . . . The immense monstrousness of it kept looming over his intelligence: because men had different goals and crests and countrysides where they lived and a thousand senseless distinctions more that vanished like dreamstuff when they died and weren't there yet when they were born, *for these,* he thought, *these shadows, these pictures from sleep with no more to them than the raving demons of mad Jack-a-moors . . . for these the earth is being . . . is being . . .* He couldn't—wouldn't—express it. His thought broke down and he stared as he paced a nervous circle on the road under the starless sky of smoke and clouds. He kept remembering again and again the blood and the dead and the ruins and wanted to scream with disgust and outrage, and muttered, instead, "Lord God, why do you draw me to the end of this bitter road?"

And he fell upon his knees there, clasped his hands, and desperately prayed, frantic, terrified . . . for a long time. . . .

At some point he heard a moan, not far away. He fixed the direction and went a few strides from the road to where the same fouled stream Lohengrin had reacted to earlier trickled, stinking, on. He smelled death and stopped. He had no desire to view those dim forms heaped and tangled everywhere, as though the army in passing had simply churned them aside like a great, hellish plow. . . .

But someone moaned in life and so he went another few yards and asked, "Who calls?"

The answering sound was almost at his feet. He stooped and saw a naked woman lying in the bloody mud where the stream had spread out from its choked bed.

She was not altogether nude, he noticed grimly. The tatters of the nun's habit still partly clothed her. Her face shone somewhat in the wavering light from one of the many isolated fires burning themselves out in the vicinity, crackling steadily.

The spear thrust in her bosom gaped, but was caked over and barely bled. She was about to die, he realized.

He uncorked his water bag and dribbled a few drops on her chapped lips. She sighed her thanks. Her large, widened eyes stared far beyond him. He felt strangely ashamed to be seeing her body even under these conditions.

"What can I do?" he muttered distractedly. "What can I speak . . . ? What . . . ?"

"Ah . . ." she whispered with a vague fluttering of breath. "There will be . . ."

"Will be? Will be what?" He was rooted to this moment, waiting for what might be said from behind death's closing door. "What? Sister?"

" . . . rain . . ."

"Rain, sister?"

" . . . snow . . . then spring . . . the flowers . . ."

He sighed and gently stroked her face.

"Peace," he whispered.

"No . . . the flowers come again . . . always. . . ."

Then he thought she was dead. Her eyes closed.

"Peace," he repeated.

"The heart is a flower. . . ." she said and then was still. He remained there for a time. The flames crackled and the faint drizzle beaded on her face and shorn head. . . .

By the time Parsival and the other two reached the end of the miles of spur and had to descend into the smoke and fog, they'd gained considerably on the vast armies that were advancing across the flaming country.

It was a blighted, dim dawn. The clouds in the sky were indistinguishable from the masses of smoke and drizzling black rain; snowed, wet, clinging soot. The winds were steady from the south and it seemed obvious that the forest fires in the brittle leaves and resinous firs were now beyond the control and intentions of the invaders. Gawain commented that they clearly were fleeing even as they attacked.

Parsival led them on steadily north, riding hard over difficult trails and untracked forest. They broke out into fairly open country by midday and met with a party of fleeing knights, nine in all: battered, soot-stained, bloody. The leader's arm dangled loosely at his side; his steed limped. Gawain hailed them and they met on a crossroads on a rolling plain. Because of a vagary in the air currents, the fog was thinner here.

"Whose men are you?" Prang demanded.

The leader's open helmet showed a blackened face streaked with the paleness of desperate agony.

"Whose men we were," he said, his voice hoarse and strained. "We fought with Modred and Lady Morgan at Dale Creek. . . ."

One of the other knights at this point simply crashed to the ground. The others were too exhausted to react.

"Where was the rest of the alliance?" Gawain wanted to know.

"I cannot say."

"The bastards are everywhere," another broke in, a stocky warrior, red-haired, helmetless, broken spear half-clenched, pointlessly, in his fist." None could reform. . . . All were swept away. I was with the Baron Leffacs and Tundril's men. . . . We were surprised and smashed to pieces. . . ." He half-sobbed. "They burn and kill everything . . . everything, beast, fowl, or man . . . !" He snarled. "God strike them! They are from hell! Devils from hell!" He pressed his fist to his lips, trembled in the saddle, as if with fever. His armor rattled from the shaking.

"Look there," Prang said, pointing north. A single knight was coming fast through the spill of grayish smoke that flowed over the field in advance of the great, black, inexorable tide.

Other stragglers, mounted and on foot, were coming out of the wooded hills, which were blotted out almost to their peaks.

As the newcomer halted, Parsival noted his plain armor. His round shield bore a single emblem and he was astounded, recognizing it: a dove-in-flight mark of the Grail knights. He'd seen it over twenty years ago at the castle that forever after had seemed a dream. . . .

"Ride due north from here," the newcomer said through his grilled helmet. "By the lake where the forest closes in again, we're forming a defense line."

"And who will hold back the flames?" Gawain wanted to know.

"The hand of God," was the reply, "if He so wills."

The knight rode up and down, peering at the men who were streaming from the woods. Parsival could hear fragments of commands and cajolements. "Courage, men . . . not lost . . . reform . . ."

"Well, Parse?" Gawain demanded of his brooding, meditating companion, who was now squinting through the stinging haze at a low hut set among a grove of old trees. He was sure he recognized the place. "What do we do?" Gawain persisted.

"Do?" cried Prang. "I know that I stand with the rest and flee no more! I fled enough for my entire life. No more of it!" His face was flushed and determined.

Gawain started to say something to him, then shrugged.

"No doubt," he said seriously, "at this point to choose your own death is as wise a course as any else."

"It's the right direction, in any case," Parsival said, returning from his reverie.

"We throw them back into their own fires." Prang was exhorting the limp armed captain of knights. "Just so I see them roast ahead of *me*." He seemed relaxed finally, grimly chipper, Parsival noted. Well, for him, the obscurities, hints, hopes, and decisions were at an end. . . .

Gawain leaned close as they spurred their horses into the general movement.

"Do we fight or go on?" he asked Parsival, who was steering closer to the hut and the trees. Now he recognized the orchards and the back fields. The freeman and his daughter—what was her name? *Ga . . . Gay . . . ? Gai?* He couldn't get it back. He remembered her eyes: greenish-gold-brown, like the forest. . . . He'd done something wrong, that was sure, couldn't get that back, either. . . . He remembered her weeping. . . . Why was there always the weeping? Was that all eyes were made for? Yes, that was the place. He pointed.

"Long ago," he told Gawain, "I was saved there, by a man who made his living from the dead."

"Well, if he be still hale, his future's assured and his fortune's at the flood," Gawain remarked.

"He was already rich," Parsival said, "I think."

"The place looks abandoned," Gawain noted.

The door was down, the shutters open. A billy goat, chewing a tuft of something, half-emerged from the doorway and seemed to eye them shrewdly. The barn had fallen in.

I never understood what Gai . . . what she wanted. . . . Perhaps I really did, though. Mayhap it's always the same for all. . . .

"The lake," he informed Gawain, "marks a beginning of the Grail country. I fled from there to this point sick with fear and fever."

He'd wandered lost. He lived on forest roots and berries, and he's ended up sick and vomiting as he rode. He'd nearly been killed by Orlius, the vengeful husband of Jeschute—whom he'd taken for a fever vision, and then fled frightened and hopeless, and from that time he was never able again to give total trust to anything, but always held something back, something just enough to spoil his family, taint his goals, and leave him blank and feeling false in hermit's robes or whatever . . . *except*, he reminded himself, *to Unlea . . . I trusted it again. . . .* He bit his lip, uneasy. *Or did I?* He shook off the question. The power still flowed. Whether he trusted it or not, he would let it carry him on this time to the end. Like Prang and Gawain and perhaps all the rest trapped here, he no longer feared the end, because at least *that* would come, with no more dread of worse later. And it *had* come. As ever promised, it had come. . . . *The power brings no joy,* he thought again as they moved in the midst of the broken forces. Another knight with dove shield and pennant stormed importantly past. More soot was raining down. The men struggled on through the stinking smoke, alternately fading and taking firm form as the billows thinned and filled and coiled. . . .

* * *

When Alienor and the children awoke in the little church, they greeted the same brackish daylight again, worse, if anything. From the rim of the hill only the vaguest blurring suggested that any landscape existed beyond a hundred steps.

She was wondering about the old woman as she got everyone packed up with their few possessions and scraps of food, soothing Tikla's misgivings and reducing Torky's morning crankiness.

"Momma," Tikla asked, "can we go home, Momma?"

"In time, my dove," she told her. "In time."

As they were starting down the hill in what she hoped and guessed was the direction of London, someone shouted. She turned quickly, hand closing on the long dirk tucked under her shapeless leather dress.

A mounted man, she thought, who came out of the fog tall and lean. As she was about to start the children running she recognized the cart driver Lampic. He was apparently mounted on his surviving mule. He hailed her, urging the beast up on the slope.

She noted that though he was sooty, muddy, and worn, he seemed fit enough. A lean, tough one. She knew the type. He'd be stronger than would seem possible.

"I've not been so far behind as you might think, woman," he said laconically. "But you kept a smart pace."

Her eyebrows knitted slightly. His manner still bothered her. Just a little *too* familiar. Still, he'd been a help.

"We're pleased to find you living, goodman Lampic," she said.

He grinned, showing uneven teeth in his askew mouth. His eyes were dark and warm. She recalled he didn't panic. She felt a certain relief that he was back because she knew her determination might outlast her actual strength before very long.

Meanwhile, to the north (beyond the rough circle of the Grail country where the heirs of Arthur were gathering for a last stand) on the far side of those rugged hills (blocked valleys intercut with fordless streams, whose tortuous paths were now jammed by groups of warriors behind felled trees) the lee side, as the river of smoke broke over it and spread there, her husband was awake, too, in that windowless wagon rolling blindly on into the desolation she was struggling to escape.

Valit was half-dressed as Broaditch stood by the door swaying with the bumps and tilts of the springless vehicle.

"You're a moon brain," Valit told him, pointing at the nude women sleeping in the lantern's flicker glow. The heavy woman was snoring beside the voluptuous Moor, who was half-wrapped in a silken sheet. "I thought of this before, in London. A man's fortune might be made in this trade. And it might easily be improved in a dozen ways."

"Well, Valit, my lad, why share this with me?" the other said, cracking the curved door and letting in a chilly draft and blurred, bleak light. He noted the murals were discolored and peeling away in spots. Minra was sitting up in the shaft of harsh daylight, blinking. Her eyes were swollen, mouth staying parted as she breathed. Her lips were chapped and dry. *Her dreams don't rest her,* he thought. She silently watched them. Valit finished dressing. He leaned down to murmur something to the heavyset woman. Then he twisted his face around to Broaditch.

"Isn't it softer to bed in hay here," he reasoned, "than wander to nowhere?"

"Stay and enjoy yourself, lad." Broaditch opened the door and poised on the steps. He called around to the driver. "You . . . you, Flell!" He craned around the side and saw the cap and bells as the jester, with an unreacting, yet voracious, expression, peered back at him. "Rein up, will you?"

"You've had enough?" Flell yelled back, fog streaming around him, as if he smoldered.

"I'm bound a different way."

"How can you tell in this weather?" He gestured around at the stained vapors.

Broaditch smiled with mild sarcasm.

"I steer from a cloud of smoke by day," he called out, "and a pillar of fire by night."

"And how d'you mark the cloud in this?" Flell pressured.

"That's the full miracle of it."

The wagon halted and the big pilgrim got down. He waved once as Minra came to the door and stood beside Valit, who hesitated as it started up again. When it was vanishing into the obscurity, he cursed and leaped down with a gunny sack over his shoulder and, to Broaditch's wonder, was followed by the flaxen-copper-haired, round, and round-faced woman.

He waited for them as the wagon went on, its curved shape giving the impression that it simply rolled away, wheelless.

Valit looked, Broaditch thought, moderately pleased with himself.

"Has this maid captured your heart?" the older man asked, deadpan.

Valit shrugged.

"This be Irmree," he explained. "She's from the German wilds." He raised his eyebrows, furrowed his forehead. "Cay-am of Camelot said me sooth: 'Better to own a spraddled mule yourself than hold the reins for a knight's stallion.' "

Broaditch began walking, shaking his head.

"So you've begun to make your fortune at last," he commented, amused and amazed.

"It takes but a single hen to begin a flock."

"If the rooster's handy." He rubbed his beard. "And in her case . . ."—he looked the ample lady over—" . . . you start with a pair already. . . ."

As they marched on into the fog, Irmree said, "Irmree." She giggled and touched her expanse of bosom, which quivered and rolled from the impact to a disturbing degree. "Irmree," she repeated, then smacked Broaditch's behind with (he thought) a blacksmith's vigor, giggling again.

"What amuses you?" he asked, wincing.

"Irmree," she informed him, and he let the subject pass. . . .

Lohengrin reached the crest of a long, rock-edged hillside that steeply leaped out of the clouded forest lowlands. He was directed to the circular, crumbled ruin of an ancient, hollowed-out fortress without a single section intact.

He sent his horseguard and captains to join the main body, which was here dimly visible moving out over a wide front through the thinning forest. The word was that the enemies were near. . . . Everywhere tents were being struck; battle groups forming up; men at arms raging commands clarified by complex curses and extraordinary maledictions; men relieving their bowels and bladders or stuffing in last bites of bread and meat; falling and being driven into line; messengers galloping across the grain of march, voices dinning, rattle, clang, slog, crunch, brisk whinnies as the vast masses moved forward like a tide into the fluctuating, ghostly curtains. . . .

Within the shattered ring of rough-hewn stones and bricks, he found a single set of steps leading down into the basements and lower levels. As he crossed the weed-overgrown interior courtyard with furious strides, he met the flabby-faced, fat, hook-nosed Baron Lord General Sir Howtlande of Bavaria, commander of cavalry army "Fang," just emerging from below. Lohengrin knew he was jealous of his own rapid rise, but they were civil to one another.

Howtlande smiled widely and raised a meaty fist to the shoulder in salute.

"Greetings at the hour of triumph," he boomed, eyes like shrewd, black, humorless pits, "Sir Lohengrin, Your Grace."

"Yes," was the controlled answer. "Is the lord master here?"

Howtlande nodded, looking faintly uneasy and even more faintly, almost, contemptuous.

"He's eating iron today," he said in a low tone, "and shitting flame."

"Mayhap he'll share my anger, as well."

Howtlande hazarded an uncertain smile. He glanced around the broken walls. The air was somewhat clearer up here, though all views were a seamless blur at any distance. Messengers and nobles hurried up and down the stairs and crisscrossed across the hilltop. . . . Somewhere out of sight there was a continuous pounding of steel on steel as armorers and blacksmiths worked as though (he thought) they were literally hammering the world into a new shape. . . .

"No one can share his anger," the corpulent commander assured him. "Impossible. I would tread quietly around him today." He smiled, bluff, except for the unchanging dark eyes.

Lohengrin tapped his foot.

"He's down below?" he wanted confirmed.

"Hmm. If he comes out at all, it's mainly at nightfall. He rides the pumpkin."

"What?"

"Ah. You'll see it before long." He leaned closer with the air of confiding a great secret. Lohengrin realized the man couldn't resist gossip, even if it endangered him at times. "He's no lover of day, not him. Why, they call him the 'bat.'"

"Who does?"

The round lord shrugged.

"It's an expression heard," he said.

"Do you believe in what he's doing?" Lohengrin suddenly demanded and watched the flabby face grow stern and dedicated. If it was acting, it was very effective and would account for the high position this man held; Lohengrin knew his martial prowess was not considered awe-inspiring.

"Naturally," Howtlande declared firmly. "He is the greatest man in the world . . . as he has said himself." No flicker of expression suggested anything one way or the other about his remarks. No great leader, Lohengrin accepted, could fail to have a few questionable advisors and instruments. . . . Men like this probably accounted for the blunders he'd witnessed along the way. . . .

Lohengrin nodded and headed for the steps. Howtlande followed for a few strides.

"Have you news?" he asked.

"Why is he angry?"

"Why *isn't* he?" A shrug. "Short supplies, objectives not taken . . . he expects perfection." He nodded, frowning. "Also, he doesn't like the smoke." He tapped his chest, indenting the flesh under the gold-brocaded silks. "Lungs. Sometimes it makes him retch."

Howtlande stopped at the head of the stairs as the other lord general descended.

"These are great days," he called after him.

The smoke had diminished somewhat and the mists thinned toward midday. The sky remained stained almost black. Wista thought (in the brief glimpses he had) that it was worse in the rounded mountains to their right. He had seen flickers of flame crawling at the churning cloud bases there.

They were crossing a cindered field, through twisted, burned-out trees. The horse hooves stirred up choking black powder. "We all look like bloody Moors now," Grontler had remarked, trying, ineffectually, to wipe away some of the charcoal dust from himself.

"We're fucked close," Grontler announced. "The ground is still stove-hot."

Wista paid no attention. He had nothing to say. He rode like a doomed man. Miles and miles of charred death and these were minor, outlying blazes. . . .

They passed a line of blackened foundations still smoking. He didn't quite look at the burned stick skeletons that lay broken on the scorched stones. He didn't have to look. He was overloaded. He needed no more sights or sounds . . . nothing. . . . He refused even to think, just rode on and on and on, aware (as if awareness weren't within him, but rather waiting at some juncture of his fate) that his moment was coming, aware that the unbearable immensity (that had overcome him beside the dying nun) would find an outlet through him like a pinhole in a dam that would drip, spatter, spray, and finally explode, bringing the whole mass down in a flood of pressure and stone. . . . All he had to do was wait; and thinking or showing any reaction in the face of all this would be impertinence. . . . Wait. . . . He would come to Lohengrin in time. Lohengrin had seen to that. Had insisted on it . . . ! Yes . . . that was somehow important, too . . . he had insisted. . . .

They rode on, horselegs spuming the pitch dust as sledders sprayed snow. . . .

Broaditch was afraid. They'd reached the foothills of the tangled, dense country he'd seen in his dreams or visions. It was just as pictured. His flesh tingled because this was the first nearly absolute proof. This cut him off from past certainties, even of hopelessness. There were laws, tides of time, and the world was a dreaming, a fabric woven and unstitched each sleep. He felt himself sweating in the chill as he accepted these things. . . . What, then, was solid when the dreamer dreamed himself, too . . . ? He took a shaky, deep breath as he recognized the waterfall spilling down the damp, dark cliff; recognized the massed pines that showed no ground, the dim outline of the general shape of this whole area, which resembled a giant mound raised by titan gardeners and set on the rolling plains. He'd never seen country quite like this in Britain. It rose before them, a seemingly impenetrable mass of rock and crosscut channels of rapid water and enknotted trees. It was harder to enter here than a fortress because there was no simple wall to scale, but an entire fractured, uneven, twisted, blocked landscape. . . .

The dreams flashed back on him: he'd floated in the glowing air above the pulsing, shining heart of this country. For the first time he felt anxious to get in there because (though his legs were actually shaking) he now believed there was a *meaning* to it. . . . He watched the mists and smoke shift the outlines, hint and cover. . . . He was afraid, yes, but the thought of going back was unbearably flat and stale. . . . There was a meaning, he was going to meet something . . . something, he suddenly thought, from the space between sleep and waking, something from neither world, and as his imagination tried to give it form (and failed to do more than stir vast, cavernous fears and draw immense, gaping faces that were not faces), he pushed himself forward a step, a single step. . . .

"So now we'll have to trek around," Valit was complaining. "A fine lodestone you are, Broaditch."

Irmree was sitting down, a thing she frequently did. She was panting faintly through parted lips.

"How can we profit by what we now have in this miserable wilderness?" Valit asked the air.

"We?" Broaditch commented. "You, lad, are welcome to all you gain thereby. Spare me a whoremaster's offices."

"What matter?" Valit shrugged. "Just words. Say I'm a Jew or a Moor, too, or a condemned Italian, and I care not so there be coin in my purse."

"In any case, get your fortune back in tow, for our way leads straight on."

Valit shook his head and spat.

"Turn me into a crow," he recommended, "and I quibble not but follow straight. . . . Or call upon your wizards and angels if you must."

"Neither pimp nor wizard," said Broaditch, starting to march, digging in his staff to additionally support his still shaky legs, wild salt-and-pepper beard riffling in the uneven breezes. "I go on."

He couldn't explain, he simply knew he now had to have the courage not to think or ask or fret or hesitate . . . above all, he had no doubt it would work. Nature had constantly been instructing him in his. Now would come the test of all those lessons, because if life had no inner intelligence, then dreams were broken, mad fragments of waking's senseless accidents. . . .

So he knew it would all be like leaping into the sea again, into the claws and fangs of those slashing reefs . . . he had to leap . . . as he'd been taught.

He didn't have to look back to see Valit hesitate, then follow.

That didn't matter, either. He had a strange impression that something somehow watching him was relieved and pleased; but that might have been a level of himself, as much as anything outside. He wondered if there was ever anything outside. . . . He knew, setting his feet on the first steep tier of heaped sharp stone, glancing up at the blackening folds of smoke breaking over the obscure hilltop, he knew that death waited at the end of this road.

Lohengrin tried to keep his outrage firm as he stormed down several levels of stairs, passing a pair of the black-armored mutes at every new turn. His hands were sweaty. It was dim and dank down here, and for all his confidence and the power his promotion had conferred, he felt flimsy, vulnerable. And he'd never actually seen Clinschor face to face. He wondered if lord master held these conferences through an eye hole in the wall. . . .

He was admitted through an iron gate into a perfumed dankness (*he chooses to live in dungeons*) and his first impressions: a long stone table supporting three tree-trunk-sized candles with incongruously tiny wicks that faintly gleamed on several lords. He recognized the powerful Lord Gobble (a short, bent man with a stiffened leg), but he stared past him, focusing on the middle-sized figure at the far end of the table, a hunched-over, large-headed, soft-featured man of more than middle age with two almost absurdly upcurling moustaches. His violently outstretched finger was pointing at a dim map on the table. All the others were bent forward, obviously straining to follow his point. Lohengrin wondered how they could see in the feeble light. He couldn't believe this was the terrible Clinschor himself, the terror of nations and kings, the afflicted master wizard who penetrated beyond life and death, the irresistible voice. . . . Then the eyes flared briefly, taking him in mid-rumbling speech. They struck Lohengrin as vacant, feline, depressed, and suited to the massive voice that was still saying: ". . . with this map the gates of the final stronghold are open. The three routes, the only three known, untangle the maze. Our armies break the last resistance." He slammed the fist of one large pale, restless hand into the soft palm of the other. Then the finger darted. "Then march here . . . here . . . and here . . . and they are trapped in the center . . . the fortress is ours!" The smoldering eyes flashed along the two lines of commanders. "No more error!" he boomed. "No more incompetence! Tomorrow

will be hailed as historically the greatest day of all time. Heroes
have returned from the past to shake the world again, to bring
determination and wisdom to a hopeless, cowardly world, to bring
fire from heaven. . . ." Here he clenched his fist before him, eyes
staring beyond them all, Lohengrin believed, into unguessed
reaches and depths. The man held the room spellbound as titanic
energy suddenly filled the stooped, unimpressive figure until he
seemed a giant. Lohengrin felt he could lose himself in those eyes,
as in staring into a starry night. As a boy he would stand on the
battlements and watch the bright rust-red speck of the planet he
didn't yet know was Mars, stare and wonder at what he imagined
was the eye of the night, a hole in heaven behind which fire
burned. More than the Moon or Venus, he'd been fascinated by
the red, burning gaze of it. . . .

". . . to bring flame and steel and strength so the giants from the
ancient past may return. . . . This is an awakening! The secret
fortress will fall, the Grail will fall, and all else will follow. . . .
Great powers from beyond this earth . . ."—some of the listen-
ers, Lohengrin noted with contempt, were obviously frightened—". . . great powers will return and God help. . . "
—both clenched fists were raised to shoulder level—". . .
God help the weak, quivering sheep who'll not stand up and be a
giant!"

His commanders roared agreement. And in the subsequent
shock of silence, Lohengrin (standing at the opposite table end
from Clinschor) spoke: "Lord master," he hesitated.

Everyone looked at him. Clinschor said nothing, simply inclin-
ing his head, giving tacit permission to go on, but offering no
warmth or support.

Rather than let the silence continue, Lohengrin plunged: "You
spoke movingly of the new world we're creating." Clinschor gave
another single nod, waited. "I believe in this. I am completely
committed."

One of Clinschor's large, pasty hands began tapping its long,
soft, thick fingers on the tabletop, rattling the map. The weak light
brought out the angular bone structure under the soft face flesh
and the deep hollows under the eyes. Lohengrin felt sweat on the
back of his palms. He couldn't explain it. He kept telling himself to
hold firm; this was a great man, yes, but still a man. . . . Even
wizards (if there really were such) were men. . . .

"Yes, Lord Commander?" Clinschor said, harsh, but even in tone.

"Who has permitted the burning and the total devastation I saw?" Lohengrin asked. "I believe you should hear what is being done in your name, Master."

The warlord nodded violently, jerking his neck.

"Yes," he rumbled, "the fire should not have been allowed to spread to the woods so soon. This was an idiotic blunder and threatens our flank!" Lord Gobble looked uncomfortable. "Still, Commander Lohengrin, my revised plans take this into account. We'll be through the dense country and into the open lands beyond before the flames are a serious problem. Now . . ."

"But, my lord," Lohengrin insisted, "the country is being utterly ravaged . . . destroyed. I—"

"On what do you base your objections?" the master coldly asked.

"Why waste the whole country?" Lohengrin felt the sweat trickle around the neck of his undergarment. "What will be left to rule, to—"

Clinschor's expression brought him to silence. His hands had just jerked into fists.

"Are you all fools?" he said looking at the low, soot-stained ceiling in exasperation.

"God!" He shook his head theatrically. "Must I have only fools around me, Duke?" he snapped at Lohengrin.

"I . . . do not—"

"Naturally." The comment was a palpable force. Lohengrin was positive he had just flushed, cheeks and ears. Clinschor leaned forward, his fists supporting his weight on the table. A massive candle with a tiny flame was nearly under this jutting chin. "This country must be sacrificed," he said, suddenly conversational, tutorial. "It is absolutely necessary and is my unalterable decision. This will be a lesson the rest of the world will never forget. With *it* in my hands, we will take care of the rest of the world. . . ." He smiled absently. "We must have very few people in this world," he murmured, "only the strongest." His eyes blazed again and Lohengrin swayed slightly on his feet in the quiet, concentrated blasts. "The world is filled with cowards, fools" He waved his hand, as if to brush them all aside with the gesture, which rocked the little flame and made the shadows in his face seem to live, swell. . . . "This has never been done. The Romans tried . . . the

Spartans. But you know nothing of this, Briton." He banged his fist on the stone. "A nation, a race, of giants! You see? You understand?" He smiled thinly, palely, straightening up, adjusting his dull gray cloak. "This will be the greatest thing ever done! The old vital powers will return. This is the mystery you cannot grasp." His hand flew before his face and began to sculpt the shadowy air, as if he held a living form there, caressing, shaping, cutting, pressing. . . . "*We* create! *We* mold! *We* build!"

Lohengrin found himself nodding, eyes misted over with unfathomable emotion. He felt suddenly flooded. This man had shown him the gates between two worlds. This man stood there open to both, and he could feel the vast forces gathering behind him, this man who had created the vastest army in the world and would soon win it all and had a plan beyond that, and another beyond the next. . . .

"Yes," Lohengrin heard his own voice saying, "yes, lord master." He thought he saw the coming world, the sweep of it, the joy of it, felt himself riding a shining crest, victorious, saw his father in a crowd, watching him pass at the head of his triumphant forces. . . .

BOOK

IV

THEY were cutting straight across the winds direction, Alienor gripping Tikla's little hand, Lampic, the lanky peasant, helping support Torkey's desperate steps.

They could hear the oncoming roar of the fire storm. The violent, twisting wind whipped not just smoke, but stinging, choking clouds of ashes into them. Eyes shut, they groped, staggered, fell, suffocating under the linen they'd wrapped over their faces. They were all effectively blind.

They'd entered a little valley in an effort to reach the clearer country visible from the previous hilltop. A sucking draft caught them. The flames did not progress evenly, although it seemed so from a distance; while the fire lapped over slopes, it raced through narrow channels like this . . . and they were caught.

The hot, clinging soot raged over them. Everything was blackness. She could hear the fire: a mounting roar of exploding trees. . . . Waves of furious heat beat at them and she knew it was hopeless even as she swept Tikla up into her arms with a mad idea that she could lie on the child and protect her. Her fear of dying had somehow gone to the little girl, so that if Tikla lived, then she lived. . . . This was the only thing real in the nightmare of unbearable furnace heat. . . . *Oh, the fools,* she thought, *the fools . . . the fools . . . fools.* . . . The fires leaped all around (she was screaming as she choked now). Their clothes flamed. . . .

"Help them!" she howled. "Help them!"

And she dove forward, pressing Tikla under herself in a last, futile act of prayer. . . .

The cat flopped on its side, purring, reveling on the deep, soft black and ruby fur rug. It squeezed its reddish eyes shut with pleasure as its master, on all fours in the dimly candlelit room, reached out a fresh braised bit of meat to its nose. The eyes opened and the rounded, speckled gray began to delicately lick the fats, red tongue lashing roughly over the flesh before the spotless-white teeth began to nibble with little head tosses. . . .

"Is it good, Itie? Hmm?" Clinschor cooed. "You like these little treats, hmm, Itie?" He beamed and gently stroked the long back and trim belly. The cat stretched and purred steadily. "You wicked cat . . . yes . . . yes . . . you know you're wicked . . . yes. . . ."

After a while he stood up alone in the dim room. He stood by the massive fireplace. A roast was cooking over a low flame. A little smoke moved back into the chamber and he wrinkled his nose. He locked his arms behind his back and rocked on his heels. His gray, unadorned robes gave a vaguely monkish quality.

The watching cat squeezed its eyes in a blink, then stared away, ears cocking after some shadow of a sound.

He was frowning as he walked, shoulders hunched.

"Tomorrow, Itie," he said suddenly, looking at the cat, which had just closed both eyes, settling onto its forepaws to doze, "tomorrow is the day. . . . I have suffered, Itie, suffered and waited for years for this. . . ." He grimly nodded again. "But my faith never wavered, not one time . . . well, not in any serious sense. . . ." He nodded again. "What a strain it is, Itie, what a strain to hold all these fools together." He sighed and shook his head. "I have to stir them and convince them over and over . . . and over. . . ." He stood perfectly still now, face slightly relaxed, as if he'd lost consciousness briefly of the invisible audience that watched him even in his most intimate moments. He always felt watched. "Itie, there are times when, like Jonah, I want to flee my destiny, hide myself, live in the countryside in quiet peace." He smiled vaguely. "Would you like that, my precious, wicked Itie?" He stooped beside the cat, which, unmoving, received this tender message. He looked fondly at the poised and indifferent creature. "You and I, eh, Itie? No more of this life for which I gain only resentment, disloyalty, stupidity, cowardice. . . ." He was now staring into the trembling flame that flared as the meat dripped. "Treachery. . . ." He sighed. "But I am called . . . I must answer. . . ." He lightly stroked the cat's head. "Poor Itie . . . Poor Clinschor. . . ." His eyes were moist. "What do they care for all my sacrifices, what I have given them?" A single tear broke free and traced an erratic, glistening course down his cheek. "I have given everything . . . everything . . . I must remain hard and alone. . . ." The overlarge pale fingers rested on Itie's neck now, which it twisted irritably free. "Ah," he said in mock pain, "so even you spurn poor Clinschor." But the creature bore his next touch. "Ah, my sweet Itie. . . ." He stared into the flames, stared as if he expected to see something take form, something answer the deepest question that he never asked. "My sweet, precious, Itie. . . ."

Gawain stood beside Parsival, facing the rolling smoke that poured endlessly across the field. He thought it was probably morning, as there was a vague suggestion of light.

For a few yards on either side, mounted and foot armies were visible ranging in a thin line with the dense mass of the Grail woods at their back.

Parsival had been standing motionless, eyes shut, as if listening for some time now. Gawain quipped to himself that shut eyes see as well as open ones here. Then Parsival stirred.

"I fear," he said, "the fire's closing us in."

"But then it needs must have overcome the enemy," his friend pointed out.

"No, Gawain," Parsival said, watching the scattered unarmored skirmishers on foot with crossbows. They were to act as spotters and fall back quickly to the main line. "If we fail here, we leave it." He was grim. "We cannot afford to die yet."

Gawain considered this.

"*You* cannot," he said.

"So you mean to give up? Listen, who's to say I'll be the one to find that place again?"

Gawain stared across the billowing field. It wasn't a question of giving up. He felt at ease for the first time in years. Whatever happened he was going to accept himself. He was going to do the best he could with all he had. There was no more necessary or possible. . . .

"I doubt well," he said, "it was ever meant to be me."

Whatever it is I thought I knew once, Parsival was thinking, *and thought I didn't know, too . . . I've been given this strength for something . . . what? Do I care? All I've become is an endless questioning, spinning like a leaf. . . .*

Unlea seemed far, far away, as if a fog of years blurred between them. . . . He found her face hard to picture. . . .

The Grail, the Grail, he thought, *they won't let me ride away from it! No . . . it won't let me . . . it . . .*

"Here we are," Gawain said tensely, snapping his helmet shut with a clang. He hefted his lance, then dropped it aside. "No sense in charging and having to fight going both ways."

Parsival watched the army emerge. The advance men were too close and the enemy was coming too fast out of the blurring, stinging clouds. Only a few were able to get off a shot before javelins, clubs, and thrown axes cut them down. Only a handful made it back to the main body ahead of the compact mass of blackened men who at first seemed condensations of the vaporous soot.

Parsival glanced down the line and saw everyone on both sides was as black as cooking kettles. He recalled his first battle, where he couldn't tell friend from foe and had ridden away in disgust. He shook his head, drawing his sword. It became all too easy after a while. . . .

The shock columns were closing fast, their screaming cheers rolling ahead, and he knew the cavalry was likely massing on their flanks. The problem was the flanks were invisible.

His body tensed and skin prickled as the clashing, roaring lines collided. He caught a glimpse of Prang meeting the first shock with lowered lance, transfixing a footsoldier and surrounded a moment later by a welter of stabbing, hacking, heaving troops. . . .

This was the easy part, Parsival thought, after all, working his mount into a side chopping war dance, sword motionless before him after each incredible slash, not having to even casually raise his shield as he almost effortlessly cleared a space on three sides of himself, men toppling, dropping, desperately ducking away. Likewise with Gawain, who, with slightly more strain and twisting, accomplished the same end.

Parsival tried to see Prang again (a little concerned) and watched the line sag away on both sides of himself and Gawain . . . then a swift charge by a cluster of Grail knights, dove banners flying, momentarily sealed the breach . . . withdrew a little, lashed out again, again, in the continuous din and writhing, choking, streaming confusion. . . . Coherence wasn't gone because, Parsival commented to himself, under these conditions it could never have existed. He already knew he'd have to fall back: through the smoking fury to his right he saw a wall of knights hacking through the flimsy line and carrying their charge into the outskirts of the rocky, steeply rising, nearly impenetrable ground at their backs.

It's over already, Parsival thought, and shouted to his partner and then, as the foot troops surrounded him once more, and he plied his terrible sword, he felt a numbing blow strike his chest and stomach, though no weapon had touched him. . . . He missed a stroke, reeling in the saddle, breaking into a chilling sweat, fighting back, felt what seemed invisible claws tearing at his heart, ripping into his chest, stifling his breath, jamming his blood, fading, fainting he fought, a spear thrust glancing off his side, a sword chopping his mailed thigh. . . . He started to whirl inwardly, dizzyingly . . . blacking out, almost . . . almost, struggled, concentrated, gathered his will (as he'd learned), began a kind of mental war chant, faster, faster, building a head of resistant energy that suddenly exploded out and blew the unseen claws away (though at the edge of the black gaps torn in his sight he almost saw red-tipped, glittering, blurring talons slashing and tearing, reaching from the billowing smoke) with a violent cry, a boom that seemed to blast *through,* not *from,* his lungs and throat. It startled Gawain, who saw the six or seven men closing in suddenly stagger as one, some flopping flat on their backs, as if the sheer sound had pounded like a giant's mace . . . and then the pair of them were riding back, breaking contact, turning into the dense woods as the endless lines and columns of soldiers flooded out of the boiling, clashing clouds. . . .

Just in the treeline now, survivors already struggling through the tangles, Gawain beside him, Parsival hoped to cross one of the twisting paths that would at least let them gain some space and time for a few breaths . . . and to hunt for a break in what he remembered were tiers and levels of tangled lanes and impassable natural barriers.

Except the flanking knights who'd shattered their right side had already blocked them off.

"We have to cut through!" he shouted to Gawain, who nodded.

The impossible terrain worked against the enemy. They could not concentrate an attack, so they all came together, moving slowly, fighting more to advance than score with blows, chopping, hacking, splintering branches, tangling lance and mace: a tall knight whirled an ax stroke at Parsival, who leaned slightly away, and the blow chugged into a tree and stuck. He didn't bother to return the compliment, just blocking and ducking, keeping his nervous horse moving through the frustrated, struggling mass of fighters. . . . Another charged him and then the horse jammed between two trees. . . . Another backed away from a thrust by Gawain and was unseated by a heavy limb. . . . Smoke cut the battle into ghostly fragments . . . a man riding headless . . . a horse dancing on another . . . a bodiless arm swinging, clutching a branch . . . two knights wrestling in the blood-dewed brambles . . . men climbing over one another, the ones underneath creating a bridgeway over the prickly tangles, screaming . . . men climbing trees to escape the press, others stabbing at them, as if cutting down fruit. . . .

Parsival kept a wall of resistance up to fend off another invisible attack. He assumed he'd been singled out, apparently by whomever or whatever had stayed after him all this time. Merlinus had told him, and he remembered it now: once open to the wizard's world, you were never safe again.

They were just breaking free, moving steadily to higher ground, riding and chopping down saplings and dead wood, when glancing back through a sudden parting of the smoke he saw a long view of the field to the forest beyond, where the great army was still pouring out. The wall of flames was now towering over them, seeming to claw at them with hands of wind. . . .

They aren't attacking, they're fleeing, he thought.

Then he flipped his shield up without knowing why and caught, without seeing it, a blow from the side that numbed his arm and rocked him in the saddle.

The smoke closed in again. Everyone was choking now and the attacking mass and scattered defenders crawled, ran, staggered, climbed into the maze of woods. Sparks were streaking through the clouds overhead and dropping all around.

Once ignited, Parsival realized, this country would go up like a waxed torch. It was better not to consider the prospect. All this happened at the same moment he turned to confront the author of that terrific blow. Gawain was just striking in front of him. Parsival recognized Lancelot, stocky, splashed with mud, blood, and soot, jointed helmet flung wide.

"We meet again!" he crowed.

Sooner than mere chance would allow, Parsival thought. *These events seem designed.* The insight stunned him; he sensed something close to him like a wordless voice, substanceless form, movement. . . .

The hot fog and stinging smoke boiled everywhere now. Breathing was largely coughing and wheezing. Horsemen and footsoldiers loomed and struck blindly at each other. Eyes streamed tears, as if friend and foe were touched alike. The fighting was resolving into a general flight. Parsival glimpsed fire starting ahead of him now; Lancelot was unimpressed.

"Come, Parsival-Bird-Head," he roared over the mad din. Chopped one of his terrific short strokes, which Parsival blocked again, loosing a slice of shield.

Gawain crossed between them out of a blinding swirl of flame and fumes.

"Ride, Parse!" he yelled. "I'll hold this lump-wit off!"

"Who's this?" Lancelot demanded, waving a hand in front of his eyes in an effort to see clearly.

"You sack of shit!" Gawain announced. "Remember me?"

"Gawain," the massively squat knight responded, "so you live. Well, I never liked you and your smart mouth. I used to tell the great king you were wretched, and don't imagine he did not agree!"

"Be fucked, you dog mess!" Gawain yelled with a sneering laugh. "You're too short to live!" And he swept in at the other, hiding his sword behind his shield, then violently lunging into and under Lancelot's savage downcut. Lancelot twisted away, hurt in the lightly protected space under the armpit (Parsival saw the flash of sparks and blood), and Gawain reeled wide, helmet split, but head intact.

What matter, Parsival thought, *reach the Grail or no, I'm trapped . . . we're all trapped . . .*

He spurred forward to join Gawain, who'd closed with Lancelot again, crashing through the smoldering brambles. The horses were wild with fear. Parsival saw Lancelot score, then Gawain. Then a stream of flame cut him off from them as he heard someone shouting a curse. . . . Now swarms of men (he first took them for spirits of the dead, on foot, weaponless, blackened, eyes rolling, wild and white) swept around him like a mounting sea: falling, rolling, falling, crawling, giving one sustained sound, as if a single monstrous beast were howling in pain, a sound that seemed the tormented outpouring of all the wracked, bleeding earth. . . . Incredibly, Parsival and his horse were partly lifted and carried on up through the flaming and blinding smoke, the smaller trees bending and snapping in this titanic human flood. . . . He could see nothing now. He heard the blaze fluttering and exploding behind and advancing on the sides in cyclonic fire-storm wind that veered madly. . . . Sparks arched out of the billows, rebounded from his armor, streaked down into the tidal mass of maddened troops. . . .

So there's no choice again, he thought, struggling to keep his charger upright as it slipped and stumbled over the soldiers trampled under as those behind clambered over the heads in front. He was almost thankful for the smoke obscuring the scale of all this. *And is there ever a choice? And does it matter?* He grunted, yanking the reins, balancing, standing in the saddle. He felt that mysterious movement again, somehow a soothing, though unimaginable, touch . . . felt (as the searing winds whipped, hot ashes rained, flames lashed, and the hosts became one bellowing voice of pain and terror) at ease, felt carried safely along, felt he could save himself, store his still-gathering power for the destination that the mass of all the world seemed lifting and bearing him onto.

Broaditch led them into the vapors, up the tangled slopes and cuts. He couldn't walk thirty feet in any direction without running into a netted thicket or gully or wall of massed trees. . . . Valit and the woman were panting in his wake. He felt free and light, partly because he wasn't going to think about this. He was done with worrying about the point of anything. He was going to react, plow ahead, and take it as it came. . . .

It seemed that every time he looked up, another impassable obstacle loomed through the mist smoke. Now he knelt on a ridge beside Valit, each helping heave Irmree up and over and she punctuated her gasping with Teutonic expletives. . . . Next they had to shoulder her from between two trees. . . . Then Valit had to be pulled from a freezing cold stream, where he'd sunk to his chin. . . . Blinded (as the proportion of the smoke in the fog suddenly increased) for several minutes, they crept on all fours along a cliff face, sweating, inching forward, steaming clouds rising from vast depths, Valit continually committing himself to his maker, until Irmree (whose breasts and belly virtually touched ground as she crept) misplaced one knee and tripped, exclaimed, and rolled over and vanished as Valit cried out, "After all this trouble, I lose her like this!"

And then he saw her stand up, as if floating in space, behind what turned out to be not a cliff, but a curve of rock . . . finally, crawling again, this time over a rushing river on a fallen tree, which Broaditch remarked was to a footbridge what a straw was to a spear. . . .

On the far side they discovered they were actually on a road.

It's possible, Broaditch thought, *it's really possible, but, my God, how faith needs constant proof. . . . It seems the weakest link between God and men, for it fades and flickers like a hero's fame. . . .* He followed this line: because faith expects, but a miracle is always a surprise. Whoever expects providence is eternally disappointed until he despairs and then with a shock he's saved again. . . .

"Which way?" Valit said. Irmree was lying on her back, breathing immensely. Broaditch had just discovered this was a crossroads. He was smiling.

"And now," he said aloud, though for no particular reason, "it's time to waver again."

"Which way?"

"Well, lad," he replied, "these vile, reeking clouds seem to come equally well down either road."

"Hark!" Valit said, cupping a hand to his ear. "What's that?"

"A horse," Broaditch answered, reasonably, listening, "and I have little doubt a rider—a knight."

"Why so?"

"Listen."

There was a faint pinging of steel in rhythm with the cantering clop-clop approaching down the left fork.

Broaditch was unsurprised. For if he had been brought to this spot by all the forces of time and heaven, then this was inevitable. If, despite everything, the great machine was run on chance, it was just a meaningless rider and they were all lost in probably every possible sense. . . . He smiled as the single horseman, sealed solidly in his armor, melted into view from the insubstantial flow.

Broaditch's expert eye noted the rider was holding a rather thin spear; for a knight. It seemed light even for a man at arms. He wore bright plate armor and his shield showed a single dove in flight, remarkably worked in gold.

He halted the charger and threw back his visor.

"How did you reach so far?" he said, surprised. "Is *he* with you? Is it possible? I am Sir Hinct. I have it, as you see. . . ." They broke, frowning. "Name yourselves," he suddenly demanded. "What is that sow doing there?" he asked, indicating Irmree. "Is she dead?"

Valit squinted one eye slyly, then hedged forward.

"Sir knight," Broaditch said, careful, watchful, already convinced this meeting had a meaning. The knight seemed uneasy, guilty. "Sir knight, we are travelers looking for our destination."

"What destination is that, varlet?" The knight's manner was changed. He was nervous and hostile now.

"The castle."

"Hah. Which castle, sirrah?"

"When last I saw it"—which happened to have been in at least a dream, if nothing more—"it shown with a splendor beyond description."

"You speak well, peasant. Are you a schoolman out of robes?"

Broaditch shook his head.

"A traveler, merely, sir knight."

"So . . . well, know that I am a messenger of that castle and. . . . Passed you any other on the road here?"

Before Broaditch could explain that they'd just found the road, Valit was seizing his first opportunity with an expression of sly determination and affected sincerity. He sidled closer to the mounted man and said, "Sir, I can see you've a long way to go." He pointed. "Consider that woman there, soft, I say, in all her parts. For a few silver coins she will . . ."

"Silver what?" the man exploded.

"Coppers, my lord, sir, mere coppers!" he instantly amended as wide-eyed Broaditch audited this exchange.

His lord sir nearly caught his crown with the spear haft, would have for a certainty despite Valit's skittering backward, except that the warrior checked the swing (Broaditch observed) just enough to miss as a kind of afterthought.

Why? He never meant to ease that blow, yet he did, Broaditch thought. *After being offered the rent of Irmree in even foggy weather, I'd have used the pointed end if it came to that. . . .*

"Out of my path, base-born scum," the furious man snarled, rearing his horse as Broaditch, staying just at the rim of his range, leaned very lightly on his staff.

"You have poor aim," he commented, trying to carefully calculate the level of response he'd get. He upped it: "You must be ill-practiced, sir knight of the skinny lance."

"You bastard oaf! Learn to curb your tongue before your betters!"

And with a snarl of social outrage he whipped up the spear, checked himself (for all his fury), and awkwardly went for his sword instead, changing hands, and something told Broaditch this was the beginning of why (again unless meaningless) he'd been herded, floated, and driven here. . . .

The knight contented himself with brandishing the blade, glancing nervously back the way he'd just come into the blank mists.

"Constrain your tongue," he advised.

"You'll never find *him* the way you're going," Broaditch tried, shrewdly, testing. "And what," he went on, heart in mouth, "if you should lose what you bear?"

The fellow's gesture clearly revealed it was the spear that mattered: old, rusty-tipped, crudely fashioned.

"The enemy is alert," Broaditch lied on, bolder, watchful.

"Why must you inflame him?" Valit interjected fearfully. He was poised to run, standing back by Irmree, who'd just risen to sit and stare dully.

The knight was suddenly calm and leaned down in earnest.

"And should I pass it on to you for safety's sake?" he asked quietly. "Before I am run down?"

Broaditch knew his improvisation had gone wrong.

"Is that your thought, sir?" he attempted.

"You foul dog!" The horseman zipped a long, looping cut that nearly took his mark cold. The raised staff, as it was riven, barely deflected the stroke. Broaditch realized he could run into the murky curtain surrounding them, but that was wrong, because if they'd met for that invisible purpose, this was his single chance and function, and if he missed it he became just a wandering, disaffected, unsatisfied ex-serf and farmer probably doomed, anyway . . . this a wordless flash as he was already leaping (Valit shouting something far, far away at the rim of the moment) in and (nothing clever) simply shoving with all his remarkable strength and battle skill so that the knight tipped wildly, surprised, flailing the spear and sword in an attempt to right himself as his opponent reached under and smacked the charger's testicles with one big fist and, staying close as it violently bucked, caught the spear with his other hand, whole body stunned by the contact, and (even as he rebounded from the horse's massive mesh armor) for an instant he could look out from himself like an expanding bubble, seeing everywhere at once, and though everything in the world was moving, yet (to him) on an indescribable level, it was still and he had forever to be aware of each slightest movement: it was terrifying and magnificent, and the fog smoke, and even the ground, became like clear, sparkling water to his vision; the knight was still falling from the horse, which was still charging away; Valit was on his knees, as if praying; Irmree stood upright. . . . His vision expanded and he saw Alienor racing in a maze of flame, clutching their daughter to herself . . . Parsival on a struggling horse borne by a mass of panicked, blinded, roasting men. . . . Everything was lit by a central radiance, as if the sun had fallen to earth and was shining through the surrounding woods, and he glimpsed the castle in the overwhelming light and the precise road that wound and doubled and crisscrossed from this point to there: that light lit worms crawling under the earth, insects in the bark of trees, swimming fish, high-flying birds that beat to escape the swirling smoke, and he saw the fire was nothing, all wispy, ineffectual . . . saw everything bathed in the streaming glow, and he had no fear for himself or any creature because he perceived they could all melt into this brightness where time was a shell of life, a faded shadow. . . . He saw they were all safe forever, felt a joyful weeping everywhere, felt the flowers waiting in their seeds, the inner names of countless leaves to come . . . pictured himself floating through the transparent, shatteringly refracting walls, merging into the pulsing rainbowed golden heart that beat and beat and breathed living sparks into all flimsy, fluttering, staggering life. . . . He knew he was seeing the Grail, the radiance of the Grail. . . .

The ground clubbed him hard. The spear rolled a foot from his grip. The knight was just hitting with a rolling, ringing crash. The hard, smoking world slammed back with a cold shock.

He sat up, dazed, catching his breath, the horse already gone, a diminishing, muffled rattle of hoofbeats. . . .

He hesitated, then shut his eyes and picked up the spear, waiting, holding his breath, afraid of it happening and not happening again . . . nothing . . . waited . . . nothing, just the smooth wood in his calloused fingers.

He stood up, motioned the other two to follow, and moved up the road the knight had emerged from. The noble gentleman was struggling, wobbling to his feet, shouting something too distorted by his headpiece to make out, hunting for his sword.

Then, as the three of them vanished into the mist and he began a halting pursuit, limping, he yelled, "Wait . . . ! Come back, you filth . . . ! Come back here . . . !"

Grontler gestured at a line of Saracens filing past into the swirling dark afternoon.

"You got to give the great lord his bloody due," he opinioned to Wista. "He brought all them swart, fucked devils thousands of miles to die here. You got to give him his due."

"Why are you here?" Wista suddenly asked.

"Eh? Why?" He twisted around in his saddle to ponder the young man. Both their faces were caked black.

"Why do you fight? What do you gain?"

"The pay, you simple bitch's boy," Grontler said affably. "What else, then?"

"Are they all here for pay?"

"How in hell do I tell that? They are unless they be fucked fools."

"All this," the young man murmured, "for pay?"

Grontler didn't hear this. A moment later he spotted Lohengrin riding helmetless a little apart from a cluster of high-ranking lords. A mass of troops stretched away beyond them into the general, condensing haze.

Wista had mixed feelings and intense nervousness standing face to face with his bushy-haired, hawk-faced lord. They'd just dismounted by a trickle of stream to give the mounts a drink and refill waterskins. The army was crashing through the forest all around through the deepening smoke haze.

"The beasts won't touch it," one of the knights was reporting to Lohengrin, who then strode a few steps to squint at the problem. He stripped off his gauntlet, stooped, and dipped his palm, then let

the liquid run out through his fingers. Wista shuddered. The hand
was stained dark crimson.

"The earth herself bleeds," Lohengrin remarked, shaking his
fingers, then wiping them on his sooty cloak. The result was a
bloody mud and no improvement.

"I have seen such things," Wista told him, coming close. This
was his first chance to really speak since being ordered to fall in
behind. "I . . . I cannot find a tongue to . . ."

"Peace," Lohengrin said grimly. "I have seen the same things."

"It is one thing to be cruel and murderous, as you were, but
this . . ."

"Peace!"

"They are destroying everything . . . everything!"

"Not 'they,' Wista the wistful." His sarcasm was a reflex. "Not
they—*we*."

"You dare to say so?" Wista was beyond being stunned, he'd
thought. "You can accept . . . this . . . this . . ."

"Ere you struggle on for words you have not, boy, consider . . ." He strode back and remounted. Wista was fascinated
by the pale-streaked, black-bloody hand. He stared at it. He
swung up onto his own horse, still staring. Lohengrin didn't
replace the mesh gauntlet yet and took up the reins with the
smeared fingers. ". . . consider this is the end of a world and the
start of a new."

Wista blinked himself out of his reverie but kept watching the
hand in spite of himself: it seemed (and he felt wild and suddenly
dizzy now) like claws with life of their own. . . . His mind kept
separating it from the arm and man, and it seemed to grip and
twist independently. . . . All the rest was closed in steel and this
alone was flesh. . . . He half-expected it to do some sudden,
terrible thing . . . blinked hard but remained light-headed and
anxious.

"New . . . ?" he wondered. "New what?"

"New world. A new world. A better one."

"What?!" He snapped out of it violently. "Are you come mad,
lord Lohengrin? What profit is there in . . ." He found his voice
and words now, full, feral, outraged. ". . . in this blood and
ashes!? Have you power to order this?! What are you? A *thing*? A
crawling thing unspeakable?! A devil? I thought you but cruel and
mistook in the shadow of your great sire, but, God's wounds"—

Wista's voice broke with weeping in his misery and fury—"God
. . . but what are you? What *are* you! What?! What?! What?!"

Now lord general Lohengrin was fuming. He leaned out from
his horse as it cantered, whooshing dead leaves as smoke puffed
between them, alternately dimming and revealing their shapes to
one another.

"Be still, weakling!" he yelled. "My father is a fool!" Then they
both bent their heads against the smoke and coughed and wiped at
their burning eyes. "I serve a man . . . a man with a holy passion
who speaks for the gods themselves!"

"Gods? What heathen . . ."

"Be still!" Lohengrin's voice was pitched ice-deadly. "We are
unleashing the greatest powers and only the worthy will survive
these days. This hour is the harrowing of the gods and the
winnowing of the earth!" He had just quoted Clinschor without
realizing it. He took them for his own words. Wista just stared at
him now, dizzy, stunned, blinking, watching the stained hand
gesture, hooking its fingers at the thickening air. . . . He stared in
silence as they rode in the massed, trampling, pounding van of the
army. The wind was building up. It sucked and twisted and
billowed the smoke. They all had to cover their faces now.
Lohengrin clapped on his helmet.

Finally Wista cried out, had to: "Do you mean to destroy
everything?!" he said over the wind, din of the troops, and the
gradually mounting fire roar coming on from the side and behind.
"Answer me!" he yelled.

They were a little apart from the others and the thickening
clouds isolated them.

Wista wasn't thinking now. His heart kept racing. His head
jerked slightly, uncontrollably. He was giddy, trembling. He
somehow knew if he thought at all he'd fall raving or weeping or
flee without direction.

"Answer me, you bastard!" his voice shouted again.

He didn't hear the muffled reply.

What can I do? What will I do? What must I do?

He nervously, unconsciously, drew his sword, seeing only the
tube of black, slitted, faceless helmet turned toward him. His
mouth was dry. He squinted into the smoke.

What? he asked himself.

"What?" he said without knowing it.

"You have no time for foolishness," Lohengrin bellowed, snapping the sooty visor open. "I give you . . ."—he coughed —". . . I give you this chance to join us . . ."—coughed— ". . . I'll bring you to *him* after the battle's done." He coughed and spat violently. Over the crackling explosions of flames there was now a roaring and unmistakable clashing that meant the enemy was engaged at last. "I must hasten," Lohengrin said. "I have a fondness for you, lad, I . . ."

Wista thought: *No! No! No!*—as if the last remark was more than he could bear, so he was crying, too, and choking, feeling his own outpouring of affection and hate and madness, too, tears streaming into the soot and gagging smoke as he struck, rising in the long stirrups, flailing the blade down as he'd been trained, seeing the helmet's dark metal spark and split, just perceiving a blurring as the knight rocked and seemed to shift himself but never saw the draw and automatic, irresistible counterstroke, that, at the last fraction, Lohengrin tried to check and twist into the flat of the blade, and then came a burst of pure white light, and a deep, spinning blackness yawned all around as his sense scattered and fluttered away. . . . He never saw his teacher, bloody sword hanging down, staring through the blinding clouds, or heard him crying out: "Wista . . . ! I cared for you . . . ! I cared . . ."

Parsival drove his horse out of the press, over the heaps of struggling men that were jamming up between the trees into a solid wall of flesh, every mad effort wedging them tighter until in places (in the filling and emptying billows) they were packed motionless except for raving heads and outstretched, clutching, waving arms as those who tried to clamber over were gripped and held and drawn back to the swelling heap as the terrible heat pressed closer. . . .

He barely struggled free: dying, frenzied men tried to hold onto the horse and his legs in an effort to be drawn along, and he'd had to slash himself free. He'd shut his eyes to do it. He was never going to simply surrender again.

He'd come out on a trail that wound up through the mounting hills. "The road you want always rises," he remembered, with almost a smile. . . .

Well, and this be not right, there'll be no second way. . . .

Behind the mass of fumes, the flames were flooding on and he hummed loudly to partly overcome the sound when they reached the tens of thousands of trapped men . . . hummed, and pushed on along the twisting way. . . . He'd caught the first massed scream that became one voice and the sputtering bursting that sounded like a fat-rich boar on the roasting coals. . . . He could not drown out the stinking wind that followed him or check the fires leaping ahead . . . saw blackened bird bodies that had rained down everywhere . . . was aware that virtually no one could be in front of him, just bare yards from the waves of fire, faint from the incredible heat. . . .

He struggled around a bend, another, swaying in the saddle. There was no hope of distancing it in these thickets. A sheet of flame crossed before him. He hesitated, but there was no turning back. He spurred the near-hysterical animal straight in and through a flash of terrible heat, and half-roasted in his hot steel, he wobbled on the narrow, torturous path. Weariness hit him like a maul blow. He held on to the laboring beast at the edge of falling with each doubling and bump. . . . Blinding flashes ripped through the clouds that he thought were his mind. . . . He felt the invisible forces close to him, warring themselves, and he thought, vaguely, spinningly, if his side lost, then the claws would get him . . . because he couldn't resist that now . . . his eyes were sealed shut and swollen. . . . Though he was a drained and battered shell of himself the power still flowed through him, and, able to see merely shadows with his right eye and nothing with his left, he was having flashes in color on that dream-like level: suddenly the landscape and sky would swell into shattering brightness, pulsing, rainbowed, and he seemed to see dark, fearful, clawed limbs and gaped-mouth shapes entangled with what appeared to be knights wearing crusted diamonds for armor, fluid, slashing, spearing, blocking . . . then smoke and flame would close in . . . another brilliant fragment . . . then the choking present, where his armor seared wherever it touched his flesh and scorched his undergarments. . . .

Broaditch was just leading the other two around another serpentine bend and thinking: *it's over.* And he cocked the flimsy spear.

"What? What?" Valit demanded.

"Look," Broaditch said, pointing at the three armed and

armored men standing in the narrow road ahead. The way was walled on the outside here (the cliff face to their left) and the warriors were shoulder to shoulder. He was puzzled, wondering how they could move freely enough to fight.

"What?" Valit repeated. Irmree whimpered.

"There, you ass!" Broaditch shout-whispered.

"Fog and smoke?"

Which was how Broaditch discovered his eyes were somewhat changed. He could see farther into the surrounding, irritating obscurity than before.

A few steps on and Valit froze, but by now Broaditch wasn't worried. He went up to the men. All wore the dove crest; all were dead, faces netted with blood within smashed helmets. They'd been propped up like this to block the way. It must have been the work of the man behind. Of course, one or more of these might have been *his* companions. . . .

As he tugged them loose to topple, banging, onto the stony surface, he realized one had been looking the other way, so there was no direction intended to their facing.

"What is?" Irmree asked fearfully, clinging to Valit, who was hardly a secure support at this point. "What is?"

"Shut yer hole!" that gentleman snapped nervously.

They went on, climbing steeply now. Broaditch was certain the knight was following and paused to cock his ears from time to time, but it was unlikely that, unless he stripped off his metal clothes, he could maintain their pace.

The climb stayed steep and the stones slid underfoot. That plus the thickening smoke had them all wobbling and puffing. Near the top Valit planted himself behind the woman and shoved as his partner tugged her arm from above while she muttered smatterings of several languages. Broaditch recognized the German, French, and English, but others were obscure.

"Pull, God curse and damn!" Valit fumed and gasped. "If she falls, I'll be undone. . . ."

"That's the price . . ." Broaditch grunted, heaving her up to fairly level ground near the crown of the hill. ". . . the price, I say, of bearing your worldly fortune . . . fortune with you everywhere."

He leaned his elbows on the wall, and shielding his eyes with his palms, started into the roiling blankness: through vague rifts and rippings he partially made out an immense, fuming, swelling, twisting pillar of dark smoke miles and miles in width, striking his fancy as a gigantic being advancing on flame feet, towering overhead, gesturing with outstretched black and glowing arms, spitting meteoric sparks, fantastic torso belted by an astonishing play of lightning, searing, flailing as the torrent of uppouring heat sucked a world-shaking storm from the tortured atmosphere. Rain and hail seethed down and terrific clouds of steam blasted from the inferno's base and he could hear the thunder's distant rattling rumble over the oceanic roaring and hissing of the marching miles of fire. . . . Then, as the view shifted with the near clouds, he caught a glimpse of the castle (he half-turned away, expecting a blast of intolerable light), the tall, graceful towers no more than a straight mile down the ridgeslope. It looked like a long, circling walk along the steep sides from here, but there it was! It was real . . . real. . . .

Well, Broaditch, he assured himself, *now you'll need faith, magic . . . everything. . . .*

He gripped the spear. Perhaps he held the key to the gate. This weapon obviously meant something. . . . His hearing seemed keener, too. He was certain he heard footsteps, clinkings, back down the twisting, walled-in trail.

Irmree was sitting down again, back to the wall, which was about five feet high on the average.

"Get your fortune up, boy," Broaditch commanded, "unless you care to wait for that gentleman behind us."

"There's always something unpleasant behind us," Valit complained. He poked Irmree in the side with his foot.

"*Ne,*" she said. "*Ne.*"

"Come on, you foreign sow," insisted her would-be pimp. "Broaditch, you gather trouble like a fishnet fish! Why did you steal that bastard's spear? You're mad!" He shook his head violently. "You're a cracked pot. . . . Rise, damn it!" He kicked her and she cursed him in some language. "Why don't you leave the damned thing here and let him find it and . . ." He kicked again and she slammed a meaty fist into his groin. He gasped, eyes popping, staggered back, doubled over.

"You have her," Broaditch said cryptically. "I have the spear. Let's hope the one proves as valuable as the other."

"Stay here, then!" Valit cried, and still doubled forward, he started to hobble down the twisting trail past where the wall abruptly ended.

Broaditch wasn't surprised when the bulky woman heaved herself up and, adjusting her long, sooty braids, waddled quickly after the young man.

"Vait," she called. "Vait . . . I am come, messire . . . Vait . . ."

Mary, Joseph, and the nose of St. Alman, be this love?

He grinned and followed after, spear across his shoulder.

Instead of the expected impact of the baking, sooty earth, Alienor felt a shock (she didn't know was cold) and suspension, then was spluttering for air, kneeling, then going with the stream's strong pull, seeing the silhouette of Lampic holding Torky, plunging in himself, just as the sheeting, exploding fire arced over and closed down all around and she had to keep ducking her own and Tikla's head to keep their faces from roasting as the healing safety of the water bore them on through the center of the inferno, as if floating in a magical spell . . . on . . . on . . . until, tumbling under a stone bridge that zipped overhead (she wondered fleetingly if it would end with them dashed to death against rocks), they slowed steadily (still as by magic) and found themselves in a wide pool beyond the limits of the flames as the country opened up into rolling fields and stone walls. . . . They struggled out through a tangle of lilypads and muddy roots until they stood on the swampy bank and looked across at the farthest edge of raging destruction in the shadow of the miles of towering black clouds. Looking the other way beyond the dark boiling that stretched overhead, beyond the advancing layers of gray, flat-bottomed rain clouds blowing from the south, she saw, with a shock of disbelief, a stunning splendor that dropped her jaw slightly in weakened awe: a rim, a pure wash of greenish-blue that at first she didn't recognize as being simply unstained sky. . . .

She was still rapt when tall Lampic, holding Torky, struggled, all angles, from the water and fell drenched, burned, half-drowned, to his weary knees and just sucked breath after breath after breath. . . .

Wista's blow had stunned Lohengrin and his left eye's vision seemed set in a blur for the time being. Through all his determination and mission and demands of command (which had been greatly reduced by these impossible conditions), he felt sick at heart.

The silly ass, he kept reiterating, *why did he seek death . . . ? The silly ass . . . why did he hate me so . . . ?*

These thoughts were unusual for him, but he'd believed he would convince the squire, teach him, and had actually looked forward to the disputes and satisfactions of the process. . . .

"Where's the master?" he roared at a knight bearing the standard of the inner circle of command: white jaws on red and black background. He felt a slow trickle of blood down his neck.

I taught him to strike hard, he thought. *I taught him that. . . .*

The knight with the banner pointed.

"Just ahead!" he yelled over the constant roar.

And a minute later he saw it: A close-packed mass of horsemen tearing through the hot clouds and the fairly open field, a dim wall of trees just beyond, rising, and the huge, black, iron wagon shaped (he thought) like a melon, drawn by three teams of magnificent armored horses, wide wheels grinding into the earth. The only opening in the curving sides were three thin-grated slits spaced around the circumference. Three armored men rode on top, one driving. Even under the soot, he made out the silver trim of the elite guard of mutes. Lohengrin had yet to discover where those men came from. . . .

A dozen more immediately surrounded the wheeled sphere. He called to the nearest: "Where's Lord Clinschor?"

The mute turned his fang-faced helmet to Lohengrin and pointed to the rolling fortress, grunting tonguelessly.

Delightful gentleman, Lohengrin commented and wondered what protocol demanded here: Did he shout? Poke his hand into the slits? Bang on the sides? He doubted the wisdom of that. He'd already learned that all the other servants of Clinschor, whatever their rank, were extremely circumspect around these devil-masked warriors.

He settled on riding close and calling out.

"Lohengrin," came the ringing bass rumble from within, "ride close here."

"You sent for me, my lord?" Lohengrin said to the slit.

"I want you with me."

"But should I not stay with my men until the battle . . ."

"The battle is won," Clinschor interrupted. "I need you at the castle of the Grail."

Lohengrin was still incredulous.

"But is this real, this Grail?" he shouted over the general din that Clinschor's steel-muffled voice had no difficulty overriding. "What is it?"

"Time enough for that."

They were close to the Grail forest now. Through a space in the clouds, masses of men were breaking like a dark surf over the rocks and rills and into the trees. Flames sprouted everywhere and sparks hissed overhead like, he thought, arrows of hell. . . .

A massive iron door swung suddenly open and Lohengrin blinked his good eye, startled by a flash of concentrated plushness: glowing ruby-covered lanterns, rich, deep rugs set off by festooned silk hangings, a gleaming black table with ivory legs, and then a shadowy Nubian servant in Oriental regalia holding the door, the master himself seated at the table in his colorless robes. The black man extended an arm as thick with muscle as a normal man's leg and helped Lohengrin lean from his saddle into the startling interior.

Inside the floor rocked and banged less than he expected. He unscrewed his helmet, looking around. Mechanics or magic? he wondered in passing.

Clinschor was facing a barred slit, talking to a rider (Lohengrin could just see) out in the smoky, flame-shot world. It was as hushed in there, he thought, as in a chapel. It seemed ironically fitting. Through the slit the world seemed strangely distant, he reflected, like a moving painting. He heard the muffled voice of the messenger from out there, but found himself engrossed in the intricate designs on the walls: golden scrolls depicting peaceful, fantastic scenes in which naked men and women floated among puffy clouds and gigantic flowers. There were astonishingly rich and fresh perfumes in this inner air. The smoke outside was barely noticeable.

He found himself sitting down on the gently yielding rug, unbidden. He was more weary than he realized. He distantly heard Clinschor's conversation. The other openings were all sealed, though he didn't notice that at first.

". . . but, master . . ."—the man outside was shouting, though the sound came through as a bare murmur—". . . most of the army is trapped by the fire!"

"Fate is fate," Clinschor snapped impatiently. "These are the risks of any great enterprise. Has the enemy been crushed?"

"Aye, master," came the reply, and Lohengrin found himself vaguely interested. He studied Clinschor, sitting by the narrow opening, arms folded across his chest, head bent forward meditatively, long, large, pale fingers restlessly opening and closing.

"Are any left to oppose us?" he demanded, with a certain redundance, Lohengrin noted, as if he wanted to reexperience the pleasure of hearing it again, although it didn't appear to satisfy him.

"None that I know of, lord master," came the tinny reply. "But under these conditions . . ."

"All are crushed!" the leader boomed with sudden fury. "And all *will* be!" he raged at the fragment of a man visible through the opening.

The wheeled fortress suddenly pitched violently and Clinschor rocked in his seat.

Lohengrin felt a little giddy. He touched the side of his skull. It hurt. The blood was drying, thickening. The blow, he decided, had affected him . . . or was there some subtle narcotic in these incredible, stinging perfumes? His vision and hearing seemed to be aware of everything from a hushed distance . . . nothing seemed disturbing, all things seemed brightly possible . . . the world seemed to shrink to a toy he could hold within the expanding vastness of himself, a clay his hands could shape. . . . He felt peaceful and almost closed his eyes, except Clinschor's voice kept pulling him back to the moment.

"Deaths feed the coming life as sacred sticks feed a sacred fire!"

Sacred sticks? Lohengrin thought from his floaty heights.

"Execute any man who turns back," the master was commanding. Then he looked at Lohengrin. His eyes tracked back and forth, seeming feverish. He didn't seem to hear the faint outcry beyond the padded, muffled iron where the knight was shouting.

"Back? Turn back?! How can anybody turn back? The flames are behind us now!"

Clinschor reached over and slammed a hinged, silk-padded wedge that slid neatly into the embrasure. The interior was suddenly shocked with silence.

"Once a field is clear," he said at Lohengrin, "we can plant as we choose." His lieutenant must have looked puzzled, for the mighty leader went on to explain: "I'm hardened to death. I am not worried about how many must die. The survivors will be fit men."

Lohengrin sort of nodded. His brain felt hot and sluggish. He watched, fascinated, the almost colorless eyes of the conqueror, which seemed to flicker with fitful inner lights, went utterly empty, and, a moment later, were hypnotic, commanding. . . . Lohengrin touched his own blurred eye lightly. He suddenly realized, distantly, that he would have to move his bowels soon. He wondered if it could be done without going outside.

In answer to a sharp rapping, Clinschor flung open the small slit again.

"What is it, Howtlande?"

Lohengrin glimpsed the fat face framed in the soot-blackened helmet. All the gold and gems were blotted over. The streaked face was sweating. For some reason it was surprisingly cool inside, no doubt more wizardry.

"Great master," Howtlande was crying out, "my army is lost . . . lost . . . !" His eyes were wild. "Only a handful escaped. . . . I—"

"Why are you alive, then?" the leader demanded.

"I rode to report, I—"

"Has the road been located?"

"I know not, master. In the confusion and burnings, I—"

"Fool!" he glanced at Lohengrin. "I remain surrounded by fools!" He stood up, swaying with the tilts of carriage and shouted through a speaking tube near the low, curved ceiling, "I want the road found! We have the map! No excuses!" He sat down facing Lohengrin again, frowning with an intensity of rancor that firmed his loose jowls. Pale fingers drummed and drummed on the tabletop. Lohengrin had a fleeting impression that this all had begun as an act to overawe others and by repetition had become part of him. . . . For a moment he felt a strange, abstract fear seeing himself mirrored in that perception as a walking, breathing collection of old poses and acts. . . . He shook his head to try and clear it. It hurt. He definitely needed to relieve himself . . . the pitching motion, the cloying, sweet air. . . . He tried to focus the still-blurred eye on the leader. The other clearly saw the pale fury of the face that seemed to hang suspended, leaning into the ruby-reddish light, mouth corners flickering with relentless inner tension.

He doesn't care if everyone dies, Lohengrin thought. . . . And then: *Do I . . . ?* He blinked, still felt remote . . . struggled to his knees and stayed there, swaying. Clinschor seemed unaware of it, lost in some inner hollow-eyed concentration. Only the large, spidering fingers stirred.

Suddenly the voice boomed and filled the padded space: "I have sacrificed everything for this . . . ! I accept all powers for myself." He was shaking, Lohengrin saw, still kneeling, as if in prayer, as what he took for a fit began: Clinschor's fists hit the boards with a crash and vibrated the rest of his body, his eyes rolled back, and his lips parted. An intricate, delicately worked golden goblet began to vibrate and clatteringly walked the length of the table to noiselessly drop, splashing a red stain of wine on the deep golden rug. "Pass all power through me!" he cried.

Clinschor was chanting now, increasingly roaring until Lohengrin felt his body and head pounding in unbearable accord. . . . He struggled first to stand, then to crawl away, telling himself it was the close, drugged air and the blow Wista had given him . . . weakened him . . . even as his swaying body started to pick up the rhythm of the maddening chant that seemed to suspend and drown out all else . . . and he felt himself starting to hoarsely bellow back, caught in the incredible crescendo (that the remaining free part of his mind believed would never stop, would mount beyond the threshold of death), and this could not be a human throat voicing what he now rocked and screamed in time with, faster, faster, faster.

". . . rowrowrowrowrowrowrowrowrow . . ."

He was certain the massive, rolling fortress itself was ringing like a squat black bell with it, that the pitchings were no longer connected with the ground, that the earth had dissolved away and they were riding a river of darkness that irresistibly poured into the blazing world, driving all things back, sucking away their color, before passing through the lord master like dark light through a black lens, then slashing into the misty earth, laying everything darkly bare before them, and he seemed to see a shape of walls, towers sinking into that river of abyss, falling, dissolving. . . . Lohengrin tried to cry out in terror, tried to twist away, but his

own sound held him and he knelt and bobbed, as if in genuflec-
tion, and raged the incantation with total body and mind, foaming
a little, his voice harsher and harsher, drawn into a continuous
snarling as Clinschor vibrated with such intensity that one arm of
his seat snapped and flew into the far wall and the black servant lay
prostrate, hands pressed to his ears, muffling himself into the
face-deep pile. . . .

Wista lay facing upward on the smoking ground. Violent winds
whipped the choking fumes and dry trees. Sparks rained down,
caught in his clothing, brushed his flesh, ignited his loose hair. He
heard nothing but felt the terrible pressure of the heat all around.
He seemed sunk in a pool of silence. With every racked breath, he
felt the blood flow out of his chest. There was no pain, only the
flames and silence. . . .

He accepted it all very naturally . . . understood . . . made no
effort to move . . . was aware of the functions of his body
separating, draining away . . . each eye blink seeming a miracle. . . .

Frell . . . he didn't want to go to what waited yet, so his mind
went to her. . . . Would she survive? Marry? Bear children?
Could he have made her pregnant? Then he tried to think about
what he'd done or tried to do . . . and he would do it again,
knowing the end, he'd follow Lohengrin into hell to strike at him
because he'd seen too much . . . too much . . . he admitted he
cared for him, too, but there was a limit to all things, and right or
wrong, he'd do it again. . . . Someone had to because the wound
that mattered may not have been made by his sword only . . . yes
. . . he saw that, blinking . . . someone had to wound Lohengrin
in a way no one ever had . . . but these things were already far
away and seemed to belong to someone else. . . . The fire and the
silence were indistinguishable from his consciousness now and his
roasting body was the flaming earth, too. . . . He watched all this
in perfect silence. . . . But was she carrying his child . . . ? His
lips may have slightly moved even as his pooling blood streamed
and his clothes flared. . . . His lips tried to pray for her or to call to
her . . . saw this lovely girl bearing away the moment, their
moment, to let it grow and be nourished from her very self . . .
that their joint life and brief touch would move and breathe and
grow and carry along its own magic time and pass into days and

sights in an intimacy he could never know. . . . And he knew (though there was really no *he* left to speak of, but simply this ambient understanding) that he died then, too, and before that and before that, that dying was to offer space to life and a shape of yourself . . . and the last thing was a picture that gleamed bright and vivid: green glow, blue skies, easy winds, fresh, opening fields of spring into hazy distances, smells, rich, fertile warmth (the flames faded to misty shadows), Frell sitting by a sky-shimmering stream where fish darted, flicked, and a bare-topped child stood with a willow wand staring through his reflection at the fleeting, clear and shadowed, sun-lanced, mysterious water, and was there himself, reaching into all of it, into them both like a wind of music—that was the last thing. . . .

Hail and rain seemed to fall in one solid sheet. The impact came on a gusting wind that hammered Parsival harder than a good jousting blow and he reeled in the saddle, metal ringing, leather cracking, charger plunging in terror as the smoke was washed away by an equally impenetrable, rattling deluge as trees and sky leaped and tilted in the crashing flare of lightning bolts that flailed the earth and ripped the air, and then his rearing mount, towering above him, caught a hissing blast on the head armor (saved the falling rider) that spasmed it, burst, and burned to the ground, while to him, as he sailed through raging space, heaven had exploded in one blinding ball of fury and his mind believed that since he was living and flying that all the power had run into him and that heaven's thunders and lightnings would henceforth be gathered within his blood and bones. . . . He blacked out only briefly when he hit the stony earth. . . .

He awoke struggling, gasping, trying to swim up to air from under the water that was drowning him (as if, his thought flashed, he was back before Gawain freed him from the stream bottom) opened his eyes, helmetless, the terrific rain beating, stinging his face, filling his mouth and nose. He sat up, coughing and spitting. . . . A flood was already pouring down the hillside, cutting a stream channel into the twisting, narrow roadway.

He stood up, rain spraying from back and shoulders and the coif of undermail that covered his head. He looked but couldn't locate the helmet, his father's. . . . He looked around: as far as he could see (twenty-five to fifty yards, at best), the fire had been drenched and beaten out. A great mass of steam was rising, billowed and ripped by the gales.

His strength, he discovered, was still there. He assumed he was very near the end now. This storm, no doubt, had just introduced the final act. He hadn't died and wasn't particularly surprised. Each event had carried him closer to whatever it was. . . . The Grail? Was it really the Grail at all . . . ? He couldn't have said. . . . It seemed absurd to consider, a vague idea, a dream. . . . He was going on, because what he thought and didn't think had nothing to do with it. . . .

Heading up the road, he leaned into the flying downpour, crossing flash floods that sprayed around his shins so that at times he waded up the hillside. He'd been called, he decided, so it couldn't help but find him. . . . He accepted everything now. . . . Everyone was dead or forever lost to him, and what hadn't burned was drowning: mother, wife, children, friends . . . the few friends . . . Unlea . . . all ghosts, all lost . . . so now with a kind of indifference (as if he were always dying and remote) he carried the power, perfectly sure this winding way would come out at the castle he blundered into and out of over two decades before. . . . He passed a log barricade that had become a waterfall. A knight with the dove crest dangled there, upside down, legs somehow caught above, arms and body flopping in the rushing water. He wondered what had killed him. . . . Lightning? The rush of water . . . ?

He slogged on through the running mud into the slashing storm, digging steel-shod feet into the steepening slope, squinting ahead, hand flung up . . . and he kept seeing, as from a distance, a trembling, floating summertime of bluish fields and mirroring rivers, a startling world drenched with golden flowers that were like staring into the sun at times. . . . As he climbed he watched those past days reel by: the boy in the coarse hides of a fool riding a bent, bowed horse into the mornings, long, scintillant blond hair stirred by the mild breezes, riding and melting into the concentrated color and lushness of the season, becoming an exhalation, a fullness, a glory forever, an awakening and glory forever. . . .

On impulse he turned off the road and climbed a short, steep, slippery cliff face. On top he was under a massed netting of towering pines that hushed the storm that lashed only high up in its branches. A few trickles and sprays were leaking through: the bulk of the ferocious downpour was outward. Through a break in the forest, he looked back and saw the still-unburned and fir-green ridges that sloped steeply down to the valley, where masses of steam and smolder spread wider and wider like a phantasmal sea under the monstrous clouds above. Far beyond he thought he saw a faint, traced line of reddish-gold that might have been the remotest of all sunsets. It was gone, covered again. . . .

It was close to dark under that roof of spiny foliage. The great boles swayed and creaked. He felt he was getting close. He suspected these were the trees he'd seen from the window of the Grail castle when he'd tried to lean out and struck his forehead on the transparent glass, the first he'd encountered. He hummed faintly. . . . Join the beginning and the end of roads, one fate was as good as another because . . . because they'd all been shadows, beautiful and dark, sweet and bitter, and he knew, finally, that he sought neither dream nor waking and aimed for a place no map outlined, no path led to, that all this warring of earth, man, and sky left untouched. . . . He suddenly began to weep here, sheltered from the relentless torrents without, and his eyes ran tear after tear, and his mind repeated: *I love them . . . all of them . . . all those pained, haunted, endlessly grieving shadows*. . . . It spoke from everywhere and nowhere. . . . He wept with loving, but for no single memory, no solitary image. . . . And so he walked in the silence of pines and with love, power, and sadness wept . . . wept. . . .

Unlea was watching her husband. She knew he was awake in the hushed, fading twilight. She sat by the window arch, looking toward the vaguely outlined bed, where he lay gaunt and pale, almost at death.

She knew he was awake. Though he said nothing, she felt his eyes. . . . The arm that ended too abruptly in silken bandages lay folded over his chest.

"I'm here," she said again, voice swallowed in the depths of the huge room. She didn't expect an answer.

She glanced through the window for a moment: saw the stretch of vague, glowing fields and the jet darkness gathered on the far horizon in vast clouds. . . . The chamber was high in the tower and she could see (though the sun had already set) the faintly traced, widely curving river she'd finally followed home. . . . Her eyes filled with lucent, glimmering, dimming illumination. . . . The night bugs were beginning to drone in the distance. . . . Then she turned back to the shadowed room that seemed murkier by contrast with the grayish glow outside.

Whatever she was thinking or remembering, she only looked at the pale shadow of her husband and said, "I am here," somewhat above a whisper. And she waited quietly in the hush of time and his silence. . . .

Alienor, the children, and lanky Lampic were walking parallel to the flank of the fire storm on the open fields. Where the trees ended drew a clear border to the desolation. . . .

The sky to the east was streaked with pale greenish-blue, and every so often a wink of honey-glowing sunlight flashed through. To the northwest they could see the tide of smoke advancing as an immense, overspreading, towering, swirling, mushrooming mass mounting higher than where the highest storm clouds themselves boiled, laced with lightning, all widening (she thought) like a dye stain in a basin of water as heaven and earth joined in black and red fury. . . .

As they climbed a rolling pasture, they could actually see the charred border of the fields like a line literally drawn. . . .

Broaditch saw the churning storm front, and as the first erratic winds whipped dry weeds and creaked branches, he knew he had to hurry, that the moment was desperate. He could just see a battlement above the pine woods that closed around the place, insubstantial and drifting in and out of view through the vapors, as if it alternately dissolved and remanifested. . . .

"I must speed ahead," he told Valit, who was squinting down the bending path. Irmree stood beside him.

"There's no going on this way," Valit said. "It's all burning up." This was the first reasonable sight of the holocaust they'd had.

"I'll go alone. You wait here, if it please you."

"Aye. Or go chat with the murderous bastard behind us, eh?" Valit spat into the wind, then wiped his face. "You'd like that, eh?"

"No."

He's a boy when all's said and done . . . an old friend's son and a little piece of mine, too . . . with his fool ideas and dreams of profit. . . . He smiled warmly. He gripped Valit's arm. *He's much like the rest of us poor fools and bastards. . . . Why, what a world he has to face and how little of it will be left . . . for him . . . or my own. . . .*

He thought again about his children. He remembered squatting with them in the sunlight under fresh skies, picking small stones out of the rough furrows where the wheat was in, their short hands poking in the rich, warm earth, their grave intentness: Tikla standing on the hill slope above the field near an ancient pair of large shade trees, leaping up and down, barefoot, half-naked, a scattering of white flowers at her feet, bouncing herself off the resilient turf, leaping, hair flying out, arms flapping, leaping as if she meant to fly (or wouldn't have been surprised), playing bird, perhaps, up . . . up . . . up . . . again . . . again . . . again . . . abandoned to the air. . . .

He held Valit firmly by both shoulders and looked into his somewhat squinty face. He shook his windblown hair from his eyes.

"God keep you, lad," he said with thick-voiced emotion that surprised and puzzled Valit, though he nodded.

"Why are you going there?" he simply asked.

Broaditch shook his head.

"I do not entirely know," he half-explained. "But I think I have been called."

"You think? But for what reason, Broaditch?" Valit was concerned. "How can you escape the fire? See how it advances. . . . " He cocked his head, almost smiling. "You said there'd be more than riches! What?"

"I like you, lad, after all's said and done. I know not what courage is, but I must tell you, go on without fear if you can, because your fate will prove the same in any case. . . . And now I can ill spare time for talk."

Perhaps, he thought, *courage is more than riches.*

He hugged the strange boy to him and impulsively kissed his forehead. Then turned and went at a rapid trot until the clouds swallowed him up. *Love well,* he thought, the image of his family still before him. Because they'd all lived, life had met in himself and them and he knew he could bear that lightly into the smoldering eye of death (where a sack of gold would anchor him to doom) and beyond . . . only that beyond. . . .

Holding the smooth, time-worn spear, he went rapidly down into acrid clouds, the ground seeming to jump wildly as the lightning intensified. The winds sucked out his clothes and fluttered his beard. The echoing thunder rolled toward him. It would be night soon. A stray spatter of rain and light hail clittered around him. . . .

Lohengrin felt weak and faintly nauseous. He'd propped himself against the curving, padded wall, bare face turned in to the muffling hangings that reeked of perfumes. The blood had caked and dried along his neck. His legs were doubled up, knees touching his chestplate.

The wheeled fortress was banging and pitching heavily now. Clinschor was gripping the silks, supporting himself by the open slit, rapping out orders to someone. It seemed as though he were speaking into a furnace. Incredible that people lived out there, Lohengrin dimly thought. He had difficulty paying attention to anything; he'd never felt so drained and hopeless and (though he would not have used the word) degraded. What had happened with the chanting left him feeling violated and apathetic, as though the other had somehow sucked energy from him in a ritual of tainted intimacy.

He shut his eyes but didn't like the darkness of himself. He hardly noticed the sweetish, heavy incenses overpowering the bitter, biting tone of the smoke.

He was thinking, with a certain petulance, that he'd be damned if he'd live to please this man. . . . He contemplated some obscure revenge. . . . He was lord Lohengrin and not to be treated in such a fashion. . . . Great Master Clinschor didn't expect to be defied. They all feared him. Well, they'd see something, then. . . . Why, if he hadn't been hit on the skull by that mad boy . . . and if his eye were better, none of this Oriental mumbo-jumbo would have affected him. . . . He nodded slightly as his aimless mind drifted from thought to thought. . . . He was no longer impressed, he assured himself . . . all fine speeches, but what did they come to . . . ? Not much . . . great armies . . . and the Grail . . . Grail . . . destroying everything, wasting everything . . . he could weep . . . waste . . . waste . . . and for the sparkling nonsense his father and the other village idiots dreamed up . . . ! Oh, a fine thing . . . a fine thing . . . great lord master wizard ball-less. . . . As soon as his strength came back, he'd see . . . he'd see a few things, the lord master would. . . . This was Lohengrin here, not those other girlish fools he surrounded himself with. . . .

Suddenly the vehicle tilted wildly and his stomach spun and he spewed sickness without moving his head, staining the silks. He was coughing, choking, still without moving, shivering a little.

I'll show that bastard . . . I'll settle the great magnificence. . . .

His head lolled and he kept shivering. He wondered if he were falling sick with fever.

They were stopped. Clinschor was shouting into the flames and smoke.

"Drive on! Drive on! This is the right road!"

Faintly from without came the words, "The wheel, lord master . . ."

"Are you hopeless imbeciles? Must I do everything myself? Drive! Drive! Drive!"

He reeled back a step and pounded his fists into the padded wall. The metal faintly rang.

Fearful he'll be burned like a capon, is he? The great fart-noise, Lohengrin thought, miserably.

A moment later, to heaving and curses and shouts, the iron ball of coach humped forward and continued its laboring, twisting climb.

Clinschor went back to poring over the map; then he rushed to peer at the mounting inferno. He muttered something as Lohengrin came suddenly alert, nerves wincing in fear, afraid he'd begin the terrible chanting again. He whimpered faintly, unconsciously.

"You'll feel better after a time," the master told him. "You adjust." His magnetic, hollow, flashing eyes held him, and for the moment Lohengrin was calm. "In any event, you have little choice. You have been started on the process—no turning back." He shook his head almost primly. "You will be changed." The stooping, pale man in the dull-gray tunic smiled with what seemed a tic, but the immense voice rumbled on, masterful, profound, ultimately certain, and the eyes were now unwavering penetration above the absurd, upcurled moustaches.

Lohengrin was sorry and a little shaky again once the voice stopped talking to him, filling him with its own somber, resonant strength. The timbre and phrasing, the flow from murmuring thunder to mounting sweep, to flashing bolts, stilled his own thoughts and left him vaguely, childishly ashamed of his carping, petty little notions. . . . It was more than just trust . . . much more than sincere faith, it was here and present, it was happening while the voice spoke and you moved in the actual flow. . . .

He shifted his body experimentally and found he was slightly better. He was sure he had no fever now.

"My personal guard has been committed to battle," Clinschor said, perhaps to himself only. He'd shut one eye in contemplation of his tented fingers. "The way to the stronghold is open. This is the hour!"

Clinschor leaned back in his seat looking meditatively at Lohengrin. He munched a piece of dried fruit. Smiled distantly, eyes suddenly remote and peaceful . . .

"I never married, you know," he rumbled, quietly. "A man like myself is denied ordinary life. But I took it as consecration. I am like a priest, in many respects . . ." He opened one hand in a rueful, self-conscious gesture. "I often dream of a peaceful old age. Once the realm is firmly established I'll give place to younger men. That is how things should be: the young follow the old, spring follows winter. The strong supplant the weak . . ." He gave a meager sort of smile to Lohengrin who was trying to move into this mood with the lord master. "I'll live in quiet and meditation . . . yes . . . I only took on these powers because no other could do it. I don't love this work, young man." Shook his head. "Not in the least. But it must be done. I was chosen, you see, as I've chosen you."

"By what or whom?" Lohengrin asked.

"By power itself. By the need. . . . My sweetest recollections are of my youth. . . . My father never understood my ideas. He had a narrow view. . . . But my mother was very intelligent. We would talk for hours . . ." He smiled with fond indulgence. "I recall once reciting a poem I'd devised . . ." Shook his head. "Oh, I was filled with great feelings. I told of the holy wars . . . in very good style for a youth . . . yes . . ." He shut his eyes, the smile flickering still. "I had ever a gift for expressing myself . . . yes . . . I want to create gardens filled with herbs and great orchards.

Once we've fixed up the world I intend to set thousands upon thousands of men at work upon that task . . . yes . . ." He rested his arms peacefully across his chest. "Men will live in these gardens. All need for grim and dark castles will be past. Such places are not healthy. I've looked into these matters. Foul humors gather indoors . . . and men should eat only fruits and uncooked vegetables. This helps develop the spirit. . . . It will be paradise regained for those strong and vital enough to merit it . . ." Shut his eyes. "Yes . . . men and women will live in nakedness again eating only the pure fruits of the earth."

Lohengrin frowned.

"Naked?" he wondered. "Like a whorestew?"

Clinschor's dreamy eyes flickered with momentary impatience.

"This will be a pure race," he replied. "All the scum will be purged from it." His eyes now stared, lidded and complacent, across the swaying interior. "Sex as we know it will have little place there. But the serf will breed and be kept alive to tend the gardens, of course . . ."

"But won't everyone die out in time if there's no sex?" Lohengrin didn't quite know whether his master was mad or subtle, at this point. Clinschor brushed him aside.

"When I was a boy," he said, tilting his head until it rested on the back of his chair, "my happiest hours were spent in the garden. Time seemed to pass so sweet and slow there." He sighed. Murmured, "This whole land will eventually become a single, sunny garden with magnificent, beautiful people walking along the fragrant, cunning paths . . . singing and rejoicing together at the mystical wonder of life . . ." Sighed.

"But, master," Lohengrin put in, frowning, "You swore to sacrifice this country as an example and—"

"This will all come later. The two things are the same."

Lohengrin was bemused.

"But what about *nothingness?*" he demanded.

"Hmm?"

"Nothingness. You showed me that we're all nothingness. Why do you talk about *gardens* and . . . you know religion is superstition yet you sound like a priest, I—"

Clinschor was frowning, serious.

"Christianity will be stamped out!" he declared. "It's political and senseless. But never imagine that I deny *God!* God is the

power of life, young man. The law of God is to destroy all
weakness, burn away weeds and filth and grow a divine man!
Yes . . . this power is beyond your personal nothingness, Duke
Lohengrin. To grow my garden I needs must turn it under with a
ruthless plow!" He smiled. "Don't think I am destroying. I am
preparing the soil." He coughed as a stinging draft of smoky air
sucked in through the loosely shut windowslit where the darkness
and fire raged. Lohengrin just stared, uncertain and feeling ill
again.

"But," he muttered, "there *is* only nothingness. I have seen—"
Clinschor cut in, fixing him with his somber eyes.

"You," he told him, "are a cloud of nothing. Like your title,
Duke. You are all words, fancies, fears. . . . You see . . . ? But
I'll destroy everything else and let the power fill you and possess
you!" He smiled and nodded, rhythmically, hypnotically. "Yes
. . . yes . . . yes . . . out of nothing all is born, my little
Dukeling . . . yes . . . yes . . . yes . . ."

And then the first blast of sheeting rain slammed and tilted that
iron mass, tearing, popping the slit open, pressure and drafts
rippled and tugged at the hangings around the interior. The
dinning on the metal shell was shockingly loud. Lohengrin went to
his hands and knees as the floor swayed and bucked. . . .

Foaming torrents spilled over the rocky ledges and poured in
muddy floods down the slopes. Parsival saw the castle lit by
lightning as he came out from under the muffling forest. The winds
were still gusting and he cut into them at a half-run. His body
shivered. The air was just the wet side of the freezing point. The
sky ripped, cracked, hissed, seemed to bend low to pound at him
as the earth seemed to dance and stagger. In all his life he'd never
known such fury: the rain would veer, spin, and needle straight
into him, billow away, feint . . . pause . . . cascade. . . .

Parsival was wading through the great moat's seething overflow
when he spotted the gate. The drawbridge looked to be half-
lowered. He put his head down and shouldered into the sucking,
twisting, pushing wind that howled and keened through every
fractional lull in the thunder. He heard the hollow rattle of his
teeth in his head. . . . As the flashes flung shadows around the
towers and walls, he was astonished by the size of the place. It was
not so big in his memory, though all else was the same.

He breathed violently and flapped his arms to warm them. Was he going to have to swim in? He was up to his shins in muddy water now. Great streams crashed down from the walls and battlements and slapped into the moat.

He thought there was just a chance he might reach the end of the bridge with a good jump. He was almost close enough to try when he felt it: the "claws" that had ripped at his heart. They were just touching the outer aura of his power, just maintaining contact, poised, waiting. . . . He felt his pulse quicken and his shivering stopped for the moment.

He was craning around, but all he could see were bounding and rebounding fragments of torn sky, quaking, woods, masses of piled stone, sheets of violent water. . . .

"Very well, then!" he shouted into the over-roar that blew his muffled words to whispers at his mouth. "I'm here! I've returned! Parsival!" Boom! Roar! Hiss! Crash! Howl! "I'm waiting!!"

Broaditch reached the back of the castle just as the worst of the mad storm hit: clouds mixing with smoke and steam, driving overhead, streaming through the towers.

He smiled wryly and accepted the fact that a long, massive tree had uprooted and fallen to bridge the rising moat. He raced across the open heath and climbed onto the trunk and (as the wind and sleet mounted to a solid blow) quickstepped across, skidding and slipping and finally diving the last few feet to keep from toppling in. . . .

Coming back, he realized, watching everything churning to froth, was going to be another tale to tell. . . .

Huddling close to the fortress wall, stumbling blindly around the periphery, Broaditch began to feel ridiculous again. There was really no proof of anything, and his mind kept wanting to smooth over the past and convert it to coincidence, confusion, dreams. . . . He found his mind preferred even the most terrifying and meaningless horrors of sword, fire, storm, and flood to the inexplicable other worlds. . . . It kept telling him to turn, crawl across that fallen tree and run, hide, survive . . . find his way home. . . .

"Home," a voice said, and he jerked his head around, holding up the spear, looking, thinking, *no doubt I spoke aloud just now and knew it not,* seeing no one in the multiple crackling blazings.

His body involuntarily leaped as a bolt shattered a tree near the moat, igniting it into a briefly steaming blaze and showing a shadow in the wall that turned out to be a fracture. He scrambled into it, clambering over wet, fallen blocks and soon found himself out of the rain in a vaulted passageway dimly, fleetingly lit by the unceasing flashes filtering in from high window slashes.

Being inside, he thought, he might as well go on as not, after coming so far, senseless as it no doubt would prove. . . . The thunder was steady, hollow, muted. . . . Even if he beheld a miracle a minute, he mused, he would still find space to doubt between them. . . . The fact was, to his mind and feelings, the only real things were these cold stones, his soaked, chilled body, the howling night . . . almost, because he sensed something that he kept saying *no* to . . . something . . . formless . . . tidal, that worked through all the chinks in all the solid blocks. . . .

He accepted being afraid and in doubt since there wasn't any choice except to curl up helpless and cower in emptiness. He gasped in a deep, deep breath.

There are no half-measures in life, he explained to himself, *no practice. It's all to a finish every time. . . .*

He went on, steadily, taking a turn . . . another. . . . The bluish flickers faded now as he arrived at a branching: one passage slanted down; the other rose and curved inward. He had no basis for choice. So he grinned. No more basis than for being here at all. And he'd never seen this forking in any visions. But he wasn't about to hesitate. That would finish it right here. He flourished the spear (for no particular reason) and plunged into the rising right-hand passage, into pitch blackness, holding the weapon out before him, tapping floor and walls as he went up and around and on past side tunnels and cross branches, grimly pursuing the irrevocability of it. . . .

How long have I been in here? Broaditch asked himself. Time was a blankness. And when he saw the warm glow of light up ahead, he was positive (in a mix of anxiety and relief) that there were others in this deserted place—even if it had to be the bearded mage, after all . . . or worse. . . . At least there would be guidance, however ambiguously expressed in mystical hintings. He allowed himself a mild smile.

However, it was an empty chamber shaped like a barrel, and he stooped, checking the ceiling height with his hand. There were three diverging doorways yawning black and vacant in the unwavering light from an immense oil lamp, whose light might burn, he could see, for years unattended.

So it was all up to nothing again. He squatted, then knelt to rest. His garments were drier. He cocked his head, thinking he heard a voice coming from one of the arches. He listened . . . nothing. . . .

He sighed. No easy way. He forced himself to get up and march without hesitation for the central passage. Since he considered there was no chance, his only hopeless hope lay in senseless—no, reasonless—decisiveness. His mind, at this point, was slyly entertained. He now assumed he was being watched and was playing to the unseen watchers. At some point they'd appear to help him. Gradually this idea moved toward conviction, except (though underlying everything he did) this belief was unstated and his surface thoughts kept denying it.

The way was narrowing steadily until he had to twist his heavy shoulders sideways and was trying to convince himself to turn back from moment to moment . . . but the idea was too disturbing: it snapped the thread he was subliminally following, clutching at . . . so he pressed on into the gradually funneling tunnel . . . felt alternately hot and cold, felt both kinds of sweat soaking him, and for the first time he noticed how neutral and pleasant the temperature was in here, not damp or chill, as might be expected. . . . He tapped on with the spear haft. . . .

He was almost dry, so how long had he been wandering?

The passageway seemed to curve constantly left, and he was going faster now, on the edge of being frantic, groping ahead with the spear, scraping himself along the rough-cut wall. . . .

He kept imagining he glimpsed terrifying spectral shapes formed from the purple-violet flashings in his eyes, and in the echo of his own feet he heard others, and the drumming of his heart filled his ears with frightening rumbles until his senses became a terror to him that he sought to escape, plunging through this otherwise stone-silent, utter darkness. . . .

On and on . . . until he saw a distant gleaming. He couldn't tell how far away it was. Part of his mind suddenly took a red-orange spot for a single, demonic eye glaring, and he almost stopped but

didn't. . . . The passage was gradually widening again, and in his
present state he believed this to be a very positive sign, going
faster now with greater confidence, sure, for some reason, that
he'd finally reached the end of his senseless winding through this
absurdly designed fortress. Perhaps this was where they meant him
to reach before showing themselves. This was clearly some kind of
test. . . . Yes, the watchers would soon show themselves. . . . His
senses were focused and stable again. Amazing what a single
fragment of light could do. He felt brisk and confident as he
stepped into the illuminated, round room and looked at the same
three dark doorways again. . . .

On the hill above the castle, Valit and Irmree were crouched
under a jut of shale cliffside sheltered somewhat from the
billowing, seething storm. His arm rested around her thick
shoulders, and her plump, blue-eyed face pressed against his chest
as one hand, very gently, with apprehension and tenderness,
stroked the back and crooked fingers of his.

The rain slashed past, spattering off the rock face, stinging
where it caught their flesh. Her hand moved over and over, softly,
almost wonderingly. . . . He glanced at her, somehow puzzled—
no, questioning. He frowned slightly. Then he turned his palm and
grasped her firmly, kissed her flushed cheek, then, hesitatingly,
her lips. . . . He pulled back, looking still puzzled. . . .

Broaditch stood a minute, heart racing, feeling sick and wobbly,
frustrated, angry, and desperate. He looked wildly around the
warmly lit chamber. Then, running, spear held out before him, he
tore through another archway, going much too fast, tip sparking,
giving a bare fraction's warning as he twisted aside and rebounded
violently from a wall, cracked his head, light flashing, staggering to
another wall, realizing this was a dead end.

He pressed himself against the stones and moaned under his
breath.

*What have I done to myself . . . ? It was madness to come
here. . . . I am full mad, yet not mad enough to be content with
it. . . .*

He slid down the rough wall to his knees and stayed like that,
bearded face to the stone.

I followed fever dreams . . . help me now . . . help me. . . .

"Help me," he said aloud, voice ringing in the chamber. Stood up in one motion, straining into the darkness. "Speak to me!" He was shouting now. "You tormentors! Show yourselves! Speak! Guide me . . . I know you're there . . . or am I truely mad and lost . . . ?" He paced in a nervous circle, the spear swaying loosely in his grip. "Help me, curse you! Get me out of this darkness!"

He stood still and caught his breath in the pitch-black silence and, after a time, smiled to himself.

"Ah," he said calmly, "so it is, nothing but myself. . . . In this my wits are whole and sound."

He gathered himself around his center of disgust, frustration, hopelessness, self-mocking outrage. He felt like a priest begging God to speak back to him in a human voice. He felt like a hypocrite-fool. He rocked back and forth, then gathered himself like a goaded bull, angry now only because there was no hope . . . no, not even angry—he just gave up, gave himself up so completely that nothing mattered in the slightest, not himself, nor darkness, nor time, nor place—no, nor wall, neither, and so he launched himself, as if he were free to move anywhere, and when he hit the bricks he smashed feet, shoulders, and forearms against them with all his strength and more and a strangely casual heart, and boomed, without hysteria, but with terrific force: "Open! Open! Open!"

And the space in him that casually watched, calmly expected what swept the rest of him along as one, then another, brick bounced free, clunked on the other side and then several at once as the crumbling, rotted mortar gave altogether and the wall dissolved around him and he stood at the hole in a cloud of dust, squinting against (to him) the blinding lightning flashing from high up in what he gradually realized was a tremendous tower whose roof was invisibly high. The thunder was a vague, hollow ringing here.

He went through and was casting about for a way out, walking carefully across the huge interior, telling himself he was never going to get involved in anything again, was going to live in Scotland, if he had to, with the savages and pretend to speak no language. . . .

The floor was smoothly tiled and he walked with a skating motion straight across the center, looking through the trembling shadows at the outside wall. He made out an archway. And then one foot slid and groped into space and he hopped frantically at the edge of what seemed to be a well ten feet across or a shadowed pit. He squatted down to gain his balance. He poked with the spear to test the depth and found it about two feet deep. The faint flashes didn't reveal the shallow bottom.

He stood up in it and wondered what purpose it served. Maybe someone ran small dogs around it or filled it with water for fish. . . . It seemed as senseless as anything else to build this great hall around it. . . .

As he was walking to the other side, he stubbed his foot on something heavy. He felt the big toe begin to mountingly sting.

"Bloody piles," he muttered.

What's this? A stone?

He picked up a massive sphere about the size of a large apple. He was impressed by the weight. Well, why not? An empty castle—no, a *huge* empty castle all a maze within, a floor with a giant basin cut into it . . . a stupid ball of metal with . . . He peered at it in the erratic illumination and thought he distinguished crude-looking writing graven around it. He shook his head. *Mayhap*, he considered, *this be the blinding light . . . gone a trifle dim. . . .* He grinned. He stuffed it into his belt pouch, which then tugged uncomfortably and banged against his thigh, and climbed back out of the "basin." Headed for the archway, still looking around hoping for the sight of something . . . anything that might faintly justify those night visions of ineffable, golden luminescences streaming through the ethereal, prismatic castle. . . . He almost bumped into a bent, straight-backed chair that sat before a three-legged table that was meant to have four. Otherwise, the hall appeared empty. He touched the table and it sagged and nearly fell. . . .

"Is this *it?*" he asked the faintly ringing room. "Is this *anything?*"

He was dizzy as the strain suddenly caught up with him. Shut his eyes and rubbed his forehead. When he reopened them he stepped back with shock, stomach tensed: a tall, bearded figure wearing a thin crown was standing by the table. He recognized him: the cowled man in the boat. . . .

"Who are you?" Broaditch demanded.

"Anfortas," was the answer.

"Are you a spirit?"

"A fisherman."

"What do you want of me?"

"Nothing more, for now."

Broaditch shut his eyes: reopened, he was alone again.

Before he could pursue questioning the vacant air, he heard a faint clashing and turned around. Far across, on the other side, there was another archway. He could just distinguish it now that his eyes had adjusted. It had sounded like a sword being drawn. He crouched, listening. . . . There seemed a glinting in the shadows when the lightning winked bluishly. . . .

Now, when I would be alone, you send me company. . . . This was addressed to his vaguely defined image of the bearded sages hovering overhead (much as he'd pictured saints and angels in boyhood, all resembling the village priest), with the chiefest among them shutting one eye and squinting the bright blue other at him. . . .

He heard another metallic pinging from the deep shadows but no voices as he turned and headed, skated, in the diametrically opposite direction toward the nearer arch. He was thinking that he hadn't come here to die for the possession of a metal ball, even were it solid gold. He ran carefully and quickly. He skidded.

The sudden jangling rattle of armored men chasing him was no surprise. But their speed was a shock. They followed wordlessly as he sprinted through the exit into a long, narrow chamber with an invisibly high roof as lightning tossed and crossed the shadows of old, upended furnishings and gleamed on the massed cobwebs he tore into, as if ripping a ghostly hole in the air . . . through a door, another long room . . . he skidded, startled by a long line of knights—*empty shells!* he realized, panting heavily now and wondering how much strength he had left. . . . The dense ball bounced wildly, staggering his stride a little . . . rushed past a blurred succession of immense tapestries whose lightning-lit images were frozen into his awareness's edge: a mounted warrior spearing what seemed a demon-faced dragon with overshadowing wings (in fragmented sequence) guarding the entrance to a cave . . . in the cave freeing a naked girl fettered to what seemed a huge, round table laden with fruits and goblets . . . climbing a steep, bare mountain peak beside the female figure, grasping a glowing star from the heavens . . . holding the star between them . . . into the next room (they all lay along the outside wall), where the picture covered the entire far wall, and he actually slowed to stare, astounded by the time and labor implied: the knight and maiden were faint outlines that seemed to have melted into the expanding star's radiance, blended into a single flaming,

and then he went through the doorway in the center (the vast
tapestry fitted around it), and tumbled down a short flight of
violently steep stairs and splashed into a cushion of water and
mud, struggling on through the flooded courtyard under the
seething, ripping sky again that seemed to reach down to pound at
him personally, glancing back only once to see several silent,
shadowy figures, darkly gleaming, rushing out in pursuit, as if
riding a swift, fell wind. . . .

Alienor was lying on her back, with the two sleeping children,
under an untreated sheep hide, feet to a low-burning campfire.
The stars were very bright directly overhead, while in the distance
she could see the incredibly coruscating storm display where the
greenish, red, and black clouds covered the sky from end to
end. . . . The thunder was a vague murmur that blended with the
sea sounds across the heath behind them. . . .

Lampic was looking at her. He sat near the quiet flames, long
face painted on the night by the warm, yellowish glowing. He said
nothing.

She felt weary, yet awake . . . and thankful in a way past
thought or expression for this free moment of life. . . .

So when he finally moved over and lifted the edge of the hide,
she understood and accepted and reached her strong-boned, warm
hands around his back without a word because something more
than just flesh ached for this, drew her sore body willingly,
violently into his, silently rubbing, pressing, startling the man (she
took note), and then, with a gasp, drawing him into the fierce grip
of her need. . . .

Clinschor's iron carriage was halted in the mud on the road that
curved around the castle and joined the track that led to the great
drawbridge over which a number of his black-and-silver riders had
just passed, led by the fat Lord Howtlande.

About the time his father was coming through the pine woods,
Lohengrin was peering out the slit at the rain billowing over the
battlements in the leaping light, inhaling the cool, wet-smelling air
that drafted in.

The shadows shook around the men and horses twisted and
scattered in the rising mud and water among the trees, along the
road, and on the field before the moat. He squinted to see: there
was an arm hooked out of a deep pool stiffly brandishing a sword
which rocked in the gale . . . a knight knelt, face forward under

water, behind upraised . . . the long tangles of a disemboweled horse twisted, snake-like, in a rapid eddy of the mounting flood. . . .

Clinschor was pacing the round interior, hands clasped behind his back, shoulders hunched. He looked very old to Lohengrin when he briefly glanced back before staring out into the wild night again: he found the terrible scenes of mere hours before already effaced or fading . . . watched the handful of remaining troops huddling under the nearby pines . . . watched as a huge rider came clattering back across the drawbridge and splashed toward the conqueror's metal shell.

"The wretch was to deliver me the holy spear," Clinschor was complaining to himself, silently observed by the big, white-rimmed eyes of his body servant. "If the traitor lives still, I'll burn away his sight and . . . and cut out his heart and . . . and feed it to the dogs." He nodded vigorously. "To the dogs!"

By then Sir Howtlande had come to the slit, his bloodless, hawk-nosed face flickering strangely in the shifting luminosity, rain whipping into his open visor. He was shouting over the din and the results were faint. Clinschor came and leaned his ear close. Lohengrin gave room, looking on now from inches away at the flabby, frowning face.

"What? What say you?" the leader demanded.

". . . a big man, he . . . so the others gave chase . . ."

"Speak!" The suddenly unleashed, incredible voice raged impatiently.

". . . he fled . . . was no knight," came the answering shout that was still smothered. "He held a spear, master."

"Catch him! Slay . . . no, bring him living to me! Living, do you hear!? Bring the spear and the filth to me!" Flecks of spittle gathered at the corners of his mouth. Lohengrin drew back farther. "Did any see the Grail?! Must I come in there myself? Have I not done enough? Must I run my own errands?!"

"Master, we are searching!" the pale, shadow-wrought face replied. "This pest hole is deserted. I have all the guard searching, but I fear they fled with it."

Clinschor snarled and leaped back from the slit, clawed the air, spitting foam, shrieking with soul-shattering violence. "They cannot!! They cannot!! I wove spells to freeze it here; none of them could bear it away any distance!!" His eyes rolled in his head. Lohengrin could see the burst vessels, as if he were about to weep blood. "Fools!! Pigs!! Filth!!" He fell upon the floor and ripped and tore at the rug and silks, mumbling wordlessly in his fury while Lohengrin, heart speeding, backed on his knees along the wall. He noticed the Nubian seemed alert, but not overconcerned, as if inured to such displays. The lord master leader was presently stuffing fabric into his mouth, chewing, snarling, rending it to shreds, pounding his fists over and over on the floor until the iron wagon resonated like a bell. . . .

At about the same moment Broaditch had just reached the tree. He felt them right at his back. He expected a blow between the shoulderblades at any instant. He heard the plopping splash of footsteps over the wind-billowed thunder.

The moat was flooding and the massive trunk was close to being floated free. He virtually shut his eyes and jumped, skidded, spun with forward momentum and managed to sustain falling (like a drunken man) almost to the other side and caught a flexible branch there as he went over and pulled himself from the water quickly, not feeling the chill yet, bracing himself (the first two were already coming across the log, bent into the terrific gusts, balancing, rocking, quick-stepping) and jabbing the spear (he still retained it) into the watery muck, heaved himself rhythmically until the great mass magnified its roll and the lead knight tumbled, screamless (he recognized the black-and-silver armor with a shock, but no surprise), splashed and vanished instantly, and the second, already falling, whipped his war ax as he lay virtually parallel to the foaming water (about to be dragged to the bottom by his steel outside), which flashed through the dancing light with terrible speed and accuracy, spraying through the gusting downpour so that if it hadn't been for an extra blast of wind, the blow would not have simply glanced from his shoulder and spun him down. . . . The others brought up short on the far side, dark, gleaming, blurry shadows, as the tree started to lift and turn in the rising water. . . .

Just about now Sir Howtlande was driving his drenched stallion back across the drawbridge and Clinschor's squat, black ball of a coach heaved on, with straining horses pulling and common soldiers pushing under the ready swords of the few remaining black mutes. The half a dozen men slipped and strained in the knee-deep muck as the huge, wide wheels sloshed and sucked by inches along the lost road now defined only by the space between

the lines of trees as the storm regathered itself and smote and
smote and smote, branches snapping and flying past, whole trunks
bending and going down. . . . Over the whole outrageous wildness, the miserable men, pressing against the barely yielding iron
bulk, over all terrible tumults, could hear a single voice, muffled,
booming, ringing within, as if the dark metal had a giant's tongue
in the red, gleaming slit of its mouth. . . .

When Parsival got there, shin-deep in the body-littered water,
the bridge was partly drawn, and as he prepared to jump the
presence he believed he'd felt following, toying with him since he
left the moors with Prang at summer's end, was there.

He held his shield of will up and let his awareness expand in a
great sphere all around him until elusively, tantalizingly, a form
seemed to shimmer before him above the earth near the castle
gate. He couldn't be sure of the actual shape drawn in tints that
suggested fire flickering behind a dark screen of smoke that the
light and dark winking of the sky had no effect on. . . . Then he
recognized it with a shock that seemed to root him to the flowing
ground, and the wind and water went away, became faint mistings,
and the lightning became vague wispings from another world, a
dream. . . . He recognized but could not describe because the
mind slid off and past with false attempts, roiling imaginings like
faces and forms seen in clouds, painting images on the mere
surface of that which was constantly changing. . . . His mind tried
to express a massively toad-like outline or an expanding, but
dwarfish, shape or . . . he smelled death, heard weeping and
wailing, felt utter chill fears crawling faceless and he wanted to
bolt and scream and somehow knew if he broke or turned or lost
focus for a fraction's fraction he would be lost, and his body stayed
locked there, draining his power out and out, felt himself floating a
little above himself at the same time . . . witnessed death after
death, burning rivers of blood, on whose shores skeletons were
hanging, multitudes on gibbets, casting others into vast, lightless
pits. . . . He wanted to cry out: *Mother! Mother! Save me,
mother . . . save me . . . save me . . . mother!!* Dark castles smoldered . . . fangs and jaws that gaped above the highest clouds
closed on the world as crippled demons pranced, fish walked, great
chickens leaped with human faces . . . monkeys paraded in priest-
ly robes . . . a great snake flew slowly overhead . . . skeletons
burning out eyes, lopping off ears . . . stuffing noses and mouths

with clods of filth . . . flaying children . . . waving bloody banners, and everywhere the weeping, weeping, weeping, endless weeping. . . . And suddenly as he was about to scream a scream that he knew would never cease once permitted to blast from within him, in that instant as his body cramped and shook violently, rattling teeth and bones and he felt himself sucked, draining away, he somehow leaped up over where he stood and his head seemed to poke into a pocket of serenity and silence (he seemed to see his body still standing in the mud below him) and his sight streamed like an irresistible light and poured through the cloudiness before him, baring and scattering the shapeless shapes, saw his mind dreaming and painting the dreams, and without using any energy at all, he (indescribably) opened his open eyes and was awake and the dreams drifted, hung a moment, then faded to thinning shimmers like a puff of smoke, and he heard himself laughing as the night came booming back and his body fell through the calm of his mind flat on its face and the splashing impact rejoined him to himself (he knew he couldn't leave yet), and as he raised himself to his hands and knees, he knew those dreams were forever gone . . . and the streaming rain was a benediction washing away the residue of ten thousand yesterdays. . . . He stood up and blinked and stretched. It was all gone and there was only the raging night pushing and pulling him. It was all gone. . . .

A little stiff, a little sore, he angled away into the streaming wind. He felt as if he'd been sleeping a thousand years. He felt rested and ready for anything. Angled away from the castle he now knew was empty and slogged steadily up the flooded road, neither elated nor depressed, simply dreamless and ready. . . .

Alienor kept looking straight up at the stars over his shoulder, head rocking in a pool of her hair on the dry grass. She let her body unbend, open, and move faster . . . faster . . . hurl itself melting into relief, letting it pour out everything, all the scorched days and shivering nights . . . everything . . . and she looked out at the stars. . . .

He wasn't thinking as he slogged shin-deep up the road that had become a river. He had an appointment in the hills above here. He recalled he had once dramatized it, painted it in red, black, and white strokes. Now he was simply ready for it.

Actually, Parsival was enjoying the great, arching bolts that suspended in motion the myriad, gleaming raindrops and racked trees. It was magnificent, thrilling. The scene was so vibrant and totally clear. . . . He watched the vivid, shifting shadows and he saw them like the light and shadows in his mind, saw it was the same thing, and now that the nightmare was past, he understood good dreams were the same, and all the endless questings from horizon to horizon took place within the little space of the sleeper's head while he never left his bed. . . . So he had nowhere to rush off to anymore, and though now he was moving as fast as possible, he was taking his time with every moment. . . . The flashes were so beautiful. He watched each pattern, each frozen moment, and each was the utter equal of the last . . . none was better or worse so he wanted no power to control or shape anything. . . . Each flash was a whole, surprising, intricate, clear, exquisite landscape, and he didn't realize he was not even seriously wishing for the storm to end because he was too fascinated. . . .

He heard a moan: a bearded soldier had partly pulled himself onto the belly of a dead horse to keep above the mounting water and was clinging there as the fury howled and tossed his hair and washed the blood from his streaming mouth and nose. Parsival saw a deep, mashed rut across his abdomen. He'd obviously been crushed by some kind of wheel. He was dying rapidly and had demonstrated amazing tenacity, still holding on as the rushing waters dragged at him. . . .

"Life wants to live," Parsival whispered, soundless in the wind. *It keeps pushing out.* . . . He saw an image: a seed pushing into the bright, mild, breathing air; the flower exhaling itself into fullness; the petals falling, all one movement, dying every fraction of the way. . . .

He stooped and gently stroked the man's forehead.

"The . . . bastard . . ." the fellow groaned. His chalk-pale face was framed by black beard and hair. ". . . run . . . over . . . us . . ."

"Peace," Parsival said, face close enough to hear and perhaps be heard over the violence of the night.

"The great . . . master . . . bastard . . . goes right . . . bloody . . . on . . ."

And he died. Parsival prayed with a word.

"Peace."

And thought: *So I'm chasing him this time instead of the other way around.* . . . He smiled. The great master. You didn't leave the dream just because you knew what it was. He had an appointment in it. He had to do his utmost asleep or awake.

So he stood up and now began to run with tremendous power, irresistibly churning through the sucking muck and currents of flood. . . .

Which was more than Broaditch could do, leaning on the bending spear, crouching close against the steep slope, certain they were behind him again.

He virtually went to his hands and knees, pressing himself into the beating, stinging gale that slammed over the crest. He happened to look back and in a sustained flurry of lightning flashes he spotted something that filled his throat with the start of a scream, and he clawed and scrambled over the hilltop and struggled on along the twisting path. It seemed a giant's skull-mask, a red, gleaming visor eyeslit glaring with faceless, blazing fury up at him from down among the slanting, shaking trees. He tottered and half-ran, overcome by a nameless terror from childhood, the lurking thing only hinted at by imagination, moving in the night shadows, stalking your naked, prickling, fleeing back. . . .

You fool . . . you fool, he was thinking in a corner of himself, *look what you've come to . . . rushed all these leagues to greet the devil.* . . .

Clinschor was howling through the slit of what Broaditch had just taken for Satan's helmeted head.

"More men! More men! Burst your hearts! Die in your worthless tracks! Only push! Push! Push!!"

Lohengrin was outside. He watched the last man at arms (who hadn't already dropped to die) staggering into the trees. They were half-swimming even here on the steepening slope. It was hopeless. He only wondered why he didn't follow after them himself.

Fat Sir Grunt (as Lohengrin termed Howtlande) and a handful of black guards were all that remained from what some claimed had been half a million men . . . And himself, too. He grinned, sarcastically.

The rain spattering through his visor did him good, he thought. It cleared his head from the sickening sweet-sour atmosphere inside the mired ball.

Howtlande was leaning down from his shivering, exhausted mount, which stood spraddle-legged in the muddy current.

"We've no better choice than this," he told Lohengrin for some reason.

"There's surely no going back," Lohengrin allowed with a sour edge of contempt. He wanted to get away, go somewhere and lie down . . . sleep and sleep all these dark days away. . . .

"He may yet be right," the puffy, hard-eyed lord general insisted. "Consider all he's done before. He may just be right."

"Right? About what?"

"The power of the Grail. What we seek here. What this war was really fought for."

Lohengrin was suddenly leaning on the hard globe, shaking slightly, silently. Howtlande just gaped down at him.

"What?" he said. "What?"

But Lohengrin just shook his head and gasped, and then his laughter became audible in a lull. Clinschor had stopped screaming for the moment, it seemed.

"Of course," Lohengrin assured him, "of course. The power of the Grail . . . yes . . ." And he broke up again, to the other's unending puzzlement. Then began to regain control and asked, "Was this a war, General Grunt?"

"What?" Howtlande cocked his ear, leaning down, as the storm picked up in force again.

Now the lord master was raging around inside away from the slit, Lohengrin noticed. He was trying not to think about any of this because each time he lightly tested the concepts, he started to bubble and shake and his sides were already sore and he felt weak. . . . He took a few deep, damp breaths, then decided he was in control. Looked up at Howtlande's intent, piercing expression and desperate eyes and knew he was lost.

"The Grail," he couldn't resist saying, knowing full well what was going to happen, "we must have the Grail."

And this time he sank down to one knee, tried to hold his sides through the armor, and rocked back and forth.

"By all means," he gasped, falling back limply into the iron, his armor clunking. "It will save the day!"

"Are you injured?" Howtlande yelled, unable, Lohengrin

realized, to hear his laughter over the storm, which added fuel to the uncontrollable blaze of humor until he was sure he was going to die. *Onward, men! Onward to the Grail!* he thought, and fell on his side in the chill flood. *The fairies are dancing away with it . . . better stop them . . . !* But the shock of the water did what his mind couldn't, and he managed to get up. The humor, he reflected, was pretty much used up, anyway. But he nonetheless carefully avoided certain phrases for a while. . . .

Howtlande kept his face close and shouted his views: "Balls or not," he rasped, "the screaming banshee has changed the world. You have to give him that. Look at all he's done! They'll not forget him soon!"

"No. I agree with that." His chest and stomach hurt. *No more,* he told himself, *no more.*

The globe of black metal was rocking itself now with the fury of what was exploding within. Then the door swung open and was banged violently into the side by the shuddering wind. The black servant, lip crushed and bloody with what Lohengrin took for toothmarks on his neck, leaped out and tore away without a sound, light garments fluttering, instantly drenched, splashing across the road and into the swaying, twisting trees. The draft howled over the opening, flapped and cracked, and then Clinschor came to the doorway and Lohengrin's first impression was of the rapidity with which his upcurled moustaches vibrated, then the rain, spraying into his face (enclosed by a gray hood), then the eyes that seemed to stare now like an old, old man's, then the wild, trembling hands that clutched and wrung one another. . . .

He's broken, Lohengrin thought, *he's broken.*

Then he spoke and the young knight found his body moving immediately, as if energy had been poured into him by the resonant tones. His sleepiness cleared up.

"Bring me a mount." He was calm, confident, commanding. "Come. The Grail is just ahead. Everything is in order."

It was, Lohengrin realized, astonished, as if nothing had happened, as if all the incredible days before were instantly dismissed. He'd wanted—expected—to see a broken, pitiful figure emerge. Anyone should have been destroyed by this, and yet here he stood . . . and he knew, with a sinking certainty, that he wasn't even really mad. . . .

"Yes, master," he realized he'd just said. This was beyond human. The fate of the world still lay centered in this stooping, indominable figure who'd just put an entire nation to fire and sword. It *had* to be beyond human. Here was the terrible scope of a god! Who could doubt the impact of such purpose? He'd clearly been let down by the weakness of other men and ill chance. But it was not too late to redeem the promise. There was a Grail; he saw that now. There had to be a Grail. It was the key, the focus, something worth countless lives and castles and villages. . . . He was taking deep breaths as he climbed on his horse and bent forward into the wake of the others, into the unrelenting pressure of the elements. . . . There was no waste. There couldn't be. It was real. He believed it was real with a sudden intensity he couldn't have explained. This man knew and he would follow him. There was no reason to return to the ruined, empty lands because he was privileged to move in this dwindled company, riding with thunderbolts, climbing to destiny at the end of the world, moving with arrogant giants whose vision ripped through the pale shreds of mortal existence. . . . He clamped his teeth together and concentrated only on that. Looked up at the dark hill above, crowned with lightning. It was true. . . . It was true. . . . It was *true*. . . .

As they climbed higher into the exploding night, he thought he could hear the voice, throbbing steadily, the sound torn and wrenched by the wild inflections of the wind . . . no words . . . just the throbbing, throbbing, throbbing. . . .

Valit felt the warm, rushing, mounting buildup that locked his body. He felt himself about to lift from himself for a moment and fall up, up, away, and out. . . . Her fingers were soft and steady, stroking faster and faster by sweet degrees. . . .

But his mind was working quite apart and abstractly: he was sketching the outlines of a plan. They had to reach a city where he could make best and proper use of her talents. She was naïve enough, in her way, whore that she was (which was at least profitable for one who had to be a woman, so that was all right) and this hard living was slimming and hardening those overloaded hams. Why, with her in good condition, he might not need to pair her right off. . . . They could save their coppers and silver pieces, then, gradually, when the time came ripe, build a fine stew and live well. . . . He pictured a good-sized stone house, some silken clothes, pewter cups, silver knives, and yes—why not?—plates like

the Jew had himself . . . yes . . . wines from across the water
. . . get far, far off from all this nonsense. Broaditch would find
no treasure. But he'd wait just to be sure. For the lowborn didn't
waste an opportunity, even a slim one, as this was. . . . He heard
himself cry out now, felt a sweet spurting that went off within like
the lightning without . . . saw several whores in a brocaded
interior, thinking that it was sense that you built a better trade
staying in one locale than wandering the country wide in search of
customers like that silly minstrel of a whoremaster. . . .

"Ahhhhh," he was just crying out as Broaditch arrived.

And was shouting, "Remain thus at your peril!"

He shuddered as her rain-washed hand squeezed the last,
ecstasyless gobbets from him. He sighed with sleepy delight and
relief even as the chill world burst in again.

"Doom is at my heels," was Broaditch's next word.

"Close," Valit ordered, and as she laced his codpiece with
expert swiftness, Broaditch peered back down the bending trail.
"Did you find what you sought?" Valit then asked, starting to
gather his legs under him.

"I know not what I found, lad," was the distracted answer. He
thought he saw a dark form mounting the hill where the rain
seemed to billow out like a great cape or pair of monstrous
wings. . . . *No,* he insisted, *fancy, but fancy.* "I've been swift and
fortunate and a fool alternately and all at once."

Never taking his sight from the crest edge where the rain lashed
furiously, yelling blown down to normal speaking tones, he pulled
the dense metal ball from his pouch and displayed it to Valit.

"This was all I found," he said.

"What did you expect?"

The older man shrugged for reply, thinking: *I should have only
expected to remain dull of wit and have stood no disappointment.*

Valit took it, weighed it in his hand. He backed away a little
from Broaditch, who squatted down, still intent on the way behind
him, about convinced the great skull was a figment of exhaustion.

Valit was excited by the density. If it were gold! He trembled
slightly. He had thoughts, flashes: pushing Broaditch over the
slope to gain a head start . . . melting a little each year and living
like a lord for a lifetime. . . . He fumbled a square-bladed knife
from his belt and scraped the surface, which peeled easily, dully.
He hadn't sat at the shoulder of Cay-am of Camelot for nothing
and quickly determined it was a sphere of lead.

"Bah," he muttered and dropped it in the mud. He wedged himself back under the rock ledge. "Here we stay until better weather," he told Irmree, who seemed to understand in a general way and settled, with bovine solidity, beside him.

Broaditch prodded him with the spear butt. Valit screamed and writhed away, as if burned.

"Ah!" he cried.

Broaditch thought he must have struck a bruise or hidden wound.

"Stay here," he cried, "and you'll meet the devil."

"Which devil . . . ? Bah." He rubbed his sore side.

Valit wasn't overimpressed by the concerns of a man who'd dragged him across countless miles of madness to secure, in the end, a lump of lead for his pains. The fellow suffered from visions and angels. . . . "More than riches," indeed. . . . Why there weren't *even* riches to begin with. . . . He embraced, snuggling Irmree, and began to consider other things he'd like her to perform to while away the time. . . . His imagination was precocious and remarkable.

"Black knights, you ass!" Broaditch thundered at him, though the elements palliated the sound.

"It certainly be that," Valit allowed, cocking a hide cap over his eyes.

There, something moved, gleamed in the last flash, back on the extreme curve of trail.

"They're coming!" he shouted, at least tried.

"A certainty," the comfortable young man agreed, pressing himself behind Irmree's bulk fairly snugly with only feet exposed to the mad weather. *High and dry,* he thought, *as the saying goes. . . . The sole knight we met not only wasn't black, but was going apace the other way from here. . . .* These reflections were comforting.

"You're Handler's son," the older man expostulated. "At least he wasn't a total idiot! We've passed through the thick and the thin and I owe you, boy, and you owe me!" In the afterimage of the last flash, he saw the outlines of approaching figures. No mistake now. The next flash glinted on steel . . . the following on an empty path, so they were now one bend away and would soon top the near crest.

"You're mad, old man!" Valit shouted from behind the woman. "You're bent by mummery and visions!" He patted her great rump as Broaditch stooped and replaced the leaden sphere in his pouch. "Take your 'more than riches' and flee the shadows!" He patted her again. "There is only this—this is real life. Nothing else! I only followed you to prove it so!"

Let others dream, he thought with satisfaction. *I've made a good beginning. . . . The cow you tie up in your yard is the cow you can milk.*

Irmree was kissing his hand. She was content. He decided to try and sleep despite the howling gusts that stuttered and drummed and sucked at their shelter. Anyway, it couldn't last forever. This was as snug a spot as he'd be likely to find, thanks to this woman's useful bulk blocking the worse of it. . . . He was quite satisfied, in his way: look at the uses she had already, and this was but the beginning. . . . He closed his eyes and vaguely heard or imagined he heard Broaditch's nagging shouts, but it all was fading and blowing away. . . . He was sweetly weary and nestled his face between her pungent hams. . . . Everything drifted off into the distant thunder roaring. . . . He added a vegetable garden to the cheerful stone house and a pond with plump geese. . . .

Mayhap they won't be seen, Broaditch thought without much conviction as he moved back toward where the path became the steep, walled road. The weight in his pouch swayed and bumped. . . .

About now Parsival reached Clinschor's deserted iron ball mired in the flooding road. The horses stood miserably in their traces. The door had been resealed. He peered in the slit but saw pitch-blackness only. The metal rang dully under the pelting downpour.

He was aware of the Nubian watching from the swampy undergrowth. He paid no attention. His senses were incredibly keen and effortless again. He went on, climbing, trotting rapidly despite his chain mail suit.

In a way he was uninterested in just what lay ahead. Details no longer concerned him because everything was the same problem. One need with a thousand faces and forms. Ten thousand fancies and shadows, but all grown from a single darkness. Only that darkness mattered, not which particular shape cast the shadow. . . .

Up a ridge and out of the trees, bucking the down-slanting gusts, he could look back over the castle towers. He understood he was being drawn to the Grail. He smiled within himself. He was always being drawn to the Grail. It was one of the rules of the dream.

He accepted that, but the point was each heartbeat surprised him. Each breath was unlike all others. Each step brought a new world into view. . . . He'd do what he must, yes, but the darkness that waited for him was incidental, even if it destroyed him—a possibility he considered perfectly likely. . . . What mattered was the mystery netted in each flash of light, the contortions of wind sketching shapes in the gleaming rainfall. . . . He still felt a little taller than himself, and that was a towering vantage point, he thought . . . because the light would also glisten in the air and on the very sword that cut him down, and each following moment would unfold the heart within the heart of time. . . . He felt twelve years old, in a way, and twelve thousand: tireless, open, fascinated, reaching out in every direction, seeing deeper and deeper into the unending reaches of everything, touching with wonder—and in one corner of all this he had a chore to do, a moment to live, to act, and he would take all the power and awareness in him and make something with it, reveal something through it, show and be and be and show . . . because it was all so incredible and mysterious and exquisite and forever. . . . He felt forever, breathed forever, and felt its pulse, and yet it was unbeat, unbreath, unlight, unshadow. . . . He would never end because he swam in the waters of forever. . . .

"Merlinus," he said. "I know you can hear me. And you were right. I've finally come home. I could have stayed there to begin with." He smiled, then trotted on, climbing, moving easily as the path zigged and narrowed, as if on calm flatlands. . . .

Broaditch had dropped back about twenty-five yards and had nearly reached where the wall began parallel to the roadway when he caught a liquid shimmer of steel in a lightning flicker barely in time to throw himself aside as the broadsword arced with a silky rip a fraction from his neck. He'd forgotten, he'd forgotten, and was he going to die for that? For stealing this worthless spear he somehow had believed was going to guide him to that light from his dreams? What madness . . . and now to die with only a leaden lump to show for it, which even Valit had tossed away, he who clung to penny whores. . . . What had possessed him to follow his dreaming to his destruction . . . ?

The knight advanced from the shadows, blade ready, helmet open. The rain foamed and tinnily drummed over him.

"Put down the spear," he commanded. The wind burbled and whistled through his armor. "Common oaf!"

The common oaf was backing up along the pathway, tilting the weapon for a desperate, hopeless (he believed) thrust.

"Put it down!" the man snarled.

Does he fear it? Broaditch asked himself. *Is it possible?*

He tried a tentative jab with emphasis on tentative, falling back a half-step even with the thrust. But he needn't have bothered: the warrior winced backward and actually crossed himself.

"So, then!" Broaditch yelled, planting himself firmly. "I have something here, have I?" He remembered the flash when he'd first touched it. He *knew* that was real and he had found the castle and . . . yet his mind kept trying to insist he'd struck his head and slept an instant. . . . No, it had been the spear. Why keep fighting the simplest things off? "The holy spear, is it?" He knew the story: the Roman Longinus had eased Christ's agony by spearing his side, and blood and water had run out, and the weapon had been transformed by the contact. . . .

It might as well be true as anything else, he thought, advancing half a step more as the knight said nothing. In the intermittent light he saw the dove crest on his steel chest. *This fellow believes it well enough. . . .*

Then he heard a mortal howl on the wind behind, overlapped by a high-pitched woman's shriek just as he was thinking: *And why did I risk drowning myself in the moat and ten other recent deaths to hold onto this thing?* And with the outcry: *Again I must. . . .* Giving it up, all of it, the image of escaping fate and finding his family and a peaceful old age, already lunging fiercely at the knight's face and seeing him retreat so fast that he slipped in the slick mud, went over backward, and went sliding down *(like a lad's sled)* the steep-inclined road beside the curving wall, accelerating rapidly, rebounding off the sides, spinning, waving arms and sword wildly, careening around a bend and out of view. Broaditch was already running back the other way, thinking: *I always have no choice . . . always. . . .* Heard another shriek. *No doubt they find her charms overpriced.* He was running. *No choice. . . .* It had to come to this, never mind mages, sages, portents, dreams, and the riptide of fate: it was himself in the end who sent him ever running the wrong way because he had no choice and the wrong way was always right. . . .

He charged the last few yards, concentrating on his footing, flimsy spear cocked as once again his mind doubted everything and told him they'd brush this toy aside and chop him to the liver. . . .

Always running one way, then the other, back and forth, bouncing and rebounding through life like a child's wooden ball on cobbled streets. . . .

He saw them seeming to jump and shift in each shock of light, metallic glitter and gleam, as the armor formed from the shadows. He concentrated on not slipping. There were so many. . . . Had they seen him yet . . . ? Closer . . . closer. . . . If he could toss them off the road, they'd roll and slide to the seething bottom.

Water from above was cutting deeply into his path and he had to jump widening fissures. . . . They must see him! Yet those visors really only let them look straight ahead, and they seemed to be involved: there was a pale shape, Irmree, crawling on hands and knees along the ledge of trail with two knights who, through the blur of rain and staggering illumination, seemed gleaming, dark demons materialized from steely night. . . .

Rage and horror hit his nerves like a blow and he bellowed fury into the wind, seeing the bluish-white glistening of a long blade being jabbed into her naked, bleeding backside. He realized they were taking time to enjoy themselves and he went a little mad. He could see Valit's sprawled legs flopped out of the partial shelter of the overhang.

They expressed the face he knew, the blank, steel, red-eyed face that was exhaled from all the ruin and horror, gathered from smoke to solid: stupid, blank, black, blunt and stupid, stupid, stupid as stone—

"Bastards!" he screamed into the lashing storm. "Stupid, idiot bastards!"

And he was upon them, hurling himself over the fallen, bleeding woman, diving at the face he'd always loathed and fled for years on years, the frozen, silver-wrought masks that formed a single pair of fanged, gaping jaws of the whole head, and he kept shouting his warcry: "Stupid! Stupid!"

Climbing in full armor was muscle and lung racking, even without a storm and slide of mud-water. Lohengrin was blinking

violet spots from his vision as they twisted up in single file to the
hilltop. If they halted he knew he'd drop on the spot. The
continual dark-light, dark-light, hurt his eyes. The blurred-out one
still hadn't come back completely. The rain had soaked through
the cloth wads he'd pressed inside the plates to try and waterproof
himself. Every once in a gasping while he thought he still heard the
voice rumbling, wailing, and howling on with the words of the
wind. . . .

Wearing and wobbling, plodding behind Howtlande's massive
back, a tireless mute coming at his heels, he suddenly was aware
that he wished he were closer to the leader. He wished he had the
strength to shoulder his way up past the others to the head of the
line. He wanted to hear his words . . . no . . . he actually (and
part of his consciousness spasmed in sheer disgust and outrage)
wanted to touch, no, cling to his hand . . . yes . . . he did . . .
he knew he did . . . but, he told himself, it was that narcotic room . . . or . . . or . . . the sickening chanting. . . . He felt
shame and raped and felt weakly (he knew too well) enraged . . .
too weakly by half. . . . He cursed himself and wanted to vomit
with spite, but no matter, he needed . . . needed to touch, to hold
him. . . . *O good God*, he thought, with terror and desire, he
needed. . . .

He felt his hands shaking. There was an edge of hysteria in his
thoughts and movements now.

*He's all words . . . ! Foams at the mouth. . . . He's disgusting
. . . ! Deformed, not even a proper man . . . just words, nothing
but words. . . .*

He kept cursing to himself to keep the other feelings back.

*I'll let him know what a pasty nothing he is . . . the blow I took
from that idiot . . . Wista. . . .*

No. He didn't want to think about that, either. He pushed it
from his mind violently, tensely, feeling trapped in this nightmare,
overwhelmed by feelings that seemed to surface from terrifying
gulfs and darkly stir the pool of his mind. . . .

And then they were on the crest and he suddenly found himself
face to face with the lord master's brooding, rain-stippled features.
Suddenly his hands were terrifically clasped by both of the leader's
and he felt gooseflesh and a strange, sweet warmth fill through his
body as the somber, flaming eyes gleamed the lightning in their
pale vacancy.

"We are very close now," he rumbled, earnestly, magnetically. "It is just ahead. Do not fail me in this hour."

"No," Lohengrin heard himself saying, spilling the words from himself. "I will not fail you, master!"

And he meant it. He knew he meant it.

Parsival saw them ahead, a cluster of knights rounding a bend on foot. He had just reached the exposed, rocky hilltop. He glanced back and saw the whole country below illuminated by the rolling storm light. For a moment he paused and understood the scope of the desolation. Only a tiny part was visible here. It was starting to look like a sea down there. He didn't care to imagine what things were floating in it. . . .

He turned and marched on. Finally drew his sword. He considered the blade. He turned the edge to catch the changing light. All their fates had led them to this moment. There could be no blame. Yes, but it had to be won otherwise. Another way. He'd tried swords enough already. This was a work of art and a teaching and a learning, too, for him. Because it was not the story, but how it would be told. . . . Nothing else mattered. He was born to tell this with his life. He smiled a little, not quite wryly. As he lost and found and lost it. . . .

He whirled the blade through the rain, posed on the roll of ridge, in an incredibly perfect, unbroken sequence of whirls, slashes, cuts, turns, drawing (in flickering blasts of bluish light) a breathtaking net of steel on the night, flowing with it in ecstasy, spinning, slicing, dancing along and over the crumbling, flooded pathway. At the end of the last explosively exquisite set of moves, he was a few strides behind the rear-most of two black-silver armored killers, one of whom had turned in time to see the finish, seeming fixed motionless by the sight, his own weapon still undrawn as Parsival in climax slashed a thousand dancing shadows to shreds, then dropped gracefully to one knee (the last cut inches from the stunned warrior) and tossed the weapon in a high, flickering arc, winking down, far down, the slope in a stopped series of flashes and was gone. . . .

The fang-jaw, masked knight took a single, short step, drawing, and cut straight for the unprotected head with terrific speed and skill because these were the last of the elite of the elite, the best of Clinschor's best. . . .

* * *

Broaditch's wrath was concentrated into a perfect thrust that struck reddish sparks, ripping through an eye hold and producing a wordless, blowing scream. Light flash: the knight reeling back, mailed hands pressed to the fanged faceplate . . . dark . . . flash: Broaditch skidded on his knees, the other fighter's sword upraised . . . dark . . . flash: Irmree had risen, wailing into the keening, stuttering wind in time to receive the downstroke (the hilt hit her shoulder), which dropped her like a lead sack . . . dark . . . flash: Broaditch, slash-sliced straight from forehead to chin, right eye blotted out by blood, literally climbing up the warrior and yelling in pain and feral rage, gripping the shark-like helmet . . . dark . . . flash, flash: pounded it against the chisel-edged rock face, in too close to be cut again, again, again . . . dark . . . flash: again, the metal already a shapeless lump, blood spraying out the holes for eyes and mouth . . . dark, dark . . . flash: again, again, again, until he fell back, weeping into the streaming rain and the knight sagged and pitched sideways . . . dark . . . flash: Valit sitting up, wounds in his chest and side bleeding sluggishly, Irmree wallowing in agony in the mud . . . dark . . . flash: Broaditch kneeling, gasping in chill air . . . dark . . . dark . . . dark . . . flash, flash: another jaw-faced killer and a knight in black and red who seemed familiar, something he should remember . . . dark . . . flash: another smaller figure between the two, unarmored, in nondescript cloak, lifting the fallen spear from the foaming mud with an indescribable look of force and triumph . . . dark . . . flash: pressing it to his lips, eyes palely flaming in the hissing, crackling light . . . dark . . . flash: glancing behind himself, the silver, jaw-faced knight rushed to the rear, red and black one advancing as the spear bearer pointed to Broaditch. . . .

Valit was supporting himself on his elbows. He felt no pain now, only a cold, empty draining . . . dark . . . flash: he witnessed Broaditch rising to his knees, bleeding, wobbling, unarmed, trembling with strain as the knight with black arms and legs and red torso and helmet strode forward, unsheathing his long blade in a brisk, businesslike way . . . dark . . . flash (the lightning seemed to him to buzz and blast close overhead now, as if this scene drew fire from heaven), flash, flash: Broaditch stumbled back, swaying in the ripping gale that flapped his clothes like sails; Irmree thrashed on the path . . . dark . . . flashhisscrackflashroarflashbang: the knight rushed him as cries and commotion broke out down to his left out of sight around the water-swept bend . . . dark. . . .

Broaditch recognized Lohengrin through the open visor, the beaked nose and mocking dark eyes that he'd seen leaning from the shadows of the whorehouse bed over the stabbed and dying lord. He accepted he was a dead man. He had no strength left for running. He would fight somehow but not run anymore. He backed up slowly, step by step, weighted pouch rocking against his leg. His bleeding eye stung like fire in the sleeting rain. . . .

Lohengrin thought: *I know this dog . . . what matter . . . ?*
"It is here!" lord master suddenly shouted, shrill behind him. "I *feel* it! I *feel* it!"
Lohengrin felt propelled forward, snarling, all his boiling emotions now concentrated against this big peasant who'd somehow just felled two knights. He couldn't wait to cleave his bones and flesh, to see the heartblood spurt and dribble. He hated the oaf for blocking the path, for resisting the sweep of events. . . . You had to kill all resisters because they confused and weakened everything . . . everything had to be swept clean and pure, purged clean by blood and fire . . . no more dull-headed resistance, no more crawling weaklings, no more craven whining, no more ugly shapes (mind raced) . . . no more nightmares no more loneliness no more sweating fear no more weeping . . . no . . . *What? What thoughts are these . . . ?* Mad with fury, snarling and roaring in his helmet, howling as he charged, already tasting the blood (*What?* his mind flickered off in a corner of himself. *What?*), teeth bared, gnashing to sink in, to rip and rend and taste the smoking blood . . . words snarling: "Weak coward! Scum!" Sword blurring in the flashes, head beating beating beating. "Die!! Die!! Die!!" And then a wordless howling roar that for a moment beat back the storm, and he slashed at the rain-blurred figure to wipe it from the earth. . . .

Parsival slid inside the mute knight's blow with that uncanny relaxed grace and pushed and tripped him over the steep, soft side. He wondered if the fellow had learned anything. He'd just discovered how his body somehow *saw* in advance where to be. In the past he'd always been too caught up to catch what actually happened in a swirl of combat. . . . It wasn't power, exactly, he considered as the next two moved up, shoulder to shoulder, blocking the ledge of path completely. . . . It was *time*. . . . He wasn't really fighting (could they see that?); he was giving himself to what had to be, and so it happened he was in the right place each moment . . . *amazing*. . . .

He stood totally still and waited. He saw they were superb fighters. He could easily die. He accepted that. He felt the time building, gathering for the next moment. He was waiting, barely breathing. He saw they were too good to move. They left him no space. To pass the curve they defended on the flooding, crumbling pathway in the crackling lightshadowlightshadowlightshadow *was* death. . . . He felt all past dreams and partial visions rushing to meet these coming moments, taking palpable form just beyond this black steel, silent pair whose heads were silver-flashing, gaping jaws. . . . He felt the shadowy presences that haunted all the shimmering, violet-golden fields of rainbow flowers where women floated like breaths of moonlight, felt the nearness of unending bright worlds where radiant animals spoke in glowing air and sunfire dripped like liquid. . . . Around this bend the worlds were meeting . . . and he sucked in a breath that crackled like the lightning and sped forward, as if the surging wind bore him altogether, catching both armored wrists in their snapping, irresistible downstrokes, twisting between them as if his big body melted, turned, still gripping, so he was now facing the same direction as they, all in one smooth floating, and something (not himself alone) pushed and they seemed to throw themselves into the air as the mad light leaped, bounced, blasted, and boomed overhead. They both hit flat on their faces, as if flattened by an invisible hand. One went right on through the crumbling side of the path and vanished. He violently twisted the second's helmet so that the eye slots were jammed, reversed, blinding him within the steel pot. The terrible jaws now faced behind.

He stood up quietly, already aware of the bulky knight standing there, flashes showing his elaborate, bejeweled chestplate and ornate helmet, which was open for conversation: "What quarrel have we?!" he wanted to know. "The war is done with . . . it were all madness . . . let us talk . . ."

"But is it done?" Parsival questioned over the storm. "Put up your sword."

"Am I a fool? Listen . . ."

Parsival moved in as Howtlande (having learned something by observation) was cunning enough to thrust, not slash, except his hilt was effortlessly caught and his weapon tossed casually away, and in the same light, graceful pirouette, Parsival whipped the lord general around (as if in a dance turn) and tossed him into the last elite guard (whom Broaditch had seen rushing back to the rear moments before Lohengrin closed with him), the force of the fat knight bouncing the other into drenching, crackling space. The next blaze of lightning showed Howtlande lying flat on his back, shoulders out over the edge, teetering on the brink of the water-falling mudslide. . . .

Valit strained to hold himself up on his elbows. He had a terror of dropping back because he sensed he would fall forever. He hardly felt everything spilling out of him now; he merely watched. . . .

He saw a low black scud of cloud, seething with mad electricity, breaking over the hill, everything quaking in thunder, the sky splitting apart. . . . He saw the black and red knight about to cleave Broaditch . . . dark . . . lightning light: Broaditch now holding something—his belt? It looked like his belt . . . dark . . . and as the raging cloud flooded over the hill, driving the rain sideways, electric blue-white violence nearly continuous, black-red skidded as he cut and his target was blown into the cliff face. The stooped man with the spear, robes flapping and shaking around him like shadowy wings, turned and began to rock rhythmically and chant, as if the night's immense violence had entered into his throat, and the astonishing sound seemed to press the elements into its own pattern, wind, rain, and fire seeming to beat like a vast, steady heart, and Valit felt the waves pushing into him, blotting at his flickering vitality. . . . The exploding night became a single, relentless voice . . . mounting . . . mounting . . . mounting. . . . He saw Lohengrin in cloudsmoke and wild light slashing and slashing at Broaditch, who spun and scrambled along the rock face, pinned by the clawing, beating wind, waving his belt overhead, around and around with the pouch attached, and it looked (to Valit's failing sight) like he threw it and struck the knight's helmet just as a series of lightning bolts ripped blindingly into the hill and burst on the path with such fury that in the wake the storm seemed to pause and then come crashing back as everything went dark in the cloud, and he had an impression that the earth had opened under him and he was falling . . . falling. . . . *Ah,* he thought, *so it is this* . . . nothing . . . a brightness . . . a last image that seemed drawn by the last brightness: a house and walled garden under meltingly sunny skies, flowers or gold coins glittering on the rich grass, and he felt himself trying to reach for it, to be there, straining, and he was blown away out into darkness and a shuddering, glowing, silver-bluish sea. . . .

Parsival bent and heaved himself into a wall of wind as that cloud exploded over them and the flashes became an unbroken disorientation. He felt more than driven rain and mud checking him, felt the pulse of the voice, and through the dark-light tumult saw a figure with a glowing spear, greenish-seeming flame flapping around him like wings, as the dream united with the world . . . saw (not with eyes) the dream figure chanting fire, swelling, haunting all time and time to come (because time was part of the dream), staining the future with the magnified sketch of this pale outline drawn into immensity like an insect flying close to a bright candle flame, playing a vast, ominous darkness over a chamber wall . . . like a shape of mounting smoke, a cloud, terrible, raging, insubstantial . . . this empty cloud floating through days and years and millennia, dimming, disturbing, poisoning the sleep of ages. . . . Years flipped past like riffled cards, days, nights, darklight-darklightdarklight, and he saw the stain of the ever-more fantastic cloud clawing over the changing landscape until the final form, like a pair of naked, grinding jaws, gaped over the smoldering world. . . . He felt it pressing at him like a wind, clawing with frenzied lightning, looming up and up and up, swallowing, as its voice became a bellow, as the mouth thundered, howled, roared, blasted, and his body (though he couldn't see it, lost in a dense cloud) shook and he was nearly wiped away, blown apart. . . . *No!* he thought. *No! No!* He strained against the wall of dream and wind, against its sentient resistance. Dug in with feet and soul, pushed, inched, slipped, heaved and heaved and heaved at the center of the voice that tore and shredded him, arms flung forward to reach for the vague figure surrounded by the luminously burning immensity and then saw the spear flaming straight at him, twisted to avoid the point but was glued by the impossible wind and muck and it caught his side with a searing pain just as the full fury of continuous lightning blew the night to pieces, and something else, as if the sun had instantly risen through the dark earth's crust, melting, coruscating, but heatless, shining through everything, lighting deep layers of rock, fires, great spaces, everything floating in its sweet, infinite suspension, burning lesser lights to glowing ghosts, light endlessly streaming from light, the figure before him a hinted, stooped, all but obliterated shadow, silent, fluttering, clouds wiped away, nothing, no form remaining in that single burst of radiance like a benediction pouring into the vast, dark, burned-out world . . . everything wiped away, the light already a mere afterglow shimmering everywhere, in all things, in burrowing worms . . . in storm-flung birds . . . little specks of shimmer (Parsival could see as the solid world resurfaced) in everyone . . . everywhere . . . even as the pain of his wound returned and time came closing back down over them. . . .

Sir Howtlande lay on his side shielding his eyes as the furious cloud burst over the hilltop. His head was still out over the steeply sloping cliff side, and he had as good a view as possible under existing conditions. He watched Parsival straining into the gale and slipping in the mud as Clinschor, a few scant yards ahead, was waving the silly spear around and booming (Howtlande thought) one of his prayers to hell or whatever they were that had always been such a mysterious business at headquarters for years. . . . The great wizard, well, there he stood, armyless, about to be cast down by that terrifying, swordless, fair-haired warrior (whom he was sure he should have recognized), prancing in the rain and mumbling louder than any human being in recorded time, as if that would save his shanks from flaying . . . ! How had he come to this? Why did he follow that loon there to end groveling in mud on a forsaken hilltop chasing a non-existent miracle . . . ? Since the wind was too much, he decided to crawl back down the slope. . . . Perhaps there were a few troops still living. . . . He could rally them for whatever pillage was still possible in this ruined land. . . .

He saw (with surprise) Clinschor hurl the spear with vigor and accuracy, ripping it into the knight's body through the chain mail links. And the damned fellow stood there rapt for a long moment with the shaft wobbling from his flesh . . . a blinding contortion of electrical violence, and he even thought he made out Lohengrin on the next bend, a hinted shape through the wall of rain, fighting and falling down, he couldn't tell if from a blow or bad footing. . . . Then he watched the fair-haired warrior pluck the head from himself and raise the shaft as he charged with blurring speed straight at the lord master, and, incomprehensibly, Howtlande felt a trickle of pity for him, for an instant seeing just a weary, vision-haunted, lost, isolated, aging man surrounded by a lifetime's ambitious imaginings, miserable, graceless, stripped by fate and fortune to a lone and meaningless death. . . .

"Spare him, sir," he muttered without hearing himself, then shook the feeling off as he refused to see the finish, starting to creep away, wallowing through the mire, the slightly abating downpour rattling and sloshing over his plates, crawling in from the crumbling edge, not seeing (because his shut visor was aimed at the treacherous path surface from inches away) the last black mute staggering ahead of him, hands wrenching futilely at his backward-facing helmet, the grimacing jaws aimed opposite his reeling steps as he banged off the wall, wobbled in the wind, made furious tongueless sounds, twisted and banged the metal, punched his own head with steel fists, as if in a demon's penance, then stepped straight into a fissure that cut across the trail and dropped silently into darkness. . . . Puffing, Howtlande labored down, bridging himself over where the knight had just fallen like some wriggling, scale-plated primal life as he half-crawled, swam, and writhed and tried, from time to time, to lift himself and use his legs, but the terrible storm drove him flat again to twist on, blinded and choked by the froth of wind-lashed muck . . . thinking, when he thought at all, about the north country that he assumed was still untouched by the devastation. . . . Yes, certainly, with a few stout lads much good work might still be done there to repair his fallen fortunes . . . yes . . . nothing was ever final. He'd rise again and be the wiser for it next time . . . yes . . . some were bound to be living. . . .

Lohengrin slipped, his blade striking sparks from the shale wall, just missing the big swine again. But he wouldn't miss *this* stroke, whirling his blade with all his cold anger and control; let him wave that pointless belt pouch at him all he pleased, the swine . . . except something blurred from the pouch like a shot from a sling through the sheets of frenzied rain and snapping, exploding clouds (he saw it come straight in the lightning winks), and then a slamming shock came through his open helmet, the crunch of bursting flesh and snapping bone, everything rammed in white pain back into his head, the bang of the impact resonating in his skull, a burst of sickening, stabbing, burning light, and he toppled into blankness, thinking, from infinite and lost spaces: *For nothing . . . finally and for nothing. . . .* Then garble and then nothing. . . .

The wind seemed to have a rhythm, Broaditch thought as he watched the lead ball zip into Lohengrin's face plate. He'd thought (sinkingly) it was a miss, but the knight moved just in time to catch it on steel and flesh. In the time of a blink he saw it appear to split in two (*it was a shell*, he began to think) and then an unbearable flame burst there, brighter than sun, and (he didn't have time to actually think) a flare of rebounding lightning (he believed it must have hit Lohengrin at the same instant) lanced into his good left eye and overloaded mind and sight and he staggered, turned wildly, felt lifted free by the irresistible, cushioning wind, fell, somehow missed the narrow ground, had an impression he actually floated in a strange peace and tranquility on the immense updraft, and then dropped fast, cried out, falling . . . falling . . . then seemed to sail again, buoyed, and felt for a moment that he might rise and drift like an ecstatic man of cloud, on and on, forever soaring . . . soaring. . . .

Parsival planted the spear in the boiling ground and dove after Clinschor without hesitation. He skidded and rolled down the frothing mudslide a foot or two behind the lord master (who'd leaped or been blown off the edge), as if invisibly linked in tandem as the shuddering updrafts puffed and slowed them somewhat . . . splashed through crisscrossing rills pouring down the incline, accelerating like sledders on the slick mud. . . .

Parsival remembered childhood and pumped himself ahead with legs and body and actually gained an arm's length and clutched Clinschor's foot, and the belly-sliding world conqueror (the watery stuff sprayed from both of them like ships' prows) writhed around and slashed with a dagger at his pursuer, only his eyes now showing in his mud-covered head . . . and then they zoomed over a last, sheer drop and fell apart, pounding into a slosh of mire and water with two terrific, sucking spumes. . . .

Parsival had his legs first and stood looking for Clinschor. . . . It had been exhilarating, breathless. . . . He noted he still felt the afterglow of the light like a tingling in his body and being; he sensed something was forever changed within him but hadn't seen just how yet, and his thinking couldn't begin to scratch the surface. . . . He looked with interest as a lump rose, straining from the ooze, looking like (he thought) the bog was rising, desperately trying to take a human shape, and rain washing the wobbling, emerging body added to this impression as arms and head melted into flesh. . . .

He smiled, realizing the same thing must have just happened to himself. He wondered how the puncture in his side was doing. It didn't hurt now and wasn't bleeding badly. . . .

He slogged with infinite slowness across the few feet between them. When Clinschor snarled and ripped the dagger at his face, he discovered his advantage of speed and skill were virtually eliminated under these conditions.

Do I perish, after all? he thought, curious, blocking the next cut but failing to catch the frenzied wrist. The panting man was wild and desperate, foam and mud dribbling from his lips as he spat and gagged and, rattling, cleared his throat. He was trying to make some kind of rhythmic noises, Parsival noted, but he'd swallowed too much pasty ooze. He made great gulping sounds in his chest, but succeeded only in producing a series of slimy bubbles and then choked and puffed, waving the blade around in short, zipping arcs.

The rain was easing somewhat and the lightning strokes diminished; the hill was still lost in piling clouds.

"You ought to have kept your mouth closed," Parsival told him over the lessening thunder.

Each step was incredibly slow as Clinschor, foaming and spitting, scraping his tongue over and over on his teeth, leaned and churned laboriously away. Parsival closed slowly, fending the frantic slashes. The mire sucked coldly at them.

"Do you understand what you have done?" Parsival asked him above the wind and fading rumbles. The flashes were becoming fainter, unspecific. . . .

Clinschor's teeth churned the muck in his blackened mouth. The rest of his bare head was washed clean at this point. He blew and spat gobs and popped his madly furious eyes in his frenzy to find his voice. Yet all he could do now was listen.

Parsival felt more than mere mud washing away from him, because if he actually had any special powers at his command, it never occurred to him to use them. Just to move and take air and see was awesome enough and magic for a lifetime. . . . He felt comfortable and expectant as this bedraggled human being frothed and flailed at him. He'd have liked to rest, but that could come later. He understood what he had to do here and now. He smiled faintly. . . . The rest would come in its own time. He felt washed down to just a very strong man confronting a terrified, tiring one in torn and sopping robes, pale chest heaving, almost fainting with the effort of each sucking movement, partly sitting on the bog at times, only his frenzy giving him energy now . . . thrashing . . . flopping (as Parsival finally took him by the fragile-seeming wrist), shouting, choking, screaming, belching out the clinging mud.

"Why did you do what you did?" Parsival demanded sternly, disarming and shaking him, surprised by his own sudden flurry of murderous energy and outrage, which was mainly disgust at the blind, ridiculous, banal, ignorant meaninglessness. "Why!? Why don't you realize what you did!?" He was shaking him. "Why!?"

Couldn't he see it? Now, after all the ugly, senselessness, couldn't this raving creature understand anything? This soft, fitful, wriggling, clawing, biting . . .

"Do you understand?!" he boomed into the dripping, startled face and froze his vicious struggles for a moment. "Do you?!" He threw one stony fist into his chest over the heart and the hollow eyes bulged, muck just dribbling steadily from the lips. . . .

Then he yelled again and lashed out, clawed Parsival's face, leaving two burning streaks of blood across his cheek and got a word or two out at last: ". . . wabla . . . bla . . . wormbla . . . wabllitfilth . . . !"

Parsival hit him in the face, saying, almost calmly, "You idiot."

Clinschor's head rocked as he was slapped once . . . again . . . he sagged, left eye already swelling shut.

"You blind, blind . . . *thing!*"

Clinschor closed his bleeding, foamy, muddy jaws over Parsival's wrist where the light mail didn't cover, screaming in a continuous, high-pitched, hissing wail, and the angry knight raised his hammer of a fist to break the pale, tendoned neck. . . . And then it washed away, was over, too, and he simply plucked the head from his arm by the lank, sticky hair, lifted him free of the mire in one magnificent, muscle-cracking effort, swayed, and tossed him away to land farther out with a glopping splash.

The easing rain was coming almost straight down now. The thunder was rolling away to the north. There was a brief glisten of

moonlight through a rent in the clouds. He saw Clinschor lying on
his side, chest laboring, feebly wallowing, his one open eye glaring
with unabated and unending fury, coughing and still, hopelessly,
spitting and spitting. . . .

What a waste, he thought, starting to slog toward a rocky rise in
the ground like a reef. The moonlight winked out and he turned to
call into the deeper darkness under the cliff shadow, where he
could no longer see the other, thinking: *How silly . . . how
silly*. . . .

"You could have done so much else!" he shouted into the
drizzling darkness. No reply. He shrugged. He hadn't expected
one. "Now, what will you do next?" he yelled over his shoulder.
"The world can barely wait!"

He reached the rocks at last and pulled himself free and knelt a
minute to regain his breath. The drizzle was misting now. The
clouds were clearing from the hill. Faint, silent flickers marked the
fading storm. . . .

But in the bog he heard the muffled, hoarse, flat, powerful
screech but couldn't distinguish any clear words, just burbling
fragments: ". . . wawawawable . . . I . . . allabla . . . willwaa . . .
baallaabaaab . . . foreverwaw . . . wolblablablawol . . . nextblubb-
waw . . . blablabo . . . blo . . ."

Parsival stood up and started looking for a safe rocky track. The
moon floated free for longer this time. The rain pittered vaguely.
The air was clean above the burned odor.

He went on without the least urge to look back. He could still
hear the streams running down the hillside behind him. He felt
expectant, ready . . . ready to start . . . ready. . . .

The moon was so clear and silent, he thought. The whole world
and tomorrow waited. . . . He was sore, cut, weary, but awake,
shockingly awake, listening to everything: the freshening breeze,
the distant crying of a nightbird, splashing and spattering of falling
water draining through the steep forests, running, running,
soaking into the charred lowlands. . . .

Broaditch opened his eyes (one was still blank) and saw the
bright moon in a sky of scattered clouds that looked like beaten
silver at the edges, going by very fast, shimmering among the
reversed trees suspended above another moon and rushing
sky. . . . He shut them again, then felt the blood beat in his head.

Reopened his eyes and understood: he lay on his back, tilted downslope, looking reversed at the flooded landscape. The country to the south seemed one vast, glimmering lake with occasional islands.

He carefully righted himself. Overflows still trickled past him. He was at least one hundred feet below the path, he estimated, peering up and around through his right eye as he began to carefully work his way back up the treacherous slide.

He wondered how long he'd been unconscious. . . . He'd have dropped all the way down and drowned if he hadn't hit this soft ridge and stuck. . . .

His head pounded and the wound on his face was throbbing. He lightly touched the sword cut, then realized, lying perfectly still, flattened to the mudslope, the slice went across the eye he was looking through. The left one was blank. The rain had rinsed the blood away and it was unharmed . . . but what had blinded the other . . . ? He remembered the incredibly brilliant, searing flash . . . had some difficulty arranging the scattered memory fragments. . . . Had lightning really hit his eye? Had that lead sphere or whatever it was attracted it? It had split open, he was sure of that, and then something burst in an unbearable flash. . . . At the knight . . . Lohengrin . . . at his head, the lightning must have hit his head. That was the only possible explanation he was interested in at the moment as he continued the long, inching climb flat on his tilted body . . . sliding up . . . balancing. . . .

Up on the road he found Irmree huddled under the overhanging rock face holding Valit in her arms and crooning or keening softly. Their blood was mixed and caked all over themselves. She was shivering. He covered her with some knight's wet, torn cloak. The almost full moonlight was very bright and he easily found (as the memories replaced themselves) the imprint of where Lohengrin had fallen and must have lain until the rain dwindled to misting, because his tracks were clear heading north on the path toward where (not far ahead) it ran behind the wall. He found a bit of broken tooth there and what probably was a thinned splash of blood.

Well, Broaditch thought, *the lightning didn't kill him, nor the blow, either. . . . But was it lightning . . . ? What had that fire really been . . . ?*

It all seemed impossible, mad, nightmarish. He refused to think about it. . . . He walked the other way and found the spear sticking straight up from the earth. He reached for it, then pulled his hand back without touching the shaft.

I've one eye left, it seems. I'll try to keep the other by watching closely what I take up. . . . He looked around, not quite smiling. *You got me here . . . if you exist at all . . . for you never show yourselves at need . . . to do whatever had to be done, I suppose, for I know not even this much for certain.* . . . *Now I only pray you never come out of your recesses.* . . . *I'll keep my good eye, thank you, from peering into dreams and lightning bolts! You have my vow on it!*

Because he was determined to go home—if it still existed. If there were one stone standing, he'd put another and another on it. He was limping and half-sighted, but, by heaven, he was going home! Let the nightmare go. . . . He'd rest and then see about that poor woman. . . . What was her name . . . ? Irmree. . . . Ah, poor Valit. . . .

He eased himself down until he was sitting with his back to the stony side looking out over the glimmering, flooded lowlands.

He was going home, no mistake about it. Let be what was. He'd cross the desolate country and see what he had to see there, if he must, but he'd get home. He sighed and wished he still possessed that Oriental pipe . . . long lost. . . . He sighed and yawned. . . . The throbbing in his head was gradually subsiding. He stretched and yawned.

Rest . . . then get on with it. . . .

He partly turned and rested his big hand on Irmree, patted and soothed her shoulders and neck with both his eyes closed. He tried to hush her keening as she pressed the young man's body to herself.

"Peace," he told her gently. "Peace . . . rest . . . we ever keep our love, I've come to think, woman. . . ." He nodded. "What we love, we ever keep. . . ."

Alienor was already up with the children when Lampic awoke. He took the situation in quickly. She'd just fed them by the fire. The boy was yawning and rubbing his eyes. The little girl was running on the grass, back and forth, trailing a length of string. The sun had just risen above the hills behind them, shining on the long wall of charred forest that undulated with the sloping countryside as far as could be seen in either direction. Here and there patches of smoky haze still smoldered.

Tikla was hopping in a little circular dance, wriggling the string, singing. He watched Alienor's fine-boned, hard, worn hands skillfully gathering and repacking the sack of dried food. She'd bound her hair back severely from her face and forehead. The streaks of gray and coppery red glinted in the pale, mild sun.

The man understood and looked faintly rueful. He blinked, thought he'd try, anyway. He still felt a flush of springtime within himself. Anyway, just having survived was something that brought youth into his heart! And the night before . . .

"So you be up and going?" he opened with.

"As you plainly see," she returned without showing anything one way or the other, "unless you come blind or your brain died in your sleep."

He slightly smiled.

"I have family in the north," he said, almost laconically. "The winters be hard, but there be compensations. . . . I was a lad in the north country. There be compensations." He watched her.

"Then you must have younger bones still than I," she informed him, still neither looking nor not looking at him. She stood up and slung the sack over her shoulder. "For the cold."

"Was it that bad, then?" He waited. Nothing. He smiled faintly. "I find you hardly old, lady Alienor."

"Lady, is it?" She had to smile and look at him now. "So you've raised my station. Be you a lord in low garments, then?"

He smiled.

"You're a right lady, Alienor," he told her, yawning and stretching, still alert to her reactions. "Say what you will."

He sat fully upright, covering hide falling away from his bare torso. His body was lean, corded, hairy.

"So I met you," he remarked, slightly petulant, "in the wrong season."

"Did you?"

"But where will you go"—he gestured with his wiry brows—"with two chappies as you have and the world as it is?"

"I came this far," she said seriously, almost grim. "And I have family in the south—at least I *had*. My father was sour to my husband. . . ." A pause. "My broad wanderer . . ."

"So he went off, then?" he asked hopefully.

She took Torky's hand and turned toward the expanse of hazy desolation. On the horizon a few massive, smoldering clouds still towered and seemed to be drifting almost imperceptibly north. One was momentarily shaped by her fancy into a squat, roundish castle . . . and then, as she watched, it additionally suggested a sentient form, perhaps a hunching troll-man or a church carving of a massive demon. . . . She blinked the images away, then turned her face back to the steady, warm sun pressure. . . .

"He went off," she said. "But if he be yet living, he'll come home . . . my broad one."

Lampic saw the way it was. He wasn't even certain why he'd pressed so long. It wasn't like him. He was an unmarried miller, fond of women to a fault, it had been said. It was not like him, but last night there had been a moment . . . a moment when he'd felt something that still lingered, mild and warm and tender in that morning. . . . No doubt it was the relief from the past, terrible days, but . . . still, he'd felt something . . . she'd been there and they'd certainly shared something which still lingered. . . .

He stood up, long, angular, and nude. It was cold in the north, he reasoned. He tugged on his woolens, then worked into his heavy shirt. He said, "Did you feel it?" He fixed his eyes on her. He paused.

She didn't even bother to ask *what*. She didn't have to. She looked at him with her dark blue, cold-sea eyes. And didn't have to nod, either, though she did, once.

"Last night?" he needlessly added.

She just looked at him. He remembered the distant thunder of the storm becoming a continuous booming, the flashes lighting the earth and sky around them where they lay . . . he shook his head to himself . . . and he'd never had such a moment with anyone, and, he insisted, she could not have, either . . . it was impossible. . . . This from a fellow known for such sayings in the villages as: "Women ease the strain a bit, but business, lads, be business!"

"I'll go with you," he suddenly said, raising a hand against her protest to come. "I'll not act, anyway . . . just for the company."

"No," she said, walking now. He was bent over, spitting to clear his throat and blowing his nose into the turf. She gathered Tikla into her wake, heading for the burned, steamy, skeletal country.

"I'll follow along, then," he found himself saying, coming on behind, lacing up the front of his rough shirt as he walked. "But you might wait and give a man time to piss . . . and break his fast."

She went on, back erect, steady, reaching into the sack as Torky ran ahead a little, and Tikla called after him, "You was scared of the fire, Torky . . . I heard you crying."

Torky didn't look back. He had a stick and was cutting the air with it.

"So?" he said.

"I was scared worse," she called to him. "I was."

"Take this back to goodman Lampic," Alienor ordered, giving the girl a hunk of hard cheese.

Think of the poor souls, she was thinking as the twisted, fallen, blackened, broken trees and mounds of stirring ashes loomed closer, *who may be living still within. . . . God keep and help us all. . . .*

Tikla ran with short, weaving steps back across the twenty yards or so to where the long man followed, rubbing his face vigorously with his palms as he long-strode, carrying the food in both her cupped hands.

We do what we can do and no more, she thought, glancing back to see him taking the cheese. Tikla's hair shone in the rising sun. Their joined shadows reached to where she was. She turned to the front again. Torky was small and pale at the edge of the silent ashes and forest bones. . . . *What we can . . .*

She heard a bird calling but couldn't see it. The sound seemed mellow as honey. She felt a spot of warmth within herself. She smiled, almost as if she nurtured a secret, a little spot of warmth that was like the singing bird, somehow. . . .

She lifted her free hand and lightly touched her hair, easing a few stray strands behind her ear. She heard Tikla saying something back there. She smiled again over the secret, soft flutter of a thing. . . .

"What we can," she whispered under her breath, serious and light at once. And she went on.

Broaditch was wading through the ankle-deep ashes, raising black dust among the charred, almost branchless trees. The sun was high and clear. The earth was still warm here and gave the season a strange feeling of spring.

He was heading roughly south, hoping to strike a road. Irmree had headed north after an incomprehensible speech. She'd kept her lover's iron pinky ring. He'd seen her pull it free. He'd watched her walk away for a time . . . then turned away. . . . The only sound in the muffled silence of the afternoon was the faint, dry whooshing of his steps. . . .

He blinked: something was gleaming in a mound of ashes. Bright silver. Coming closer, he saw it was a sword, melted almost shapeless except for the blackened hilt. Near it a blob of helmet was half-buried. . . . Farther on his foot kicked against a plate chestpiece with no trace of even bones, much less flesh. . . .

He went on . . . wondered how many days it would take to walk out of this devastated zone. . . .

He paused once in hours, thinking he heard a bird call somewhere in the blasted forest. He listened intently . . . nothing repeated, if it had been real to begin with. . . .

The sun was slanting down behind the trees that seemed black scrawls against the sky as he topped a low hill and looked at where a slender crease of stream curved away, shockingly bright and clean on the powdered blackness. He realized that the rains must have washed it clear. . . . It was a wonder of beauty to him. The sun spattered sparkling light reflections that flashed on the somber banks. . . .

He was following, winding with it at almost a stroller's meditative pace when he saw them up ahead and shielded his eyes (his sight was equal again) against the brightness. He went on steadily toward them. They didn't see him: the long, lean man was bathing his feet; the two children were wading; the determined-looking, copper-and-gray-haired woman was sitting a little apart, hands dextrously sewing a piece of garment while her eyes looked toward the quietly flowing water. His first reaction was that he thought he was going to like her. He liked her look, her worn, strong, attractive face, and it wasn't until she turned her head (and the blue eyes locked on his) that he recognized her and understood again that there were really no accidents, that fate was simply guiding him out of the shadows this time, that the tide was lifting him. . . .

He stopped a few steps from her, not looking at anything else but those dark-sea eyes, which seemed richer than he would have believed, as if age deepened and warmed and worked them into jewels. She was blinking, that was all, blinking, and he couldn't tell if she actually wept. It wasn't necessary. . . . He knew the man was watching him and that the children had stopped playing, but there'd be time for that. He was still taking in, relishing, the stunning moment, the richness. . . . He didn't want to speak yet.

Her hands were motionless in the shapeless garment. He noticed everything, as if his senses were washed clean: the gleam of the thorn needle, the tracks of dark thread, the coppery tints of her hair, the lines in her face that (he understood) were simply shaped by what was inside, were the writing of the soul in time's script and were beautiful . . . her breathing . . . he was afraid to speak. . . .

The moment stretched out and then: "Well," she said, without even smiling yet, though he was, "you might have let us know you were coming."

He smiled and stretched out his arms. *Alienor*, he thought, as if it now were certain.

"How, woman?"

She shrugged.

"Sent a crow with word, I suppose," she said, and now he saw the tears. The sun flashed on them. Her voice was suddenly a little husky. "You seem weary," she said, not moving yet, as if she, too, were afraid to press the moment. . . .

He nodded, said nothing. He turned and looked at Lampic, who was watchful, feet still dangling in the stream. He looked at his children, standing knee-deep in the water with the incredible sunlight shatteringly enhaloing them, as if they stood at the heart of brightness, as if their bodies were shadows and the shimmering, soft glowing were their true substance.

"My doves," he finally said. He felt Alienor standing beside him, felt her strong hand firmly join into his. He heard her light, uneven breathing, felt her . . . felt her. . . . The children still hadn't moved and he remained held by the rippling glow . . . felt the warmth of her hand, gripped it, as if to press the two into one piece of flesh. . . . He shut his eyes and reopened them. "Now it begins," he said. "Now it begins. . . ."

Parsival was several miles north of the burned-out woods and had just reached an ancient, sunken road that curved away across the open fields into the glimmering, violet wash of twilight.

He abruptly stopped and turned around. The wind was cool and he could distinguish a distant, faint, charred hint on the air. . . . He was suddenly remembering his wife and daughter lying in the grave he and Prang had dug outside the castle, saw their pale forms . . . he'd washed off the dried blood. . . . He confronted the image in his mind, as if he were actually facing them, because there was a message, a meaning: the fragile, silent women gazed, as if from a dream, wordless and profound, and then he understood and knew why he'd stopped—he had to find his son. Yes . . . he had to try and find his son . . . Lohengrin. . . .

He was already unconsciously starting to walk back the other way as he took the feeling in. . . . Gawain or someone had said he'd been fighting with the invaders, and his own inner senses told him the young man was alive. He had no doubt of that. . . .

Yes, he thought, walking faster through the fading wisps of dusk, yes, he had to try, for the living, as well as the dead. . . . Everything was suddenly lucid: go back to where he'd seen the Grail light, to the very point, that was important, pick up the trail from there, because that was the true beginning of his new life. . . . He was already in his new life, he thought, walking out of a dream into the lucid air, where the first stars were trembling out, Venus like a soft eye following the sun down. . . . His new life would start where all his roads had ended and would start with his son. . . . Yes . . . yes . . . *my son* . . . *my son.* . . . *We start from there.* . . . Perhaps he'd find Gawain again, if he lived, and he might . . . he might. . . . He looked steadily at the richly bright evening star as the road curved away from his direction and he headed across the smooth fields, past dim, clustered blots of trees.

The world, he suddenly thought, *will start there.* . . .